IN COLD
PURSUIT

IN COLD PURSUIT

◇
◇
◇

Sarah Andrews

ST. MARTIN'S MINOTAUR ⚏ NEW YORK

This is a work of fiction. All of the characters, organizations, and events portrayed in this novel are either products of the author's imagination or are used fictitiously.

ISBN-13: 978-0-312-34253-1

To the good people of McMurdo Station, Antarctica—

and some of the bad ones, too

Acknowledgments

This material is based upon work supported by the National Science Foundation under Grant No. 0440665. Any opinions, findings, and conclusions or recommendations expressed in this material are those of the author and do not necessarily reflect the views of the National Science Foundation.

My sincerest thanks go to the National Science Foundation Office of Polar Programs for their support of science education and outreach. It was through NSF's Antarctic Artists and Writers Program that I traveled to the locations depicted in this book to do the research necessary to bring to the page this story and the descriptions of scientific research and discoveries it conveys. In particular, I wish to thank Marilyn Suiter, who first invited me to speak at NSF; Guy Guthridge, who invited me to apply for an AAWP grant; Kim Silverman, who picked up where he left off; Julie Palais, who connected me with glaciology programs; Tom Wagner, who connected me with geology programs; and Dave Bresnehan, who managed McMurdo Station while I was there.

This is not a work of science fiction, which is a genre characterized by "what if?" questions posed by either suspending certain facts of science or by projecting future occurrences based on not-as-yet-invented technology or not-yet-discovered features of nature. Instead, I write fiction about science, which presents fictional characters but actual scientific findings, or events of nature that are within the bounds of what would actually occur at a given location. Thus the scientific research and findings presented in this book are borrowed from current science events, but the scientists have been replaced by fictional characters and situations, and, need I say, no one was actually murdered in the creation of this book.

I am deeply indebted to Kendrick Taylor and Noel Potter for their technical input and for reading complete drafts of this book while it was in preparation. Todd Hinkley of the National Ice Core Library kindly tutored me on the care and interpretation of ice cores, David Ainley vetted the penguin bits, Gary McClanahan corrected the tractor scenes, and a great many others kindly responded to a hail of e-mails, there always being one more detail I needed to get just right. These people include Neal Pollock, Sam Bowser, Matt Huett, Jim Mastro, Ted Scambos, Mark Fahnestock, Ashley Davies, Dorothy Burke, Nicole Bonham Colby, Kristeen Dewys PA-C, Erich Junger, and Maureen Bottrell. Eileen Rodriguez once again corrected my hideous and confused use of Spanish. Richard Alley's *The Two-Mile Time Machine: Ice Cores, Abrupt Climate Change, and Our Future* was a key published resource in the growth of my understanding about climate as interpreted from ice cores.

It has been my pleasure to have assisted many fine geologists in honoring James W. Skehan, S. J., Professor Emeritus, Director Emeritus, Weston Observatory, Boston College, by naming a character after him in this book. I thank R. Laurence Davis, Kate L. Gilliam, Helen Greer, Arthur Mekeel Hussey, Noel Potter and Helen Delano, Paul Karabinos, Priscilla Croswell Grew and Edward S. Grew, Christopher Hepburn, and good old Anonymous for contributing considerable funds to the Geological Society of America Foundation to establish this honor.

Before I deployed to Antarctica to research this book, a great many people coached and assisted me in preparing my field plan. Primary among them were Christine Siddoway, Stewart Klipper, and Karl Kreutz. I gleaned essential understandings from research papers presented at West Antarctic Ice Sheet Workshops 2005 and 2006, which were ably run by Robert Bindschadler of NASA.

Once in McMurdo Station, I received key scientific inspiration and guidance from Kendrick Taylor, Karl Kreutz, Christine Foreman, Douglas MacAyeal, Nelia Dunbar, Phil Kyle, Kathy Licht, and Sam Bowser.

The good people who support McMurdo's infrastructure were also keys to the success of my visit. Being a part of that great army that travels on its stomach, I wish to thank all the Raytheon Polar Services personnel who worked so hard to serve three incredibly delicious meals per day under the superior guidance of Sally Ayotte. Trevor and Erik had us eat freeze-dried sludge with chocolate bar chasers at survival school, but I thank them as well. I am grateful to the personnel at Berg Field Center who stocked such warm sleeping bags, snug tents, and leak-proof pee bottles, and those at Science Support Center who taught me to drive a Pisten Bully. Thanks go to the fine pilots and personnel of Helo Ops who got me where I needed to go (especially Paul Murphy, who let me use his name, and Melissa, who always had a smile), and the staff at Crary Lab, most especially Micheal Claeys, who sustained me with hugs. Thanks also to Peter Somers, Barb Wood, Jean Pennycook, John Wright, Mariah Crossland, and Cara Ferrier, and thank you, Warren Dickinson, for showing me around Scott Base. McMurdo runs on the backs of all those who sweep the floors, drive the shuttles, maintain the shops, recycle wastes, generate power, purify water, and process sewage; though your acts may seem humble, they were essential in creating the environment in which research can be done in a forbidding environment. There are perhaps one thousand people I need to thank, such as Holly, who kept my computer running, and the marvelous man whose name I didn't get who gave me a disc of his favorite photos, so THANKS TO ALL OF YOU!

Field deployment in Antarctica is not undertaken casually, and many people worked hard to keep me safe while they tried to educate me; moreover, they made room and time for me during the incredibly hectic schedules Antarctica squeezes from its researchers. For teaching me about ice on Clarke Glacier, I am indebted to Karl Kreutz, Bruce Williamson, Mike Waszkiewicz, Toby Burdet, and he who prefers not to be named. On Cape Royds, I could not have had better teachers about penguins than David Ainley and Lisa Sheffield, and am indebted for archaeological information about early explorers to Neville Ritchie, Alasdair Knox, Robert Clendon, and Doug Rogan, representing the New Zealand Heritage Trust. In Arena Valley, I wish to thank Jaakko Putkonen, Greg Balco, Daniel Morgan, Bendan O'Donnell, and Nathan Turpen.

Scientific field work was not the only Antarctic field deployment that informed my research. For the great kindness of sending me on a traverse to Black Island Station, I wish to thank Fleet Operations director Gerald Crist; traverse foreman Katrine Jensen; Gary McClanahan, who taught me to drive a Challenger 95 and kept me smiling; Ron Rogers, who taught me to drive a certain Delta named Flipper; and James, who showed me how to hurl flags off the back of Flipper. At Black Island, I could not have been in better hands than those of station manager Tony Marchetti and cook Jessica Gonya.

The fixed-wing aircraft of Antarctica and their personnel were wonderfully generous with me, taking time to teach me about their aircraft, the navigation and cargo transport thereof, the trapping of nonexistent rodents, and the fine art of inventing fun in the Coffee House (Tractor Club membership being free, life-long, and irrevocable). I wish in particular to thank Colonel Ron Smith, USAF JTF/CD Support Forces Antarctica, and Colonel Max Della Pia, Majors Samantha East, Dave Panzera, Mahlon Hull, and Marty Phillips, and Master Sergeant John Rayome of the New York Air National Guard 109th Airlift Wing. I wish also to thank the USAF captain who let me onto the flight deck of the C-17 flying south (name lost with a missing notebook) and Flight Lieutenant Chris Ferguson, Flying Officers Kane Stratford and Leigh Foster, Sergeants Natti Hodges and Stever Knapton, and Squadron Leader Stu Balchin of the Royal New Zealand Air Force, who let me stand in the cockpit flying north rather than die of discomfort in the cargo section of that plane. It was over their shoulders that I watched the long, white cloud of Aotearoa slide over the horizon.

I wish to acknowledge the murder and mayhem in the minds of Rachel Murray, Micheal Claeys, Jean Pennycook, Brendan Stamp, Roger Harvey, Andrew Heister, Deborah Kunze, Charlotte Lees, Robert Lloyd, and Steve Croissant, who provided assistance and input during the Howdunnit Contest I held while in McMurdo to find out how Antarcticans might best kill each other. The winner was Brendan Stamp for his most elegant "Death by Biodigestion," which involved running the corpse through the sewer system, whence it would be shipped home to Point Magoo, California, unrecognizably as "cake."

Thank you, tried and true Kelley Ragland for your ace literary input.

Now on the purely personal side, I with to thank the Girls' Night Out group—Nancy Saylor, Vicky Hill, Gabbi Shader, and Emi Takacs. You can't imagine how much your all-white-foods send-off meant to me. And last but in no way least, I thank my husband, Damon, and son, Duncan, for understanding my itch for adventure, and for making their own sandwiches, washing their own clothes, loving me without judgment, and even driving me to the airport so that I could go to Antarctica.

IN COLD PURSUIT

As the coast of Antarctica came into view from the US Air Force C-17, those who had been to the ice before stayed seated, earplugs in place, trying to catch up on the sleep they had lost while crossing from North America to the jumping-off point in New Zealand. The new hands climbed out of the webbing perches that folded down from the naked walls of the fuselage and crowded around the two small portholes in the passenger doors, trying to get a squint at the measureless white world they would inhabit for the coming months.

Valena Walker was more assertive than the rest. Taking advantage of the fact that she was, by some quirk, the only woman on board, she moved to the desk at the bottom of the steps that led up to the flight deck and asked the loadmaster if she could climb up there for a better look. He gave her an appreciative smile, spoke into the microphone on his headset for a moment, then waved her up.

Climbing up the steps was somewhat difficult. As was required of all passengers—pax, in military jargon—traveling to Antarctica, she was dressed in ECWs, extreme cold weather gear. She had slipped out of the giant down parka emblazoned with its US Antarctic Program patch but still wore two layers of polypropylene underwear, thick black wind pants with suspenders, and, most cumbersome of all, giant blue boots. FDXs, they were called, another abbreviation for the growing list of Antarctic speak. The boots were glorified couch cushions with Vibram soles. The thick, insulated fabric and leather toes and heels of the uppers were a fetching royal blue. Inside these voluminous outer layers were two thick felt inner soles and quilted liners, and just to make certain she was warm enough,

Clothing Issue had supplied her with extra-thick wool socks. Her feet were damp with sweat. Nothing daunted, she thumped up the steps and presented herself on the flight deck.

Nothing could have prepared her for what she saw over the pilots' shoulders. Beyond the arc of the windshields lay . . . what? Those were mountains, certainly—they had to be part of the Transantarctic Range, as by her reckoning their flight path was taking them over Victoria Land—but everything was backward. Instead of dark, tree-swathed masses capped by snow, the mountains were bare fins of naked rock sticking up through . . . ice . . . which was . . . incredibly white—no, bluish-white—and . . . it looked oddly familiar . . . it looked . . . like . . .

It looked like whipped cream! How strange. A whole continent made of pie topping. And beyond the mountains, the whiteness rose and became the horizon, endless, unimaginably vast. The Polar Plateau, a sheet of ice miles thick and as broad as the continental US. Add to that the ice sheet of West Antarctica, and it was seven *million* cubic *miles* of ice, too great a number to comprehend. And there were no familiar objects to suggest scale.

Valena turned to the captain. "How high up are we?"

"Thirty-five thousand feet," he replied.

Six and a half miles. The confectionary swirl of chocolate mountains notched by whipped cream glaciers went on and on, trackless mile after mile—*no, think in kilometers now,* Valena reminded herself—hundreds, no, thousands of square kilometers spread below her with not the tiniest mark of human passage. Nothing in this alien landscape offered her eye a reliable scale. Nothing lay beneath them but delectable whipped cream ice and chocolate mountain kisses. She saw not a tree, not a road, no cities, no towns, not even a lonely hut, no marks of man, and for that matter, no animals, plants . . . nothing but ice!

The coastline swung majestically out from under their route, revealing an embayment strewn with another pattern of white and blue, reminiscent of lace, even stranger than the flowing cream topping and edible mountains.

Smiling at her amazement, the captain spoke to her again. "This is Terra Nova Bay. Look at that glacier down there, where it flows into the ocean, see the cliff it forms! Imagine how high that has to be to be visible from way up here."

Terra Nova, named for the ship Sir Robert Falcon Scott had sailed south for his last great, and fatal, attempt at reaching the South Pole! The very sound of the name shot a thrill through Valena. She had wanted to come here ever since her grandfather had read aloud to her and her cousins from *Endurance,* the story of Sir Ernest Shackleton's ill-fated 1917 attempt to cross the continent overland. Something in that story—their joy in adventure and their willingness to release themselves into the void—had filled her heart with longing, and she had followed that urge like a beacon down all the years that had culminated in this day.

"Are those ice floes?" she asked. It was early November, springtime in the southern hemisphere.

"Brash ice, to be specific." Suddenly, the captain was all business. "It's time for you to get back to your seat."

"Will we be landing soon?" Valena asked, hoping to stay just a few minutes longer. "Can we see McMurdo Station from here?"

He shook his head. "It's still half an hour to the south, but we're heavy, so we'll be flying around low and hard to burn off some fuel. Otherwise we can't land. The sea ice runway is only seventy inches thick."

"Seventy inches? That's six feet."

"We don't like to take chances."

"Take your time," Valena told him. "I've come a long way, and I've been planning to come to Antarctica for sixteen years. I don't want my visit to end just as I arrive."

"Sixteen years? You barely look that old. Younger than my daughter."

"I am twenty-four," Valena answered, more stiffly than she had intended. It bugged her that people underestimated her age. She needed every bit of respect she could get to make it in the competitive world of science.

The pilot's attention lingered on her face, examining each of her features with a look of intellectual abstraction.

He wants to know my heritage, she decided. Everybody asked sooner or later, or looked like they wanted to, but it never made it any easier for her to take. She wanted to tell him, *You're right, keep looking, I don't fit in anywhere. But here I am in Antarctica!* She stared back at him, willing him to look into her eyes. When he did, he flushed slightly, and the muscles of his cheeks bunched into an uncomfortable smile. Having extracted this price for his curiosity, she thanked him for allowing her on the flight deck and went back downstairs to her seat.

An hour and a half later the jet touched down and rumbled to a stop on the sea ice runway next to Ross Island. Valena was sitting in the seat closest to the passenger door but could not see out through its tiny round window. *Antarctica is right out there,* she told herself. *No longer a dream. I am here at last on the ice.*

An enlisted man moved to that door and popped it open. Instantaneously, all moisture on the aircraft shattered into ice as the warm, humid New Zealand air she had been breathing was sucked away into the emptiness of *outside.* It was as if some cold monster had put its lips to the doorway.

That's exactly what did happen, Valena thought, her mind reaching out into the frozen white wilderness beyond to take in each and every sensation. *But that monster is Antarctica!*

She stabbed her arms into the sleeves of the giant red parka that had been issued to her in Christchurch. Instantly, she felt warmth returning to her as the dense surrounding of down cuddled back heat that it gathered from her own fragile flesh. The parka was heavy and bulky, like a wearable sleeping bag. *It's true,* she realized. *It really is this cold here. And this dry.*

Falling into line behind the other passengers, she juggled her duffel bags and stumbled down the steps onto the ice. The ice! "See you on the ice," her professor had told her, as he'd left Reno two weeks ahead of her. So this was what was meant by that salutation! She staggered around in a drunken pirouette in her loose, toasty warm clothing and voluminous boots, taking in the scene. The ice spread flat and cold and white for miles in every direction except to the north, where the island rose in steep volcanic cones from a chaotic fringe of ice pressure ridges. The thin civilization of McMurdo Station clung like a mass of barnacles to an amphitheater of naked black basalt between the nearest cones. She set down her duffels and reached into one of the array of patch pockets that encrusted the front of her parka, searching for her camera.

"Keep moving!" someone barked. "You can take your pictures later!"

Valena turned to face the man who had spoken so brusquely. Why was he in such a hurry? Like everyone else around her, he was covered from chin to mid-thigh in the blaze red of a huge, standard-issue expedition parka, and from there down by the black insulated wind pants. He had pulled a brightly colored fleece fool's cap down tightly over his brow, its levity incongruous above his scowl. Staring past her into nothingness, he swung his arm briskly from the shoulder, exhorting her to hurry toward a looming red vehicle that had been cheerfully emblazoned in white letters as IVAN THE TERRA BUS.

Valena craned her neck. Ivan was huge. Its passenger compartment was not much bigger than that of a standard school bus, but it was mounted atop six balloon tires, each taller than Valena. The driver's side door was accessed via a ladder that was bolted to the side, and on the passengers' side—well, most large buses had steps, but this was a full staircase. Everything here was completely out of scale with anything she had seen before.

She picked up her duffels and shuffled toward the bus. Climbed the stairs. Found a seat. Looked around. The other passengers stared out the scratched windows, exhausted but wired. She gazed from face to face, trying to figure out which of these people were scientists like herself—here on grants from the National Science Foundation or NASA—and which were employees of Raytheon Polar Services, the contractor that provided all the infrastructure support that would soon put her out in a field camp on the ice, far beyond the jarring hustle and bustle of this arrival.

The scowling driver climbed aboard, closed the door, and put Ivan in gear. Off they went across the ice toward the island and its harsh jumble of steel buildings. At the edge of the ice, the road pitched steeply upward, then turned between the hash of metal buildings. Like the bus, some of the structures had names painted on them: Royal Society. Hotel California. Everything rolled past too quickly in a chaos of impressions, until the bus pulled up in front of a wooden building that looked like a Swiss chalet. It looked like part of a movie set, no more real than anything else she was seeing.

The driver opened the door and got out. The other passengers rose and headed down the aisle toward the stairs. She followed them, peering through the windows for her first glimpse of her wandering professor. Emmett Vanderzee had a way of getting lost sometimes, mostly in his head, but he was a brilliant man, and the work he was doing was essential. He and an assistant had come south a week ahead of her, "to look after a few details from last year," he had told her.

But where was he? All the people gathered outside to greet the arrivals looked alike in their red parkas, like a gaggle of bad Santa Claus impersonators. Even so, Emmett should have been easy to pick out: he was tall and angular, and, even bundled in a big red parka, his pale narrow face and long curving nose and crooked smile would be visible, a combination of attributes that gave him the aspect of a curious camel. If he wasn't wearing a hat she would spot his thin rooster-tail of unkempt, graying hair, and if he had forgotten his sunglasses, she would see his soft, inward-gazing blue eyes.

She looked from face to face. He wasn't there. Perhaps he was waiting for her inside the chalet, where everyone from the bus was now heading, first stacking their orange duffel bags on the porch. She followed along, peering into every face she passed, growing anxious. He'd said that there would be a briefing that would go by way too fast for a "fingie"—whatever that was—but that he would *be there*, to help her put everything in context and so that they could get right to work preparing for their field deployment.

She pushed through the door into an airlock, passing a sign instructing all visitors to take off their crampons before entering, and continued through the inner door into a small assembly room that had been prepared with chairs, a screen, and a projector. Emmett wasn't here, either.

The in-brief was an overwhelming flood of instructions presented by an array of National Science Foundation and Raytheon section chiefs in rapid monotones. To check out keys to your dorm room, go to building such-and-such and see so-and-so. To check out a vehicle, see this blah-de-blah in building mumbled number. Raytheon employees have training sessions here and science grantees will meet there. Don't bug Raytheon personnel in the dining hall; make an *appointment* to see them in their offices. Wash your hands after using the bathroom and before meals so you don't spread the crud. Put your sunglasses on even when passing between buildings; if the UV doesn't get you, the blowing grit will. Don't leave McMurdo before you've gone through Happy Camp. Don't go anywhere without checking out. After hours, call the fire department for phone numbers. Fill out this form. And this one. And this one. Make sure you recycle. Do this, don't do that. Don't screw up. Don't. Don't. Don't.

The United States, Reno, and the Desert Research Institute seemed long ago and far away, figments of another planet.

At last this firing-squad introduction to How to Survive in McMurdo was over and everybody was standing up. They had arrived too late for supper, so someone was handing out another round of sack lunches. Eating seemed a good idea, but what was she supposed to do after that? Where in hell was Emmett? Or, where in . . . the ice?

She heard her name being called: "Valena Walker? Is Valena Walker here?"

She turned. A tall, bearded man was moving toward her. "Ah, there you are," he said, reading the name tag on her parka. "Would you come into my office, please?" He gestured toward an inner door. He wasn't smiling.

Valena followed him, her big blue boots thumping on the floorboards. Something was wrong, that much was now certain. Her stomach felt like it was full of sand.

The man closed the door behind them. "Have a seat," he said.

Valena sat, clutching her flight lunch. What was his name? During the in-brief, he had been introduced as the National Science Foundation's top representative here in McMurdo, *el jefe*, the man in charge of all of the scientists, but had used up copious amounts of his welcoming message trying to persuade everyone that they should not believe or spread rumors. She now watched him acutely as he paced slowly across the room, searching his stiff posture for clues about what he was about to say. Had Emmett been injured? Was he sick? Where *was* he?

The man reached the far wall of the room, turned, started back. He wasn't looking at her. He was staring at the floor. That was bad.

"Is something the matter?" she asked, feeling like she was reading from a poorly written script. This was not how it was supposed to be. She was in Antarctica. She had worked hard, had excelled in science, had moved heaven and earth to get into the Antarctic program, and now . . . where in hell was Emmett Vanderzee?

"I'm George Bellamy," the man said. "Well, you know that; I was just introduced to all of you right outside that door." He stopped pacing, his face twisting with discomfort. "Well, uh . . . I have some bad news for you. Uh, very sad, um . . . well, your PI—uh, the principal investigator of your project, Emmett Vanderzee?—uh, well, he I am sure meant to be here to greet you, but, ah . . . well . . ." He crimped his face into an unfunny smile, as if he'd just been stung by a bee on one cheek.

"Well then, um . . . where is he?"

"He's on an LC-130 Hercules," he said.

"An LC-130. Oh, I see. He's been delayed coming in from checking his field locations, then . . . or whatever it was he had to do before I got here."

Bellamy blinked. "He—no, no, he's been redeployed."

"Redeployed?"

"He's going *north*," Bellamy snapped, as if speaking to a student who had been caught daydreaming.

"North." Valena quickly computed the implications and permutations of the word. *Okay, this man is speaking in present tense, so that means that Emmett is not dead, but why would he be heading to New Zealand?* "Has Dr. Vanderzee been injured?" she asked.

Bellamy shook his head vigorously. "No. No . . ." He began to pace again.

Valena tracked his movement. *Well, if Emmett's not dead, and he's not sick or injured, and whatever is wrong with him is making this man really, truly uncomfortable, then what exactly is the problem?* She cleared her throat. Waited. Spoke. "And he's on a plane going north because . . . ?"

"Hm. Well, I can't tell you that, exactly. In fact, I am not sure, myself. And the less said about this, the better." He let out an uncomfortable laugh. "McMurdo is a rumor mill. We must be careful not to feed it!"

"Rumor?"

"Now, as regards your status here, I'm sorry to say that we can't get you on a plane until at least Tuesday."

Valena jumped to her feet, dropping her sack lunch on the floor. "Wait! Isn't Emmett coming back?"

"Well, that is to be determined, I suppose." He presented her with a dismissive smile, a man done with an awkward duty. Stepping behind his desk, he said, "Now, you must be tired, so you'll want to get situated in your dorm room, and—"

Valena raised her hands in entreaty. "But I'm here to do research for my master's degree!"

Bellamy shook his head sadly. "I know this must be a terrible disappointment. We should have caught you in Christchurch this morning and saved you the flight, but we did reach the other student on your project— Taha Hesan? He hadn't left Reno yet, so we were able to put him on hold. But, well, now you're here, so . . . well, as I say, we can get you out in a few days. I'll just need you to be discreet."

Valena's self-control began to slip. "He's not coming *back?*"

Bellamy flipped a hand toward the ceiling in frustration. "This *could* all be cleared up, I suppose, and we'd get Dr. Vanderzee on the next available flight south again, but scheduling here in Antarctica is always tight. The next several flights south are filled, and there are frequent delays due to the weather. Antarctica is the land of delays! Nothing ever quite goes according to plan, and after a while it wouldn't be worth continuing, because the season will simply fly by."

"*What* could be cleared up?" she said, and then, her voice hitting a keen pitch, demanded, "Tell me what's going on here!"

"Dr. Vanderzee . . . had to leave to attend a hearing."

"A hearing? What kind of hearing?"

Bellamy's face darkened ominously. "A man dies in your camp, there are matters to be cleared up. Surely you understand that."

A thin ringing noise filled Valena's ears. She sat down and tried to brace her elbows on her knees, which felt oddly gelatinous. "That journalist died of altitude sickness," she said.

"Indeed he did. And I'm sure that will all come out in the hearing. Now, Ms. Walker, I'm sure this is all a shock to you, but . . . well, I really can't tell you anything more, because you see it's all got to be kept confidential, and I need you to, uh, keep everything I've just said to you in strictest confidence. The US Antarctic Program does not need this kind of publicity!" His hands suddenly seemed to have left his voluntary control and began to fly around like great sallow moths. "We do the finest science, and we struggle and slave to get the word out, and now this!"

Valena stared up into his face. "I am here to continue Dr. Vanderzee's excellent work." She wanted to add, *And this is not going to stop me,* but her words had grown thick, and she couldn't get them to come out of her mouth. Huge government programs were an abstraction to her. Her priorities lay in her thesis work and what lay beyond it: having participated in Emmett Vanderzee's critically important study of rapid climate change, she intended to roll on through a doctoral program, thereby earning a position at the DRI—the Desert Research Institute in Reno, which was world famous for work in cold deserts like Antarctica—and begin her own projects, which would bring her back to the ice again and again. "I—I'll phone the other people on the project and get back to you in the morning with a revised plan," she managed at last.

Bellamy nodded his head like a woodpecker. "Certainly. Certainly."

Even though she was swathed in layers of down and fleece, Valena felt cold. She was ten thousand miles from home, exhausted, and had no idea whom to turn to for help. Bellamy had an agenda, and it did not include her. If she didn't get out of his office soon, her tears would flow, and she did not want him to see them. She needed time to think, to get her emotions back under control. She stood up and headed out of his office and toward the outer door.

"I need your word that you will keep our conversation in strictest confidence," Bellamy called after her.

Valena turned, said, "I'm scheduled for survival training day after tomorrow, and—so that's what I am going to do."

"As long as you exercise the utmost discretion. We probably can't get you on a flight until Wednesday, anyway. Watch the bulletin board near the entrance to the galley. They'll post your flight north. Make sure you're on it."

Valena's chill suddenly turned to heat. She turned and gave the big man with the pale hands a quick but defiant stare, then shoved open the door that led into the airlock, bowing her head against the cold blast of air that awaited her outside.

2

THE DORMITORY ROOM WAS A NIGHTMARE. VALENA HAD BEEN AS-signed to a barracks room with seven other women, two of whom were abject slobs. Their duffels spewed clothing, and their skis formed tripping hazards between her bunk and the door. The bunk beds and freestanding closets had started out cheap and had been badly abused from there. And being last into the room, she had drawn an upper bunk. What was it going to be like if she had to get up in the night and pee?

It was a struggle to tuck in the sheets and army blankets issued by Housing. She had to duck her head to clear the ceiling while kneeling on the bunk itself, and every time she moved, her knees twisted all previous smoothings. She wanted to scream.

What is my problem? she asked herself. *I've hiked or skied to fourteen of Colorado's highest summits and have kayaked the Grand Canyon, camping in the most primitive conditions—loving every minute!—so why does this room seem so stark?*

The woman on the upper bunk of the bed to her right began to snore loudly. Valena stared across the dim room toward her, wondering how anyone could fall asleep in such a setting.

She lay down on her back and stared at the ceiling. Time inched by. It was past 9:00 p.m., perhaps 10:00. Her stomach growled, reminding her that she had left her flight lunch in Bellamy's office. She tried to push hunger out of her mind by meditating on the landscape she had witnessed after leaving the Chalet. Too upset to think straight, she had marched the short distance out to the edge of the slope that led down toward the salt ice of McMurdo Sound and stared at the towering peaks of the Transantarctic

Mountains, which marked the edge of the continent. Ross Island, where she stood, was separated from them by at least thirty miles of frozen ocean.

In the broad daylight of a springtime evening seventy-seven degrees south of the equator, the mountains had danced alluringly. Everything south of the Antarctic Circle saw daylight for the six months of the year that the South Pole faced toward the sun during its annual revolution and darkness during the six months it faced away, so during Valena's planned eight-week visit, the sun would not set.

But George Bellamy had just told her that she would not be staying even *one* week. She willed herself to forget her fears and cherish this first solo moment with the land she had longed to meet, but the sting of disappointment was too intense to overcome, and after a short while she had turned toward Building 155, where this horrifying room awaited her. Now her only view was of the stains in the ceiling. She mapped them slowly, trying to trace a route that would lead her out of her troubles.

Half an hour later, she was still staring at the ceiling when another of her bunkmates came into the room. Valena closed her eyes and pretended to be asleep. She was too wired and too tired to talk to strangers, and her old bugaboo of feeling isolated in a crowd had set in with unusual force. She had heard stories about McMurdo, that people came here the first time for the adventure, a second time for the money, and the third and every other time because they had figured out that they fit in nowhere else. Did she fit in here?

The unseen roommate stepped quietly through the room, making only the softest sounds of zippers unzipping and the muffled thump of shoes landing on floor, then a rustling as she slipped between the sheets. A moment later, the sound of singing erupted from the hallway, the door again opened, and two more of her roommates entered, giggling, tripping over the skis, whispering to each other to observe the request another roommate had posted—DAY SLEEPER, GOING ON SHIFT AT MIDNIGHT, HAVE A HEART. It took them twenty minutes of muffled laughter and thumping around to settle down. Saturday night in Antarctica.

Finally, from sheer exhaustion, Valena slept. When she opened her eyes next she had no idea what time it was. The light that filtered through the sheet someone had tacked up over the window was every bit as bright as it had been when she fell asleep. Soft breathing and gentle snoring rose from all the pillows around her. She began to doze again herself, so tired that her body seemed to be spinning. This jolted her awake, and another quarter hour passed before she again found sleep.

The next time she awoke, there was no getting back to sleep. She rose, grabbed her toilet kit and a change of clothes, and went looking for the shower room, which proved to be as Spartan as the bunk room.

Ten minutes later, freshly washed and dressed in clean jeans and a purplish-blue turtleneck sweater, she shrugged her way into the big red parka, grabbed her backpack, which held her laptop computer, and set off in search of her office at Crary, the science laboratory on station where all grantees were given office space. If she had only three days to figure out how to not get sent home, she figured she'd better get cracking.

Apart from the shadows on the far mountains being cast to her right instead of her left, Sunday morning looked surprisingly like Saturday evening. The wind had picked up, blowing grit from between the broken sheets of ice that covered what passed for a street, and even with her parka cuddled to her chin and the hood up, the cold bit quickly through her blue jeans. She began to shiver.

She hurried down a path and up to a stile that crossed a gang of eighteen-inch-diameter pipes that snaked between buildings. She ran up the steps and down the other side and crossed to the steel building with the big refrigerator doors that had been referenced during the in-brief. Insulating her hand with the cuff of one parka sleeve, she grabbed a steel door handle and slipped inside the airlock.

The inner doors of the airlock were locked.

Remembering the card key that had been issued to her when she had picked up her dorm room key the evening before, she dug through the pockets of the big red parka, ran the card through the slot in the card reader, and continued inside.

The interior of the building felt a little more like home: pale, institutional, off-white walls with glass display cases. The nearest one was filled with dinosaur bones collected out in the Transantarctic Range, remnants of a long-ago time when the whole continent lay closer to the equator, making it warm enough for lizards. Posters explaining scientific findings of various research projects papered the walls. Hallways branched off to left and right, and a long ramp led downhill to more halls as the building descended the side of the bluff on which it had been constructed. She turned and headed along a short hallway to the left, instinctively searching out the administrative offices.

There was no one present at any of the desks in the office marked DIREC-TOR. *Of course—it's Sunday,* she reminded herself. *That's the one day Raytheon Polar Services gives its personnel. They explained that at the in-brief.*

As she walked back down the hallway toward the entrance, Valena spied a dark-haired woman sitting at a desk inside another office. She paused. The nameplate beside her door read BRENDA UTZON. "Can I help you?" the woman asked kindly, peering at Valena over her glasses.

Valena braced as the woman's gaze slid over her face, taking in what everybody noticed: the unusual angles and curves of bone and flesh, the seemingly mismatched colors of her skin and eyes. Even though people usually liked what they saw, their evident surprise told her again and again that she was different. She muttered, "I'm, um, looking for my office. I just arrived."

"What event number?" the woman asked.

"What event? Oh, yeah, my project number. I'm with Emmett Van-derzee's group. I-543."

"Oh, you must be Valena Walker. I'm so sorry about Emmett."

"What happened?" she asked. Bellamy might have told her to keep her mouth shut about what he'd told her, but if other people wanted to open theirs, well, what was the harm in that?

"Oh, you don't know? You poor thing. Well, they didn't tell us much, either, but in a place like this you can't really hide anything. We saw the marshal take him into custody."

"Into . . . *custody?* Wait, Bellamy said—"

"Well, they tried to make it look like they were just going for a stroll, but they put him in Hut 10, right where they put the last fellow they incarcerated."

"*Incarcerated?*"

"It's like a little house. You can rent it for parties. They put the young man who attacked another with a hammer in there. Put him on suicide watch, in case he was going to try to hurt himself, but he was actually quite cooperative, I hear."

"Emmett Vanderzee? Suicide?"

"No, I'm sorry, I'm talking about the man who hit the other one with the hammer. Three years ago."

"They have a marshal here? Where's his office?" *I should go talk to him,* Valena decided.

"Yes, they do. Chad Hill, the NSF man in charge."

"I thought George Bellamy was in charge."

"He's on the Science side. Chad is Operations. Somebody had to be the local law, so he went up to Hawaii a few years back and was deputized, or whatever you call it." She lowered her voice to a whisper. "Everyone wants to know if he has a pistol!"

"A pistol?" Valena squeezed her eyes shut and opened them again. None of this was making any sense.

"There are no weapons here in Antarctica. That's part of the Antarctic Treaty, I think. Anyway, there's no need for them. Who in their right minds would fight a war here? They'd freeze their behinds off! And there's no hunting allowed here, either; that's absolutely part of the treaty, or is it the environmental protocol?"

Valena heard Brenda's words but was stuck back at the beginning of the conversation, trying to imagine her highly intellectual, ironic, tall, skinny professor being marched into a makeshift jail. The idea of Emmett Vanderzee being held under armed guard was nothing short of ludicrous. Valena shook her head, trying to clear it. What was going on here?

Brenda spirited a huge bag of corn chips off the table behind her and offered the open end of it to Valena. "Take some," she said. "It's why it's here."

"No thank you," she said. Five minutes earlier, she had been so hungry that her stomach seemed to have grown teeth, but now it felt like she had eaten clay. Her professor was in jail and she was nowhere. Fourteen years of effort had gone up in smoke.

Brenda's soft brown eyes glowed with concern. She said, "Well, breakfast's being served in the galley if you need it. I don't go over until brunch on Sundays, usually, which starts at eleven. You do know that it's Sunday, don't you? So many get mixed up when they cross the international date line. I'm just over here writing my e-mails because the computers are faster here than the ones in Building 155, and I don't have to wait in line. But you were asking where your office is. Biology is on this level. Glaciology and geology are down on the second phase. Down the ramp and to your right."

Valena began to back out of the room. Somehow having someone care about her made her feel even more lonely and exposed. "I'll just take a look downstairs."

"Okay. When are you scheduled for Happy Camp?"

"You mean survival school?"

"Yes, Snowcraft 1. Are you in the Monday-Tuesday class?"

"Yes."

"Well then, have a good rest today. You can't go much of anywhere else until you go to Happy Camp. Maybe there's a movie at the Coffee House. We had a showing of *March of the Penguins* last week, and it's always a good laugh when they show *Madagascar*. I just love those psychotic penguins: 'Cute and cuddly, boys!' "

Before Brenda could say anything more, Valena gave her a vague wave and moved quickly along the hall and down the ramp.

VALENA FOUND A door marked with a plaque listing Emmett's name and event number. She inserted her key. The door opened to evidence of Emmett's somewhat chaotic office housekeeping. His equipment was stacked everywhere. Big shipping cases and duffels, file boxes filled with air photos and satellite imagery, mountaineering equipment. She unzipped one of the larger black duffels. It contained an enormously thick sleeping bag and layers of closed-cell foam matting.

They didn't take away his equipment, she noted. *That's a good sign.* As she stared at the jumble, it occurred to her that Brenda had not spoken to her as someone who was about to be sent home. That meant that her fate was not generally known or perhaps even clearly decided. And that meant that there were possibilities. She now looked at the heap of equipment with a keener eye.

His cloth attaché was stowed underneath his desk, as if he had left it there just a moment before. With a certain sense of invasion, she opened it, but she found only a few unused tablets of lined paper, some pens and mechanical pencils, and his electronic camera. She noted that its memory chip had been removed and that his laptop computer was missing, too. *The marshal took his digital media as evidence,* she decided.

Then she realized, *I'm thinking like a detective.*

For the first time since that horrible moment the evening before when George Bellamy told her what had become of her professor—and her plans—Valena felt her heart lift. She let her mind follow the concept of detection down a narrow, turning passageway of thought. The world seemed to spin and shift, now taking in one point of view, now considering things from yet another.

Why would they arrest him now? If that journalist's death wasn't an accident, and Emmett killed him—which is absurd!—they would have arrested him a year ago, when it happened.

Then she turned these thoughts around another way. *What evidence exists that suggests that the reporter died through anything but mischance? What new evidence has come to light that justifies a change in their conclusions?*

She ran what she knew of the story of the death in Emmett's camp through her mind. This amounted to precious little. When it happened, she had been in her first semester at UNR, the University of Nevada at Reno, where she had enrolled for her master's degree. She had worked the summer before at the National Ice Core Laboratory in Denver, processing cores Emmett had collected, to prove her interest—and her capacity to function in the negative thirty-two degrees Fahrenheit cold of its vaults—and had enrolled immediately in Vanderzee's glaciology class, the only class he taught at UNR, so that she could show him how smart and dedicated and hard-working she was. Her plan was to get him to take her on as a research assistant out at the Desert Research Institute, where he kept his laboratory, become indispensable, and persuade him to take her with him to Antarctica.

"Hello."

Valena turned to see who had spoken.

It was a woman, leaning in the doorway with arms folded. Blond. Thirties or forties. Fit. Easy smile. Intelligent eyes. "New here?" she inquired.

"Yes. I'm Valena Walker. Glaciologist. Just arrived yesterday." It felt good to identify herself not as a hapless graduate student who was about to be sent home, but as a professional.

"Kathy Juneau," the woman said. She pointed up toward the upper level of the lab. "Biologist."

Valena tipped her head a bit to one side. "I thought there was almost no biology to study down here. Are you a marine biologist, then?"

"No, freshwater. I'm here to collect a cubic yard so I can extract a carbon sample, then archive it for scientists worldwide to study."

"Carbon?"

"We're studying the carbon cycle as it occurs in lake water. This is about the only place on earth we can do that, because everywhere else carbon is washed in from surrounding vegetation and other organisms that live outside the lake."

"Oh. Right. I had heard that there were lakes under the ice."

"This particular lake is not underneath a glacier. And the microbes that live in it can be found most anywhere, but here there's essentially nothing growing in or around the lake except these microbes."

"You mean, like, there's no vegetation?"

Kathy smiled. "You *are* new. Haven't you noticed? Look outside the window. Tell me if you see any trees, grasses, even algae."

Valena did as she was told. All she saw was ice.

Kathy said, "We do get influx of penguin guano, but we can easily identify that contribution and subtract it out."

"Penguin guano?"

"Yes. The lake is at the edge of an Adélie penguin colony. However, the lake has not been kind enough to thaw yet this year, so in the meantime I am finding other projects to keep myself busy. In Antarctica, one must be adaptable."

Valena sighed. "I'd love to see a penguin in the wild. Is it far to this lake of yours?"

"Fifteen minutes by helicopter, a couple of hours by tracked vehicle or snow machine."

"Not a casual visit."

Kathy shrugged a shoulder. Getting anywhere in Antarctica is a logistical undertaking. First you'd need to have your survival training, then sea ice training—you have to go over the sea ice, because cutting across land is too dangerous; crevasses and such, and the sea ice is not to be trifled with, either—and you'd need basic training on the use of a vehicle, presuming you have no helo hours. Then you'd also need someone to go with you, as one does not go anywhere alone here, and then there is the matter of permits—the colony is of course protected, so they require that you justify your visit on grounds of research—and then—"

Valena held up a hand. "That's almost too much to take in."

"It is rather overwhelming, at first. It took me three seasons to really begin to learn the ropes."

Valena stared at her feet. "This is my first season, and it looks like it's going to be incredibly short."

"I heard that Emmett left. What was that all about?"

"Something about that death in his camp last year."

Valena thought fast, trying to come up with a statement that would not defy George Bellamy's edict. She settled on being vague.

Kathy said, "I was afraid it might be that."

Valena searched her face for information. *Were you here last year?* "I signed on late to this project and I really don't know what happened."

"So far as I know, the story goes like this: the deceased was a journalist from the *New York Financial News*. He arrived in Emmett's camp without acclimatizing to the high elevation as he had been told to do. He developed altitude sickness—symptoms similar to pneumonia, but it will kill you quick—and, well, he died. There was a storm, so they couldn't get him out in time. Storms are huge here. They stop everything dead." Kathy stared out the window for a moment. "Sorry, bad choice of words. Anyway, when the winds dropped and they could get a flight in, the journalist's body was brought out stiff. In Antarctica, refrigeration of corpses is not a problem." She shook her head. "It was terrible bad luck."

Yeah, thought Valena. *The worst kind of bad luck. The kind that's contagious.*

Kathy's eyes briefly narrowed again in thought, then she smiled ironically. "It's the original locked-door mystery. They all went in alive, and one came out dead. If there was foul play, it follows that one of them did it." She shrugged a shoulder again. "Or all of them. Well, if I can help in any way . . ."

"Are any of the people who were in that camp here again this year? Anyone I could talk to?"

"I imagine so. I don't remember the names, though. I was thinking more of help getting oriented around here. Where to find things, how things are done."

"Oh. Well, one thing, how do you make a phone call from here?"

Kathy pointed at a guidebook that sat on the shelf above Emmett's desk. "You mean back to the world? It's all in there. But if an outside line is what you want, the dish is down."

"The dish?"

"The satellite dish that carries the telecommunications. Some engineers are working on it this morning. They're trying to increase the bandwidth without the expense of putting in a new one. Everything's about resources here. Everything. It all has to come in by plane or ship from somewhere far, far away."

"How about e-mail?" asked Valena. "Oh. I suppose that uses the same satellite."

"It does, but you can pick up mail that's already arrived and been put in a queue, and your outgoing messages will go out when the system comes back up. You can't use your own computer until IT hooks you up to the system, but you can use the computers upstairs in the library."

Valena shook her head in amazement. "McMurdo is a lot bigger and more complex than I imagined it would be."

"This is a premier research institution. That requires infrastructure. And this base is the jumping-off point for myriad smaller field stations and field camps, not to mention the Pole. This whole continent is a research laboratory."

A wave of sadness and frustration broke over Valena, and she looked away.

Taking this as a hint that the conversation was over, Kathy said, "Well, welcome to Antarctica, Valena," and headed on down the hallway.

Valena lifted her gaze again to the office's one small window. It looked out across the frozen sea toward the dancing run of mountains. High ice clouds had formed, painting a dizzying wave over the far-off summits. In the foreground, the four-jet-engine C-17 on which she had arrived dwarfed the smaller turbo-prop LC-130s, which rested in trim ranks beside the ice runway with their noses pointed eastward, their tall red tails lifted to the west. Even though it was still early morning, the sun was somewhere high overhead, casting short shadows to the southwest.

The scene was breathtakingly beautiful, a symphony of white and blue, but instead of lifting her heart, it seemed a tease, a chimera. *All of this is so close, so tantalizing, and yet if I can't get Emmett back down here . . .*

Looking out across the cold wilderness she now began to comprehend the form that death took in this environment, for everybody involved. They were isolated from the world, and when the wind blew, they might just as well have been the first explorers with no radio, no planes, and no ship to save them.

Shaking her head in an attempt to dispel the ghosts of anxiety and loss, she left her laptop and backpack on the desk, relocked the office door, and headed back up the ramp to the stairs that led up to the library.

Crary Lab's library proved to be a broad, airy room with windows that ran all along the wall that looked out over the ice. She gazed through them awhile, again lost in the cold majesty of the scene, and then sat down at one of the computers that hummed in the center of the room. She hit a key on the keyboard to wake it up. Nothing happened.

A man who was sitting at a nearby machine turned toward her, reached over to her mouse, moved it a bit, and gave it a click. The desktop screen came up. "Cussed thing," he said, in an accent that betrayed an upbringing somewhere in the American midwest. He had a beard and soft brown eyes that seemed telescoped back by his thick, steel-framed glasses.

"Thanks."

He smiled and went back to work at his own machine.

Out of the corner of one eye, Valena studied the soft curve of his nose, the curly fringe of his mustache, his closely cropped hair shot with early gray. Almost palpable kindness radiated from him. Again, and a little more loudly this time, she said, "Thank you."

He glanced back her way and gave her a wink. "You're welcome." He continued working.

"I really appreciate that."

He took his hands off his keyboard and folded them across his chest. Tipped his head her way. Regarded her with a gentle smile. "First time on the ice?"

"Yes."

"Me, too. I've been here about a month. I was minding my own business one day and a colleague said, 'They've got jobs in Antarctica. Want to go?' and I said, 'Sure, where do I sign up?' How about you?"

"I have always, always wanted to come here," she replied. "Or at least, ever since I was a kid and my granddad read to me about Shackleton's winter in the ice and all that. I wanted to come here and know what he loved so much about it that he would take such a risk. And . . . I hoped that I would love it that much, too." Now she felt embarrassed. She hadn't told anyone any of this, ever. Why was she blurting it out now, and to a total stranger?

The man held out his right hand to be shaken. "Michael."

"Valena," she replied. "Nice to meet you, Michael."

"Been to Happy Camp yet?"

"The survival training? No. I start tomorrow."

"Really? Excellent! We'll be there together." He got up and crossed to the coffeemaker, poured some for each of them, handed one to Valena, and sat back down in his chair. "Excuse me, please. I've got to finish this and then get over to the chapel in time for tai chi." He focused his eyes on his computer screen, lined his fingers up over the keyboard, and dove back into his work.

She turned to her computer and tapped into the Internet, bringing up her e-mail account.

She wrote to Taha Hesan, the other graduate student who was supposed to be coming to the ice to serve on Vanderzee's project. He was a doctoral candidate. She had gotten to know him only slightly as they prepared for the trip.

Taha

I am here in McM and V is not. NSF says that they got hold of you and told you not to come. I don't know how much they told you about why, but here's what I've got:

1. V was removed from the ice under guard.
2. It's got to do with the reporter who died in his camp last year.
3. Presuming the worst, V is being charged with

She paused a moment. It didn't make any sense to be writing this. A renewed sense of shock gripped her. Her fingers felt cold on the keyboard. Shaking herself free, she deleted "with" and simply put a period to mark the end of the sentence. Then she added:

Please write ASAP to let me know your plans. My plan is to proceed as if V is returning soon. Do you have any idea what needs to be done to prepare for fieldwork? I have Snowcraft I (Happy Camp) tomorrow and Tuesday—your Sunday and Monday; I keep forgetting that I've crossed the international date line into tomorrow—so I will be incommunicado for two days. Anything you can do from your end to help V and supply info that will keep our project going I would appreciate.

Valena

She hit send and then sat with her fingers suspended half an inch above the keys. *Who can I go to for help?* she wondered. *Who would know where to start with a mess like this?*

Suddenly the answer came to her. She would write to Emily Hansen, a woman she had gotten to know during her undergraduate studies at the University of Utah. Em had been doing her master's there at the time, and she now worked for the Utah Geological Survey. Her specialty was forensic geology, and she was famous for the work she had done unraveling crimes. Yes, that was it, write to Em; she could tell her how to proceed, and she could keep her mouth shut, so it would be okay to tell her everything!

Valena looked up the Utah Geological Survey Web site to find an e-mail address for Em, then tapped out a message stating what had happened, ending with:

> I'm trying to figure out how to proceed. How do I get people around here to tell me things? And does Antarctica fall under some kind of international tribunal or do American scientists accused of endangering American journalists fall under American jurisprudence?

Remembering her manners, Valena asked after what was new in Em's life, signed herself, "Affectionately, Valena," thought better of it, given the gravity of the situation, and changed "affectionately" to "yours" and then hit send.

She glanced over at Michael. His face was calm and tightly focused on something he was reading. She thought of offering to freshen up his coffee but didn't want to seem too earnest about getting to know him. She had heard that the ratio of men to women in McMurdo was seven to three, so it might be unwise to seem too friendly.

Turning back toward her Internet account, she wrote an e-mail to send to her list of interested friends and family, extolling the beauty of the view out the window and trying to put in words just how big it was and how tiny this frail outpost of humanity seemed by contrast. In thus doing, she at last plunged herself into an enjoyment of having made it to Antarctica. Time flowed and the clock crept past 10:00 a.m. and approached 11:00. Valena's stomach growled, breaking her concentration, and she decided to get some food.

She found her way downstairs and out through the heavy doors of the airlock, out across the yard past a row of tracked vehicles, up over the stile, and back toward Building 155. The icy wind was blowing toward her, and she could smell cooking fumes coming from the exhaust system. A short, stubby tracked vehicle ground past the upwind end of the building, and a few seconds later, she smelled gasoline. Just as quickly as it had reached her, the odor dissipated and was gone.

Both odors were oddly overpowering. *Why?* she wondered. Then she noticed that there were no other odors around her, no stink of rotting compost, no soft scent of flowers. *Rocks and snow have no smell,* she realized.

Valena continued into the building, then turned into the dorm hallway to her left, so that she could leave her parka in her room. Deciding to look her very best, she doffed the turtleneck and slipped into a creamy white fleece pullover that clung to her curves. She then continued down the main corridor toward the scents of food and people. The air smelled of sweetness and grains—waffles?

Following the flow of people swarming in for the meal, she arrived at a TV monitor that was scrolling information about movies, flight schedules, and the weather. It was a robust fourteen degrees Fahrenheit outside, negative ten degrees Celsius. She checked the flight schedules and saw that her name was not on any of the manifests. This was the first bit of truly good news she had had since arriving.

Next she headed for the hand-washing station. DON'T SPREAD THE CRUD, a sign on the wall above the sink advised. Following the instructions listed, she used plenty of soap and scrubbed assiduously for fifteen seconds, pondering how little Emmett Vanderzee had told her about survival in this harsh and bizarre environment. She tried to give her absent-minded mentor the benefit of the doubt, but his lack of advisement bothered her. Had he not, in fact, been the leader she had thought he was?

And if he was not that kind of leader, just what was he? A murderer? The thought was absurd. But was he a bungler? Had she bet on the wrong horse?

She grabbed a sheet of paper toweling and began to dry her hands. People filed past her on their way to brunch. Most made eye contact, smiled, and nodded; some said hello. What had Brenda said? In a place like this, you can't really hide anything. That meant that Valena was about to meet several hundred people who might have ideas about where to look for things that were supposed to lie hidden.

Valena turned toward the dining hall. It was time to get acquainted with more good citizens of McMurdo Station.

3

DAVE FITZGERALD CRUISED THROUGH THE FOOD LINES IN THE GALLEY in search of something hot and filling. It had been a long, cold week rolling snow into ice out at Pegasus runway, and he needed to stock up for another.

Building this landing surface at Pegasus was a satisfying challenge. It was built in layers, using the only road metal they had in Antarctica: snow. He and the other heavy equipment operators out of Fleet Operations used a 966 Cat loader with a snow-throwing attachment to coat the runway, then drove a Challenger 95 tractor up and down the runway pulling a Reynolds box, laying the snow out in a smooth three-inch layer. Next, they transformed the three inches of snow into an ultra-hard-packed, one-and-a-half-inch-thick surface of white ice by dragging 124 tons of weight carts behind the Challenger. The weight of the rollers caused a process that metallurgists called sintering, in which the structure of the fine ice crystals they called snow were compressed and reformed into a dense, interlocking crystal lattice hard and smooth enough to land jets. Each layer took about three days of working around the clock, and it would take ten layers to get the desired effect.

Building runways and dressing the flagged routes that led out to them was slow, exacting, and satisfying, his favorite kind of work, and the solitude of the long hours in the tractor in all that gloriously empty space was eased by a weather-tight cab and the Armed Forces radio station that piped in classic rock. But riding back and forth in the cold for nine hours a day, six days each week, built up an appetite. It looked like the Belgian waffles were the cure today, and hey, how about some eggs and bacon and a little dessert? He moved over to the sweets table. What was this little confection that the kind pixies from the kitchen had left for him? Looked like lemon bars. And oh, that fresh-baked bread, mm-hm!

Dave forked two of the lemon bars straight onto his tray and picked out a nice, thick slice of bread to chew on while he waited in line for a waffle. He snagged a little bowl of stewed fruit just in case all those folks who touted diet pyramids knew what they were squawking about, loaded up two glasses with milk, grabbed a fork and a knife, and turned toward the waffle line. Having slept in after an evening sipping Jim Beam and Cokes at Gallagher's, he was hungry as a bear.

"Hey there, Dave," said the chef as he reached the front of the line. "Fix ya up with a waffle here?"

"You know you can," Dave replied. "Hey, you were doing purty well at the pool table last night at Gallagher's."

The chef winked. "Gotta shark me some extra dollars. When I get out of here I'm going to travel up through southeast Asia. Ride an elephant, all that."

"Sounds great." Dave gave him a friendly smile. The folks who worked in the galley were really decent. They took the job of feeding the horde of people who flowed through McMurdo very seriously and greeted each soul who stood in their lines with dignity and professional pride. He especially liked the omelet guy. He was older than the rest and had learned exactly how Dave liked his eggs, but waffles were only an option on Sundays.

"Here ya go, man. Check out the strawberries. They're fresh!"

"They look wonderful," said Dave, scooping several spoonfuls onto his waffle.

"Go for it. We got a whole load of freshies in from Cheech yesterday with that late flight. Cool, huh? Yeah, loads of lettuce, too; they'll be up for dinner. Man, I'm salivating just thinking of it."

"Me, too. I never was a fresh foods man before coming down here, but now I'd walk a mile in tight shoes for an orange or a banana. Hey, is it true that you sometimes get spiders and such on the lettuce?"

Waffle Guy grinned. "Yeah."

"What do you do with them? Put them in the compost?"

"Oh, hell no! We keep them as pets!"

His waffle acquired and heaped with strawberries and whipped cream, Dave turned toward the galley to choose a seat. He craned his neck to see if Ben, the biologist he had enjoyed visiting with the morning before, was sitting up in the beaker zone. No luck. He spotted his roommate Matt at one of the tables where the heavy equipment operators tended to sit and headed over to join him.

Matt had his turquoise blue contact lenses on, which always had a startling effect. He drove various loaders and a mammoth forklift built by Caterpillar. It could lift enormously heavy loads, like the big metal shipping containers that brought materials in from the States and carried waste materials back. It had a big counterweighting butt emblazoned with a cartoon of Garfield and its nickname: Fat Cat. "Morning, Dave," Matt said, without glancing up.

"Matt." Dave settled down and shoveled into his eggs. For several minutes the only noises from their table were the soft sounds of munching and forks hitting china.

"Yup."

"So, you goin' to Black Island this week?"

"Hope so."

"You gonna drive the Challenger, Flipper, or one of the snow machines?"

"Dunno."

"Whatcha haulin' out there?"

"Water."

"You and me, we're like an old married couple," Matt said finally, as he pushed aside his plate and moved his coffee closer to his large chest. "That was four one-word sentences out of five, and a total of only two words over one syllable."

"You ought to go back to teaching, Matt."

Matt laughed. "But I hate kids, remember? That's why I came here. You see anyone under eighteen in this room?"

Dave looked about him. "I'm not sure as I see anyone under thirty."

"Over there by the milk machine. The DA who's putting in the new box of nonfat."

"What's 'DA' stand for, anyway?"

"Dining assistant."

"Oh. Thought maybe the *D* stood for dog. They work purty hard for their wages, and they sure are the bottom of the totem pole around here. They never go anywheres. Imagine coming all the way down here and never seeing the outdoors, even, except one day a week, and you'd get a different day off than everyone else, too."

"You're changing the subject. What do you think of her?"

"Aw, hell, Matt."

"You like her?"

"She's cute."

"I know her. I could introduce you."

Dave blushed slightly, a change in coloration that only really showed around his eyes, where the glacier goggles protected the skin from tanning. "A bit young for me, Matt."

"What, you looking for long-term commitment and deep meaning? You've been here, what? Eight weeks? And you haven't hit on a single female. C'mon, folks will think you're gay."

Dave grinned. "Think *we're* gay, you mean."

"No, really, man, you gotta start checking out the chicks."

Dave looked around. "Half of *them* are gay," he said, now trying humor to throw Matt off his case.

"Why, because they aren't climbing into your lap?"

"You gotta admit some of the women here are tougher than both of us put together."

Three more men walked up to their table, arranged their trays, and sat down. Dave idly took a census of their gastronomic decisions. Steve, a Fleet Ops comrade who had stood his share of shifts out at Pegasus, weighed in with a nice-looking cheese and black olive omelet, while Wilbur, who ran a loader on the road being constructed up past the layout yard, had decided on a big bowl of the homemade granola heaped with Greek yogurt, nuts, and stewed fruit. Joe, who was helping construct the floating ice dock that would service the supply ships, had gone for the waffles. As they forked their first mouthfuls of food and swilled their first ounces of juice, coffee, and water, Dave took a big draw on one of his glasses of milk, wondering what kind of nonsense the gang of three was going to come up with this time.

Steve delivered the first volley. "Any new babes to check out? I hear where yesterday's C-17 made it in from Cheech, so it's possible." He glanced around the room, scanning the tables.

Matt said, "Chasing skirt's bound to be one big exercise in frustration in a place where the ratio of bucks to does is seven to three."

Joe said, "What are you, gay?"

"It's the thrill of the hunt. Oh, Wilbur, there's your honey now," said Steve, eyeing a young computer tech who was just emerging from the waffle line. "What's her name?"

"Burnie."

"Short for Burnadette?"

Wilbur shook his head. "Nope, short for burns my ass. She just storms through the dining room like she's some grade school principal in pursuit of a kid accused of shitting in someone's lunchbox."

"Nice tits," said Joe.

Wilbur shot him a look.

"I don't mean yours," said Joe. "Hers! You gotta admit, she's got tits made in heaven, and when she rolls her ass like that—"

"Stop it!" said Wilbur. "She ain't giving me any, so I can't stand to watch, so I ain't, and I sure's hell wish you'd quit giving me the blow by blow."

"What is it you guys named her?" Dave asked. "You have such a way with language."

"We call her Hell No," said Steve. "Guess why."

Wilbur said, " 'Cause that's her answer. The tight-assed—"

Dave said, "I gotta wonder if you boys might do better if you went it alone, rather than hunting as a pack."

"Dang!" said Wilbur. "Here comes Wiggles!"

Joe swung his face around to catch every last ripple of movement. "My, my, my. I do like what she's done with all those chocolate bars she's been eating."

Steve snickered appreciatively. "Cadbury's ought to hire her. She'd be an inspiration to all young women who think anorexia is a beauty plan."

Steve asked, "What's the deal with the load from Cheech?"

"Only one female name on the flight manifest," said Wilbur. "At least, I think Valena is a woman's name."

"What's her other name?"

"I forget."

"Walker," said Joe. "Valena Walker."

Matt said, "Yankee last name, first name ending in A, sounds like a babe to me. But they're mostly bringing in beakers these days, so she could be one of those brainy ones with less hair than you have."

Joe put a hand on his bald spot in mock affrontery. "I beg your pardon."

Something near the food lines caught Matt's attention. He went on point and let out a series of small beep noises, like a machine that was honing in on a target.

Wilbur said, "You got your forklift stuck in reverse, Matt?"

"There *is* a new one!" said Matt jubilantly. "Check her out! And if that's what a beaker looks like, sign me up."

"Where?" said Steve.

Joe said, "One o'clock high. Blue jeans, white fleece pullover, and oh, my my."

All eyes swung toward the approaching woman.

"Exotic," said Steve. "Gorgeous. Strong. And *built*!"

"What do you think?" asked Wilbur. "She black? Latino? What?"

"I see some Asian in there, too," said Joe.

"And tell me about those cheekbones!" said Steve. "Native American? Hawaiian?"

"Carries herself like a dancer," said Dave, sneaking another look.

Matt swung his attention to his roommate. "I didn't know you were a poet," he said.

"I mean she moves real purty."

"I'll show her how to move," said Wilbur.

The woman stopped about fifteen feet away and turned, scanning the crowd. Dave watched her closely out of the corners of his eyes. There was indeed something marvelous about her, but also something sad, almost haunted. The tension in her shoulders made her look uncertain of herself, almost scared.

Wilbur began to utter inchoate gurgling sounds.

Right then, Dave wished that he could shoot Wilbur out of the universe like a watermelon seed. This woman needed comfort, not drooling. He began to rise from his chair. He didn't have a plan, but perhaps he would speak to her, ask if he might be of assistance. But no, she had made her choice and was moving quickly toward a table up at the far end of the room by the windows, where the computer geeks tended to sit. He lowered himself back into his seat.

"Sitting with the dweebs," said Steve. "Must be a new techie. Or yeah, a beaker, even."

"You think?" said Joe.

Wilbur let out a theatrical sigh. "Yeah, hang it up, men, she won't have no time for the likes of us."

Dave mapped the gentle curves of her spine as she settled into a chair. When he returned his attention to his own table, Matt was staring at him, observing him frankly. "What?" said Dave, so that only Matt could hear him.

Matt raised an eyebrow.

Dave bowed his head and lifted his fork to his mouth, pretending that he noticed or cared what was on it.

4

"MIND IF I SIT DOWN?" VALENA ASKED THE PEOPLE AT THE TABLE BY the window.

"Make yourself at home," said a man wearing a fleece hat that featured a band of fake fur that stood out like a fright wig. The other denizens of the table—two women and another man—continued their conversation.

Valena settled into a chair and stuck a fork into her eggs.

"No Belgian waffle?" the man with the hat asked, even before she got the first bite to her lips.

"Couldn't wait." She stuffed the forkful into her mouth and chewed. Relief surged through her body.

"I'm Peter," he said.

"Valena."

"Well, if you don't go back for a waffle, don't miss Wednesdays. That's cookie day around here, and you don't have to wait in line. Where are you from?"

"Reno."

"Cool. What do you do here?"

"I'm here to study glaciers. How about you?"

"I'm an energy conservation specialist."

"I see. Where are you from?" she inquired, completing the symmetry of the conversation.

"My storage locker is in Idaho."

Valena blinked. This was the first time she had ever met anyone who didn't think of himself as being from somewhere.

The man who was sitting to her right said, to no one in particular, "Well, I'm going to go get in line and buy some hooch," and got up and left. He was replaced by a tiny woman with high cheekbones on a face so heavily tanned that it evoked the original meaning of the adjective. She put one foot on the chair and squatted on it, letting the other leg dangle. "Who are you?" she demanded, leaning a little closer than Valena quite found comfortable. "You're new. I'm horny as hell."

Valena could smell alcohol on her breath. "Does everybody here drink on Sundays?" she asked, trying to sound casual.

"Oh, hell no. Usually I spend the day skiing. But today I'm real horny. You're just a kid, so don't worry. Yeah. You're just a kid. Are you any fun? Huh?"

"Don't mind her," said Peter. "It's just her way of saying hello. Love me, love my hormones. Take it easy on her, Cupcake, she just got here."

"I like in-your-face," Cupcake said. "It keeps things fresh."

Peter said, "Fresh is what you are, love."

Cupcake now leaned even closer to Valena and examined her face with frank interest. "You're a little bit of everything, ain't ya?"

"What do you do here?" Valena said evenly, trying to back her off.

"I drive heavy equipment. Come for a ride?"

Valena said, "This is an interesting town. Just like college, only more so."

Cupcake said, "Yeah. The food sucks, you get no privacy, but instead of 'What's your sign and what's your major?' everybody asks, 'Where are you from, and what do you do here?' Gets real boring, huh?"

"Oh, I'm finding the food quite tasty," Valena said.

The woman eyed her appreciatively. "You're good."

"Thanks. What did you say your name was?"

"Muffin."

"I thought it was Cupcake."

"Okay then, Cupcake." She moved her gaze pointedly to Valena's left hand. "No wedding ring."

Valena shook her head. "No wedding ring and no dice."

"Aw, you're no fun."

Valena began to smile. "Yeah, well."

The woman seated across from her said, "I'm Doris."

"How do you do, Doris?"

"About as I please today. The rest of the time I gripe a lot."

Valena asked, "Is there something I'm not quite understanding about Sundays in McMurdo?"

Doris said, "We work nine hours a day, six days a week. On Sunday, we kind of get out of hand."

Another man came to the table, plopped down in the empty seat to the right of Doris, draped an arm around her, and fixed a grin on Valena. "Who are you?" he inquired.

Cupcake said, "This is Valena from Reno. Sounds like a song."

The man began to make up a tune, and sang, "Va-le-na from Re-no, she really knew her ice, she was so very nice, that Va-le-e-e-na . . . from . . . Re-e-e-no!"

Then he held out a hand. Valena took it. He bent forward and rubbed his cheek to it as if it were a cat. He began to purr.

Trying to pull her hand away without being too abrupt, Valena reflexively asked one of the two standard questions. "What do you do here?"

"I do Doris," he said, giving her a salacious grin. "Life is good."

Valena yanked her hand away.

Doris said, "She needs that hand to eat with, sweetie. And she's a grantee. Treat her nice. What did you say you did, Valena?"

"Ice. Stable isotopes."

"Whatever," the man said. "Beakers. Cut 'em some slack and they talk weird at ya." His grin moved from salacious to soupy.

Peter said, "Always remember, were it not for the beakers, none of us would be here."

"What's a beaker?" Valena asked.

Cupcake said, "Scientist. As in, the glassware. A fingie beaker at that."

"And 'fingie' means?"

"F-N-G. The second two letters stand for 'new guy.' "

Valena choked on her orange juice, and it came out her nose. Coughing and laughing, she put a napkin to her face.

Peter said, "So, Valena, whose project you on, or are you McMurdo's youngest PI?"

Valena tensed. Here was her opening. "I'm working with Emmett Vanderzee."

"Oooooh . . ." said Cupcake, letting the sound rise and fall. "Man, you really got hosed!"

Valena waited, hoping someone would offer information, but all eyes were on her, waiting for the same. Taking a deep breath, she said, "Can anyone tell me what happened? I just got here last night and, well, all I know is he's been sent north."

Cupcake patted Valena on the shoulder. "Eat up," she said. "I got some-one you should meet."

5

TWENTY MINUTES LATER, HER BODY LOST UNDER THICK POLYPROPY-
lene underwear, wind pants, wool socks, floppy blue FDX boots, mittens,
a fleece hat, and the capacious acreage of her big red parka, Valena found
herself hustling to keep up with Cupcake. "Are you certain I need this
many layers?" she asked. She was beginning to sweat, and her blue boots
flopped like clown's feet.

"We're still in the wind shadow of the buildings and these hills. Why
do you think they put this armpit of a station where it is?"

They emerged from the cover of the buildings and headed away down
a trail in the volcanic rock that formed the island.

Valena pulled off her fleece hat and stuffed it into a pocket. The gravel
of the trail moved oddly under her feet, and she looked down to study it. It
was formed of bashed-up scoria, a volcanic rock filled with little air bubbles because it had flowed out of the ground frothing with rapidly expand-
ing gasses. It was odd to think that in this world of ice, the island had been
born of fire. She had been to Hawaii, where volcanic rock weathered
quickly under invasive vegetation and other organisms, but this scoria was
so cold and perennially bound in ice and snow that nothing could grow on
it or live in it, nothing to break it down into soil. She glanced around, con-
firming to her still disbelieving eyes that there was not a single nonhuman
organism anywhere in sight: no trees, no grass, no moss, no lichens, not
even a bird in the air. The great blue-white landscape of ice and distant
mountains was punctuated only by the line of aircraft parked on the ice,
the few ski-mounted small structures that attended them, and this odd
gathering of humans.

They kept moving. Cupcake led the way down the long, shallow slope toward a point of land that jutted from the end of the peninsula on which McMurdo Station had been built. Valena was having trouble walking in the big, soft boots. "Who are we going to see?" she asked, trying to get Cupcake to talk more so that she would have to slow down. She threw open her parka, which was so warm that she had not, in the twenty-four hours she had been using it, ever actually zipped it up; she had used it instead as a wrap.

"You are about to have the honor of meeting the master blaster."

"Master . . . what?"

"Blaster. Didn't you—oh, right, you just got here, so you don't know. They're blasting the road that leads towards Castle Rock, trying to straighten it, for some goddamned reason. He'll be out at the hut today. He goes out there every time they open it up and let us wackos in. I think he likes to photograph ghosts or something. Anyways, you can corner him there and ask your questions."

"And I want to ask him questions because . . . ?"

"He was out in your dude's field camp last year."

"I see."

"Gotta go right to the source around here. Otherwise, all you hear is rumors. That, and suppositions. It's like this place is a halfway house for paranoiacs."

Valena asked, "What's this hut he's photographing?"

"Discovery Hut. Actually, it was a warehouse. I guess they lived aboard the ship, which of course got stuck in the ice. Those boys were good at getting things stuck. You're lucky; they don't open it to visitation very often."

"*They* lived aboard the ship? Who built it? When?"

"Scott, 1902. His first expedition. Got his butt to eighty-two south, had to turn back. Not the 1911 expedition where he froze to death."

Sir Robert Falcon Scott! Valena drew in her breath with surprise. Scott's first attempt to reach the South Pole was mounted just two years into the twentieth century. He had arrived aboard a ship named *Discovery*. *And this is the hut named for that expedition! She thought. I am walking on ground on which he walked!*

As she continued down the trail, her heart now racing with excitement, they came out from the lee of the hills that surrounded McMurdo and were caught by an exhalation of frozen air off the ice sheet. Valena was instantly cold, so cold that her muscles began to contract. She hurriedly put her hat back on, pulled up the hood, and tried to get the slide of her big red parka's zipper engaged. As she fumbled with chilling fingers, the wind found its way down her neck. The zipper was jammed. She tried it again and again, reseating it, pulling at it, cursing it.

Twenty strides down the trail, Cupcake turned around to see why Valena had dropped behind her. "Oh, hell, hasn't anyone given you the short course on how to work the zipper on your big red yet?" She strode back toward Valena and grabbed the two sides of the track, yanked the one on Valena's left down sharply, slapped the slide from the other side onto it, and whipped it up to her chin, all in the space of three seconds. "You gotta let it know who's boss," she said. She opened it again. Showed Valena how to hold the pieces properly, tugging the left side down sharply and holding it taut while she worked the right. "Now you try it. Yeah, that's it. You'd think they'd make it idiot proof, considering that your life depends on it, but there it is." As she turned around to resume her march, she said, "It's like just about everything else down here: it's essential, you need a short course to know how to do it, and that course doesn't exist."

"I've got survival training tomorrow."

"Happy Camp. Have a party. They'll put a five-gallon plastic bucket on your head to simulate a whiteout, like that's going to really learn you." She shook her head. "It's not their fault. There's just entirely too much to absorb. I've been down here seven seasons, and some days I feel like I'm only just getting the hang of it."

Five minutes' additional brisk hike brought them to the end of the point. There, the ground dropped off precipitously on three sides, plunging fifty feet to the frozen sea below. The ice met the land in a jumble of heaved-up slabs where the winds and tides had worked it, like puckered waves stilled by a snapshot in the act of slapping the shore.

Someone had erected a cross at the summit of a small rise at the very end of the point, and just below it, Valena could see a gently sloping roof made of wood and built in the shape of a shallow pyramid. It was supported by posts. Valena assumed that this must be a protective canopy erected to preserve the original structure, which must exist as ruins underneath; after all, she reckoned, more than one hundred years of fierce Antarctic weather had thrashed it since Scott's men had built it.

One hundred years, thought Valena. *Not much more than the average human lifetime*. In all the lifetimes of the human species, great civilizations had arisen and fallen and been built again on all six other continents, but here in Antarctica, the touch of humanity was this new, a tiny foothold on an unimaginably large expanse of ice. This had been the last continent to be located, the hardest to reach, and by far the most difficult on which to maintain even this fragile encampment. Less than two hundred years ago, there was no southern continent on world maps. In the 1770s, Cook sailed around a southern sea choked with ice but could only hypothesize that land lay beyond it. So obscuring was its veil of ice that land wasn't sighted until 1820, tantalizing yet unapproachable through a ship captain's spyglass.

Valena moved closer to the cliff to look off toward the Transantarctic Mountains, drawn simultaneously by emptiness and fulfillment and the fear that she would not make it to the continent itself but instead be sent home in an agony of frustration.

"Don't wander too close to the edge," said Cupcake. "That cross there? It's for this guy Vince somebody, who was the first man to die in McMurdo Sound. He fell off this cliff in the middle of a blizzard. They never found his body."

"I shall proceed with respect, then."

Cupcake pointed at the hut. "When you're done ogling the scenery, join me in there."

The sun was high in the northern sky, throwing shadows to the south, the reverse of what she had grown to consider normal back home in North America. She shook her head. Her world was turned upside down and inside out or, more accurately, outside in. As a particularly strong gust of frozen wind bowled in off the ice, Valena turned and followed Cupcake to the low, square structure.

Two women stood underneath the overhanging roof by a door that led into the hut. "Please brush all the snow off your boots," one instructed, as she welcomed them in out of the wind.

Valena scraped her enormous blue boots. "Where does the original hut begin?" she inquired.

"This *is* the hut."

"But the wood looks almost new!"

"Things don't rot out here."

The windows were small, sparse, and recessed under the veranda, so the interior was dim, its darkness exaggerated by a thick accumulation of soot on the walls and ceiling. Two pairs of antique outer pants hung on a clothesline. Heaps of strange substances were stacked near one wall.

Catching her inquiring gaze, a man who was standing there wrestling the legs of a camera tripod said, "Hundred-year-old seal blubber. Want to try some? It's good with garlic."

Valena gave him a smile. He was a moderate-sized man of husky build and was endowed with pendulous mustaches that bristled with gray. He wore a blue watch cap, and instead of the blaze-red Valena wore, the shell of his parka was made of light brown canvas. A pair of faux tortoiseshell half-glasses gave him an oddly professorial air, and he gazed through them now at the leg-extension catches on his unruly tripod. With a final tweak, the last of the legs slid down into place. He jiggled it around, getting it into position, and then, apparently satisfied, he opened the top of his parka and produced an old Nikon F2 camera, which he clipped onto the top of the tripod.

Cupcake appeared at his elbow. "Oh, good, you've found each other. Ted, this is Valena. She's a student of Emmett Vanderzee's."

Ted closed his eyes for several moments. When he opened them again, he wasn't smiling anymore.

Valena waited.

Cupcake said, "Valena just arrived yesterday afternoon, and it was news to her that her professor wasn't going to be here to greet her."

Ted closed his eyes again and sighed heavily. "That's very bad luck for the young lady, but what exactly do you expect me to do about it?"

"I want you to talk to her. Tell her what you know."

Pain suffused Ted's voice as he said, "I know very little."

Cupcake put a hand tenderly on Ted's shoulder. "But you were there, so you know stuff."

"I was in the camp, but I wasn't there when the guy died."

"Then tell her that much."

Ted finally reopened his eyes and looked deep into Valena's.

"Anything you can tell me would help me understand," Valena said. "Anything at all."

Ted looked away. After a moment, with great consternation, he unclipped his camera and began folding up his tripod.

"I'm sorry," Valena told him. "I didn't mean to interrupt your work. Would you like me to meet you later on, maybe? When you're done?"

"No, young lady, I am now done for the day, trust me on that. But we're not going to talk about this here."

Cupcake said, "When someone dies out here, it really gets to people, especially if they knew the person, even if he *was* a raging jackass." Focusing her sharp eyes on Ted, she added, "Especially if you think you could have changed things had you stayed in camp. It wasn't your fault, Ted."

"Then it was nobody's fault. That's what's so ridiculous about yanking Emmett off the ice. He didn't kill that man any more than I'm the Queen of Sheba."

"In a previous life, Ted. That's why you're so good at contacting your feminine side."

"Stuff it up your tailpipe, Cupcake."

Ted dropped his camera into a ziplock bag, then opened his parka halfway and tucked the bag inside the top of his bib overalls, up against a layer of navy blue fleece, and pulled his zipper back up to his chin. With a softly paternal tone, he advised Valena, "If you take your camera indoors when it's cold, the condensation will screw it up. And the battery has to stay warm to work. It will die at these temperatures so fast you wouldn't believe it, but if you warm it up again, it comes back."

"When are you going to get a digital camera?" Cupcake chided.

"Sweet thing, I am a devout Luddite. I will still be shooting film when you're gumming your soup in some home for the ancient and insane." He glanced over his shoulder at Valena. "Kind of silly shooting print film, considering that I don't see the results of my work until I go back north, but it's what fires my rocket."

Outside in the glare and reflection of twenty-four-hour sunlight and wraparound ice, Ted led the way up the short hill to Vince's Cross. There, he set down his gear and looked out across the frozen sea toward the continent. "You know your landmarks yet, Valena?" he inquired.

"Not really."

"That bit of meringue is the Royal Society Range, just one small section of the Transantarctic Mountains. Scott named it in honor of the sponsors of his 1902 expedition. You'll find lots of stuff like that around here, things named for people who never set foot on the ice. The Transantarctics run for three thousand kilometers, and here and there, glaciers flowing from the Polar Plateau flow down valleys onto the West Antarctic Ice

Sheet and the Ross Ice Shelf. To get to the Pole, you have to climb up one glacier or another and then continue on across the Polar Plateau. He had to drag his supplies up over the mountains somewhere, but where? You want to go inland as far as possible across the ice shelf before you start to climb, because the higher you get, the colder it gets, and the pole is 9,200 feet above sea level."

He pointed southward, to the left of the range, toward a group of lower summits that stood somewhat closer. "He headed out past those islands. That's White Island to the east, then Minna Bluff—keep an eye on Minna; if it disappears, a storm's coming and you have about two hours to take cover—then Black Island, Mount Discovery, and the Brown Peninsula. Black Island is the closest, at about twenty-five miles hence.

"They came in by sea, not like us lazybones who fly down; they were at sea in the wildest weather for weeks. They sailed in during the height of summer when the ice was broken out, all the way to this point, and dropped anchor, spent the winter, and started out south the following spring. That was the way of it. They couldn't get close enough to make the pole in one season, because the ice freezes out hundreds of miles to sea, and it doesn't break out until December or January, and some years not at all. So they had to wait for their access, then unload their supplies and begin to set up depots, then hunker down and wait out the long winter night. When the sun rose again, they went out around White Island and continued south across the Ross Ice Shelf. The ice is riddled with crevasses where it flows around those islands, so that must have been a joy. That's my job, you see. I blow up things that are in peoples' way around here."

Valena nodded, letting him know that she understood, though she wasn't certain that she did.

Ted said, "So he took his best shot, picked a glacier, and made his climb. Then he was not only fighting the cold, but also the altitude. He crested 10,200 feet. That first attempt was unsuccessful, you'll recall—only got to eighty-two south." He threw up his hands. "*Only* eighty-two south? For Christ's sake, can you imagine the effort that took? They did it on foot, dragging a sledge—just a few miles a day, the conditions were so bad—and with no idea what lay beyond, because no one had been there before. They had to turn back at eighty-two or die. Why? Because they'd dragged their asses up that glacier. It burns up a lot of energy when you keep falling into crevasses, and let me tell you, you can't always see them before the snow that's bridging them falls out from underneath you."

"They were lucky to be alive," said Cupcake.

Valena listened intently. She could never have imagined the dimensions of Scott's undertaking without standing here at the edge of the ice—the barrier, they called it—with the wind buffeting her, her cocoon of down and polypropylene all that stood between her and certain frostbite. *And this is a balmy spring day,* she reminded herself.

Ted said, "Well, that's how it goes around here. You drum up the money to make a try at a goal—the geographic pole, or some key bit of scientific understanding—and then off you go into all that ice and you do your best. Thing is, you'll never do it perfectly. You'll never learn everything you set out to know. You'll never be perfectly satisfied with yourself, or your accomplishments. But you go, and go again, until you make it or you die trying."

Cupcake said, "You're stalling, Ted."

Valena turned to look at the man. She had to turn her whole body, because the hood of her parka was in the way. She waited.

Ted dropped his gaze. "Your Dr. Vanderzee is a smart man, a driven man. He had questions he wanted answered. He drove really hard to get to them. And now he's been turned back, short of his goal."

The use of the past tense was not lost on Valena. *Had* questions. *Wanted* answered. *Drove* hard. As evenly as she could, she said, "I'm here to continue his work."

Ted nodded. "Good. Good."

Cupcake said, "Tell her what it was like up there. She needs to know, Ted."

"Yeah, I'm stalling. That damned newspaper's been hounding me since last year—nice way to spend my off time, dodging weasels with microphones—and now here we are with federal marshals hauling scientists off the ice. It's just not good. The next thing we'll have is some kind of fundamentalist preachers down here telling us the earth is flat."

Cupcake said, "I missed something in your reasoning, Ted. How'd you get from the *Financial News* to Bible thumpers?"

Ted set his jaw. "It's all one ball of wax." He stared at his boots, kicked at a shard of ice. "And I don't mean honest, God-fearing people, I mean the jerks who take advantage of them. It's all a game of opportunism." He sighed. "Okay, what do you need to know, young lady?"

Valena said, "Who was in the camp when it happened? And why's the newspaper been hounding you? I mean, there was a certain amount of ruckus on the grapevine at the University, but, well, I suppose Dr. Vanderzee did his best to keep it out of sight."

Ted nodded. "He's a gentleman, your Emmett, when nobody's poking him with sharp sticks. Well, okay, kid, let's head for somewhere warmer so I can calm myself with a nice, cold beer."

Cupcake said, "Gotcha covered, Ted. Got a six of Monteith's Black in the fridge."

"Lead on, m'lady."

They walked in silence back up the trail to McMurdo, cut along the top of the bluff toward a row of dormitories, and ducked inside the last one. Cupcake's room was at the far end of the corridor on the ground floor. Valena surmised that Cupcake must have greater rank than she did, because the room was shared by only two people.

Again, it was like college: all furniture except for the beds had been arranged in a line down the middle of the tiny room to form a barricade, dividing it into two. Cupcake had the far section and had arranged India-print bedspreads to give it the ambiance of a tent. Her mattress was on the floor. Half-burned incense lay about in little stone trays. The effect evoked a Far Eastern bordello.

Cupcake opened a midget refrigerator and pulled out a can of suds for each and settled into a cuddly heap on the mattress with Ted.

Valena grabbed the only chair. More and more, she felt like she had passed through a looking-glass into an obscure form of hell. *It's like going to college with your mom and dad and everything you never wanted to know about them,* she decided.

Ted popped the opener on his can and drained half of it in one gulp, sighed, and gave Cupcake a wet kiss on the cheek. "You're okay, Dorothy."

"Dorothy?" asked Valena.

Cupcake swatted Ted across the chops. "Damn you! It's bad enough being called Cupcake without you trot out that old horror. Dickhead!"

Ted kissed her again, going for her lips this time.

Cupcake growled, letting it slide into a purr.

"Should I come back later?" Valena asked.

Ted patted Cupcake on the knee. "She's got a low kindling point, eh? But go ahead and ask your questions."

"Who was in Emmett's camp last year?"

Ted sighed. He used his beer can to count off fingers on the opposite hand. "Vanderzee. Bob Schwartz and Dan Lindemann, the two grad students—the only other grantees—and yeah, they're down here again this year. Bob's with a crew from the University of Maine, and Dan . . . well, I forget, but I've seen him."

"Oh, great! Maybe I can talk to them."

Cupcake said, "Sure, you can go over to Mac Ops and give Dan a whistle."

"What's Mac Ops?"

"The radio relay station. It's right over there—that building with all the antennas on it, upstairs from the Airlift Wing, next to the weather station. They monitor all frequencies around the clock, and each field camp has to check in at least once out of the twenty-four."

"How far away is the U Maine field camp?"

"Out in the Dry Valleys somewhere. Under an hour, by helicopter."

"Can I maybe hitch a ride out there?"

Cupcake laughed sardonically. "No, you can't. Between NSF building the new South Pole Station and Raytheon trying to make a profit, things have gotten screwed down so tight you can hear their assholes squeak. Used to be you could hitch a ride anywhere they had an empty seat, but those days are gone."

Valena said, "Okay, so there were two grad students in Emmett's camp last year, and of course Emmett himself. That's three. Who else?"

Ted continued counting on his fingers. "Sheila Tuttle, that's your cook, an Aussie. She'd be Raytheon. She's up at Black Island this year. Good place for her. She's kind of a grouch."

"There was a cook?"

"Hard work, those high-altitude camps. You need someone looking after the calories. Of course, she had other duties as well. Nobody in a field camp ever finds himself with time on his hands unless it's storming, and then you just try to catch up on your sleep." He went back to his count. "I borrowed David from Fleet Ops to help me with the machinery. So he was

Raytheon, too. Then there was William what's-his-name, the dogsbody, also Raytheon."

"Dogsbody?"

"The Boss sent him along to do some heavy lifting." He started his counting over again with his thumb. "Manuel Roig, mountaineer; Raytheon. They sent him in with Sweeny to babysit, keep him out of trouble. Hah. Calvin Hart, who was Emmett's helper, so I guess you can put him on the grantee list. I think he's out in deep field helping with the drill for the WAIS Divide project."

Cupcake said, "Oh, yeah, Cal. Wasn't a scientist or anything, more like a ski bum, but Emmett said he was a good guy to have around. He told me, 'He'll do anything I tell him to and he doesn't complain when it gets cold.' Contrast that to Schwartz and Lindemann, who are both whiners."

"That's eight," said Valena, making a mental note to keep her complaints to important things, like, My leg just fell off.

"There were nine, aside from me, and like I said, I was gone before it happened, so who did I forget?" He stared at the ceiling, tapping a ninth finger. "Oh yeah, the deceased. Though of course he wasn't dead when he got there."

"He had a name," said Cupcake. "Morris Sweeny."

Ted gave her a look. "You'd know?"

"Yeah. I'd know."

Ted put his lips together and whistled. "You don't miss a chance, do you?"

"Am I missing something?" Valena inquired.

Ted glanced her way. "Our Dorothy's telling us she played a little Wizard of Oz with the man."

Cupcake shrugged. "He was okay. Nothing great."

"So how come Mr. Sweeny died?" Valena asked, steering the discussion away from what either was or was not great about the reporter's capacities in bed.

Ted took another good guzzle. "The guy arrived on schedule, but Emmett had been delayed getting started and was still out in the mountain camp. Emmett wanted to have him on the ice sheet, out at WAIS Divide, not up at altitude."

Cupcake cut in again. "I don't get what that WAIS project is all about.

And what's up with the acronym? Everybody's got to have a goddamned acronym around here."

Valena said, "It stands for West Antarctic Ice Sheet. They're setting up to drill a continuous core, or sample, of the ice."

"I don't know what you want with all that ice," said Cupcake.

Without thinking, Valena shifted into science teacher mode. "The ice is made up of snow that fell a long time ago, trapping some air with it. So we collect a core, a long cylinder that goes from the top of the ice sheet to the bottom. Ice has layers, one for every year, just like tree rings. If you know what you're doing you can read the layers just like you're reading the pages of old weather reports.

"I was just jerking your chain," said Cupcake. Don't you guys have enough cores? The Russians got one at Vostok. I read the newspapers, and I've seen Al Gore's movie. You look at the CO_2 in the core and it gives you the temperature." She made a horizontal zigzag through the air, mimicking the classic illustration of rises and falls in CO_2 and temperature, then threw the sharp rise onto the end, indicating the spike of CO_2 and corresponding rise in temperature with modern burning of fossil fuels. "So we're all going to hell in a handbasket. Why blow a gazillion more dollars drilling another core?"

Valena shook her head in frustration. "Vostok is on the East Antarctic Ice Sheet. This continent is huge! Would you look in Cincinnati if you were trying to find out what the climate was like in Las Vegas? We need as much information as you can get from as many places as we can get so we can continue to refine the climate models. We know from Greenland cores that the climate has changed many times, and quickly. Ten degree changes in a time period of as little as ten years. Like as if you moved from Los Angeles to San Francisco or Atlanta to Pittsburgh."

"Climate changes happen that quickly?" asked Ted.

"Yes. The variables that change climate—like change in the amount of sunlight reaching the earth's surface, or the level of greenhouse gases— build up and up and up, and it looks like not very much is happening, but then the climate system crosses a threshold and bang, it's a new game, like flicking a switch. The ocean currents flip to a new circulation pattern and ecosystems either adapt or die. If changes like we've seen in the cores happen today there will be huge social impact until our water and agricultural system gets back in synch with the new climate."

"We'd be fighting over every single resource," said Cupcake.

"Right," said Valena. It doesn't help that we're doing a global-scale experiment by increasing greenhouse gas and altering the thermal balance of the earth. We could be pushing toward one of those thresholds."

Everyone was quiet for a moment. Then Ted said, "I don't like being part of that experiment. I mean, good planets are hard to come by."

Valena said, "And we drill here because this is where most of the ice is, and because it's important to understand whether global climate changes start in the Arctic or the Antarctic. There are ice core records from Greenland that go back 104,000 years; that's pretty good, but we can do better here. We want to see how climate changed in the past when the amount of greenhouse gasses changed, so we need an Antarctic ice core from a place where it snows a lot—like right smack in the middle of the West Antarctic Ice Sheet—so we can read the years."

Ted said, "But why put the WAIS project out on the divide? It has the worst weather in Antarctica. It's a logistical nightmare to get the drill and all the housing and everything in there."

Valena said, "The worse the weather, the more snow accumulates, and the more snow, the better we can read the annual bands in the ice, and better we can refine the gas and isotope analyses."

Cupcake said, "You're stalling again, Ted. So it was WAIS that the reporter was supposed to see, not the high-elevation camp. But they were still setting up the drill last year at WAIS and building the covering structure. What was he going to do out there?"

Valena said, "It's a huge project that involves about twenty different PIs. Before you go to the expense of flying in that huge rig and setting up the building that will house all that brainpower, you do some test drilling to make sure the condition of the ice is what you expect. So there would have been drilling last year, just not the big rig yet."

"But let's get back to the high camp," said Cupcake, popping the top on another beer.

Valena, said. "So the guy showed up there instead of WAIS Divide, and he got sick. And you were there working with explosives, Ted?"

"No, Emmett had a drill going getting shallow test cores from that location, but he also wanted to get some bigger block samples, and that's where the other muscle and I came in. But then suddenly here's this guy from New York at high altitude, and he hadn't come up in stages like you're supposed to. Emmett told him to sit tight and rest, not exert himself until he was acclimated, but he was one of those macho types who just couldn't stand himself unless he was breaking a sweat. Said he was really fit, shouldn't be a problem. He'd been in the military, said he could handle it fine. He was a real piece of work, all cocksure and not listening to reason." He shook his head. "Things got off to a bad start, lots of arguments."

"About what?"

"Guy stuck his bare hand on one of Emmett's ice samples, for a start."

"He didn't!"

Cupcake asked, "Why's that a big deal?"

Valena said, "The whole point is to get uncontaminated data. The ice is like a big deep freeze that keeps past climate records intact. The instant you introduce modern contaminants—well, then it's worthless. We only handle the ice samples with special gloves. When someone puts bare hands on them, it's as if someone spat in your beer."

Cupcake curled her upper lip in disgust.

Ted said, "Yeah, so it went downhill from there. Things get pretty intense when you're camped out there on the high ice together, even at the best of times. It's cold, and the cold intensifies the effect of the thin air, and you're doing dangerous work handling machinery, and then here's this chucklehead breathing down the good doctor's neck, and bugging the help with what he liked to call 'interviews.' Hell, I call it cornering people and bugging them until they blow their tops. Schwartz popped off at him pretty good, Sheila looked like she was going to hit him with a fry pan before the first meal was done, and even cool Cal was cutting a wide margin to avoid him. It just wasn't right. You have to be able to depend on each other in a place like that, and this guy's shown up looking for a fight."

Valena said, "Was he trying to argue that the climate isn't warming?"

Ted said, "Yeah, there was a lot of arguing about a story for the *Financial News*."

Valena said, "Emmett probably wanted to take the guy to the source and show him how the work was done and maybe correct some of his confusion, open a healthy dialog. It was a reasonable idea."

Ted said, "Yeah, it would have been reasonable if the guy had been inclined to listen, but it sounded to me like he was going to write an exposé on what a waste of the taxpayer's money Emmett's efforts were. But he got sick."

Cupcake said, "It was altitude sickness, right?"

Ted nodded. "That's what they tell me."

"You'd left by then," Valena prompted.

"I'd pulled out to come back here just a couple hours before he started showing symptoms. Caught a ride in one of the Twin Otters they had moving through the area; they're your smaller ski plane. It had stopped to pick up some fuel from the cache. That was the other reason some of us were there. We were digging up fuel barrels that had gotten buried in the snow. Damned windy place." He shook his head. "The storm came in really fast, just barreled down off the plateau, a particularly nasty herbie."

"That's a hurricane-force storm," Cupcake explained to Valena. "They usually come from the south. Air pours off the big ice sheet that covers East Antarctica. You can get sustained winds up to a hundred miles per hour, and the gusts . . ."

Ted nodded. "Laurence Gould, who came here with Admiral Byrd in 1929, wrote about a wind so strong that when he reached up and grabbed the strut of his airplane, it blew him out like a pennant. And he was not a small man." He shook his head. "Anyway, Emmett radioed in that evening to say that Sweeny was in real distress. They got the doctor from the hospital here on the horn at Mac Ops, and they decided that it had to be altitude sickness. They couldn't evacuate him, as there was no way they could land any kind of aircraft. Visibility was down to zero, a total white-out blizzard. So the flyboys got creative and sent in a Herc to drop supplies."

"LC-130 Hercules," Cupcake explained. "The Hercs are the big workhorses down here. They carry the heavy loads in and out of field locations, haul everything that goes to Pole, and they make all the flights from here up to New Zealand during the times when the ice runways are too soft to land wheeled aircraft. The Herc's got skis they can lift up, so's they can land on wheels up in Cheech."

"And they've got some damned fine pilots," Cupcake went on. "They're career officers from the Air National Guard. Great guys."

Ted said, "Anyway, they figured they'd fly over Emmett's camp, drop a parachute with a Gamow bag and other medical supplies. A Gamow is like a pressure tent. You put the guy in there, pump it up, and it's like bringing him down to sea level. Fluids in the lungs clear. He lives."

"But he didn't live," Valena said. "Because they couldn't find the camp in the storm."

"Oh, the plane found the camp," said Ted. "Problem was, the camp couldn't find the chute. When you're in condition 1—zero visibility—the dictum is, don't go anywhere. Stay in your tent, or your vehicle, or your building, wherever you are. You've noticed the monitors by the main exit doors?"

Valena nodded. She had seen the lighted overhead signs that scrolled the information. "They've said 'condition 3' each time I look at them."

Cupcake said, "That means clear and no restrictions. Condition 2 is watch out and pay attention, get to where you're going and don't mess around. Condition 1 is stay put. Don't go out. Remember that."

"Yes, ma'am. So they had a total howler."

Ted continued, "Yeah, and Emmett ordered everyone in camp to stay put, not that anyone was foolish enough to go out. You couldn't see your hand in front of your face. Of course, the newspaper holds this against him, because they've never been in such conditions. The toughest thing they've ever had to do is cross Fifth Avenue to buy a cruller." He shook his head vehemently. "That asshole had no business coming down here." He finished his beer. "You got another of these, Do-roddy?"

Cupcake pointed at the little fridge. "You know where to find it."

Ted popped another open and drizzled several ounces into the maw between his whiskers. Belched. " 'Scuse me. Yeah. So they wait for the first break in the weather—things are only up to condition 2, and ragged at that—and out they go." He shook his head. "Didn't find it. Storm closed in again. Back to the tents." Ted fell silent. "They had to wait until the storm abated. Took another two days. First chance, a Herc came out and loaded them up. Sweeny was frozen solid by then. I saw it land. They brought the body out in its sleeping bag. Hell of a long sleep that boy was in for."

Everyone was silent for a while.

Ted sighed. "They held him overnight in the ice core storage unit over by Crary Lab and then shipped him out in the cargo hold of a C-17. It didn't matter that he was an asshole. If you lose anyone down here for any reason, everyone feels like they've had a hole torn in them, and in a very real sense, everyone is accountable."

"But the storm," said Valena.

"Yeah, the storm," said Ted.

"It wasn't your fault," said Cupcake. "What could you have done differently?"

Ted had finished his second beer. His big hand crumpled the can like it was made of paper. "I should have hauled his ass out of there with me on the Otter. Or William was almost done with his work. I could have sent him out, and then I would have been the one to stay. Maybe I could have found the damned chute."

Cupcake had an arm around him. "No one found it," she said.

The big man hung his head. "Yeah, right. Not until five days ago they didn't."

6

BRENDA UTZON POURED HERSELF A CUP OF TEA AND HEADED DOWN the ramp that led to the lower levels of Crary Lab, leaving phase 1 for phase 2 and continuing all the way down to the aquarium. She had seen Michael heading down this way, and she had a job for him.

She was always fascinated by the maze of tanks with their burbling waters being circulated by humming motors. It was usually her pleasure to stop and stare into the nearest aquarium, a small Plexiglas arrangement labeled CRARY TOUCH TANK. The biologists kept examples of Antarctic marine creatures in there so that visitors could see who lived underneath the sea ice and to keep them from sticking their hands into the other aquaria, which housed the creatures they were actually studying. But today Brenda was on a mission. Instead of stopping to look, she hung a right and knocked on the door to the electrical tech's shop. "Michael?" she called. "Are you in there?"

"Just a moment," she heard, through the heavy steel door. Presently, Michael opened the door and let her into his sanctum. It was lined with shelves packed with widgets and gizmos that kept all the equipment in Crary Lab ticking. He was new this year, but in the short time he had been on board, she had come to know him as a gentle, caring man, and she had a job for someone with just those characteristics.

"What can I do for you, kind lady?" Michael inquired. He was perched on his swiveling stool, his back against the side counter. On the counter in front of him lay the disassembled parts of some bit of equipment that Brenda did not even try to comprehend, but from the scent of the air, she could tell that she had interrupted a job of soldering. Why was he working on a Sunday?

Michael reached to one side and dragged another stool out from under a counter. "Have a seat. I don't get much company."

"Thanks, Michael. This is nice down here. So, you're going to Happy Camp tomorrow, am I right?"

"At last. I've been bumped twice, but now's my big chance. I'm looking forward to being able to hike past Ob Hill."

"Oh, I know, it's kind of constraining to be in this great, huge place and not be allowed to go anywhere."

Michael nodded.

Brenda said, "Well, I was wondering if you could help look out for someone who's going to be there. She's just a kid, and she's having a rough time."

"Oh?" Michael's soft brown eyes softened further. "What's the problem?"

"You've heard about the scientist who was taken off the ice under guard?"

"Yes."

"Well, the young lady I'm concerned about was his graduate student. Scheduling missed the chance to turn her around in New Zealand, so she's here. She came in on yesterday's flight. I saw her this morning and she looked pretty scared, like she didn't have a friend in the world. Because she's here and there won't be another flight north until Wednesday, George Bellamy said she could go ahead and attend Happy Camp." She shrugged her shoulders in what she hoped was a fetching approximation of innocence. "So anyway, I was hoping you could keep an eye out for her."

"Sure," said Michael. "Sounds rough."

"Yeah. Imagine working hard enough to get in on a grant to work in Antarctica and then having it snatched out from under you."

Michael began fiddling absentmindedly with a loose bolt on his countertop. "How old is she?"

"Well, she has to be mid-twenties, but she looks like she's about eighteen. Nice-looking girl, sort of unusual-looking."

"I think I've met her. Valena?"

"Yes, that's her. Valena Walker."

"Wow, and she was Vanderzee's student? Rotten luck. So what's the scoop on that, anyway? I heard the basics—that someone died in his camp last year, and that now they think he killed the guy—but what happened? I mean, he walked out of here last year a free man, and this year something's different?"

"Well, that's what we'd all like to know." She leaned closer and lowered her voice to just above a whisper. "There was of course a big flap about it last year. It's very bad when someone dies on the ice. Not only does it scare everybody—morale plummets—but also it's a black mark on NSF *and* Raytheon. When I left the ice at the end of the season last February and returned to Denver, I was amazed at how much trouble it had created at headquarters. The newspaper the deceased man worked for kept badgering everybody for details, as if we had been keeping things from them, which we hadn't. Heavens, how was I supposed to know anything, for instance? I never leave McMurdo. I certainly wasn't at Dr. Vanderzee's camp when it happened. But sure enough, I got a call as soon as I returned to Denver. I'll bet they'd have phoned me here if they could have figured out how. They even got hold of e-mail addresses for the winter-over personnel and asked questions of them."

"What did they ask you?"

"Oh, you can just imagine: If someone's never been down here, they don't know how things are. They demanded that someone go out to Dr. Vanderzee's camp and investigate. They didn't understand that after February, nobody flies anywhere. The planes and helicopters leave the ice, and there's no way someone is going to try to make a run up to the mountains in the dark. That would be suicidal."

Michael's gaze drifted toward the window. She saw his jaw sag as he considered what it would be like to be out there in that cold, and in that darkness. The window was tiny, triple-paned, and set in a very thick wall. Staying warm in Antarctica was not a joke. "But something changed," he said.

"I came in at WinFly—early September, before Main Body comes in October. Nothing had changed by then. Then two weeks ago the investigators arrived with Emmett. I don't think I'm supposed to be talking about that, though."

Michael ran his thumb and forefinger across his lips, sealing them with an imaginary zipper.

She looked anxiously over her shoulder. She hadn't liked the investigators. They had set up shop in the lab manager's office, which was next door to hers, and they had treated her as if she were their private secretary. "They asked a lot of questions."

"I remember them hanging around up there on phase 1, but I didn't realize who they were until they were gone," said Michael. "One of them came down here to get a repair on a piece of equipment, but they didn't tell me what it was for, just as you say."

"Right. Real closemouthed."

"But they found something that suggested that it wasn't just death by mischance."

"Apparently. I don't know what they found, but they had the Airlift Wing fly them out there, and when they came back, they came to me and had me phone Chad Hill and tell him to come over. *Tell* him to come. Imagine. Chad's one of the two top reps for NSF on site and a federal marshal to boot, and they were ordering him around."

Michael's face glowed with concern. "And then what happened?"

"Well, Chad said he'd take care of it, as it was his jurisdiction, but they said they were on their way out next flight and wanted Emmett with them." She had let her voice rise to normal speaking tones, but again dropped it to a whisper. "I was right there in the office with them, because they had me making arrangements for their departure, calling the people at the Chalet. I overheard the whole thing."

"That must have been very upsetting for you."

"Yes." This was why Brenda liked to talk to Michael. He understood her feelings without having to be told, a gentleman in the truest sense of the word.

"You look like you need a hug."

"Oh, boy, do I." She sighed, and stood up to meet him as he wrapped his big, strong arms around her and squeezed. This was the best and worst thing about Antarctica all in one: How kind everybody was, and how desperately she needed their kindness, considering how deeply she missed her friends and family back home. It was wonderful coming to the ice. The landscape was more beautiful than anyone could imagine, and the community was wild and full of fun. But always there was that longing for those who were not here with her.

Michael patted her hair, cuddling her closer to his massive chest. "There," he said. "It's okay. There. And don't worry, I'll keep an eye out for your little gal Valena."

7

VALENA WENT STRAIGHT FROM CUPCAKE'S DORM ROOM TO THE BUILD-
ing with all the antennae on it, in search of Mac Ops. It was building number 165, according to the little map she had picked up at the in-brief.

She climbed up the stairs over the pipes that ran between buildings and
down into a bald gravel yard, then let herself in through the main door,
which, like most doors in McMurdo, was built to keep out the cold. The
hallway inside was narrow and led unceremoniously through a catacomb
of offices to a staircase, which she climbed. At the top of the stairs she
came across a man sitting behind a desk. Arrayed around him were maps
and charts of the continent. "Can I help you?" he inquired.

"I'm looking for Mac Ops."

"Down that way. This is the weather station."

Valena headed down another network of hallways and again got lost.
She found a room labeled 109AW SKIER OPERATIONS. Inside were two men
in uniform. "Can I help you?" asked one. His name tape read LANSING.

She stepped into the doorway. "Well, I'm looking for Mac Ops, but do
you guys fly those LC-130s lined up out there on the ice?"

Lansing pointed at the dry-mark board he had been writing on. "Yes,
ma'am, we do. That's all the flights that are scheduled for the next week,
though it looks like the weather's going to dish up some cancellations.
Storm coming."

"My bad luck. I'm going to Happy Camp tomorrow."

"A little storm will add verisimilitude to your exercises. They won't
have to put five-gallon white buckets on your heads to simulate a whiteout."

"They really do that?"

"I'm not making that up, Ms. . . . Walker," he said, reading her name off the tag on her parka.

"Valena," she said. "And you're Mr. . . . I don't know your rank . . . Lansing."

"Master Sergeant John Lansing at your service."

She awarded him a smile, thinking she might possibly harvest some information here. She decided to oil the gears with some background chat. "Thank you. So this is a military base?"

"Not exactly. McMurdo was built as a Navy base back in the fifties, but they pulled out in the nineties. The US Air Force flies the C-17s and we fly the LC-130s. The lone C-130 out there belongs to the Kiwis, the Royal New Zealand Air Force. The US Coast Guard brings in the icebreakers. Otherwise, McMurdo is now civilian."

"Are the planes here year round?"

Lansing shook his head. "No, ma'am, the fuel lines would freeze. We fly our birds home to New York."

"New York?"

"We fly out of Stratton Air Force Base, near Schenectady. We're with the New York Air National Guard."

"So this is something you do just a few weekends each year? How do you get all the way down here in that time?"

Lansing chuckled. "Not all guardsmen are weekend warriors. Skiers are full-time. I came down a few weeks ago. I'll go home for Christmas, then back again in January and February, to wrap up the season."

"Hah," said the man who was sitting behind the desk. He had settled back in his swivel chair with his hands folded across his fatigues to listen to the conversation. "You aren't going home for Christmas. They'll keep you in this jug until you're gray and pushing a walker."

Lansing lifted his chin at his compatriot. "I'm already bald, so what's to go gray?"

"You're a long way from home for a long time," said Valena. "You must miss your families."

Lansing acknowledged this with a brief pursing of his lips.

"So then, it's not just a jug to you. What is it, the setting or . . . ?"

"The food," said the man behind the desk.

Lansing raised an eyebrow at his colleague. "I haven't gained an ounce since high school, which is more than I can say for you. You're just going to have to lay off those desserts."

"What does bring you?" asked Valena, now shamelessly pursuing his confidence.

Lansing pondered a moment, taking her question seriously. "You're a scientist, so I'll assume you always knew what you wanted to do. But me? No. Some of us find our way by trial and error. I was an above-average student, but I didn't see the advantages of going to college. I was bored with all the hoops you have to jump through. So I decided on a hitch in the military, figuring I'd make a difference by doing my bit for my country, and then pursue my little corner of the American dream."

"That's you," said the other man. "Our beautiful dreamer."

Lansing rolled his eyes eloquently before continuing. "I left for basic training three weeks after graduating high school, then went on for advanced training. I spent six years in. When my hitch was up, I got a job as a computer salesman. It was a good job, and I made quite a bit of money selling. But to be honest, my life was a hollow shell." He shrugged. "Then one day I realized that the only time I felt right—you know, fulfilled— was when I was around my buddies in the Guard."

The other man said, "Gosh, honey, I didn't know you cared."

Lansing picked up a pencil and cheerfully threw it at him. It clattered across his desk and into his lap.

"Hey!" the man said. "Enough with the government property!"

"So you reenlisted," said Valena.

Lansing said, "I was a reservist at that point, but when the opportunity came for me to get a full-time job in the Guard, I jumped at the chance." He chuckled to himself. "I took a ten-thousand-dollar pay cut, but my self-esteem rose, my self-confidence returned, and once again I'm part of something and making a difference. And I've returned to school, heading toward retirement with a degree in hand." He smiled into space a moment, then brought his attention back to Valena. "But you've got something on your mind, and it's not my life story. What can I do for you?"

She blushed with the realization that he had seen through her craftiness. She decided to lay it out straight. "I'm working with Dr. Emmett Vanderzee, and I understand that someone from here flew him out to a high camp day before yesterday. I'd like to talk to the pilot. Might that be you, by chance?"

Lansing laughed. "No, ma'am, I'm just a ground-pounding, nonaviating, enlisted puke." He sat down at his desk and tapped a few keys on his computer and read from his screen. "You want Major Bentley," he said. "He's not here just now. Anything else?"

"Well . . . I'm told that your Airlift Wing flew the missions that dropped the medical supplies in his camp last year, and also that you brought the group out after the storm abated."

Lansing nodded, a slight movement in a body held upright and straight. The other man glanced back and forth between them, alert but silent. "Again, Major Bentley's your man."

The clock was ticking. Thoughts and associations cascaded through Valena's mind. Did these men trust her? Could she ever hope to have a life as comfortably structured as theirs, with its built-in sense of belonging? She hadn't always known what she wanted to do with her life, and in fact wondered if she was all that sure even now. She looked Master Sergeant Lansing up and down, taking in every inch of his uniform. She had considered joining the military—melting into something larger than herself, the ultimate extended family of choice—but had opted instead for scientific pursuits. She said, "Cool. Well, I've got to find the radio station."

"Mac Ops is down that way. Come back anytime, we love the company."

ONE MORE KINK down the hallway, Valena found the transmitter station: a room filled desktop to ceiling with radio equipment.

The array of switches, microphones, telephone handsets, computer monitors, and lighted dials wrapped around two sides of the room, and charts labeled SEA ICE MAP and LANDING LOCATIONS were tacked to the remaining wall spaces. A young woman sat at the center of the desk eating a brownie and sipping from a quart-sized Nalgene water bottle. She turned around in her chair and smiled at Valena. "Hi, can I help you?"

"Yes, please. I understand that I can call people in a field camp from here."

"Sure. Who do you need to call?"

"His name is Dan Lindemann. He's somewhere in the Dry Valleys."

"There are nine different events out in the Dry Valleys right now. Do you know which one?"

Valena's brain suddenly felt tired. "No."

"Is he the PI?"

"The principal investigator? I don't think so."

"What category of event, then?"

"As in . . ."

"Geology, glaciology, biology . . ."

"Glaciology."

"Well, that narrows it down. Let's see . . ." She hit a couple of keys on her computer and referred to a list. "He's out on Clark Glacier with Naomi Bosch. Do you want me to get him on the radio for you?"

"Radio?"

Just then, a slightly garbled, static-ridden voice came in over a speaker. "Mac Ops, Mac Ops, this is Whiskey-218 on Mount Aurora, how read?"

"Excuse me a moment," the woman told Valena, then leaned toward her microphone and keyed it. "Go ahead, 218."

"Can you pass a message to the Boss at Fleet Ops? Over."

"That's affirmative, 218. Standing by to take your message. Over."

"Message follows: Sorry, cannot make Black Island traverse. Over."

"Let me read that back. Cannot make Black Island traverse. Is that correct?"

"Please emphasize my gratitude for the opportunity. I hate to miss it. Thanks for your help. Whiskey-218 clear."

"Mac Ops clear." The woman glanced at a clock. "Naomi's event number is I-299. They're due to check in at eighteen hundred, but they're a drilling camp, so somebody's usually near the radio. Do you want me to whistle them back?"

Valena said, "I take it if I talk to them on the radio, that's not very private."

The woman shook her head. "Depending on conditions, about half of the continent can hear you. Or should I say, everyone who's tuned in to that frequency." She smiled uncertainly, wanting to please. "It is the main frequency for all the science events in that area."

Valena's heart sank. The discussion she needed to have with Dan Lindemann was not for anyone else to hear. She stared at her feet, trying to figure out what to do next.

The radio operator asked, "Do you need to get a private message to them?"

"Yeah."

"You can write it out and take it down the Helo Ops. Maybe they have someone stopping in that camp sometime soon, and they could drop it off. I'm not sure when you'd get your reply, but it's better than nothing. Oh, wait." She tapped a few more keys on her computer. "No, sorry. I was thinking maybe they had an iridium phone out there, or Internet, but they don't have them at that camp."

A hundred miles from the nearest flush toilet, but they might have satellite phones or Internet, thought Valena. "Where's Helo Ops?"

"Just down the hill. You can't miss it."

It took Valena several minutes to find her way back out of the building and through the maze of trails and pipelines that led to the road down to the helicopter pads, but at last she succeeded, managing not to slip on any of the ice-glazed banks of snow she had to surmount to make her short-cuts. She could see four helicopters, two larger ones with four blades and two smaller ones with only two blades. She found her way past a dive locker and a gymnasium to the building that housed the offices and storage bays for the helicopter crews. It was closed. *Of course,* thought Valena. *It's Sunday, everybody's day off.*

She turned and looked back up at Mac Town. The tumbling architecture of Crary Lab, which had been built in steps coming down the steep hill, seemed forbidding, a palace for people whose professors did not get arrested. She stood for a while with her hands in the warming pockets of her big red, trying to decide what to do next. *Back to the galley,* she decided. *It's almost dinnertime now, and maybe I can find Major Bentley there. Everybody has to eat. But first, I'll stop through Crary and see if there are replies to my e-mails.*

At Crary, she found only junk mail. Ten losses at computer solitaire followed, further depressing her mood. Finally, she went online and noodled around on the *New York Financial News* Web site, discovering what she could about Morris Sweeny. Little of significance appeared from her search. He hadn't been at the paper long before he came to Antarctica and died. But then she noticed something odd: none of his articles were about science. He appeared to report primarily on politics. *So why jump onto this story?* she wondered. *Because it's political?*

HALF AN HOUR later, Valena once again beheld the dining room of the galley, this time holding a tray laden with pork chops, canned vegetables, and two desserts. She stared across the room, trying to figure out which of the uniformed personnel present flew the LC-130s. She felt an urge to march back over to Cupcake's room and demand that Ted point out Major Bentley, but she imagined that Cupcake and Ted were by now either pretty well gassed up and taking the kind of flight that doesn't leave the room or sleeping the good sleep that should follow it.

At last she sorted out the insignia on the fatigues worn by several of the people who were sitting at the table nearest the coffee urns and soft-serve ice cream dispenser. There were no empty chairs at the table, but Valena sucked up her courage and said, "Hi, I'm looking for Major Bentley."

A man with a graying buzz-cut and military-short mustache leaned back and gave her a friendly smile. He swatted one of his mates on the elbow and said, "Hey, you were just leaving, give the lady your seat."

The man jumped up, nodded courteously, and disappeared with his empty tray.

Valena sat down. "Are you Major Bentley?"

"Nope. He's not here. Anything I can help you with?"

"Know where I can find him?"

A slender woman dressed in olive drab fatigues said, "He's in New Zealand. He'll be back tomorrow, weather permitting, though the weather does not look like it's going to permit tomorrow."

"Anything *I* can help you with?" repeated Buzz-Cut, leaning toward her with growing interest.

Valena looked at his rank insignia. A seven-pointed leaf. Did that indicate that he was a major? "Ah . . . well, I'm with . . . I understand that he—"

A woman with sleepy green eyes who was wearing a dark blue uniform appeared at the table. "Hey, is Waylon coming back tomorrow?" she inquired. "I'm just dying for a vegetable that didn't come out of a can."

"Oh, hi there, Tractor Betty! Arr!" Buzz-Cut made a wild pirate's face and bent his right index finger at the first knuckle, as if it had been cut off.

"Arr!" answered Betty, making the same gesture without changing her almost comatose expression. "I forgot. Is *Tractor* Waylon coming back tomorrow?"

Buzz-Cut said, "You bet. But as for being a vegetable that didn't come out of a can . . . well, maybe Waylon ain't your man."

Raucous laughter broke out all around the table. Tractor Betty grabbed a chair from a nearby table and sat down on it backward, leaning her chin on its back. In response to the frivolity, she lifted one corner of her mouth.

Buzz-Cut turned to Valena. "Betty here is a firefighter, and a darned good one. You can measure that by the fact that there are currently no fires." He put a hand to his chest in mock grandeur. "*I* am a pilot. The name is Hugh. Marilyn here is a navigator. Larry is a loadmaster, and these other guys are sorry reprobates. And you are?"

"Valena."

Hugh drew his brows together to indicate great seriousness and said, "Hey, Valena, here's a critically important question: do you like tractors?"

Valena looked back and forth between the flyboy and the firefighter. "Sure. My granddad let me drive his Case out on his farm in Idaho during the potato harvest."

Hugh threw his arms into the air with delight. "We're in!"

Betty said, "The Tractor Club meets Tuesday evening. Coffee House, seven p.m. Be there."

Valena managed a wan smile. "Uh, fine. I'm heading out tomorrow morning to Happy Camp, but if I'm back in time, uh . . . sure . . . if ah, Major Bentley will be there."

Hugh said, "He'll be there if he possibly can. Tractor Waylon is club protocol officer."

Betty asked, "Why'd he take this mission? I thought he had his time in."

Buzz-Cut Hugh's jolly smile faded for a moment, revealing the military officer who dwelled a quarter inch beneath the party boy. "Duty called. You know he was pretty well up past his eye sockets in that situation, finding that evidence and all, so he volunteered to carry the lad north." He shook his head. "Sad situation." He took a last draw on his coffee, tossed his silverware into a heap on his tray, and stood up. "I'm on in five. See ya," he said, and left.

Major Marilyn Wood glanced at her watch. "Yeah! Outta here." She disappeared the same direction as Major Hugh.

Betty turned her heavy-lidded eyes on Valena. "So. What do you do here?"

What do *I do here?* Valena wondered. She decided to present the official version. "I'm here to do research for my master's thesis. Glaciology."

"Oh. Climate change. Huh."

"Yeah, climate change."

"So, is it?"

"Is it what?"

"Changing."

"Yes, it is changing. Always has, always will. Climates change whether they are perturbed by human activities or not. It's important to know how they vary and why. *And* we're trying to document things like whether or not the amount of carbon dioxide we've dumped into the atmosphere by burning fossil fuels is indeed unprecedented, and learn how fast this ice might melt, and what additional changes might occur as a result."

"So you think we're changing the climate. By driving cars and such."

Valena took a moment to observe Betty carefully, searching her dead-pan expression for clues to where this conversation might be going. Since becoming involved in climate research, she had found herself in this conversation increasingly often. Sometimes it was with colleagues, who liked to engage in rousing debates over the interpretation of data. Sometimes it was with neighbors or family members or strangers in the supermarket. Some people truly wanted to know what she had learned, while others just wanted to argue, suggesting that she was selling lies intended to scare people or upset the economy.

Valena looked around the room. Each and every person present was either doing scientific research or providing the infrastructure that could support that research in this severe climate, but that didn't mean that those in the latter category believed in what the "beakers" were doing. Was this firefighter looking for information or a fight? And if it was a fight that Betty wanted, just how big a pain in the neck was she prepared to be? As big as the reporter who had bulled his way into Vanderzee's camp and then had the temerity to die?

I'm getting paranoid, thought Valena. Finally, she decided to answer the question with the kind of precision that usually rocked people back on their heels. "I don't *think* we're changing the climate. That would suggest that it's just an idea. I'm a scientist, so I think quite a bit, but I make a distinction between thoughts, ideas, hypotheses, theories, and facts. Is it a fact that by burning fossil fuels we're increasing the amount of CO_2 in the atmosphere? Yes. Our studies document the fact that levels are higher than they have been in 650,000 years, and data not yet fully analyzed extend that number to 850,000 years. Not only is the level of CO_2 higher, the rate of increase is greater. Fortunately, the latest studies indicate that we are not near any thresholds, so it is unlikely that the increase in greenhouse gasses will soon lead to an abrupt climate change—huge change that occurs within a decade—but we—the science community—know that the additional CO_2 has already committed us to a change that will have significant social effects."

"Your computer model says so."

"*All* of our computer models say so. There's not just one model. There are about a dozen, and they all agree. Very sophisticated models built by teams of people who know one hell of a lot."

"And you believe them."

Valena stared into her plate for a moment. "It's not a belief thing. Science is not a faith-based endeavor." She thought a while longer, then added, "Science is a system of observations, predictions, and tests. The models are predictions based on observations. The best way to prove if the models are right is to do an experiment. For that, we'd need two planet earths. On one we don't change the atmosphere, and on the other we do. Then we wait fifty years and compare the two. The problem is that it's really hard to get funding for that, let alone find a replicate of planet earth. So we do the next best thing, which is use computer models.

"All of the models agree that climate will get warmer. In some places it's not the heat that's going to be the problem as much as the lack of rainfall. Think about the Middle East, southern Europe, North Africa, and the western US with twenty percent less rain. Think about a complete revamping of those agricultural systems and the movements of people that would have to occur. Environmental refugees. The reservoirs on the Colorado River, the lifeblood of states from Colorado to California, are only half full now. We're already doing the experiment, but we only have one planet."

Betty asked, "But if climate changes on its own, how do you know what part is our fault?"

"Back to the models. When we model the climate of an earth without humans, we can't make the climate do what it's doing now. We have to add anthropogenic greenhouse gasses."

"You think we should make policy decisions based on a computer model?"

Valena smiled wryly. She liked the astringent intelligence behind Betty's questions. "These are exactly the questions you should ask. Every major business makes large economic decisions based on computer models; they hire the hottest minds out of computer schools to do exactly that. So then you have to make a choice: you can make your decision based on the best available scientific interpretation of the data, or you can guess. Either way, you have made a decision, so you might as well discuss the science, learn what it means, learn what you can do to cut back on burning of fossil fuels. Maybe you decide the benefits don't justify the costs in your case, but at least you will have made an informed decision."

The firefighter sat quietly across the table from Valena. "Yeah, well, speaking for myself, I like putting fires out. I prefer it cold." She gave Valena a wink, the biggest change in facial expression she had displayed since arriving at the table. "I'm due on shift. See ya," she said, and she hopped up and left.

Valena regarded her pork chops. They seemed to have aged in the ten minutes since she had forked them onto her plate.

A young man in olive drab fatigues sat down next to her in the seat Hugh had vacated. He arranged his tray in front of himself, took a sip of his apple juice, turned to Valena, smiled, and said, "So, where are you from, and what do you do here?"

8

THE NEXT MORNING, VALENA AGAIN ROSE EARLY. SHE HAD ONLY A FEW hours to make something happen, and she didn't have to worry that it might not yet be light out.

She had packed a duffel containing her ECWs, her little yellow Rite-in-the-Rain notebook, camera, and a toothbrush the night before and had laid out the clothes she would wear until it was time to go to Happy Camp. That way, she could slip into a layer of long underwear, jeans, sneakers, a fleece sweatshirt, and her big red, grab her duffel, and get out the door without waking any of her roommates.

Breakfast was not yet being served. She headed instead first over to Crary Lab and checked her e-mail, in expectation of a reply from Taha Hesan. No luck there, but there was a reply from Em Hansen. Valena tapped on the message to open it. For several long moments, nothing happened. The slowness of the computer made her writhe.

Greetings Valena,

That sounds like a nasty shock, and there's nothing I can say that will make it any better, but my very best advice as regards investigating this crime is as follows: LOCK YOURSELF IN THE CLOSET UNTIL THE URGE PASSES. If it is murder, and your professor did not do it and whomever did do it is there to be discovered, he will probably discover you before you discover him. This is not a healthy scenario. I am sure that having your professor jailed feels like a personal violation, but if you came home to find your house broken into, you'd be stupid to charge right in there, precisely because whoever broke the door down may still be inside. The police have dogs trained to go into houses where security has been breached. Don't confuse yourself with a dog. There are just too many ways to die in Antarctica.

Stay safe. Stay alive.
Em

Valena read the message three times. Finally, she wrote back,

I am certain you are right, but I only have one shot down here. Surely if I just gather background information that the authorities might have missed, I'll be all right. By the way, do you have any good connections there, in case I find something they should know? And is there anyone at the *New York Financial News* who knows something about why Morris Sweeny came south? Sweeny reports politics, not science, so why was he here?

Valena pressed send, then logged off the computer and descended the stairs into the lower levels of Crary Lab. By the time she was halfway down the ramp that led from phase 1 to phase 2, she had let Em's advice slip from her consciousness and had focused instead on her feelings toward Taha. Frustrated to the point of thinking vile thoughts about the other student on the project, she let herself into the office she was supposed to be sharing with him and Emmett Vanderzee.

Her professor's personal gear was still there, right next to the big packing boxes of equipment that he had shipped from Reno. She got to digging through the duffel bags and found that he had already checked out some field equipment. Inside she found an enormously thick sleeping bag labeled "Arctic Storm"—a confidence builder, certainly—and a neoprene sleep mat. In the hope that Emmett might have hidden any kind of clue deep inside his duffels, she emptied them out and restuffed them. She finished none the wiser.

Just then, Doris walked into the room carrying a laptop computer. "Hey, Valena, how's it going?"

"Oh, fine. I guess. Trying to figure out what all Emmett left behind. Looks like he left his gear but took his computer with him."

"No, he didn't." She placed the one she was carrying on the desk. "Emmett was having trouble getting this hooked up to the Internet here. Sorry it took so long to fix."

"No, don't apologize! Otherwise it might have been taken as evidence or something."

Doris put a hand on the laptop and, in a tone dripping with irony, said, "Wow, I didn't think of that. You think I should report it or something?"

"No, no, no, no, no. You just leave it right there."

Doris raised one eyebrow coquettishly. "You can get it to him, right?"

"Absolutely. You just put it out of your mind, okay?"

"Whatever you say, champ." Doris left the room. A few steps out into the common area, she turned and said, "What's weird is that there wasn't anything wrong with it, but he made a point of entrusting it to my care the morning before he headed out into the field with the feds." She gave Valena one last quirky smile and disappeared around the corner.

Valena considered kissing the computer. She quickly turned it on and dug into the communications software to find Taha's home phone number, then pulled out the prepaid telephone card she had brought from the US and picked up the telephone.

She thought it somewhat miraculous that she could even hope to place a telephone call that would cross the ten thousand miles that separated them, but possibility and likelihood proved two different things. She opened up the guidebook that had been issued her at the in-brief and began to dial. The first number asked for an outside line. Next, she punched in her prepaid calling card number, her PIN number, and finally the number she wished to call, for a total of over twenty-five digits.

A rapid beeping indicated that the small handful of outside lines were all currently busy. Following further instructions, she hung up and sat down to wait, as the phone would ring when a line became available.

She waited.

And waited.

It was excruciating. This was not how her first days in Antarctica were supposed to go. She was supposed to be helping her professor with the final preparations for going into the field, far away from things like offices—as far as she could get.

Her gaze wandered back to Emmett's laptop. It appeared that he had left the computer for her to find; shouldn't she therefore look through it?

She put the computer on her lap and turned it on. Its filing system was easy to navigate. e-mail here, spreadsheets there, visual images another place, and extensive files for all his correspondence and the papers he had written and talks he had given. Everything was arranged chronologically. She paused a moment, wondering what to do if she found something personal and embarrassing, or worse yet, something incriminating.

"I understand you want to talk to me," said a baritone voice behind her.

A jolt of adrenaline slammed into Valena's muscles. She had to fight the urge to slap the laptop closed, instead simply swinging around in the chair so that whoever was at the door could not see the screen.

A man not much older than Valena was leaning into the doorway from one side, just a head and one hand peering around the door jamb.

You sly devil, she wanted to say. *Sneaking up on me like that!* He looked familiar, like someone whose face she had seen in photographs, but whom she had not met. "Hi there," she said. "I'm sorry, but I'm not sure who—"

"Bob Schwartz," he said. "I used to . . . ah, work with Emmett."

Now Valena did close the laptop, and, as casually as she could, set it on the floor, slipping it behind her day pack. "Well, hey, this is lucky. I didn't know you were in McMurdo."

"I'm just leaving. Catching a Herc out to WAIS Divide in about two hours. Working on one of the projects that are coming out of that core."

"I guess you've heard what happened. To Emmett, I mean."

Schwartz scowled and shrugged his shoulders. "He left, is all I heard."

"Left? He was hauled off the ice by some federal agents. Arrested."

He shrugged again. The scowl became more petulant.

So little reaction? You did know this. You're lying. "Yeah, well, I'm trying to get some information about what happened last year. I was hoping you could fill me in."

"What's there to tell? This asshole journalist bullied his way into the high camp and then croaked. It sucked. So, what's up with Emmett? They saying he lost the Gamow bag on purpose?"

Valena watched her fellow climate student closely, trying to catch every little twitch of muscle or inflection to his speech. "I don't know. Do you think there's anything to that idea?"

Once again he shrugged, just one shoulder this time. "Ask Cal when he comes in from WAIS."

What are you hiding? Valena wondered. "So Cal Hart's coming to Mc-Murdo? When do you think he might arrive?"

"Don't know. Maybe he'll return on the plane that takes me out there. If we get to go today. Weather out there always sucks. Well, I'm outta here," he said, and started to turn away.

"Wait. Help me with this: you're up there at high elevation in a tremendous storm. The Airlift Wing drops a chute with the Gamow bag. Where were you?"

"In my tent!" He glowered at her, his eyes like needles. Then, in a more sulking tone, he added, "With Dan Lindemann. We stayed the hell out of the way. We were not there. And I've told this to the feds half a dozen times already!"

"*You worm*, thought Valena. *You nematode*. So you were just finishing your doctorate with Emmett, am I right?"

"Oh, now don't get going on that crap! I did what I had to do. I had a career to look after!"

"I—"

The phone rang.

Valena leaned over and grabbed the handset off its cradle. "Just a moment. I've got to get this call through, and then we can—"

But she was speaking to an empty doorway.

Valena wanted to chase after him and get more information—a half dozen questions now spun in her brain—but she didn't want to lose the line out. An electronic voice was asking her to punch in her calling card number again. She did.

A few seconds ticked by, during which time she listened to the sound of ten thousand miles of electronic space. At last the sound changed, but alas, it changed to a busy signal.

Valena slammed the phone back into its cradle. Spitting mad, she began the whole process again, once again heard the "hang up and wait" signal, and did so. She folded her arms fiercely across her chest and stared at the phone.

Moments ticked past.

She kicked the office door shut, swung her swivel chair back toward the desk and pulled Vanderzee's computer out from behind her pack. Clicking quickly through his filing system, she came up with a category that commanded her interest: FINANCIAL NEWS, it said.

When she opened that subdirectory, she found three more, listed alphabetically: LETTER TO EDITOR, OTHER CORRESPONDENCE, and SWEENY ARTICLE.

She glanced at the clock at the lower right-hand corner of the laptop's screen to see what time it was. Breakfast was under way now, and she had about an hour and a quarter before she was due at Happy Camp. In that time, she needed to eat, come back here to change into her ECWs, and get to the Science Support Center, where the class would gather. She decided to take a quick glance at whatever LETTER TO EDITOR had to offer, because, she reasoned, letters were lots shorter than articles, and OTHER most likely had something to do with follow-up communications based on whatever ARTICLE and LETTER were about.

As she opened the first file, she heard a knock at the door. She slapped the laptop shut again and looked up, imagining that it might be Bob Schwartz thinking better of his escape. But when she stood up and opened the door, she discovered that it was Michael, the man who had helped her with the computer in the library the day before.

"Good morning," he said. "All ready for Happy Camp?"

"Oh, uh, sure. Just trying to get a few things done first."

He nodded. "Great. I'm on my way over to breakfast. Care to join me?"

Valena glanced at the telephone. "I'm sort of waiting for a call."

He shook his head. "You wait and wait for a line, and then they aren't home."

"It was busy the first time," she said.

"Well, I'm off."

"See you over there."

Michael disappeared down the hallway whistling.

The phone rang. She picked it up and dialed. This time the connection went through, rang three times, and was answered. "Hello?" said a woman's voice.

Valena recognized Sahar, Taha's wife. The image of her dark eyes and prim scarf came to mind. "Hello," said Valena, marveling at how clear and immediate the connection was. "Um, is Taha there, please?"

"Taha? Oh, no, he left hours ago. Who may I say called?"

"This is Valena."

"Oh! Valena, where are you calling from?"

"Antarctica."

"Oh, my, well, that is a long way away. Is it very cold there?"

"Well, not where I'm sitting. It's maybe—" She stopped herself, unwilling to use her precious long-distance minutes with pleasantries. "I'm sorry, Sahar, but I don't have much time to talk. Is—um, well I wanted to ask Taha a few questions about what the NSF said to him about the situation down here."

"Situation? Taha told me very little, except that his travels were delayed. Taha does not like to worry me," said Sahar, letting her voice drop to a deeper register.

"Does he seem . . . upset at all?"

"Well . . ."

Valena could almost hear the gears turn in Sahar's mind. She was a very traditional wife from a culture very different from the one Valena understood. It was clear that she did not like to be outspoken on personal matters. She and Taha had come to America from Palestine so that he could pursue studies in desert systems, but he had gotten the bug to study the coldest desert on earth, Antarctica. Taha was very bright and hardworking, a prize student for any professor.

Finally, Sahar said, "I think he is quite concerned. Can he call you back? I am certain that he would like to talk to you."

"No, he can't call here, and I have to leave, anyway. Can you relay a message for me? Please ask him to answer my e-mail as best he can. It's important."

"Oh, certainly, Valena." She paused. "Is something wrong there? I am wondering why he is delayed."

"I'm certain that everything will work out," she heard herself say. She offered a cheery closing salutation, hung up the phone, and then sat for a moment, contemplating her next move. *Get a message to Lindemann,* she told herself.

Quickly, she dug into her kit and produced her notebook paper and a pen. After a short greeting explaining who she was, she wrote:

Emmett has been removed from McMurdo under guard, apparently under arrest. I need to talk to you about what happened last year.

Thinking better of this approach, she scribbled that out and tried again. And again. After the fourth try, she realized that she had no idea whose side Lindemann was on, much less whether it was at all smart to contact any of the eight people who had been in the camp, at least in this manner. Several things could go wrong. Her message could be intercepted or lost, or one of them could turn her in to George Bellamy. Or worse yet, if anyone had anything to hide, this would put him or her on the alert.

Her mind burned with negative possibilities. If she was unlucky, she'd get sent north as soon as Wednesday, a disaster not only for her master's thesis research but also for any hope of helping her professor. At least today she would attend Happy Camp, which would get her out of McMurdo and onto the ice she had dreamed about for so many years, but while there she could do very little to find out what had happened or hope to move toward a reversal of fortunes.

It was time to get moving, to get breakfast so that she could be on time for her class. She got up and was about to leave when it occurred to her that the laptop might be gone when she returned the next day. She pulled her own laptop out of her bag and put it on the desk, folded up his computer, slipped it and its power cord into her bag, and prepared to carry it off to her dorm room.

She turned toward the doorway and almost collided with yet another man. All the long muscles of her body jerked, and she almost dropped the bag.

"Hello," he said. "You'd be Valena, right?"

"Yes."

He was tall and blond and no more than five or six years older than she was. He was smiling at her. He was good-looking and very fit. "I'm Cal Hart. Emmett's assistant."

So you're in town. Not at WAIS Divide." Her mind raced. How long had he been standing there? Had he seen her switch the computers? She forgot completely all the questions she wanted to ask him. "I was just going to breakfast," she said.

"Let's eat together," he said.

"Sure, ah . . . that would be good. I was hoping you could fill me in a little on what happened. You know, to Emmett."

His smile crumpled, revealing a tender boyishness. "I wanted to ask you the same." He put his hands in his pockets and hung his head, shaking it in bewilderment. "I got back and he was gone."

"You were in the high camp last year when it happened," Valena said. "I was hoping . . ."

Cal lifted his head and looked at her, his eyes round with surprise and innocence. "It was awful," he said. "I . . . I'd never seen a man dead before."

A third man appeared just outside the office door. This one was middle-aged, slim and bearded. "Cal!" he said. "Can I have a word with you?"

Cal turned. "Sure, Jim."

"In my office?"

"Sure." He glanced over his shoulder at Valena. "See you at breakfast," he said, then he turned his attention to the man named Jim.

The two men walked away, leaving Valena with the weight of the computer in her backpack. *Did he see me make the switch?* she asked herself again. *Should I leave it here?* She thought only a moment before hurrying off to her dorm, backpack and computer in hand.

9

Major Hugh W. Muller, "Tractor Hugh" to select cohorts, sat at his desk in Building 165. He stared into the computer screen in front of him, trying to decide whether to involve himself any further in the mess he and Waylon Bentley had found up in Emmett Vanderzee's high camp or to let it ride. It was impolitic to say a word. It was unprofessional to even blink. But it was quite possibly immoral to do nothing at all.

Master Sergeant John Lansing appeared at the door. "Got a moment?"

"Sure. What's up?"

"A young woman came looking for Waylon yesterday. She's a student of that beaker Waylon hauled off the ice on Saturday."

"I met her, too. Nice kid."

"I'd sure hate to come all the way down here and have to turn around and go home."

"What are you suggesting?"

"Nothing." He put his hands in his pockets and began to whistle a little tune.

"Okay, I got you on radar. Get out of here."

Lansing grinned and disappeared from the doorway.

Deciding on a measured step, Hugh switched to his e-mail screen and typed a few sentences to Major Bentley:

Hey there wise guy. You getting your fill of greenery? Okay, enough frivolity, what happened when you offloaded the professor? Feds still treating him like a criminal?

Thinking better of it, he backed up and erased *like a criminal* and typed in *the same*. He smiled. He was rather enjoying this cloak-and-dagger stuff, speaking in code and so forth. Waylon would know what he meant. Waylon had been ready to drop the feds out the cargo door at altitude, the way they'd spoken to the professor up there at the high camp. This was Antarctica, where people depended on each other or went down fast. It was ridiculous to go after them like they did.

Hugh typed,

So here's the latest: it seems that Herr Doktor Professor has two students this year, and they only managed to stop one of them from coming south. The other one's here, and wow is she a pistol. Wants to clear his name.

Hugh thought for only a few tenths of a second before adding,

You want to play?

He signed himself "TH" and hit send. Then he leaned back in his chair, arching his back into a big, much-needed stretch. The tension of that visit to the high camp—and what they'd found there—had bitten holes in his sleep every night since. Something had to give.

10

At ten minutes to nine, Valena settled into a seat in a small classroom on the second floor of the Science Support Center. She had time to burn, enough to begin to fidget and replay the conversation with Ted and Cupcake for the hundredth time, the conversation with Taha's wife for the tenth, and begin to chew on the visits from Bob Schwartz and Cal Hart.

She itched to ask someone whether she would be back from Happy Camp in time to attend the Tractor Club meeting, whatever that was, so that she could meet Major Bentley, but she didn't want to draw attention to herself or in any way seem anything but gung ho about survival training for fear that, considering her status as a short-timer, they would decide that she didn't need the training.

All she knew about Happy Camp was that she would be required to demonstrate that she could sleep in a tent on the ice and light a camp stove without igniting the tent or herself. She presumed that her ECWs were warm enough that she would in fact survive, but she was yet to be convinced that a sleeping bag and a tent were going to keep her warm enough to actually sleep. Sleeping aside, if it was true that everyone in McMurdo went through this training sooner or later, and she had so far not seen anyone with missing fingers or toes, then it must be that survival training was . . . well, effective.

Promptly at nine o'clock, two young men came into the room and announced that they were Happy Camper School teachers. One had black hair and eyes and skin that was a burnished mahogany brown everywhere his clothes, hat, and glacier goggles did not touch. His nose, cheeks, chin, and lower forehead made a rich, dark contrast to the paler skin around his eyes, making him look like a negative image of a raccoon. He said, "Hi, I'm Manny, and this is Dustin." He gestured toward the other instructor, whose freckled skin seemed more chapped than tanned. "We're going to have an hour or so of lecture here where it's warm, and then we'll be heading out to Snow Mound City." With that, he picked up a dry marker, approached the erasable board at the front of the room, and launched into a discussion of the five mechanisms of heat loss: conduction (wet clothes), convection (moving air), radiation (keep covered up), evaporation (don't get so warm that you sweat), and respiration (heat that you exhale is just plain gone). This last was important also because exhaled air was replaced with air that was incredibly dry. It seemed that dehydration was a big problem in Antarctica. ("Drink, drink, drink. Your pee should be clear and copious.")

Valena dug in her pack for her water bottle and took a swig. She found herself preoccupied with little things, such as what it was going to be like to pee, and what kind of sleeping bag would be issued, and what they might have for lunch. These were all things that Emmett Vanderzee had not thought to explain to her. She had thought that he would show her the ropes. But he was not here.

Her attention wandered to her classmates. Michael from Crary Lab was there but was studiously taking notes, so she checked out various young men in the class. None particularly grabbed her interest, so she got to examining the visual aids, such as a mock-up of a helicopter seat and harness, which they were expected to learn how to exit in a hurry. Her gaze came to rest on a second dry-mark board toward the back of the room. The lecture from a previous class had not been erased. The subject was altitude sickness. Symptoms. Triage. Treatment. Valena wanted to get up and examine it more closely but, again, did not wish to attract attention to herself. Over the next two days, she wanted to be just another face in the crowd, not that poor kid whose professor got hauled off in handcuffs.

Back at the front of the room, Manny was discussing how to recognize hypothermia ("Pay attention if your partner develops the 'umbles'—fumble, mumble, grumble, stumble") and the early stages of frostbite ("You'll get pink and numb, then next comes a white patch. After that, it goes stiff and sounds wooden when you hit it. If it goes beyond that, we're talking blisters and blackening"), how to keep warm ("You are the furnace, and you need fuel—eat, eat, eat") but not too warm ("If your goggles steam up, your core temperature is too high: take off a layer"), and so on. The three mechanisms of heat gain were metabolic (eat more than you burn), exercise (both voluntary and involuntary . . . such as shivering), and radiation (cuddle up to something warm; the old saw about getting naked with some*body* warm was apparently no longer as popular a solution).

Finally, they were told to exit through the back of the building and load into the Delta.

What's a Delta? Valena wondered, until she stepped out through the doorway and got her first view of their over-the-snow transportation. It was another mammoth vehicle with fat rubber tires that loomed taller than she was. This one had a cab that was cantilevered out in front of the front tires, which in turn sat in front of a huge pivot point; the front wheels did not swivel, but instead the whole front end swung to make the vehicle turn. Mounted on the after end of the frame was a big, rear-entry passenger box with a chain ladder hanging below the door to permit awkward entry. They clambered up the ladder and packed in together tightly, Manny cheering the twenty students on with, "Come on, you can cuddle in tighter than that!"

Valena felt a hard shove in her ribs. She turned to recognize Doris, the computer person, trying to cram in closer to her. "What are you doing here?" she asked.

Doris gave her an exasperated look. "I managed to escape this last year, but they've finally caught up with me," she said. "And don't ask me why I'm in Antarctica if I don't like the out-of-doors, okay?"

"Whatever you say, boss."

Manny had the last few firemen hoist in cardboard boxes full of flight lunches. "Hold those on your laps. Okay, now when we get there, don't go opening this door from the inside. We'll be opening it from outside, and you could take our heads off with it. But if something goes wrong, like we crash or something, there's an emergency exit in the roof." He pointed. "Okay, everybody happy?"

Several Happy Campers gave a thumbs-up.

Manny slammed the door.

Suddenly they were twenty people packed as tight as sardines in conditions that were brand new to each of them. Gazes turned inward, and all conversation stopped. Valena heard the muffled sounds of Manny and Dustin climbing into the cab and starting the engine, and a moment later, the whole rig lurched into motion, bouncing and rolling on its giant tires.

They wallowed off toward the east, up around Observation Hill, and down toward Scott Base, the New Zealand research station that lay three miles by road from McMurdo. Valena craned her neck to look through the battered windows, anxious to see whatever she could of this fantastical environment. Ob Hill was formed of more of the black volcanic rock, with bands of reddish scoria. As they came around the far side of the divide that lay between the two research stations, she caught a new view across the ice, looking south toward Minna Bluff. She noted with some dismay that it appeared to be clouding up. *We've got two hours to find cover,* thought Valena. *Or create it, out of snow and ice.*

Valena listened to discussions that sprang up around her. There were several firefighters aboard, a raft of scientists, and miscellaneous office personnel from McMurdo, all wound up and excited to be getting their basic training in Antarctic survival. The firefighters were all men and looked like they needed a fire to fight. They were twitchy and restive and talked only to each other but immediately proved their worth. "Damn!" one of them cussed. "We're filling up with fumes." He pounded on the front of the box for a moment, trying to get the driver's attention, but soon gave up.

"They can't hear us," said another. "They're in a separate compartment, and they're probably listening to tunes."

"Damned surplus equipment," muttered the first firefighter. He got up and popped the emergency hatch in the roof. The same cold monster that had sucked the warm, humid air out of the C-17 worked its same magic on the fumes.

Valena dug a chocolate bar out of one of the flight lunches. *Eat, eat, eat,* she told herself, peeling away its wrapper.

❖

HAPPY CAMP WAS not as great a challenge for Valena as it was for the few participants who had never braved wilderness camping before. She already knew how to use the tiny stoves and pitch the dome tents, and while she had never camped on snow she had backpacked in the Rocky Mountains and had done her share of skiing. She had wondered why Vanderzee had asked her how many pairs of skis she owned. She had answered three (one pair downhill, one mountaineering, one skating). He had thought that quiver small, and now, as she shoveled snow to build a crude survival igloo, she understood. He had wanted to gage her level of experience with and enthusiasm for snow.

Antarctic snow was a species apart from any of the broad variation of the white stuff she had experienced before, affording a different range of uses. They built their shelter, or "quinzy," in the style of the inland Inuit of Canada, by shoveling snow into a heap, packing it until it reset into a lightweight version of concrete, and then hollowing it out. To expedite construction, Manny had them make a heap of all the duffels containing their sleeping bags and mats and shovel the snow on top of them. "We'll punch a hole in the side and pull them out once we've got a good shell," he said.

Valena took the first shift standing on top of the mound and jumping up and down on it to pack the snow tight. To no one in particular, she called out, "I can't believe that this is going to create a structure that will stand."

"The snow here is a lot colder and drier than you may be accustomed to," said Dustin. "It's strange stuff. It packs hard."

Getting the first duffel back out from under the heap was an immense challenge, considering that it was weighted down by four other layers of duffels and a tightly packed shell of snow, but a couple of the firefighters took it as a challenge. When the structure had been emptied, Valena crawled in with a shovel and carved away all excess thickness, smoothing the walls and leaving a flat floor about eight feet in diameter. Then she poked a small air hole through the roof and began to close the hole made to remove the duffels by making a patch out of the snow she had scraped off the inside. It was quiet and snug inside the little arch of snow. The walls were thinner than she had expected, letting light shine right through, which offered a blue glow.

At the same time, Michael dug a tunnel into the wind-packed snow on the downwind side of the hut, under the wall, and up inside it, leaving as much of the floor as possible intact as a platform for sleeping bags. When they were done, there was room for exactly three.

"Snug as a bug in a rug," said Michael.

Valena smiled. "I'm going to call it home." She rolled out the two layers of thick neoprene and the enormous sleeping bag that the instructors issued to her, choosing the middle space so that if she rolled over in her sleep, she wouldn't kiss the frozen wall.

The wind had picked up while they were finishing the inside of the quinzy, but she could not hear so much as a whisper while inside. In fact, the only sounds she heard were her own breathing and the sounds of people walking around in the cold snow outside. *It's less than ten degrees out,* she reckoned, recalling how cold it had to get back home before the snow squeaked like that. She was glad that she had chosen the quinzy. It would keep her warmer than a tent.

Most of the other Happy Campers pitched tents. Some pitched two-man mountain dome tents, but Manny also issued them two Scott tents, which were tall, teepee-shaped rigs designed in the early days of Antarctic exploration. "You can stand up in a Scott tent," he said, explaining its virtues, "and two or three of you can sleep comfortably on its floor, but given that the fabric's heavy and the poles are not collapsible, the style would be useless anywhere sledges or helicopters were not available to assist transport. They are, however, stable in a high wind." He demonstrated the fine art of pitching the tent, first laying it out on its side with its top pointing into the wind, then hoisting it up and downwind using two of the guylines. A wide skirt around the base was then laden with snow to prevent the wind from turning it into a parachute, and the ends of the guylines were wrapped around bamboo sticks and buried a foot down into the snow.

The snow fascinated Valena. She had grown up in Colorado and Utah, where snow was usually light and fluffy unless it was allowed to sit around city curbs too long, in which case a few cycles of freezing and thawing turned it to ice and slush. This snow had a completely different quality, being born colder and kept frozen. The wind packed it into slabs, which Dustin now demonstrated could be quarried into blocks. This they did, piling them three courses high to form a wall that surrounded the little city of dome tents, connecting the Scott tents to the quinzy. When they had started to build it, Valena had thought it a mere exercise in survival training, but now she realized that it would provide a serious and important part of their comfort in the coming hours as the wind was gusting up to twenty knots now.

It was getting on toward the end of the afternoon, and Minna Bluff had long since disappeared entirely. Two of the firemen had gotten one of the little bivouac stoves going inside the Scott tent, so Valena joined them by climbing in through the sphincter of fabric that formed its airlock and availed herself of a cup of instant hot chocolate. Its warmth was welcome and the sugar hit her like a bomb. Settling herself on the small wooden crate in which the instant drinks had been packed, she allowed herself a short break.

One of the firemen said, "I don't know about that Dustin fella. He has the latest outdoor gear, but I think he's more show than go."

The other said, "Manny's okay, though. He's had a lot of experience down here. He's been a mountaineer other seasons."

"Yeah, so why's he teaching Happy Camp instead of getting the hell out of Dodge?"

"I hear he was out at this high elevation camp last year when somebody died of altitude sickness. It wasn't good."

Valena jumped into the conversation. "Really?" she said. "Do you mean Emmett Vanderzee's camp?"

The man nodded. "Mm-hm. First time they've lost someone in years."

So Manny is Manuel Roig, one of the people Ted told me were in camp with Vanderzee when the reporter died! Quickly she got up and wiggled back out through the airlock in search of the instructor.

Outside, the wind had increased another five knots and low clouds were beginning to press downward into the scene. Manny and Dustin were in the center of the corral, waving people together for a chat.

"Okay, you're on your own," Manny informed them, crouched down into the lee of the snow-block wall. "Dustin and I are going over to the instructor's hut for the night. You've got shelter, food, water, and a latrine. Do not, I repeat, do not leave the flag route while transiting to the latrine. As you can see, we are no longer in condition 3. This is getting toward condition 2. If it gets down to condition 1—if you can't see the flags—do not go to the latrine, you're bound to get disoriented and lost. Everybody understand?"

"What do we do if we can't get there?" someone asked, provoking a smattering of nervous laughter.

"Well, then you get creative," said Manny. "Bottom line, if you have to choose between peeing your pants and risking your life, what would you do? Okay, so Dustin and I are just half a mile down the road in the I-hut. Doris here has a radio, so anyone needs us, just call. See you at nine tomorrow morning for the next part of training. Have your stomachs full, the tents down and your sleep kits packed. Sleep well!" And off he went, with the redoubtable Dustin trudging along behind him.

Valena huddled down behind the snow-block wall and tried to reason out what to do next. On the face of it, there was very little that she could do except prepare something to eat and then climb into her sleeping bag inside the quinzy so that she could stay warm, the better to survive the night. The idea had strong appeal. She was jet-lagged, short on sleep, and now physically exhausted from shoveling snow. Sleep was the cure for all, and then she would be ready to question Manny when "morning"—that period of slightly brighter light that came after the period of slightly less bright light—arrived.

But first, she had to eat. She headed into the Scott tent and dug around through the food box, hoping for something palatable. There was nothing there but freeze-dried instant backpacker's dinners, granola bars, and chocolate bars. Black Bart chili with beans sounded like a bad idea in the tight confines of the quinzy, so she chose a packet that claimed to produce beef stroganoff. Following the lead of others around her, she tore open the top of the bag, ladled in a cup or so of boiling water, zipped the bag shut, and stuffed it inside her parka to keep it from growing cold before the contents rehydrated enough to become edible. She then located an eating implement—a sort of spoon with teeth—and headed back outside to again huddle inside the wall.

In the time it had taken her to get dinner, the world beyond the small grouping of tents had narrowed to a soft bluish gray, the sky and the surface of the snow-covered ice all one tone with the faintest darker line marking the seam between them. In this soothingly minimal environment, she took a moment to try to sort through her feelings. Ever since the shock that had awaited her arrival, she had been obsessed with disappointment and her determination to avoid being sent home. Oppressive cold with little shelter brought both exhilaration and a sense of desperation to her mood. She wrapped her arms around herself and squeezed the foil packet of food closer to her chest, holding it to her heart. Surely there was a solution.

Another human swollen with red parka and black wind pants shuffled to her side and sat down. The parka hood turned her way, revealing a pair of goggles, a rime of ice-encrusted beard, and the tip of a very red nose. The ice crimped briefly into a smile, then split horizontally, revealing a mouth. "Hi," the man said. "You're Valena, eh? Emmett's student?"

"Yes."

"Yeah, I heard you were here. Bum deal. Makes no sense at all."

"I'm inclined to agree with you . . . ah . . ."

Noting her attempt to figure out who he was, he moved his left arm away from his chest, revealing his name tag. DR. JAMES W. SKEHAN, it read. "Folks call me Jim," he told her. "Emmett and I are at DRI together."

"Sure, I know who you are," she said, embarrassed that she had not known who he was when he snagged Cal Hart from her office door before breakfast that morning. "I wrote to you last year to see if you were accepting students."

"I'm glad you were able to get on with Emmett. You should be proud. Your record looked very good, and he doesn't take many master's candidates."

She wanted to say, *Yeah, and it looks like it was my bad luck that he did,* but instead she said, "I'm truly glad to meet you."

Skehan unzipped his parka just enough to produce his dinner, which he opened up and drank, having put in more liquid than Valena had. He chugged it down in two long swills, then folded up the bag and tucked it into one of the four big patch pockets on the front of his big red.

"I hadn't thought of that technique," said Valena.

"You can only do it with certain ones," he said. "They ought to supply a large-diameter straw."

"What are you doing in Happy Camp? You've done tons of work down here."

"They've got a rule about how many years you can go without a refresher. It doesn't matter that I've spent those years working in Greenland. No, back to Happy Camp, my boy!" He did not sound happy at all.

"Perhaps you can help me understand what happened in Emmett's camp last year," Valena said. "I knew there had been a death, but—"

"I sat down with you because I was going to ask you what *you* knew about this whole mess. I just got here Thursday. Emmett was in the field, so I didn't see him. Then he came back, and . . . well, I didn't hear anything until midday Saturday, when Emmett was already on the plane going north. They really kept things quiet."

Valena pondered this statement. If the rest of McMurdo had the news, why was Skehan ignorant of it? Didn't the townies talk to the beakers? "What exactly was the gripe between Emmett and the journalist?"

"When the now-famous article appeared in the *Financial News* calling Emmett's work on rapid climate change a hoax, he—"

"He called it *what*?"

"Yeah, imagine that, a newspaper decides to debunk careful scientific research. Last time I checked, scientific findings were juried by peer scientists, people who understand the data and methods; but no, now our findings are to be judged in the newspapers by people who don't know data from dung, or worse yet, people who are pushing a political or business agenda."

"Sweeny took it on himself to say Emmett didn't know how to do science?"

"It wasn't Sweeny. The article was written by Howard Frink, who's making quite a name for himself for bashing science. His technique is to quote things out of context and misstate findings by applying them to things they obviously don't fit, the same way the religious right attacks the Theory of Evolution. It's like throwing out half the rules so you can change the game into whatever suits you."

"So Emmett invited him to come to Antarctica so he could educate him?"

"Sure, but did he come? No. No, he sent Sweeny. Frink couldn't be troubled to come to the source. Can't risk that, he might learn something contrary to his precious beliefs."

"Is Frink a fundamentalist?"

"Fundamentalist, neo-con, flat-earther, who knows? He's in with anything to the right of Attila the Hun. We're all going to hell. Ironically, he called Emmett's work 'the interpretations of an alarmist.'"

"Wow, that's scary."

"It's the fact that he could get that printed in the *Financial News* that's scary. Frink's in with the industrialist camp that doesn't want to think about all those nasty little correlations between increased atmospheric CO_2 from the burning of fossil fuels and the rise in global temperatures, reduced water resources, nastier storms, and environmental refugees. Thinks all our data that indicate that climate can change dramatically in just a few years is some wacked-out conspiracy to destabilize the saintly progress of commerce."

"He said all that? I always thought the *Financial News* was a conservative paper, as in, not into sensationalism."

"He made his statements in the kind of terms you have to read twice to spot how scathing they are. All about how liberals who rest on university salaries are undermining marketplace competition with skewed data and conjecture. Sure, let's just pump even more carbon into the atmosphere in the name of competing with the Chinese. Before that, it was Japan. Next, it's India. It's always somebody we're supposed to be afraid of. I say it's just the money maggots—excuse me, mag*nates*—wanting to keep on living beyond what's reasonable, zipping around in private jets and running huge pumps to keep their swimming pools pristine and chill or heat their houses to seventy degrees." He shifted slightly, working a kink out of his back. "The other problem with printing that kind of nonsense is that the other journalists are lulled into thinking that they are correct in the way they are reporting the story."

"And what's that?"

Skehan said, "In journalism school they are taught to always present the 'other' viewpoint. Anything less obvious to them than 'two jets flew into the Twin Towers today' requires that they give point and counterpoint, as if science is just a matter of opinion and that any opposing 'opinion'—that the increased rate of warming is caused by alien abductions, say, or by homosexual marriage—should be presented with equal weight."

Valena felt the stiffening cold of the ice-block wall seeping through her clothing. She pulled her neck gaiter up over her nose and spoke through it. "I guess you're pretty certain that the climate is warming," she said, intending irony.

"And you're not? Whose student is it you said you are?"

"Emmett Vanderzee's." Irritation was seeping into her with the cold. She respected her professor, but also wanted to kick him for getting into trouble. "But I'm supposed to keep an open mind, right? Which also has me asking questions, like how come Sweeny got sick and why did he die?"

Skehan said, "He got sick because he went to high elevation too fast. The real question is why Emmett was pulled off the ice."

"As in, what new evidence points to foul play."

He turned his goggles toward Valena. "You really don't get it. Sweeny's death was gasoline on the fire. Not having the gear that would save him was a terrible accident, but you can't convince the media of that. Frink has been using it to build his case against Emmett, keeping the story alive. There's nothing like a dead journalist to get a story on the front page."

"But *was* it an accident?"

"Yes, but an accident that happened thirteen thousand miles from New York in a place no New Yorker or Kansan or poodle-walking bridge player from San Diego can possibly imagine. It would have been great if Emmett could have gotten a whole team of media in there immediately to prove what actually happened, but that wasn't possible. *He* couldn't even get back in there to look at the site."

"Why not? Why did he leave without knowing what happened to the air drop?"

"There were more storms forecast, and everyone was already beat up from the last one. Emmett had to pull the whole camp out as soon as he could. And that was a lucky thing—in fact, the sane and rational thing to do, for everybody's safety—because another did come in right behind it, and then another. Big ones. When they say 'high winds' here, they mean hurricane force. If Emmett hadn't pulled out when he did, they'd all have been pinned down for at least another three weeks. The cook tent would have been torn to shreds, and then maybe even the Scott tents.

"Emmett wanted to get back in there to find that damned chute and document what had happened, but NSF was in no hurry to run another flight in there. The risk of getting stuck was too great. Then in no time flat it was the end of the season, and everyone went home. Maybe you don't understand yet what a narrow weather window we have here. It's already the end of November. Even if Emmett were here, you'd be lucky to mobilize into your camp within the next week. First it's storms and then it's fog. Once the fog lifts, then there's a backup of everybody trying to get where they want to go. Then you get the first really good day of flying weather, and it's Sunday and the pilots are on their days off. Antarctica is the place where they invented the expression 'hurry up and wait.' "

"Let me guess: the *News* thought it was all a cover-up."

"They made it sound like he lured the guy down here and ran him up that mountain with the express purpose of killing him."

Valena shook herself to work her muscles and create heat. "Well, did he? I mean, is there any truth to it at all?"

Skehan snorted. "Oh, ye of little faith. You're kidding me, right? I can't believe you would have come here with him if you believe him capable of that."

Valena stared into Skehan's goggles and frozen beard. She said, "What's faith got to do with science? Look, I don't really know the man.

He's got a great reputation as a scientist. I was thrilled to get onto his project. But now here I am without him, and if Bellamy gets his way I'm on the next plane home. I don't want to go. I want to stay! I'm here to do science, not perform acts of faith."

Skehan sighed. "Emmett wanted the guy to wait in Mac Town until they were done at the high camp and ready to move lower down, but with the storms and all, they were behind schedule. Sweeny said he was on a tight schedule himself, and if he did not get into the field in two more days he was going to return to Wall Street and write his story. NSF freaked at the thought of what he would write after coming all that way and not getting to the field. So they sent him up. Emmett really did not have much choice in the matter. He could have refused, but every project has to do media outreach, so a refusal could have come back to haunt him. The guy insisted that he had done plenty of high-elevation mountaineering and knew what he was good for. And maybe that's all true. Maybe he already had a respiratory infection going into it and didn't even know it. A lot of people show up here with the crud after all those hours in a commercial jet, or they catch it as soon as they get to McMurdo."

Valena said, "So the man got sick and they couldn't get him out fast enough."

"Emmett ordered a Gamow bag. The Airlift Wing flew it in on an LC-130 and dropped it on a chute. It was blowing to beat the band. Eighty knots sustained, gusting to who knows what. Emmett went out to get it. He took Cal Hart. They saw the chute in the distance, blowing, apparently dragging its cargo. They chased it, but suddenly the gusts got so huge that they were blowing along like sheets of newspaper. They had to use their ice axes to stay fixed, to keep the tents in sight. Then things deteriorated to condition 1. They had to claw their way back to the tents and hunker down so they didn't get lost. When the weather lifted, Emmett went out again, but he couldn't find anything, not the chute, not its payload, nothing."

"So he ordered another one."

Skehan's face remained aimed at Valena's for several seconds. "I don't know the answer to that question."

"I mean—"

"You mean did he just let the guy die. Listen, you go ahead and think what you want, but try to get one thing straight: down here it's tragedy when someone dies, no matter how little you might like him. It's a personal loss. And just because you're a wet-behind-the-ears grad student is no excuse to miss the really important point here: scientists don't go around killing people just because they're mad at them. That's for mafiosos and presidents, not scientists. Scientists want their adversaries to stay alive, so they can *prove them wrong*!"

Valena opened her mouth to say something, but Skehan had jumped to his feet. With one last unreadable stare, he stalked off into the gathering storm.

11

Valena woke during the night with a desperate need to pee and lay in her caterpillar-thick mound of sleeping bag considering her options. She read her wristwatch. It was one o'clock in the morning. She had climbed into the quinzy early because she had discovered, after her disastrous discussion with James Skehan, that she had let herself get dangerously cold. After dancing around and swinging her arms to warm up, she had swilled one last cup of hot chocolate and retired to her sleeping bag. Once inside its enormously thick wrapping of synthetic fibers, she had discovered that she was also extremely tired and had gone to sleep.

Now that the call of nature had brought her awake, with no idea what time it was, the illumination coming through the snow walls being nearly identical to what was there when she fell asleep, she realized that she was no longer alone. Doris snored gently to her right, and Michael from Crary Lab was sleeping to her left.

Realizing that there was no way she was going to get back to sleep if she did not relieve herself, she unzipped her bag as quietly as she could and struggled into her ECWs. She had gone to bed wearing two layers of long underwear, wool socks, and a fleece hat, with her big red parka pulled over the bottom half of her bag for an extra layer of warmth. She wiggled into her wind pants, raised their suspenders to her shoulders, shrugged her way into the parka, pulled on her boots, hat, and gloves, then stepped down inside the exit tunnel and crawled outside.

She popped up into a world that was even less welcoming than the one in which she had gone to sleep. The sky had gone low and wooly, though even in this tiny hour of the night it was as bright out as four o'clock in the afternoon back home.

It was blowing thirty knots, she estimated, kicking up loose snow that slithered as blurred white snakes across the packed surface of the ground. She counted flags along the route that led to the latrine and could see five. Given that they were spaced about twenty feet apart, that meant that visibility was down to less than one hundred feet.

Valena considered just hopping over the wall and taking care of business right there but did not want to find out the hard way how cold or unpopular that was going to make her. Five flags was good enough for her, though it was time to get moving or the point was going to be moot.

It seemed a long walk to the little wooden shack that housed the latrine. Ten flags out from camp, she looked back. The camp had disappeared. Everything was a blurry grayish white, a world of snarling wind and uncertain footing.

Turning back toward her goal, she continued into the murk, buoyed by a growing sense of liberation. This wildness was what she had come ten thousand miles to experience, and her sense of glory was diminished only by the increasing urgency of her bladder. At length the little wooden shack appeared, resolving itself from the soft grayness first as a brownish smudge and then as increasingly distinct edges gathering into a solid form.

When she pulled the pin from the clasp that kept it closed, the plywood door to the latrine flew out of her hand and banged open. Backing into the building, she had to use both arms to pull the door shut. *As if anyone could see me*, she thought, *but I'm not dropping my pants in this wind*. After pulling almost hard enough to give herself a hernia, she got the door closed and lowered the drop seat of her wind pants and the layers of underwear beneath it. The Styrofoam seat on the latrine was a shock for only a moment.

On the return trip, her sense of isolation was so complete that anxieties began to grow in her tired mind. *Am I walking the wrong direction?* she wondered, and, after another five flags, worried, *Shouldn't I be there already?*

At last the vague outlines of the two Scott tents loomed from the blowing plumes of snow, followed by the edges of the block wall and the quinzy, and soon she was close enough to see over the wall into the little town of mountain dome tents. She was home. *Funny to think of this as home*, she mused, as she slithered back down the rabbit hole that led to the quiet warmth of her sleeping bag.

She lay snug in her bag wondering if this was the kind of weather that had brought death to the reporter from the *Financial News*.

Hours later, she awoke as Doris climbed over her and began hurrying into her clothes. "Nature calls," said the computer specialist, pulling her last zipper up and disappearing down into the hole. Ten seconds later, she reappeared, popping up like a prairie dog, her eyes huge and her hood and shoulders covered with a fine sifting of snow. "I can only see three flags!" she gasped. Indecision stayed with her but an instant, and she was gone.

Valena listened to the squeaking of many footfalls outside the quinzy. It sounded like most of the rest of the camp was already up.

Michael rolled toward her and presented her with a divine smile. "Good morning," he said. "It was nice sleeping with you."

Valena laughed. "You too, Michael."

"Why don't you roll up the gear and I'll get us some nice hot tea," he said.

"You've talked me into it."

Michael got into his clothes and descended into the hole. He, too, returned a moment later with a fringe of tiny snowflakes. "It's all the way down to condition 1. I hope Doris isn't caught halfway out or back," he said. He headed back down into the tunnel.

"Wait, aren't you supposed to stay here if you can't see where you're going?"

"I'll follow the wall from the side of the quinzy to the Scott tent," he called from the tunnel. "I just can't wait to know what sort of freeze-dried mush awaits us for breakfast."

Valena slithered into her gear and crawled down the tunnel to take a look. Outside, the world had gone completely white. She could vaguely make out the shapes and colors of other campers struggling to take down the dome tents in the wind, and they were less than ten feet from her. *So this is what it was like when Emmett Vanderzee went looking for the chute,* she thought. *No wonder he couldn't find it!*

Twenty seconds staring into the buffeting void was plenty. Valena dropped back into the tunnel and returned to the snug safety of the snow hut. Alone inside the quinzy, she went about the tasks of packing up the sleep kits. Life had telescoped down to just a few simple necessities. She was at peace.

Her solitude was shattered by the return of Doris, who looked like she'd been dusted with a liberal coating of confectioner's sugar. She said, "If I ever try that again, tell me to pee my pants instead, okay?" She then dug inside her personal duffel and produced the two-way radio Manny had given her, fiddled with the knobs, and made her call. "I-hut, this is Happy Camp, how read?"

Fine static poured from the speaker.

Doris repeated her call. Five seconds later, Manny's voice came through the instrument. "Happy Camp, this is I-hut, go ahead."

"I-hut, we have condition 1, repeat, condition 1. We have the camp almost struck. We are leaving the two Scotts up until we see you. Request early departure. Over."

"H. C., we have same conditions. We'll come get you when conditions permit. Until then, stay put, stay hydrated, and eat all the chocolate and oatmeal you can stand. You copy?"

"H. C. copies," growled Doris.

"Check in each hour on the hour. Over."

"H. C. copies. Each hour on the hour."

"Anything else?"

"No." She stared at the radio for a moment, then added, "Clear."

"I-hut clear."

Doris switched off the radio. Her face was a mask of tension. "I'm a computer geek," she said, as much to herself as to Valena. "What am I doing here?"

"Having the adventure of a lifetime?"

Doris turned her gaze toward Valena. She took a breath and let it out abruptly. Under her breath, she muttered, "Beakers."

12

THE FIRST CALLS THAT SIGNALED THE STATE OF EMERGENCY CAME shortly before noon. It was the Boss's voice over the radio that got Dave's attention. "Challenger 283, this is Fleet Ops, you copy?"

When the Boss was answered only by silence, Dave put down the tool he had been using to break ice off the steps of his own Challenger and headed toward Building 17, the tight little prefabricated unit that housed the offices of Fleet Operations.

What was condition 1 out on the ice was condition 2 in Mac Town, which as usual had its own local version of the weather. It lay cuddled in the shadow of surrounding hills, which dampened the winds enough that it was still possible to walk from building to building without the hazard of getting lost. But most of the heavy equipment operators worked out on the sea ice grooming the runways and flag routes. Those who had been on night shift, at work as the storm closed in, had either managed to head back in to McMurdo before visibility got down below four flags or had hunkered down at the runway galleys. Everyone who had come on the day shift in McMurdo had stayed in McMurdo.

Inside Building 17, Dave found Cupcake and a handful of other heavy equipment operators swilling strong coffee and munching stale Chips Ahoy cookies. "Hey, Dave!" Cupcake said. "You manage to keep busy this morning?"

Dave poured himself a cup of coffee. "Yeah."

"You're such a good doobie. Whatcha been up ta?"

"This and that." To change the subject, he said, "I heard Happy Camp is pinned down with condition 1."

"Naw, they're on their way in now," said Wilbur. "It's starting to lift by the ice runway, too."

The radio coughed into life again. "Challenger 283, this is Fleet Ops, you got a copy?" His voice had a pleading note to it.

Silence.

Cupcake turned to Dave. "The Boss is calling Steve. Is he out there in this?"

The radio squawked again. "Challenger 283, this is Fleet Ops, come back please."

Joe said, "He was on night shift out at sea ice runway, but he knows what to do when he can't see where he's going. He must be in the galley or something."

"Yeah," said Dave. "He knows to stay put and catch up on his sleep."

"Then why ain't he responding?" Wilbur asked. "He ain't such a heavy sleeper."

The radio crackled again. "Challenger 283, this is Fleet Ops, come back please."

A thin static filled their ears, but no reply from Steve.

Wilbur said, "He don't usually ask 'please.' Sumpin's up."

Dave stood up and moved into the Boss's office, which had a window that looked out over the sea ice. The scene was still dark with storm clouds. A hundred yards down the hill from the building, he could just make out the blurred form of someone trudging up the hill toward the post office, leaning into the wind, parka hood up and cinched close to the nose.

The Boss sat at his desk with the radio microphone in his hand. He looked up as if drawn from deep thoughts. "You heard from Steve this morning, Dave?"

"No, I have not." He looked out the window. A gust of wind was abating, and he could see a dance of swirling snow that led clear down the hill onto the ice. "I can see the tails on the Hercs sticking up out of the blow. It's clearing up."

The Boss gave him a look. "I may be sitting with my back to the window at this moment, Dave, but I have been looking out from time to time. It requires only that I push with one foot to swivel my chair the requisite one hundred and eighty degrees. I have the technology."

Dave offered no rejoinder. The Boss was firm, but he was a nice guy.

Getting cranky like this meant that he was worried. Dave said, "What's the sitch, Boss?"

"I sent him out there last night with 283 before it got bad, because I wanted someone there in case things improved enough to get a flight in and the runway needed plowing. I knew he'd be pinned down for a while, but he doesn't seem to mind the food out at the runway galley."

Now the man was not only being polite, he was apologizing and explaining. This was bad.

The others had followed him into the Boss's office and now stood clustered around the man's desk. Cupcake said, "Yeah, Steve'll eat anything. You think maybe he's just gone in for lunch?"

"No, they just phoned me to ask where he is. They're counting heads, like. They said he was there for breakfast, but they haven't seen him in a while."

"They think he went out to take a nap in the Challenger, maybe?"

"They checked. It's not there."

"Maybe he turned his radio off, or maybe—"

The Boss keyed his mike one more time. "Challenger 283, this is Fleet Ops. Kindly respond, Bucko."

They all tensed as the radio crackled, but when the static resolved itself into a voice, it was a woman's. "Fleet Ops, this is Mac Ops, do you have a problem you wish to report? Over."

The Boss stared into space. Admitting to Mac Ops that he had a problem was admitting to himself that one of his people was at serious risk. He keyed the mike. "Mac Ops, we have a man not responding to radio coms. We are trying to ascertain his position. Over."

"How do you wish to proceed? Over."

"I guess we'd better give him another couple minutes and then go find him." After two or three heartbeats, he added, "Over."

"Mac Ops copies. Call back in five."

"Fleet Ops clear." The Boss picked up the phone and dialed the sea ice runway galley. "Can you see his tractor?" His face tightened as he listened to the answer to his question. "Damn. Keep me posted anything changes. I'll do the same." He hung up. Leaned back in his chair. Puffed up his cheeks and blew out a long, wheezing breath. Stared at the ceiling.

Dave and the others shifted like a group of cormorants fighting for positions on a rock. The minutes ticked by. Nobody said anything.

"Fleet Ops, this is Mac Ops," the radio sputtered.

"Go ahead, Mac Ops," the boss replied.

"I've got Search and Rescue on coms. Conditions have improved, so they're going to take their Haaglund out along the flag route toward the runway. Over."

"Thank you for that. We're going to send another Challenger. Say conditions extended area. Over."

"Mac Ops copies Challenger aiding search. Conditions east and south still alternating 1 and 2. Cape Crozier currently condition 1 and Black Island condition 2. Conditions east: Penguin Ranch reports condition 2 and clearing, no one is at Cape Royds to report, Dry Valleys report high clouds and one hundred miles visibility. Mac Ops clear."

"Fleet Ops clear."

Cupcake turned to Dave. "We'll use your rig," she said and headed toward the door. Dave slapped the toggle on the coffee urn to refill his insulated mug, grabbed a pack of juice boxes, and followed.

"We're coming too," said Wilbur, as he and Joe hurried after them.

"You won't all fit in the cab," Cupcake snarled. She stood in the open doorway, one hand on the knob to block their passage. Snow sifted in, covering her shoulders. "Besides, you idiots care too much. You'll get in trouble, too. Stay here and help the Boss. Come on, Dave." She grabbed him by the cuff and pulled.

Dave and Cupcake hurried along the line of parked tractors. They could hear the boss hollering at Joe and Wilbur, ordering them to stay put. "You got emergency rations in your Challenger?" asked Cupcake.

"Sure enough." They were running now.

Cupcake waved Dave up the flight of six steps that led up over the front of the treads toward the cab of the towering tractor. "It's your rig, you know it better," she hollered.

Dave roared the big engine into life, then spun the steering wheel with one hand, reaching for the gear lever with the other, thankful for the machine's exquisite power steering. He slapped it into second out of the ten forward gears. The huge tractor lumbered authoritatively down past the line of parked vehicles and, at another touch of the wheel, turned out onto the road that led down past the gas pumps toward the main road and the transition from land to ice.

The view ahead was daunting. Conditions had indeed improved from total whiteout, but ragged gray storm clouds still packed the sky, their maelstrom of wind and frozen moisture obscuring all but a few glimpses of the mountains. The wind scoured the great plane of ice that opened out before them, kicking up a blur of moving snow. The horizon was lost in shades of blue and gray.

When they reached the juncture between the land and the frozen sea, Dave stopped and unclipped his microphone. "Mac Ops, Mac Ops, this is Dave Fitzgerald with Challenger 416 at the transition. Two souls on board. We are proceeding via flag route to ice runway and beyond to assist with search and rescue, over."

"Challenger 416, this is Mac Ops. Call in every quarter hour to report your position. Sooner if you find him. Over, out, and Godspeed."

BRENDA UTZON HEARD about the missing tractor driver as she joined friends for lunch. News of Steve's disappearance was rolling through the galley like ball lighting. As she settled into a chair, the woman who managed McMurdo's library leaned forward and passed the word. "SAR is out looking for a missing tractor driver. Guy named Steve, from Fleet Ops. How I hate this."

Brenda glanced around the galley. Friends were stopping friends in the aisles between the tables. Facing the demon as a group, as a community, as one soul with a thousand faces. One man lost in an Antarctic storm made all hearts beat in one anxious rhythm.

The PA system popped into life and George Bellamy's voice filled the air. "May I have your attention please for an important announcement. This is to confirm that a search is under way for a missing person. If anyone knows the whereabouts of Steve Myer, please contact the Firehouse with that information. In the meantime, please stay calm and do not attempt to assist in the search without direct instructions from the Search and Rescue team under the direction of Manuel Roig. Repeat, do not attempt to assist without instructions from proper authority. Conditions are still variable between 1 and 2 and . . . and we don't want anyone else going missing." The PA channel remained open for several moments. Everyone in the galley stayed frozen with ears cocked toward the speakers, waiting. Finally, Bellamy added, "Uh, that is all for now," and closed the channel.

Brenda shook her head. She was not personally acquainted with Steve

Myer, but that didn't matter. The US Antarctic Program was a community built on interdependence, and that meant that a part of herself was missing.

She looked down at her tray full of food. Suddenly it did not look appetizing. She really liked the thick, creamy soups that the kitchen staff turned out, but just now this one smelled awful. She pushed it away. "I think I'll just go back to my office and get back to work," she said.

MAJOR MARILYN WOOD found Major Hugh Muller at his desk in the Airlift Wing offices. "You heard?"

"About the missing Cat driver. Yes. Any news?"

"Not yet. Anything back from Bentley?"

"I was just typing him another e-mail. This is what I got from him this morning."

Bentley's message glowed from his screen:

Listen, chucklehead, you weren't there last year when we loaded that corpsicle onto the bird. It was not pretty. I agree that there was something funny about what we found up there this year, but I vote we leave this one to the proper authorities. What's over is over. Kick it upstairs to the Colonel and be done with it.

Marilyn said, "By that I take it that he means that you and I are *im*proper authorities."

Hugh snorted. "Right." He wrote:

Okay, dipstick, we'll hold short for takeoff, but let's keep our engines warm. SAR is at this moment out on the ice looking for a missing somebody. They just found his tractor between the runway and town but he's not in it. I tell you, the Hughster has a nose that smells rot in all its forms, and ol' Wrong Way Wood here is flaring a nostril, too. Something is going south down here, bigtime, and when we say "south" down here, we mean SOUTH.

Hugh hit send and leaned back in his chair. "Loadmaster got everything dialed in for emergency takeoff with medical crew?"

Marilyn snorted softly, as if to say, *Need you ask?*

Hugh said, "I sure don't like sitting when something like this is going on."

Marilyn's face had set like stone, but her words came out light and easy. "What say we get ourselves out to the runway and drink that galley's coffee for a while? This pot's almost out."

13

After helping the other Happy Camp participants unload the Delta into the cargo bay at the Science Support Center, Valena went looking for Manuel Roig

"Didn't you hear?" Dustin asked. "He's gone off with the search and rescue team."

Valena wrinkled her brow. "But we're already rescued."

"Not you, someone else. *You* were never in danger. *You* had food and water and fuel and tents and each other. This guy's out there alone in the storm in a tractor. Scratch that, *without* a tractor. They just found the one he'd been driving and he's not in it."

"How strange," Valena said. "Why would he leave his tractor in this weather? I mean, shouldn't he have stayed inside it and waited for the storm to let up?"

Dustin gave her a look of appraisal. "Go to the head of the class," he said.

"Then something's wrong. I mean, really wrong."

Dustin said nothing.

"What's his name?"

"Steve Myer. Now, if you'll excuse me. Class is dismissed. I have to go help with the search myself."

Valena nodded. As she watched Dustin disappear out into the storm, she ran down her mental list of people who had been with Vanderzee during his previous season on the ice. Steve Myer was not a match.

Em Hansen's words of caution flashed in Valena's mind. Waiting for those hours on the ice, unable to see farther than she could have thrown a cinder block, it had begun to come home to her that this was not a safe place. Caution was necessary for even the simplest, most basic things, like staying alive.

Uncertain what to do next, she left the building and walked back along the rutted road that led to Building 155 and her dorm room. Suddenly the banks of melting snow and ice that bordered the path seemed painfully fragile. Life was finite in Antarctica, almost insignificant when opposed to the overwhelming expanse of ice that surrounded her. She had cruised through Happy Camp with arrogance, pleased with herself for having withstood its hardships with such ease, confident that theirs had been a practice situation made uncomfortable for the sake of training. But now a real Antarctican doing a real Antarctic job was missing and presumed in real trouble. A tractor driver. Valena pictured her grandfather on his farm tractor, pulling the potato harvester, caught in a sudden storm.

Grandpa. Being a practical man, he had let her drive the tractor when needed because she drove it well. Through hard work, she had built a place in his life.

Rounding the corner past the McMurdo General Hospital, she humped her duffel up the steps to the entrance into Building 155. She pushed open the door and walked inside.

Life seemed oddly normal within the building. People were walking here and there up and down the hallways, one stepping into the coat-room alcove to fetch a parka, another moving into the computer bay halfway down the main hallway, a third rushing up the steps that led to the galley.

Valena stood at the nexus of the hallways, glazed with fatigue. Blinking to adjust her eyes to the interior light, she glanced around, taking in details of her surroundings. A TV monitor mounted on the wall presented various data, the screen changing every few seconds. It presented local time: 13:32. *Military time,* she told herself. *Subtract twelve; so it's half past one in the afternoon. Damn, lunch is over.* While waiting to be brought in from Happy Camp, she had eaten a couple of helpings of reconstituted freeze-dried crud, but her stomach longed for something more recognizably foodlike, and the idea of sitting on a chair at a table in a heated room while she ate it seemed downright heavenly.

The monitor rolled to a different screen, this one listing the flight schedules for the day, all canceled. Valena closed her eyes and opened them again, correlating this information with her immediate concerns. *Flights north have all been bumped forward a day, which means that I won't be sent home tomorrow!*

Smiling with new hope, she headed down the hallway that led to her room with the lovely concept of a hot shower blooming in her imagination. Halfway to the door to the dorm rooms, she noticed a pair of bulletin boards housed behind locking glass doors and stopped to take a look. They appeared to be passenger manifests: southbound flights coming from New Zealand and those going onward to Amundsen-Scott South Pole Station to the left; northbound to New Zealand to the right. Today's lists were in place, but marked CANX, which, she reasoned, must be military-abbreviation-ese for canceled.

She spotted her name on the northbound list for the next day's flight, confirmed that the flight was marked CANX, and let out a sigh of relief. Also on the list she found Calvin Hart's name. It seemed that everyone working for Emmett Vanderzee was being sent home.

Not surprisingly, the southbound manifest did not list Emmett Vanderzee's name among the arriving flood of scientists, all of whom must be pacing the streets of Christchurch waiting for the weather to clear. And she realized that Major Bentley would be stuck in New Zealand as well. She would not be questioning him at the Tractor Club meeting tonight. It seemed that every good thing that happened in Antarctica had a bad side as well.

Valena headed down the hallway toward the dormitory rooms and the hot shower and clean underwear that awaited her there. She told herself that, after showering, she would check her e-mails and would find a message from Taha or even one from Emmett, saying that everything had been straightened out and that they would join her just as quickly as they could. She would then celebrate by going to the little store she had spotted near the entrance to the galley and get some postcards to send to her grandpa and the teacher from grade school who had first gotten her interested in science. And then she would take a walk in the wind and the snow.

Taped to her dormitory room door she found a note from an administrator at the Chalet, which read:

We've managed to squeeze you onto an LC-130 flight to New Zealand Thursday morning. Sorry for the delay. Please see me in the Chalet for details.

Valena let herself into the room, dumped her duffel, and trudged sullenly toward the Chalet.

"It's the earliest we could get you out," the administrator explained when she got there. "Sorry. But your situation is rather unusual. We're used to people staying here a bit longer before they redeploy."

"I don't mind staying, really. In fact, I'd like to stay. Prefer it. *Greatly* prefer it. I was hoping there'd be some word from Dr. Vanderzee. That he'd be coming back."

The woman gave her a you-poor-thing look. "Sorry," she said. "At least you don't have to go through any more in-briefs. Or out-briefs, for that matter. You haven't been anywhere and you're not a PI, so there's no paperwork to fill out."

Right, I haven't been anywhere at all. Suddenly, a thought occurred to Valena. "Could I become the PI?"

"I don't think so." She looked across the assembly room toward George Bellamy's office. "I suppose you could ask, but . . . well, no. I don't think so, dear."

Valena stared at Bellamy's door. The expression "a snowball's chance in hell" filled her mind, consuming all hope. "Well, if for any reason you need to bump me from that flight, you just feel free to do so, okay? I'm supposed to be doing research for my master's thesis, and I can just hunker down in the library at Crary and get plenty done. Really."

The woman fixed her stare on her computer screen. "Welcome to Antarctica," she said.

Valena said good-bye and headed out the door and turned away from 155 and away from the heartbeat of McMurdo before the tears began to roll down her cheeks. She was not given to fits of crying. Tears were pure humiliation: hot; useless; sad evidence of the collapse of her dreams. Right now she needed privacy. She ached for solace. She sought the out-of-doors.

The weather was clearing, the sky opening wide in its blinding pale blue. She followed a road up past several weather-beaten Quonset huts toward the conical prominence of Observation Hill. With each step away from the strange ant-hive of human endeavor called McMurdo, she felt more safe, more self-contained. It was difficult to make the hike in the enormous blue boots she had been issued. They were designed for staying warm while standing still on the ice, but the soft sides provided no ankle support, and the thick, stiff soles and layers of felt provided no arch support and the quilted liners tended to work around sideways, making her socks bunch up.

She was high above McMurdo when she heard the engine of one of the helicopters down on the pad below Crary Lab whine into life. She turned and looked down on the scene. The rotors began to turn. Was this a crew of scientists heading out across the ice toward the continent? They could be geologists going out to study the history of the landforms in the Dry Valleys, biologists on a mission to study the single-celled life forms that scraped out a meager existence in one of the frozen lakes there, or perhaps a team of glaciologists on their way to study a giant iceberg that had calved off the edge of the Ross Ice Shelf.

She surveyed the severe landscape. The wind had dropped to its usual nattering levels and the snow had stopped falling. The clouds were breaking up in the south, replaced by a high, scattered overcast. She could now see beyond the ice runway, clear past Black Island, and the first of the peaks on the Transantarctic Range were beginning to resolve themselves from the clouds.

Even though the blades were now turning so quickly that she could see only a blur, people were just loading into the helicopter. She thought that strange until she noticed their sense of urgency and a white van parked nearby. An ambulance? Was this a medical crew departing? Did that mean that search and rescue had found the missing man?

The helicopter lifted off, pivoted, and skimmed along the contours of the hill, then turned and accelerated away toward the end of Hut Point, staying so low that it skimmed barely fifty feet over a small wooden hut that was parked on the ice. It thudded heroically as it shrank into a dot and disappeared around the point.

Valena sat down on the clinkered ground, watching it go. Then she noticed that someone else was on the trail below her. Not ready to give up her privacy, she rose and continued up the steep slope toward Scott's cross. The other person continued to gain on her. She picked up her pace, but still the other lone hiker overtook her before she reached the summit. Only as he came quite close and she saw his wild hat did she recognize him. It was Peter, the energy conservation engineer whom she had met in the galley during Sunday brunch.

"They've found Steve Myer," he said. "Isn't that a relief! I thought I'd come up here and watch them bring him in, offer my spiritual support."

"Do they usually send a helicopter?"

"There's nothing *usual* about this. In fact, nothing like this has ever happened, not so far as I can recall."

"It looked like they sent a medical crew. That must mean he's alive. Maybe he's really cold and they need to warm him quickly."

Peter looked uncertain. "Maybe that explains why he wandered off. Like maybe he's all confused or something."

"Does that happen much?"

Peter shook his head. He had kind, inquisitive eyes.

They stood together at the cross for several minutes in silence. Finally, they heard the return passage of the helicopter. It began as a faint pattering and grew again into a thunderous rumble as it emerged around the point, flying low and fast toward the helicopter pad. Someone had turned the white van around and opened its rear doors, waiting to receive the patient. The wild mechanical bird settled, and, even before the whine of its engine changed pitch or the whirl of the blades diminished from a blur to the spinning of individual blades, the personnel on board disembarked. In one quick motion, they transferred a stretcher from the helicopter to the van. Someone closed its doors, and they were off uphill toward the hospital.

"Well, they're hurrying," said Peter. "That means he's still breathing. But what was he doing clear out around the point? I mean, even if you're confused from some kind of injury, you don't wander that far." He shook his head. "I don't know Steve except to say hi, but he seemed a reasonably smart man. Better than smart. In fact, he used to be a pharmacist."

Valena cocked her head in question.

Peter chattered on. "Oh, yeah, you get all kinds down here. PhDs driving Cats just to be here. People get jealous of me because I'm actually doing what I was trained for." He smiled shyly and looked intently into her eyes, as if mapping her.

Uncomfortable with this scrutiny, Valena turned toward the cross that dominated the top of the hill. "So this is a monument to Sir Robert Falcon Scott," she said.

"Oh yeah. Right. He didn't make it. Died just a hundred miles or so out there on the ice shelf, coming back from the pole."

"They didn't have helicopters back then."

"Or radios to call for help. Or McMurdo Station, for that matter."

They stood shoulder to shoulder, looking down at the amphitheater of buildings, Quonset huts, gravel roads, fuel tanks, miscellaneous vehicles, and layout yards that was McMurdo. "What a strange place," said Valena. "It's kind of like a mining camp, only without the mine."

"Oh, it's ugly as hell, there's no way around that. But we call it home."

Valena turned her attention back toward the far distance from whence the helicopter had returned. "What's out there, anyway?"

"There's a flag route leading around to the north toward Cape Evans and Cape Royds, with a fork continuing straight west to the Penguin Ranch. Beyond that there's a drilling project . . . something about the ocean floor."

"The ANDRILL Project," Valena said.

"Yeah."

"They're gathering data from the sediments that are dropped by the ice as it slides off the edge of the continent. The ice carries all sorts of clues about climate variation."

"That's what you're doing here, right? Gathering climate data from the ice?"

"Yes. When we get our core back to the States we'll analyze the stable isotopes of oxygen and hydrogen in the water, the gasses caught in the bubbles, and also the fine dust that settled out of the air into the ice." She began to walk back down along the trail, descending the hill.

"Peter followed her. I didn't know that there were different isotopes of oxygen and hydrogen in water," he said.

"Oh, yes, there are," she said, bending down to tighten the laces on the soft FDX boots in the hope that her feet would not slide forward inside them. "Most of the O in the H_2O that makes up the snow that recrystallizes to form all this ice is good old oxygen 16—eight protons and eight neutrons—but a small percentage of oxygen has extra neutrons, making oxygen 18, which is heavier. The thing is, the ratio between the two—how much 16 versus 18—is governed by the temperature of the clouds from which the snow falls."

Peter said, "Oh, I get it. You can figure out when the global climate was warmer and when it was cooler by measuring that ratio."

Valena shrugged. "The isotope ratios are a proxy for temperature. It's simple physics. The laws of thermodynamics. The hydrogen in the water molecule is a slightly different story. Hydrogen typically has just one proton, but sometimes two. We call that deuterium. How much deuterium you find in the ice is a reflection of the temperature of the water that evaporated to form the cloud. So by analyzing the isotopes in the ice, you can read the surface temperature of the ocean waters up in the tropics where the water left the ocean and entered the atmosphere as vapor."

"So even though you drill in Antarctica, it's not just about Antarctica."

Valena laughed. "Why would the taxpayers who are paying for this research care how cold it is in the middle of Antarctica? We chose the WAIS Divide site because it will give us a global record. We'll study the dust in the ice to figure out where it came from and how hard the wind was blowing. That tells us about atmospheric circulation patterns throughout this hemisphere. The amount of salt tells us how far into the ocean the sea ice extended around Antarctica, another indicator of ocean currents and global temperature. Organic compounds tell us about marine productivity in the southern oceans. The chemical and optical properties of summer snow and winter snow are different, so we can make measurements on the ice core that identify each annual layer of snowfall. It's like counting tree rings, really *old* tree rings. But the gasses, they rock."

"Gas in the ice?"

"Yeah, when the old snow gets buried by the new snow, it gets compacted into ice. The gas that was in the snow, like twenty percent of the volume, gets trapped in the ice. Grind up the ice, free the ancient air. You can study methane, CO_2, nitrogen, free oxygen. The ice is the only way to get pristine samples of the ancient atmosphere."

"You're going to do all that?"

"Not me alone. It takes a team of twenty PIs, each with their own research team and lab, working for years to pull this off. We're just getting started."

Valena was enjoying sharing her enthusiasm with Peter. He was easygoing and sweet, a soothing companion, and talking about her research topic moved her out of her tangled emotions and into the pleasure of the mind.

They reached the bottom of the hill and began to stroll back down the road that led toward the center of McMurdo. Valena said, "There are people here who study the way the ice flows off the continent. That's important because we need to know how fast it moves, so we can know how quickly the ice that's on the land can flow off into the ocean, and what influences that. Just recently, we at last have really good and complete satellite imagery of the entire continent, but just as we're really getting things dialed in, NASA gets funding cuts and we can't get as good coverage to monitor the ice movement, or how fast it's retreating. It's all very frustrating."

"Budget cuts. Not good."

"Right, and there are people who'd prefer that we not spend even as much as we are to study these things, or who don't believe there's any point in it."

"I've heard the argument that the additional greenhouse gasses are a very small percentage."

"Sure. Greenhouse gasses always exist in the atmosphere—heck, you and I are exhaling CO_2 right now—but it's that percentage that is added by burning gasoline in our cars or coal to fire electric power plants that makes a profound difference in how much heat is trapped. And right now, the US and China are building several times as many coal-fired plants as we've had in the past, and each one is bigger and is going to burn more coal. We've learned to scrub the particulates out of the stacks, but still they will emit CO_2. Tons and tons and tons of it. And per BTU generated, coal throws a lot more carbon into the atmosphere than other fuels."

"That's not good."

"That, in fact, is bad. They argue also that the global temperature has been rising for other reasons, such as the natural oscillations caused by things like the earth's orbit and that's true. Either way, we need to know as much as we can about climate so that we can plan accordingly. During the ten thousand years that our species has gone from a bunch of hunter-gatherers to crop raisers to industrialists and from a world population of a few million to six billion, the climate has been unusually benign, making all that crop growing and industrialism possible. The likelihood that it would continue that way was low. The likelihood that the climate would become less predictable is high. But why kick it over the moon? Answer me that."

They were approaching Crary Lab, and they stopped to talk in the middle of the road in front of it. "Because they either don't believe it's going to make a difference or because they don't care, I guess," Peter offered.

"I can think of a third possibility."

"What's that?"

"Because they don't know. And that's my job. To come up with the facts and take them to the people, so they'll all make wiser, better-informed decisions." Impulsively, she reached out and tapped the front of his parka. "And people like you, whose job it is to make us all more efficient in the way we heat and cool buildings, can not only figure out how to use less fossil fuels but also make decisions about other ways to heat buildings so we can quit using fuels that throw CO_2 into the atmosphere."

Peter considered this. "You keep talking about CO_2. How about the methane?"

Valena rolled her eyes. "Well, first, CO_2 is the bigger problem, simply by volume, and second, it's darned hard to persuade people to give up dairy products or to put methane scrubbers on cows. That's the major source of methane emissions that humans can influence. Landfills would be second."

Peter leaned toward her, incredulous. "Cows?"

Valena grinned. "Bossy and Bessie, you bet. Factory dairy farms are a big deal. The factory farms are also a problem because of their impact on groundwater. And once they foul up one area, they move them to another and foul that up, too."

"How do you know all of this?"

"I spent a lot of time on a farm when I was a kid. And I did an internship with an environmental firm in California during college, just to make sure which way I wanted to go for graduate school. My undergraduate degree was in geology."

"And you decided to go into climatology."

"Glaciology. For climatology you have to put together oceanography, atmospheric science, geology—"

"Geology?"

"Yeah, so you know how the continents move, which strongly influences—"

"The continents move?"

Valena opened her mouth to say yes, but then saw the twinkle in Peter's eyes and instead swatted him across one shoulder with a mitten. "What are you, a flat-earther?"

"I am the center of the universe. Didn't I mention that?"

"Come on inside Crary, and I'll show you dinosaur and fern fossils found underneath all this ice that prove that the continents move, Bishop Ussher."

"Who's Bishop Ussher?"

"A sixteenth-century monk who calculated the age of the earth from Biblical scripture. He came up with October 23, 4004 BCE. And then we can discuss the way particulate pollutants have dimmed the earth."

Peter's eyes were twinkling again. "You're into lots of thinky stuff, aren't you, Valena?"

"Yes, I am."

One of the heavy steel doors on the front of Crary Lab opened and a woman came out. "Hey, Peter!"

Peter turned around. "Oh, Doris! I saw the helicopter come in. It looked like they took Steve to the hospital. And I heard they found his tractor not far from the runway, so I mean, wow, how'd he get clear out there?"

Doris shrugged. "I don't know. We'll have to wait until he regains consciousness. It doesn't look good."

14

AN E-MAIL FROM TAHA HESAN WAS WAITING FOR VALENA WHEN SHE checked the computer at Crary Lab.

> Hello Valena,
>
> I know nothing that you do not. I was told only that there was a delay and that I should wait. This is very bad. I have spoken to the president of DRI and he says that everything possible is being done in Emmett's defense. Emmett has not written to me but I imagine he is very busy with lawyers. They have him in Hawaii. At least that is a long way from New York City, where his accusers have their camp. We must wait and pray. I will write to you if I learn anything more. Meanwhile please work hard in McMurdo to make certain that everything is ready for our field encampment should matters improve.
>
> Yours most truly,
> Taha

"Bummer," Valena whispered under her breath. She glanced at her other messages. The reply from Em Hansen was still there, as were the cheery greetings from her friends back in Colorado. Somehow, these last seemed as insubstantial as frost on the window, far away and separate. She exited the mail program and rose to head down the hallway toward the galley.

She was swept up into a hubbub of men who were slapping one another on the back. "Yo! My man! Way to go! Hey man, how'd you find him out there?" they were hollering.

The hero among them was grinning a down-home kind of grin, all aw-shucks and glittering with unconscious pride. He was a hardy-looking man with dark, shining eyes and brilliant white teeth, and as he walked, he rolled his broad chest and muscular shoulders with strength and ease of carriage. When his gaze briefly connected with hers, he blushed, his mahogany tan turning ruddier and the spaces around his eyes that had been protected from tanning by his glacier goggles turning pink.

Valena looked away. Had he found her features odd or disturbing? So many people stared. It made her feel ugly and increased her sense that she fit exactly nowhere. In this place, where she had somehow hoped to find a break from all that, the strange looks hurt bitterly.

The crowd swept the man along with them toward the galley. "No shit, Dave," one of them caroled, "it's like you're clairvoyant or something. He's out there in how many thousand square miles of ice and you drive right to him! He wasn't even wearing a big red! Shit, man, he was in Carhartts!"

"Oh, stick it up your butt, Wilbur," the man said. "Out there, anything that's not white sticks out like a sore thumb, and he wasn't all that far from the flag route."

The crowd turned the corner. Valena heard additional cheers emanating from the galley. She followed along more slowly and dawdled over washing her hands. When she at last picked up a tray and took her place in the cafeteria line, the ruckus had moved on into the main part of the dining hall. She stood for a while, watching well-wishers journey up to the man named Dave, patting him on his shoulders, scruffing up his hair. He good-naturedly swatted them away.

"Bunch of sexist wackos," said someone behind her.

Valena turned to see who had spoken. It was Cupcake. "Oh, hi," said Valena. "Guess they found the missing man."

"*We* found the missing man," said Cupcake. "I was with him in the Challenger. Yeah, he spotted him first, but only because I was scanning the *other* hundred-eighty degrees of the landscape."

"Sorry to hear," said Valena. "I mean, I don't like discrimination wherever you find it."

Cupcake took a long, candid look at Valena's face. "I'll bet you don't," she said. "Just what are you, anyway? Quarter black, quarter Asian, quarter Cherokee, and quarter WASP?"

Valena's head jerked at the epithet that finished the list. "I haven't heard that term in a while."

"And never attached to you, I'll bet," said Cupcake.

"Excuse me," said Valena. "Like I said, I despise discrimination." She set her tray down and left the galley through the door she had entered.

It took half an hour lying on her back on her bunk staring at the ceiling for Valena to pull herself together enough to return to the galley. She was extremely hungry, having eaten nothing that day but instant oatmeal, a chocolate bar, cocoa, and half of a stale sandwich, washed down with a six-ounce box of juice that she'd had to whack against her palm to break the frozen parts up into slush so she could suck it through the tiny straw that came with it. After twenty-four hours of exposure to cold at Happy Camp and the hike up Ob Hill, her body screamed for calories, and she reckoned that she was dehydrated.

Stuffing her feelings behind her best attempt at a game face, she hopped down off her bunk, ran her fingers through her hair, and headed back out to the galley. Once there, she picked up another tray and loaded it with broiled fish and a medley of vegetables that had obviously spent a lot of time in a very large can. She ladled a large wad of mashed potatoes on top of them, doused the whole mess with gravy, and headed for the drinks bar. There she mixed orange with cranberry juice, and in a separate glass, drew a volume of water. She guzzled the first glassful on the spot and then filled it again. Turning, she grabbed a fork, knife, and spoon out of the central island and then turned toward the dining hall.

The celebration involving the man named Dave had expanded, and now Cupcake was right in the middle of it. In fact, she had perched herself jauntily on the edge of the table and was giving one of the men a Dutch rub. People were offering her high fives, and one man came along and hoisted her right off the table to give her a squeeze.

Valena stared out across the room, trying to figure out which way to dodge the party. Suddenly, a man stood up from the first table to her right and waved to her.

"Hey, Valena!" he hollered. "Over here!"

It was the mustached guy from the Airlift Wing. He was sitting with the same sleepy-eyed woman firefighter. Valena lowered herself strategically into an open seat that allowed her to keep her back to the party. "I'm sorry," she said, "but I can't remember your names."

"You've probably met two hundred people in the few days you've been on the ice," he said. "I'm Hugh, and you've met Betty."

Betty said, "Here, have some wine. I'm celebrating not being out there searching for that man." She produced a bottle of New Zealand merlot and a glass and poured three fingers for Valena.

"Thanks." Valena settled in and ate several forkfuls of fish and potatoes before risking a sip of the wine. Even under the best of circumstances she was a cheap drunk, and going at it on an empty stomach while dehydrated seemed a bad bet, especially considering her mood. "So he's going to be okay?"

Betty said, "He's out cold, and I do mean cold. The docs have decided to warm him up a bit before they have the marvelous Major Hugh here medevac him to Cheech."

Hugh said, "I don't know what their problem is. I told them we could carry him up on the flight deck to make certain he stays warm, but they got all wiggy about how drafty our dear Hercs are."

"Why's he unconscious?" Valena asked. Each bite of food was having an almost magical effect on her. Her mood was lifting rapidly.

Hugh looked at her a moment with an expression that said, *You're smart*, before answering, "Wouldn't we all like to know that. Hypothermia alone doesn't put a man into a coma except on the way to the great beyond. If he went out from the cold alone, he'd probably be awake by now, or he'd be just plain dead." He shrugged his shoulders. "What do you think, Betty? You've got all that fancy medic training."

The firefighter mirrored his shrug, her face impassive. "Ask those Cat skinners over there. They found him."

Valena risked a glance over her shoulder at Cupcake. Feeling Valena's eyes on her, the heavy equipment operator extricated herself from an arm-wrestling match and sauntered over to their table with her hands in her jeans pockets. She bumped a hip against Valena's arm. "See you found yourself some vino. Mind if I have some? I'm dry."

Betty pushed the bottle toward Cupcake. "I hear you're the woman of the hour. So what's the story?"

Cupcake picked up the bottle and drank out of the neck. Smacking her lips, she said, "Looked like he'd been hit."

Betty's laconic eyebrows rose a millimeter.

Hugh said, "You mean like a bruise?"

"Hard to say," said Cupcake. "Rumor has it ol' Steve had a glass jaw."

"The McMurdo rumor mill," said Betty. "The source of all wisdom."

Cupcake said, "Could have taken a fall climbing off his Challenger, hit his chin, gotten stupid. Or at least, that's the official story. Well, thanks for the vino. Gotta get back to whooping it up." She wandered off, hoisting the bottle for another good toot.

Valena noticed that Hugh's eyes had narrowed ever so slightly, like he was concentrating hard on what had been said. She said, "Funny how people are getting hurt around here."

Hugh's eyes shot her way, the very quickest of glances, then he looked away again, staring into space. Finally, putting his party-boy smile on, he said, "Well, we can't solve that mystery just now, so let's make plans instead. Valena, you're still on for Tractor Club tonight, right?"

"Sure," she said. "I wouldn't miss it."

"Good. It's at the Coffee House."

"Coffee House?"

"It's a wine bar," said Betty.

Hugh grinned. "They got three bars here in greater metropolitan Mac Town: the Coffee House, Gallagher's, and Southern Exposure. The Coffee House is that Quonset out there by Derelict Junction," he said, pointing with his thumb over his shoulder. "They show movies sometimes, and you can do keen things like play Candy Land or Scrabble. A regular playground for intellectuals. Gallagher's is mixed drinks, hamburgers, and pool, more the singles scene, but if you hit the schedule just right and you can stand it, they have line dancing. Southern Exposure serves a rather different clientele."

Betty said, "You want to learn some new words for 'hey, baby'?"

Hugh pursed his lips. "Betty, my love, so scathing thou art. I've learned some of my best jokes from the boys who frequent that dive." To Valena, he added, "But I'll warn you, you even walk past the exhaust fan on that joint and you're up ten thousand feet in density altitude."

Betty said, "That's flyboy-ese for 'They smoke like chimneys.' As a firefighter, I am trained to consider rapid oxidation of flammable materials a negative thing, even if they're sold twenty to a pack."

Hugh said, "Drinking and smoking are only two of the addictions common to McMurdo Station. Consider our own dear Frosty Boy," he said, pointing at the soft-serve ice cream vending machine. "You'll notice the sign on it that informs the ice-cream-craving populace that the Boy is out of juice until tomorrow. That's because more than a few McMurdans are known to have a Frosty habit. If they were to keep that machine loaded up all the time, it would probably blow the food budget, so they stoke the Boy only once each week, and that's all she wrote. The DA who loads it cusses a blue streak. Evidently the Boy takes his toll on even those who do not partake."

"And those who do?" Valena inquired.

"Oooh, on that magical day they load the Boy, the patrons fall on it like it's nectar. But the funny thing is, they don't eat it plain. They apply it to most anything else they are eating. They apply it with gusto. They apply it with vigor. They apply it with passion, verve, and originality. They apply it indiscriminately."

"Frosty Boy in the morning coffee. Frosty Boy on your breakfast cereal," Betty drawled.

"Frosty Boy on sandwiches has been tried," said Hugh, "but it's the suppertime dessert crowd who really have it down."

"Frosty Boy on brownies with some of that cherry sauce and some of those chocolate ants on top," said Valena, spying tubs of other accoutrements arrayed around the machine.

"She's quick!" said Hugh, rolling his eyes toward Betty. "Gotta keep an eye on our Valena! Ah yes, how many ways people use that soft-serve Frosty Boy goodness on the lovely desserts this galley puts out for the faithful!" His smile was aglow.

"They can't stop themselves," said Betty laconically. "They are enthralled. Like vermin to the bait,"

Valena could feel something coming. "And so . . . ?"

The brilliance of Hugh's grin rose to twenty thousand candlepower. "So we have to trap the vermin!"

"Trap?" asked Valena. "You mean, like a mousetrap?"

On cue, Hugh whipped mouse trap out of his pocket and handed it to

Valena. "It comes with a trapping license. All very ecology-conscious. Thus we observe both the spirit and the letter of the environmental protocols of the Antarctic Treaty."

Valena turned the trap over and saw the card that was glued to its back. "Antarctic Trapping License," she read. "Bearer is authorized to trap fur-bearing mammals on the continent of Antarctica in accordance with 'the Treaty.'" She looked up at Hugh. "And you put this by the Frosty Boy machine. How's hunting?"

Hugh almost burst his face smiling. "Not *by* the machine, right there on the floor below it! Catch the little critters on the approach! We even sprinkle some of those chocolate ants on the floor all around it."

Trying to keep up with the twists and turns in this conversation, Valena said, "I didn't know there were mice in Antarctica."

"Not a one," said Betty. "The largest land animal that spends its entire life on this continent is a half-inch-long wingless midge. All those birds and seals only come to land to breed and pup."

"There's the odd skua," said Hugh. "A penguin or two."

Betty said, "Or twelve hundred, if you go up to Cape Royds."

"They've got twelve hundred penguins on Cape Royds?" Hugh asked.

Betty said, "Twelve hundred *pairs*."

Valena said, "They do? Right now?"

"Ask the penguin guy. He's sitting right over there." Betty gestured toward a very fit, middle-aged beaker who sat at a nearby table, munching a brownie while he read one of the summaries of world news from the *New York Times* that could be found lying about on some of the tables.

Valena sighed. "Penguins. But no vermin."

"I didn't say that," said Hugh, his smile vanishing. "Just no mice or other rodents. But we do have the sort of vermin that run around on two legs." He gave her a very penetrating look, his smile gone. With that, he stood up from the table, grabbed his tray, and left.

Valena waited, watching Betty to see if she was going to drop another conversational bombshell, but the firefighter only yawned, stretched, said, "See you later," and got up and left the dining room.

Valena's eyes shifted immediately to the penguin scientist who was reading the paper. He was halfway through his brownie, chewing slowly. He turned the page on his *New York Times* summary. He began reading the last page.

Springing into action, she hurried with her tray into the scraping room and dumped things into the appropriate recycling bins—food scraps here, burnables such as paper napkins there—and stacked her plates and glasses where the dishwashers could reach them, dropping her tray onto a third stack and her silverware into a bin filled with antibacterial solution. Rock music pounded from the far reaches of the adjoining dishwashing room, where two men in rubber gloves and aprons stood aiming a big spray nozzle at the encrusted plates.

She hurried back to the food lines, poured herself a fresh glass of milk, and grabbed a brownie, one of the butterscotch kind with chocolate chips. Then she drew a bead on the penguin guy and headed to where he was sitting. "Um, hi, can I join you?" she inquired.

He said, "Please do."

She lowered herself into a seat across from him. "The firefighter lady says you work with penguins," she said.

He nodded. "Betty."

"Can I ask you some questions about them?"

"Sure." He laid down his news summary and laced his fingers together on the tabletop. "They've just finished mating. The males are on the nests. The females have taken off to feed. They'll be back in a couple of weeks."

"So they're not emperors? Because they walk around with the eggs on their feet, right?" She was digging into her paltry storehouse of penguin facts, trying to sound knowledgeable.

"They're Adélies."

"Littler."

"Yes. All other species of penguins are smaller than the emperors." He waited, watching her politely.

"Can I . . . is there any way I could see them?"

The penguin guy nodded. "I'll be going out there again tomorrow. Perhaps you'd like to come then."

"That would be wonderful! But um, how do I get there?"

"I'm flying. Helicopter."

"Is there a spare seat?"

He shrugged his shoulders. "Most likely. The only problem would be getting back."

"Can't I ride back in the helicopter?"

"No. They'll drop me and take off to the next location. They usually head off to Marble Point next, on their way to the Dry Valleys. They have a very full schedule."

The Dry Valleys, she thought, *I could go for that!* But she said, "Is there another way to get back? How far is it?"

"Oh, about twenty miles. You could come up around the edge of the island on the sea ice on a snow machine, or check out a Pisten Bully or a Haaglund, if you've got one in your event budget. And you'd have to find someone to ride with you."

"I know. You can't go anywhere alone around here."

He nodded. "It would be better if you waited until you can put together a plan, then come out with someone else. Tomorrow isn't such a good day for me anyway."

Valena closed her eyes. Penguins. Real, live penguins living where penguins really lived, doing what penguins really did. But tomorrow was her last day. "I'll stay in touch," she whispered.

15

WHEN CUPCAKE TIRED OF THE VICTORY CELEBRATION IN THE GALLEY, she doused her dishes at the dishwashing window, grabbed her parka, and headed over to the hospital to see how Steve was doing. No one was seated at the desk near the entrance door to tell her to go away, so she walked through the catacombs of rooms until she found the action. The sight of Steve all trussed up to keep his neck from moving, oxygen mask covering half his face, and IV drips going in and out of him made her suck in her breath.

A short, round nurse turned around and saw her. "Hey, Cakes," she said. "Who let you in here?"

"I did. How is he?"

"Still out," said another nurse. "You shouldn't be in here."

"Let her stay," said the doctor. "I've got some questions for her."

Cupcake asked, "Is he sleeping?"

"You wish. This is a level 3 trauma with subdural hematoma. So tell me, do you believe this crap about he slipped on a step?"

"Not for a minute."

"Then what happened out there?"

"Wouldn't I like to know."

"Hazard a guess."

"Someone hit him with a board."

"Are there boards out there?"

"No. Shovels, maybe. Is there an edge to that bruise? I never got a good look since you got him cleaned up."

"Here, put on a mask first. He's had fluid leaking out of his ear, which means the lining around his brain's ruptured. It happens a lot in closed head injuries. They can get septic really easily, and then you've got a head injury and encephalitis."

Cupcake put on the mask the nurse offered and bent over her fallen comrade, examining as much of his face as she could see. "Aw, shit," she said. "If he'd slipped on the tractor, he couldn't have done that."

"Because . . . ?"

"Is his skull fractured?"

"Yes." The nurse pointed at the X-rays.

"To do all that on the bottom step of a Challenger, his legs would have had to fly out sideways, like someone grabbed them and yanked them out from under him bringing him down like a hammer. And I don't see any tread marks from the step or anything." She shook her head. "But even that isn't what tells me it wasn't any falling off any steps. Tell you the truth, I suspected as much before I came in here."

"Give," said the doctor.

Cupcake pointed. "Whatever hit him, or whatever he was hit *with*, made him bleed. There was coagulated blood all down the side of his head when we found him."

"And?"

"He never wore a hat. And his hood was pulled up onto his head."

"Which means?"

Cupcake walked over to where Steve's ECWs were laid out on another bed. She turned the hood inside out. "There's no blood on it, see? That means that when the injury occurred, and the blood dried, his hood was down. How long does it take for blood to clot, even in the cold? Several minutes, I'd bet. So it was down. In that blizzard would *you* take your hood off, even for a minute? No, you wouldn't, which means that he wasn't outside when it happened, or he'd just stepped out and hadn't pulled it up yet."

"Point well taken."

"Right, and even if any of that made sense, I can't buy the idea that he hit his head and walked off into the storm. Someone would have seen him, and when you're that screwed up, you don't get into your Cat, drive it a ways, then get out and take a stroll."

"Right."

Cupcake shook her head. "You know what I think? I think some son of a bitch sapped him and dumped him out on the ice, thinking that we'd never find him in time."

The doctor looked at her watch. "I agree. His blood pressure is dropping, and vital signs are unstable. If we can't get them under control soon, we're going to have to take the risk of flying him to the ER in Cheech, or that son of a bitch will have succeeded anyway."

16

VALENA SETTLED IN WITH A CUP OF TEA AND WAITED FOR MANUEL Roig to come into the galley. The minutes ticked past, and she got herself a second dessert, and then a third. As the hour for the food lines to close neared, the dining assistants came out of the kitchen and began to remove the steel serving tanks from the steam tables, and she began to wonder if she had missed him, but at last she spotted him through the windows, coming out of the hospital. He crossed to Building 155 and a few moments later arrived in the serving area. There he crossed to the wall adjacent to the kitchen doorway and opened a cupboard door, revealing a warming locker. Waiting there for him was a plate loaded with food.

Valena made one more pass back through the food lines, nailed some fine-looking devil's food cake and a cup of decaf coffee, then headed back toward the corner of the room where she'd seen him sit down. He had his head bowed over his plate as if he was either at prayer or nearly asleep. He didn't look up when she approached his table, even though there were very few people left in the galley.

For a moment, Valena felt sorry to disturb him, but urgency won out over manners. "Manny?"

He looked up as if suddenly wakened. "Oh! Uh . . . Valena, right?"

"You're good."

"I'm tired. Excuse me, please, it's been a long day."

"May I sit down?"

"Of course. I don't mean to be rude." He made a tired gesture toward the chair across from him and returned his concentration to his dinner.

"You were out on the search for the man who got lost. I hear he's in the hospital, beginning his recovery."

"Yes, we were lucky, *gracias a dios*."

"How did he get to where they found him?" she inquired, immediately sorry that she had applied the wrong pronoun. Manuel had said "we" and she had demoted that to "they."

"Walked, I suppose."

"How far was it?"

Manuel made a gesture with his fork and looked glassily through the walls of the building and the rocks and ice beyond. "Five, six miles."

"How far from his tractor?"

"Call it four, four and a half."

Valena nodded slowly, thinking. "So, how fast do you think a man can walk in a whiteout? Maybe two miles per hour, tops? And how likely do you think it would be that he'd be able to do that in a straight line?"

Manny raised his gaze from his dinner to look at her inquiringly. "Depends on whether he was following the flags. They found him not far from the route. And conditions might have been less severe where he was walking. It cleared to the west before here in McMurdo. We won't know until he wakes up."

"So three hours he was walking, minimum. Was he not a very hardy man?"

Manuel's eyes drew into a squint. "*Why* are you asking?"

"Because I think it odd that he would succumb to exposure that quickly. It's cold here, sure, but I noticed that when the storm came in last night it actually got a little warmer overall. Even with the windchill factor. So a grown man properly dressed for the conditions walks for three hours and suddenly keels over in a coma?"

"He seems to have fallen off the bottom step of the Challenger and hit his head. Got a concussion. It can really screw up your judgment. In fact he hit it hard enough that he started to bleed inside."

"Is that the theory?"

"Theory? What are you—oh, I get it, you're a scientist. Always a theory. So, multiple working hypotheses, you've got to have at least one more. What's the null hypothesis? He didn't have an accident? Someone hit him? Dragged his body five miles and dumped it on the ice. Nice way of thinking."

Valena stared at her hands.

Manuel said, "Perhaps there was something else wrong with him. He had a small stroke or something, enough to make him stupid enough to get out of his vehicle during a whiteout. Why? What's this to you? Listen, I don't like to be unfriendly, but like I say, it's been a long—"

"Valena interrupted. I'm supposed to be heading out to the field with Emmett Vanderzee," she said.

Manuel put down his fork and closed his eyes. Cleared his throat. "Oh. Well, I suppose then there's a connection, in your mind at least. Forgive me, Valena, but I just can't tell you how tired I am. Today was in fact the worst day in my life since I left Emmett's camp."

"Why?"

He opened his eyes and glared at her. "I do not wish to lose another man to the ice."

"Look, I'm being pushy, I know. But I was hoping you could tell me what happened last year at Emmett's camp."

Manuel bowed his head again. "I'd rather not. Oh please, I'd rather not."

"You're teaching Happy Camp, babysitting fingies instead of going up into the mountains with field parties. Why? Was it that bad?"

For several moments, Manuel said nothing. Then, in a harsh whisper, "You simply cannot imagine just how bad it was, Valena. It was my job to keep that man alive, but instead I watched him die. I heard him take his last breath." He picked up his fork and stabbed at his meat. His hand was shaking. He tried to lift it to his lips. He set it down and left it there.

"So you stayed in the tent with him while Emmett looked for the chute with the Gamow unit?"

Manuel clenched his teeth. "You think you saw a whiteout this morning? That day was infinitely worse."

"Then how did you look for the Gamow bag? Did you tie up together with ropes?"

"No. Yes! Toward the end we did. As mountaineer, I was in charge, so yes, I had everyone rope up because we were working close to a crevasse field. In places, the surface was sheer ice, and our crampons were of little comfort. If anyone lost their footing and landed on their belly, they'd slide for thousands of feet, accelerating before they hit something. So yes, we were tied in. But that was after the storm had begun to abate. You must understand that no one could do anything while it was blowing. We heard the Herc fly over, we heard the pilot call us over the radio to say he'd made the drop, that it should be right on top of us, but we could not find it."

"Major Bentley," she guessed. "He was the pilot in the Herc."

"And he was the pilot with the crew that came and took us out."

"How big an object was this they dropped?"

Manuel shook his head in frustration. "You ask this. Everybody has asked this. 'A four-foot cube of wood and iron with a big, orange parachute on it and you can't find the thing,' they say. And what do I have to tell them in reply? Nothing. We could not find it, I tell them. It was nowhere."

"Four feet on a side?"

"That's what the loadmaster told me later. He packed the thing on a four-by-four wooden pallet. It was too light, he said, so he put a fifty-five-gallon barrel of fuel on it, to give it weight. And I tell you, it was nowhere to be found. It was almost like they hadn't dropped it at all." He made a slashing motion with his hand. He was getting angry.

Valena decided that it was politic to change the subject slightly. "Who was there? Were you all in the same tent?"

Manuel stared at the tabletop. "Why are you asking all these questions?"

"Because I'm supposed to be on a flight out of here Thursday morning. I've got less than thirty-six hours to clear Emmett or I go home. I'm supposed to do something called bag drag tomorrow evening. My little clock is ticking down."

"I don't know what I can do to change that."

"I'm trying to help my professor, Manny! And yes, I'm trying to help myself. If he returns, I stay. So tell me, please. Who was there? Who was in which tent?"

Manny looked up again. "So many questions! Okay. Okay, I've told this a thousand times to the FBI, but I'll tell you, too. There were eight in camp. Emmett, me, the . . . dead man . . . the cook, the two grad students, Emmett's assistant, the blaster's assistant, and the other guy, the gopher. That was it."

"The cook, is she here this year?"

"She's out at Black Island."

"Lindemann's out in the Dry Valleys."

"Yes," he said, trying to sound patient. "He's up on a glacier in the

Olympus Range. I heard he got on with that crew from the University of Maine."

"Why didn't he stick with Emmett?"

"How should I know? Your academic politics. I stay out of that."

"The blaster's assistant? What was his name, David?"

"I don't know. Maybe he's around. There are probably a dozen Davids on the roster this year."

"That last one. William somebody."

"William was a punk kid. I doubt they hired him back."

"A punk. What, as in homicidal?"

Manuel threw up his hands. "As in not very competent. Had to have everything explained to him. What he was doing in Antarctica, I'll never know."

"So, were you all in the same tent while you waited for the drop?"

"No. We had four Scotts and a cook tent. Most people hung out in the cook tent, because it was warmed by the stove, and it's the largest—eight feet across and sixteen long. Scotts are tall, but not very big across, as you'll remember from your training today. You can sleep three people in them, but two is better. I was in the cook tent with Sheila, helping her with the sick man. I think Bob and Dan were in their Scott tent most of the time."

"Bob and Dan."

"Schwartz and Lindemann. They have first names. Dave was with us most of the time in the cook tent. So was William, eating cookies. They shared a tent with Ted, but Ted had left. Cal Hart—that's Emmett's friend—he was in the tent he shared with Emmett, reading Nietzsche. I had a dome tent right next to Sheila's Scott, but we were both in the cook tent that day. Emmett went from tent to tent, making sure everyone was okay."

"How did Emmett get from one tent to the next?"

"They were close together. It was no more than a hundred feet from one end of the camp to the other. And we'd seen the storm coming, so I had strung ropes so we could find our ways from one tent to the next and to the latrine."

"And Emmett went out in the storm looking for the chute?"

"As soon as he could see his hand in front of his face, yes. He took Cal with him. Safety in numbers. He wanted that man to live! I kept telling the

FBI men that, but they believed what they wanted to believe. The chute was gone, I tell you! It probably blew into a crevasse and was immediately covered with blowing snow. I went out and helped as soon as it was safe. We all did. Then it began to blow again. We just weren't lucky. End of story."

More gently, Valena said, "I'm still trying to understand what it was like there, Manny. Since coming here, I've learned one thing, and that is that this place is like no other place on earth. Half the time, I feel like I've left the planet. I'm on Mars, or the moon. What was the camp like? How high were you? How steep was the terrain? That sort of thing."

Manny leaned onto his elbows and ran his hands through his hair. "We were at 10,500 feet. Add to that the effects of the cold and of being five degrees further south than McMurdo. The higher latitude increases the apparent elevation. Call it 12,000 feet. And the ground is rough. It's not so much how steep the terrain is, it's the ice. Crevasses. You just don't screw around up there. And then here's the reporter, straight up from sea level. He looked okay for a day, almost two, then down he went."

"And everybody's certain it was altitude sickness."

"What else would it be?"

"Something else, if federal agents are hauling scientists off the ice a year later."

Manny shook his head. "The doctors here at the hospital looked at him, and you bet there was an autopsy. His lungs were full of fluid. No big bacterial or viral growths, so it wasn't an infection. And there were no toxins in his tissues, so you can't pin it on anything he ate. No punctures, no nothing."

"They checked for punctures?"

"*I* checked for punctures. We had a medical kit there. All the field crews carry one, very extensive, with some pretty heavy drugs in them, including for pneumonia—and yes, we were administering that drug—and we had it because you never know when somebody's going to get sick when you can't get them back out to McMurdo. So yes, I checked him over."

"Why?"

Manny leaned back in his seat and bared his teeth in frustration. "Because there'd been such a commotion."

"Tell me."

"It's no secret that the man fought . . . *argued* with Emmett. Nothing physical."

"Argued about the science?"

"About everything. About Emmett's techniques. About what was for dinner. The man had a real burr up his butt. He chewed at Emmett and a couple of the others, harassed them like there was no tomorrow."

Valena sighed. "Apparently there was no tomorrow for him."

Manuel squeezed his eyes shut.

Valena said, "I'm sorry, but I have just a few more questions. The feds: they came down this year and started asking questions. Why? Could you tell anything from what they asked?"

Manuel shook his head. "Talk to the fellows in the Airlift Wing. The feds arrived on one of their LC-130s. They asked a lot of questions. Then Emmett took them out to the field camp. They were gone six or seven hours, long enough to fly out there, stay a few hours, and come back." He stared into space past Valena's shoulder, as if watching the scene unfolding. "And when they came back, that was it. They had Emmett by the sleeve. I watched them come in off the ice. They marched him off to Hut 10. I hear they interrogated him all night and into the next morning. Nobody could believe it was happening. I went to the door of Hut 10 and was told to leave. Early afternoon the next day, they packed him into a Herc again, and were gone." He swung his gaze to Valena, focused his eyes on hers. "That was Saturday."

Valena thought a moment, then asked, "I'm sure there's something else I should ask you, but I don't know what it is. I know so little about this place."

Manuel looked at her a long time, then said, "Ask yourself why he didn't have a Gamow bag in camp. Why he had to send for one."

"Who, Emmett?"

"Yes. It's standard procedure to have one along." Having said this, Manuel appeared to deflate, as if something that had been stiffening him had finally escaped. Then he said, "You want to know anything else, you'll have to ask the Airlift Wing personnel who went into the field with them."

Personnel. Plural. Of course, thought Valena. *There's more than just a pilot on those planes, there's a whole crew!* "Who else went out there with Emmett and the investigators?" she asked.

"I don't know. There'd be a crew of at least five. Pilot, copilot, flight engineer, navigator, loadmaster. More, maybe. I don't know that much about the military here. They stay kind of separate."

You just have to go talk to them, she thought, but then she recalled the undecipherable look in Hugh's eyes. Had he actually been giving her information, or had he just been toying with her?

She looked at the tired mountaineer. "Thank you, Manny. I'll leave you in peace now." As she rose from the table, she thought about all the questions she would ask this man and all the other citizens of McMurdo if she was not afraid of being downright rude. *People here ask where you're from and what you're doing here, but what I'm beginning to wonder is, why are you here and what are you hiding from?*

17

THE COFFEE HOUSE WAS MADE FROM TWO SMALL QUONSET HUTS CON-
NECTED at right angles. Half buried under a sad-looking bank of dirty,
thrice-frozen snow that had been thrown up by the plows, the little water-
ing hole seemed to be holding onto the past as much as to the ground. The
corrugated iron arches were old, battered, and painted an unappealing
shade of brown. At the point where they joined, a small plywood airlock
had been constructed, so long ago that it now sorely needed paint. Valena
pushed open the outer door of the airlock and passed within.

Inside, the atmosphere was comfortingly dim. The structure had no
windows, creating the illusion that the sun had actually set, returning her
world to low-latitude normalcy. She passed down a short hallway that
housed coat hooks and a bulletin board displaying photographs of a number of local women dressed in ball gowns as they carried out their daily
routines on the ice; driving Cats, riding snowmobiles, cooking chow for a
thousand people or so. The shorter Quonset opened off to her left. It was
filled with derelict couches that faced a large-screen TV. Nothing was on,
but one couple sat familiarly close on an eight-foot-long divan that featured fuzzy, grass-green upholstery. They had their arms around each
other, and if their wineglasses had been any closer together, they could
have dispensed with one and simply shared the other.

Valena turned right into the other Quonset. The inside of its low barrel
arch had been paneled with knotty pine, yielding an arched rendition of a
hunting cabin, though without the crackling fire, stuffed heads, and frosty
windows looking out over pine-dappled landscapes. Into this space had

been stuffed a bar, behind which stood a bartender, and a great many small, square tables surrounded by miscellaneous hard-backed and over-stuffed chairs, another McMurdan monument to scavenging. Various pairs and groups of people sat around talking, swigging vino, and playing cards or board games. A huge man in canvas overalls played darts with a woman who couldn't have weighed over ninety pounds.

Valena looked right and left, searching the room for Major Muller. He wasn't there. She finally spotted Betty the firefighter sitting with a group of people at a table toward one end of the room.

Betty raised her sleepy eyes as Valena approached. "Hey, glad you could make it," she said. She gestured to her left, toward a man in military fatigues. "May I introduce Tractor Larry, who is standing in as protocol officer for Tractor Waylon. That guy with the turquoise eyes next to him is Tractor Matt. Next to him we have . . ."

The names began to blur in Valena's mind. She had met entirely too many people in the past few days. Appellations seemed to descend into a netherworld even as they emerged from Betty's lips, almost as if she were on television and the sound had been turned off. Even the faces were beginning to merge into one big composite southlander, a hardy soul of intermediate gender who eschewed fashion for warmth, easy care, and fitness. In fact—she realized, now that she thought of it—Antarcticans, while attractive people on the whole, wore no fussy shoes or constraining clothing and almost no jewelry, and she saw not a lick of makeup on any of the women present. She smiled. In a very true sense, she was home. She took a seat next to Tractor Matt, a burly man she had last seen whooping it up in the galley with the man who, with Cupcake, had found the missing Cat driver.

"May I serve you some wine?" asked the flyboy to her left.

"Ah, sure. What are we having?"

"Red, I think." The man pulled one of three bottles out of the center of the table and poured. As Valena took a sip, another flyboy said, "Got any Georges to send north?"

"Georges?"

"One-dollar bills. We're bringing Susan B. Anthony, Sacagawea, and Jefferson south and sending George home." He produced some two-dollar bills and one-dollar coins from his pocket. "Even exchange."

Valena pulled her wallet out of her back jeans pocket and emptied out most of her folding money, holding back her New Zealand currency and the two US twenties that lurked behind them. "Here's a five to contribute to the wine money," she said. "And here are all the ones I have."

"Good woman." The man pounced on the money, swapping her two-dollar bills and dollar coins for the singles. The five he approached differently. Producing a stamp and green-inked stamp pad, he printed little green antique tractor symbols all over it. Then he hit all the singles as well, apparently for good measure. Then he ceremoniously slipped his tractor stamp into a special pouch. A block of wood lay next to his hand. It was about three by four inches, and adorned with large green letters that read MOATS.

"What does 'moats' mean?" asked Valena.

The man grinned. "It stands for 'Mother of All Tractor Stamps,' " he said. He turned it over, revealing a very large version of the antique tractor symbol on the other side. "Come to think of it, I'm behind on my job here," he added, charging the enormous stamp with ink. He examined each of the wine bottles in turn and rolled the tractor onto the labels of those he had not previously hit.

The man with the stamp raised his voice a bit and addressed the group again. "As president *pro tempore* in lieu of Tractor Hugh, who could not be with us this evening due to grave and unavoidable duties in the line of duty and so forth, I call everyone's attention to . . ."

Larry said, "Some more new business."

"Yeah. Tractor Larry, as the meeting of the Tractor Club is already in session, how do we proceed with the introduction of this new candidate?"

Larry rubbed his buzz cut as he mulled this question. "I believe that, in emergency situations such as these, we can use the abbreviated form. In any case, we must start with introductions."

Valena interrupted. "Is it okay if I do this even if I'm about to leave?"

"Leave?" said Matt.

"Uh, yeah. I just got here Saturday evening, but my—uh, Professor Vanderzee had to leave. So they've scheduled me to go out on the next flight north." She glanced at Larry, wondering if he'd be the pilot of the plane that took her away from the ice.

Matt said, "So they aren't even having you go ahead and do your scientific research?"

"Not unless I can get my professor back," said Valena. "Or find a job all of a sudden. Anyone have employment for a beaker who's mislaid her professor?"

"Aw hell," said Betty. "Most beakers don't even lay their professors, much less *mis*lay them."

The crowd broke into cheerful laughter, with hoots of, "Good one, Tractor Betty," and, "Oooo, it burns!"

The man with the stamp said, "Then we must proceed with speed on two accounts. Okay, let's go around the table and introduce ourselves to the candidate. Members please state your names to the candidate."

"Tractor Betty."

"Tractor Larry."

"Tractor Matt." Matt made eye contact more pointedly than most, then hopped up and wove his way between the tables toward the bar, where he leaned an elbow next to a man who was perched on a stool there working on a bottle of white and engaged him in earnest conversation.

Meanwhile, the introductions continued around the table. "Hi, I'm Valena," she said, when the process ended with her.

Betty said, "What now, Tractor Larry? Hell, I never knew it was so difficult to remember all this crap. Where's Tractor Hugh when we need him?"

"We ask the candidate the Questions," said Tractor Larry. "Valena, we must ask you two important questions, which you shall answer as honestly as you can. Are you ready?"

"Sure," said Valena.

The man with whom Matt was speaking at the bar had twisted around on his stool and was looking at her.

Larry said, "Okay, here's the first question. What is your name?"

"Valena."

All present nodded in approval.

"Okay, you are doing well," said Larry. "Now for the second and more crucial question: Valena, *do you like tractors?*"

Valena looked from face to face. All now gazed on her with feigned solemnity. Confused, she said, "Oh, sure. I love tractors."

A great cheer went up from the table, arms flying upward with delight, all faces beaming with happiness.

"Huzzah," said the protocol officer. "Tractor Betty, you may proceed with the investiture."

Betty turned her heavy-lidded eyes toward Valena. "Valena, I now pronounce you Tractor Valena. You are a duly invested member of the Tractor Club, and therefore endowed with the rights and privileges thereof, or something like that."

All raised their glasses, roared, "Tractor Valena," and took a drink.

Valena asked, "What exactly are my rights and privileges?"

"In unison, they announced Membership is lifelong, free, and irrevocable!"

"Well, how nice," said Valena. She felt unaccountably pleased.

Matt resumed his place at the table.

Larry said, "Now the best part. The story."

Betty said, "Oh, yeah. Okay now, Tractor Valena, we proceed to the best part, the solemn invocation, or some such. Tractor Valena, you may now tell us a story about tractors. What's the rule on that, Tractor Larry?"

"It can be the truth, a lie, or a story," said Larry.

"Yeah, that," said Betty.

"Me?" said Valena.

The assembled broke into cheers.

"Yeah, you," said Betty. "Give us a tractor story."

Valena's mind went blank. She stared from face to face, trying to think of what to say. Her gaze dropped to the Mother of All Tractor Stamps, and the jaunty green tractor reminded her of an ancient one that occupied a special corner in her grandfather's barn. "My grandfather has a 1929 Case L," she began.

An appreciative "Oooo" ran around the table. The men performed heavenward looks of spiritual transcendence. Larry held his hands to his heart.

Out of the corner of her eye, Valena could see the man at the bar rise and move toward their table. He was looking at her. To her audience at the table, she said, "Grandpa is proud of that tractor. Sentimental, even. He inherited it from *his* grandfather along with the farm. He keeps it oiled and fueled, and on very special occasions he drives it. Like in parades, that sort of thing. And sometimes around the near meadow." An image began to arise in her mind, of brilliant sunshine, the dogs running along behind, grasshoppers scattering . . .

"A fine man!" said Matt. He looked like a cat who had caught a canary.

"A fine tractor!" said Larry.

"Yes," said Valena. "He . . . once he let me drive it."

"Oooo . . ."

"Or rather, I sat on his lap, and he let me steer." The heady scent of the old man's sweat, the warmth of his skin and the hard and soft edges of his ancient bones and body felt through his cotton duck pants and plaid shirt came back to her as if it were still happening. How she had longed for that moment, the official "now I am eight years old" grandchild ride, with all the cousins watching. They were cheering, proud of her, for the moment not calling her those names . . .

And then Great Aunt Dilla had emerged from the kitchen door. She blew out onto the porch like a storm, roiling in her dark intensity, her head coming forward in a threat, and shrieked, "Get that child off that tractor!"

All the cousins turned. One laughed, a toxic little snicker.

She felt Grandpa's leg stiffen as he stamped on the clutch. The tractor rolled to a stop. Dilla was coming at them now, her stiff legs with their varicose veins moving like a man on stilts, her craggy hands whipping this way and that like vicious attachments on a machine of death. "I will not have it! I don't care what your wayward daughter brings home in her twisted notions of Christian charity, I will not have her drive that tractor!"

Grandpa had stood up for her, scolding his sister, saying, "God sees your lack of charity!" but the joy of the moment was ended. Gone forever. The cousins were smirking and sneaking looks at her. The tractor had stalled. A cloud had swept across Valena's heart and it was still there.

"What did it sound like?" asked Matt.

Valena's mind snapped back into the low, arching room in the Coffee House. The people seated at the table with her came back into focus. "Sound?" These people were smiling *with* her. Their merriment was shared, and at no one's expense.

The wraiths of remembered cousins slunk away like feral cats and curled up in the shadows at the far corners of the room, their dark eyes blinking at her from the gloom.

She heard a strong male voice behind her. "Are you Valena Walker?"

She turned to face the man who had approached from the bar. "Yes, that's me."

"I'm in charge of Fleet Ops. I hear you have some time free, and that you know how to drive a tractor."

Valena looked up at this man, at his kind, calm face, his aura of bemused command. "Yes, I do. I've driven all the tractors on my grandfather's farm in Idaho, and some of those up and down the way from his. I've helped with the harvest several times. It was fun."

"Ever driven a truck in soft dirt? Or snow?"

"Countless times." She smiled. "There's a matter of finesse."

"Then I'm wondering if you'd be available to assist one of my crews. I'm a man down, as you may have heard." Sadness rippled across his face. "Steve Myer. He had to be flown out to Christchurch this evening, and he was scheduled to go on the Black Island traverse tomorrow to resupply the telecommunications station there. This involves hauling water and other essentials over the ice shelf and fixing the flag route along the way. We have a good weather window and we need to take advantage of it, but we need a full crew, and like I say, I'm down one driver. Matt here said you might be available to assist us. Are you interested?"

Larry said, "I'd give my left nut for a trip like that."

Black Island, thought Valena. *That's where the cook from last year is stationed this year. And . . . and it's away from here! Out on the ice! An adventure!* "I'd love to!" she said excitedly. "But, ah . . . well, how long does it take?" *If we can get out there and back in one day, I can do this!*

"Oh, you'll be gone overnight," said the Boss. "It's sixty miles, and at least thirty of those need new flags set every two hundred feet, slow going. You'd be driving one of our Deltas, carrying the cargo, and maybe you'd like to take turns on the snow machines. And then of course we'll have one of the Challengers along to groom the trail ahead of the Delta. A Challenger 95. I'll bet that's a mite bigger than any you had on the farm."

"Oh, it is! But . . . I'm supposed to fly out on Thursday."

"I imagine I can get them to delay your flight a day or two."

"You *can*?"

"Try me."

"Then it's yes!"

Cheers broke out around the table. Someone started a chant of, " 'Lena, tractor, 'Lena, tractor!"

The Boss patted her on the shoulder. "Good. You be at Building 17 first thing tomorrow—that's seven in the a.m.—and have your ECWs with you. You got a sleeping bag?"

Matt said, "She can use mine."

"There's one in my office at Crary Lab," said Valena.

"Great. Matt, you help her get her gear up to 17?"

"Sure thing, Boss."

"Oh, I'm sure I can handle it," said Valena. "It's just a big duffel."

"Then it's settled. Make sure to get a good breakfast in you, and you'll probably want to take it easy on the joy juice this gang is pushing on you. You don't want to dehydrate out there."

Appreciative laughter broke out around the table. Matt gave her a wink.

"I'll be there," said Valena. "Straight up, sober, and ready to drive." She was grinning so hard that her face hurt. *This is a lot better than driving a 1929 Case,* she decided. *A whole continent's worth of better!*

VALENA FELT A psychological jolt when, five minutes later, she stepped out of the lock into the blinding light of Antarctica. It was almost ten in the evening, but the sun was still well above the mountains.

"Confusing, huh?" said Matt, who came out behind her. He smiled merrily at Valena. "Get some sleep. It's a long way to Black Island, even if it is only sixty miles."

"I'm on my way," she said, but she tarried awhile, taking in the odd sight of nighttime sunlight glinting off far glaciers. "Thanks again, Matt. I really appreciate your sprinkling pixie dust for me."

"Think nothing of it." He gave her a wave and headed toward his dorm.

The door opened again, and Larry came out. He marched toward her, saying, "So, Betty says you're an okay kid."

"Kid? Well, next to you, I guess."

"I'm forty. Not quite old enough to be your father, but I mean to make a point here. I have some serious business to discuss."

"What is serious business?"

"You've got to understand something, Valena. When we fly one of those planes somewhere, we're on mission. It's our job."

Valena nodded. "So you have something to tell me, and it does not go beyond me."

"Right. I'm part of the Wing, so pretty much what I understand is 'salute and execute.' We've got to have people who will take action without questioning things."

"I see," she said, not certain that she did.

Larry moved closer to her and snaked one hand around the small of her back. "We are taking precautions. Anybody sees us talking, they'll just think I'm hitting on you. Okay?"

Valena tried desperately to relax. "Okay, on my great-great-grandfather's 1929 Case, you have my word."

Larry nodded. "That will have to do. So what happens when something strange comes up? Like you're out there flying your mission and you see something that maybe you weren't supposed to see, or that you weren't required to see, maybe, but it's important."

"Like when you pick up a corpse that's supposed to have died of altitude sickness," said Valena.

"Or something else, like when you fly certain investigators out to the site where that someone died of altitude sickness, and they found something that suggested that maybe there was more to it than all that."

"Such as?"

Larry put his lips close to her ears. "You never heard this, and if someone puts the thumbscrews on you, you don't know where the notion came from, right?"

"Why, is this information dangerous?"

"Understand that we're here because you're here. The Airlift Wing flies in support of science in the polar regions. We think what you're doing is important. We're not doing this *just* because we love to fly our planes." He lifted his chin toward McMurdo. "This whole place is here to get you guys into the field and out again." He pulled her even closer, and began to whisper. "Last Friday, one of our crews flew certain people out to a certain site to make sure things were as certain people said they were."

"I see."

"Okay, so here it is: this crew flew the feds out there. Your professor was along to show them how the camp had been set up. Over the winter, the winds had swept the place clean. It was like nothing had ever been there, except for just a few things."

"What things? Come on, give," she said, leaning her body against his.

Larry gave her a smile that didn't match what he was saying, and ran a hand up one of her sleeves. "The wind blows hard up there," he whispered, breathing into her ear. "It blew like a banshee all winter, really smoothed the place out again, like no one had ever been there. Except that things were buried there."

"Buried?"

"Yeah. See, last year when your professor wanted in there, we made several flights. Precautionary. First, we had a mission make a reconnaissance flight, to overfly it to make sure we could land on it. The weather's hell out there, so it's seldom clear. Well, for a rekkie flight we need severe clear from ground up to mother sun, so we get the shadows we need. We fly it low and slow with a photographer going click-click-click taking pictures,"—he grabbed her tighter with each click—"and we're mapping out the snow cover to make sure it will hold our ship when we land. No crevasses. Hopefully no snow swamps."

"Snow swamps?"

"Really soft snow. Hasn't been packed hard yet."

Valena answered his squeezes with a coy pat on his chest.

He grinned. "Right. So we don't land unless we're sure we're not about to snag a ski in some mother-sucking crevasse or bury the whole bird in ten feet of vanilla fudge."

"Got you."

"But what ho, the powers that be also wanted to make a fuel depot out of the place. It is strategically located, it would seem, so they schedule not only our mission but also a mission to drop twenty barrels of fuel. That's AvGas for Twin Otters and MoGas for snowmobiles. Right, so we need severe clear for our rekkie mission, but the air drop can go off under cloud cover. So guess what? Our rekkie gets CANX-ed six days running, but the fuel drop goes off on schedule. So now what do we have?"

"Some kind of a delay?"

Larry put his other hand on her other sleeve and massaged her arms through all the layers of down and polypropylene. "Did I mention the storms up there? Wow. Blew like hell for three days after they dropped those barrels. Then finally we get out there for the rekkie and I can show you photographs of those barrels, or what little was still sticking up through the snow."

"They got buried?"

"Mother Mary and Jesus, they got buried! We could only see the edges of a few of them sticking out."

Valena said, "So you are in a zone of accumulation."

"Where the barrels landed, yes. Your professor was collecting ice about a quarter mile away, where the wind kept scouring the fresh snow away."

"Zone of ablation."

"What you said. Right, so when we took your man in last year, Raytheon sent extra personnel to dig up the barrels."

"Did they find them all?"

He slid one hand from her arm up to her cheek. "It's a lot of work to dig up a barrel that's been buried in that much hard-packed snow. You may have noticed that they need a snow saw to quarry blocks of it at Happy Camp."

Valena nodded.

"Now take it to high elevation."

"Even more work."

"Now add weather, repeatedly forcing you to retreat to your tent."

"Gotcha. So some barrels were left."

"Seven, to be exact. So this year we took special equipment in to find the rest. Ground-penetrating radar works like a charm in such conditions. Shows us where all the bodies are buried." He laughed mirthlessly at his own joke. "Right. We wanted to know where they are, so if we ever truly need them, we can retrieve them. So anyway, when we made the flight last week, we took along some special equipment."

"A crew with ground-penetrating radar?"

"Emmett Vanderzee. And the federal agents. And yes, we had radar."

"And you found something."

"Right. Let's call it an additional radar signature."

"You were missing seven barrels, but you found eight signatures?"

"Exactly. The eighth was not far from the others."

"And what was making the eighth signature?"

"Three guesses, and the first two don't count."

"You found the barrel that was with the Gamow unit. But what was it doing that far away? Surely your accuracy is better than a quarter mile."

"Our accuracy is within one hundred feet. The place where it was located was a quarter mile from the camp, about where the first barrel would have been dug up."

"I'm with you. But there was something about the condition of this air-dropped Gamow unit when it was found that got Emmett hauled off the ice."

Larry's expression darkened. "Yes, there was." He raised his other hand to her face and traced her cheekbones with his thumbs.

Valena murmured, "And this is where you are telling me something that I never heard."

He leaned so close that he was almost kissing her. "You never even heard that we found the unit."

"Never at all," she said, staring into his eyes. "But there was more." She waited.

Larry spoke very softly. "The chute was underneath the sled."

"You mean—"

Larry pressed his lips to her temple. "Precisely," he breathed. "Someone had purposely bunched up the chute and stuffed the whole works in one of the excavation holes left when they pulled out the first thirteen barrels. Someone had buried it so that it would not be found. And that, dear Valena, is why the reporter with the altitude sickness died in that camp."

18

THE EDGE OF ANTARCTICA DROPPED AWAY TO THE SOUTH AS MAJOR
Hugh Muller piloted the LC-130 out over the Southern Ocean, willing the
craft to move faster than it was built to fly. The man behind him was not
doing well.

He turned to look at the stretcher, which they had managed to lift up
onto the flight deck and mount on the bench at the back wall. The man's
hand protruded from under the fleece blankets they had wrapped around
him. It was gray.

Hugh returned his attention to his job, to the controls, to anything that
would occupy his mind and help him think positively.

The evening was clear and the air was still, and the miles of ocean slid
by, turning increasingly gray as the sun dipped toward the horizon. It
would be dark by the time they reached Christchurch. Too bad; he always
loved to watch the cloud-shrouded islands of New Zealand slide down
over the horizon. *Ao Tea Roa*, the Maoris called it: the Land of the Long
White Cloud.

As they crossed sixty degrees south latitude, Major Marilyn Wood's
voice reached his ears through his headphones. "Leaving grid navigation," she said, referring to Antarctica's system of grid lines laid parallel
and perpendicular to the Greenwich meridian. In the world north of the
Antarctic Circle, lines of longitude approached parallel, but over Antarctica, the lines of longitude converged until they were too close to be useful
for navigating, necessitating the grid system. And the magnetic south pole
was somewhere off the coast and in the ocean.

Hugh looked at the compass in front of him. From its grid course of

170, it spun 180 degrees, coming to rest pointing 350 in the standard system, his bearing for Christchurch.

The minutes rolled past, and a lengthening twilight covered the sea. His copilot yawned and stretched, then murmured that he was going to get a cup of coffee. He glanced at his wristwatch; it was 1100 Zulu. That made it 2200 McMurdo and New Zealand time. Back home in New York it would be 0600. His wife would be waking soon, putting on the coffee, putting the dog outside to do its business. In half an hour his younger daughter would awaken, then his son, and finally his older daughter. She was the night owl in the family, next to him. He loved Antarctica, but he loved his family much, much more.

A hand came to rest on his shoulder. He looked up to see the strained face of the doctor. Her lips moved, but he could not hear her words.

The strange tricks of wave skip over the curve of the earth brought radio calls from San Francisco Approach to his headphones. Home, half a world away, was calling to him. Suddenly, his need to hear his wife's voice weighed on his heart with a thousand atmospheres of pressure.

19

Valena headed for Crary Lab to retrieve the sleeping bag that Emmett Vanderzee had checked out for her and stored in his office. She marched down the path between the buildings, dodging around banks of filthy snow and ice, her mind spinning with the information she had just been given. Was Emmett Vanderzee a killer? Somebody had prevented aid from reaching that reporter, and if James Skehan was correct—that Sweeny had made Emmett's life a living hell, misstating his findings at a national level, keeping him busy defending his right to do science rather than doing the science itself—then, regardless of Skehan's assertion that scientists prefer a live adversary to a dead one, Emmett might have seen the chute, chased it, and buried it just to shut the man up.

Was he capable of such an act? She did not know.

She jogged up the wooden steps that bridged the gang of heating pipes that ran between buildings, grinding on these questions.

At the top of the stairs, she stopped, suddenly transfixed by an object mounted on the railing. It was a sundial. She had noticed it before, but it hadn't really sunk in that it read as a twenty-four-hour clock.

She realized that until this time she had hurried almost everywhere she went like an astronaut so busy doing her job that she forgot to look out the window of the spacecraft. Standing still for the first time, she noticed that a poem ran up the steps and down the other side, carved into the soft pine, an anonymous gift to all who passed this way. And there were unusual objects on the steps. A mobile made of shiny discs. Plastic toys nailed to the wood. And underneath the steps, a scrap metal sculpture of a troll swinging a sword or some kind of axe. The whimsy of Mcmurdo Station suddenly delighted her.

Putting herself back into gear, she crossed the ground between the steps and Crary Lab. With a smile, she noted that it was beginning to seem usual to get into her office by pulling open a heavy steel door that looked like the entrance to a walk-in freezer. Though it was the reverse walk-into-the-warm-place door.

Inside, she ran down the ramp that led to phase 2, hung a right, and hurried to the door of her office, pulling her key out as she went. As she closed the last few yards of distance, her brain registered a change in the way things looked: the door stood open, and there was nothing whatsoever inside the room except her computer and the furniture that was attached to the wall.

She came to a stop with the key at the ready position, four feet from the yawning doorway. This did not compute. Did she have the wrong phase of the building? No, Vanderzee's name was still on the plate in the bracket beside the door. She stepped forward and looked inside. Everything, down to the last pen and pencil, was gone. Why?

A man cleared his throat behind her.

She turned. It was Michael, the electrical technician. What was he doing there at ten at night?

"They told the head office to pack up his equipment and ship it to Hawaii," he said.

"Who told the head office to do that?"

"The feds, I guess. The people from Berg Field Center picked up the field equipment."

"But I need—"

"Wow, was any of that equipment yours? I got them to leave your computer."

"No . . . I . . ." Yes, that was her laptop and she had taken Emmett's. Did that make her an accessory after the fact?

"Anything I can help you with?"

Her heart pounded. Somebody had killed that man, just as surely as if they had run a knife through his heart, and now more than ever she wanted to know who had done it. The Black Island traverse was the next task and she needed a sleeping bag in order to join it. She needed to be at Building 17 with that sleeping bag at 7:00 a.m. "When does Berg open?"

"I don't know. Seven-thirty? Eight?"

Valena began to tremble. Just when things were looking up, they came crashing down.

"Hey," said Michael. "You look like your puppy died."

The trembling was getting worse. She could feel her lips begin to go. "I n-need a sleeping bag," she said.

Michael stepped toward her and put his arms around her, scooping her up into a great, warm hug. "There," he said. "There."

The tenderness of that hug unhinged her and she leaned against him, fighting tears. "I'm just so—I don't know what to do!"

Michael ran his hands down her back, stroking her like a kitten. He said, "Surely there's another sleeping bag to be had in this great expanse of ice. When do you need it?"

"Seven tomorrow morning. I—I'm supposed to help drive some equipment up to Black Island." With that, she remembered that there was another person whom she could call on for help. Matt. *Tractor Matt. Because membership is free, life-long, and irrevocable . . .* Her tears immediately began to subside. She straightened up, wiped her cheeks with her sleeve, and said, "How can I get in touch with Matt?"

"I don't know. Matt who?"

"I don't know his last name."

Michael let his hands drop from her shoulders. "Come with me."

Valena followed him up to the library at the top of the lab and watched as he sat down at one of the computers there. He woke up the screen and clicked quickly through a menu that brought him around to what looked like a phone list. "Matt with two *t*'s, right?"

"I have no idea."

"Well, that's the standard spelling." He typed the name and clicked the mouse. "Okay, we have three Matts in McMurdo just now. Not bad, out of twelve hundred people, a third of which are women. One's a cook. Looks like the second is in the carpenter's shop. And number three is Fleet Ops. What's your guess?"

"He had a khaki parka."

"That rules out the kitchen. You've described a tradesman, so he's either a carpenter or a heavy equipment operator. What else do you know about him? Who introduced him to you?"

"He—" The wheels inside Valena's mind were finally turning again. "Wait, he knew the Boss, who's in charge of the people who are driving out to Black Island. Is that Fleet Ops?"

"Bingo. Here's his number." Michael pulled a pen out of his pocket, wrote the number on the palm of his hand, got up, crossed to a telephone, and dialed. When the call was answered, he said, "Excuse me, but I got a young lady here in search of a sleeping bag. Can you help her?" Grinning, he handed the phone to Valena.

"Yes, is this Tractor Matt? Oh, thanks. Yeah, I thought I could get the one out of the lab, but no dice. Can I still borrow yours? Hey, thanks. Yeah, just drop it off at Building 17, and I'll get it there. You're a champ."

After hanging up the phone, Valena turned to Michael and threw her arms around him, mashing a huge squeeze on him. "Thank you, Michael."

"Hey!" said another male voice from somewhere behind her. "I hear love blooms even in this cold excuse for a continent, but so quickly!"

Valena jerked clear of Michael and turned. It was James Skehan. He didn't look as big without his ECWs, but that did not abate the embarrassment she felt. It cut like a hot knife clear down to her socks. "We were just—what business is it of yours?" she demanded.

Skehan held his hands up in mock defense. "Whoa! I didn't mean to step on any tender toes here. Just being sociable. So how goes the detective work?"

"What do you mean?"

"I saw Manny Roig an hour ago at Gallagher's, and he was telling folks all the questions you were asking. Sure sounds like a Sherlock Holmes job to me."

Valena felt the blood go out of her face. This was bad. She glanced from Skehan to Michael.

Michael had adjusted his face into a mask of pleasant civility. She realized too late that she was asking an employee of Raytheon to defend her to an NSF grantee, and a very powerful one, at that. Would Skehan, or Roig, or anyone else for that matter go to George Bellamy and report her before she could leave McMurdo Station in the morning?

Skehan's beard hid most of his expression, and his eyes were equally opaque.

"I think I'll get some sleep," said Valena, as she hurried toward the door.

20

THE NEXT MORNING, VALENA DODGED DOWN THE HALLWAY AND INTO the galley exactly as the food lines opened. She carried a day pack that held her essential little yellow notebook, her camera, a water bottle, hat, gloves, and a change of skivvies. Everything else needed for the Black Island traverse she already wore on her body, from two layers of polypropylene underwear right out to her blue FDX boots, wind pants, and big red parka. She quickly filled her water bottle with orange juice, then hurried around the room grabbing anything and everything that would fit in her pockets without soaking through them. She did not want to chance running into George Bellamy or anyone else.

The man standing behind the omelet griddle watched her run past. "Hey, what's the hurry? Can I fry you some eggs this morning?" he inquired.

"Me?" she asked, stuffing a corn muffin into her mouth.

"You look like an owl in a searchlight factory. Going out into the field?"

"How'd you—"

"You've got your big red on. People usually leave them on the coat hooks out in the hall."

"Oh. I'm . . ." She looked over her shoulder. A few people had come into the lines behind her and were moving slowly past the homemade granola.

The man said, "I know that look. I had a daughter once, and she got to looking like you do each time some boy she didn't want to meet up with was chasing her. Come here."

Valena stepped toward the griddle.

Lowering his voice, he said, "You that young thing who's going to Black Island with Fleet Ops?"

"I—"

"Just tell me what you want on your eggs. Thing is, you don't want an omelet, because that stuff that's already whipped up is made from a box. These eggs over here are still in the shell. See? Now, here . . ." He pointed at a row of small stainless steel bins with his spatula. "These are toppings you can have. What you say is, 'Give me three *fresh* eggs with,' well, whatever you want on them. Then you put this thing on"—he handed her a paper chef's hat—"and you head through that door into the kitchen. Back beyond that big, gruff guy who's baking bread—don't mind him, his face broke like that ten years ago—you'll find a little office or two, nice and private. Young ladies need good nutrition and a place to sit down so they can hope to digest it. Okay? I'll make your eggs up and send them along to you. Now, what do you want on it?"

Valena managed a faltering smile. "I'll take cheese, black olives, and mushrooms, please."

"Good enough. When you're done eating, the folks back there will hand you a box of flight lunches to take up the hill to the Boss. Anything else you need?"

"No, sir, I think that'll do it."

"Git."

Valena got.

At a quarter to seven, she left Building 155 by the dock door beyond the kitchen carrying the box of flight lunches. Turning her face away from the sea ice, she climbed the hill that led up to Building 17. The call to adventure rose in her heart, and it was time to get the hell out of McMurdo. The place was making her crazy with its strange mixture of kind people and frontier-town haggardness. And if the Boss had any trouble making his need of her free assistance stick with the NSF, it would be to her advantage—and his—if she could not be located in McMurdo.

It was a bright, cloudless day with little wind. She could see why the Boss wanted to take advantage of the weather to get his crew out to the telecommunications station. She turned and walked backward up the hill so that she could look out across McMurdo Sound. Black Island seemed to float above the glistening ice, a vague slash of distant volcanic rubble rising from the frozen sea. Sixty miles was a long way to go on a tractor. *I'm going to drive a Challenger!* she told herself.

Turning back around, she continued her climb with a big, fat smile on her face. Presently, she heard the crunching footfalls of another pedestrian on the road. Glancing nervously over her shoulder, she saw a woman carrying an orange duffel. She was a freckled kind of pretty, her cherry-glossed lips a contrast above the collar of her Carhartt jacket, which was streaked with grease and grime. "Hey," she said.

"Hey yourself."

The woman grinned, snapping a mouthful of gum. "You must be Valena. I'm Edith."

"Edith?"

"Yeah, I'm your crew foreman. You're replacing Steve, right?"

"Right." Valena's mouth sagged open. It simply had not occurred to her that her crew would have a foreman, much less a good-looking girly woman.

"I'm starting you out in the Delta with one of the guys," said Edith, "but then you can take your turn on the snow machines if you like. We'll also have a Challenger, but that will be pulling a goose—that's a sort of plow thing on skis—so with apologies I'm not going to let you learn how to drive it while we're off the main routes because if you screw up we're stuck. You can drive it on the way back tomorrow, after we get off the soft stuff. Dave will be driving it. He'll teach you."

"Dave." *There was a David on Ted's list,* thought Valena. *Manny called him Dave.*

"Yeah, he's our Cat skinner."

"Not a blaster."

"Dave? No, he drives a Cat. The blasters are part of another outfit."

"That's a common name."

"You'd be amazed how many Daves we have this year. Some years we'll have only one Dave and thirteen Alistairs. Anyway, then we got Wee Willy and Hilario. So the Boss says you've driven heavy equipment during a potato harvest."

"Yes, I have."

"Aces." They had arrived at a small prefabricated building. "Okay, here we are: Home sweet Building 17. You can load those lunches straight into the cab of the Delta."

Valena turned. Instead of a passenger box on the back, this Delta had a flatbed on which had been loaded a huge PVC water barrel, several large wooden packing crates, and a heap of bamboo poles tipped with bright nylon flags. There was a short person on top of the load dressed in Carhartts. He was wrangling a water hose into the barrel to fill it. *This will be either Dave, Wee Willy, or Hilario,* she presumed.

She got the box of sack lunches up into the Delta, taking a moment to look the machine over more carefully than she had when she had been a mere passenger on her way to Happy Camp. Its wheels were almost as tall as she was. It had a huge engine mounted behind the front axle and the cab, which was a six-foot cube cantilevered out in front, hanging about shoulder height above the ground. Unconcerned with aerodynamics, its designers had simply constructed a metal box with square corners, giving the cab the appearance of having been added as an afterthought, like a brick left sitting on a board. It had two doors on each side, with the handles set at the bottom so that she could hope to reach them from the ground. Access to the cab was up metal ladders, the bottom rungs suspended from metal chains. The whole mess had once been red but was now faded to a soft rose, and the forward doors had been embellished with a lovely cartoon of a leaping porpoise above lyric yellow lettering that read FLIPPER. Somehow this did not inspire confidence.

She reached up and yanked open the forward door and shoved the box of lunches and her backpack in onto the floor, then climbed up the ladder to the running board. From there she could maneuver the lunches and her pack onto the backseat, which was already heaped with other peoples' duffels. The windshield and other windows were flat slabs of glass, and the dashboard was olive drab metal with placards listing the vehicle's weight, which was eleven tons. Long windshield wipers hung on pivots from the tops of the windows. The whole thing looked like a stage set for a World War II film about the mud-ridden life of the GI.

Valena climbed down and gave the door a healthy slam.

At the sound, the short man on the flatbed turned and saw her. "Oh, hey, you're the new Steve," he called. "We're all filled up. Have to fill this thing at the last minute, as it would freeze if we left it overnight. Let me screw this lid on and we'll get on our way. Oh, and I put Steve's sleeping bag into the cab for you. It's behind the driver's seat."

"Thanks."

Half a minute later, he had climbed down and was standing on the ground in front of her, pulling his gloves off and stuffing them into his pockets. He was short and swarthy and had coal black hair, dark brown eyes, and wide cheekbones.

"Are you Hilario?" Valena inquired, pronouncing the name with the Spanish accent she had learned from friends in Colorado.

He gave her a look of appraisal. "Latina?"

"*No se,*" she replied. *I don't know.*

Hilario tipped his head and stared at her. "You don't *know?*"

"I was adopted."

Hilario flashed a row of even, white, teeth. "Aw, screw it then, you're Latina. *Chica* fine as you I claim for *todos los Latinos.*" He threw a hand over his head like a bullfighter.

"Well, thank you," said Valena.

The door to Building 17 opened and the Boss stepped out. "Hilario, come in here, please. And get Edith, will you? Dave and Willy are already in here."

"Sure, Boss." He turned and called to the crew chief.

"Does he want me in there, too?" asked Valena.

Hilario shook his head. "Don't sound like it." He disappeared into the building, with Edith close on his heels.

Valena stood in the door yard and waited. Time was ticking past. She wanted to get moving. She burned to get out onto the ice. She itched to speak with Sheila Tuttle. And she wanted desperately to step beyond the reach of George Bellamy. Something was wrong, she could feel it in her gut. When he had stepped outside the door, the Boss had not looked as jolly as he had the night before. In fact, he had looked upset. Had he been told he could not have Valena's help? Did that mean that the traverse to Black Island was scratched until Steve could recover?

What was taking them so long? Were they talking about her? Were they changing their minds, deciding that she wasn't up to the task?

I'm getting really, truly paranoid, she chided herself.

Two more men in insulated canvas clothing came hurrying along the road. "What does he want?" one asked the other. "Dunno. But I don't like it," said the other. A truck pulled up, and three more men hopped out and hurried into the building. The last slammed the door behind himself.

At least this means it's not about me, Valena decided.

Ten minutes passed. It felt like an hour. She began to get cold. She pulled up her hood and hopped from foot to foot.

Finally, the door opened. One of the last men to enter shambled outside, walked to the far side of the road, and stared up into the surrounding hills. He stood with his back to Valena. Lit a cigarette. Hung his head. Kicked at the ground.

A second man came out. His eyes were red and swimming with tears. He wiped his sleeve across his nose. When he saw Valena, he averted his eyes, pulled up his hood, and hurried away down the road.

The next time the door opened, Edith and Hilario came out. Edith's eyes were red-rimmed and staring. "I can't believe it!" she was saying, her voice tight with sorrow. "It's just awful!"

Valena cleared her throat.

Four more heavy equipment operators came outside, shuffled a few feet away from the door, and stopped. Stared at the ground.

Edith began to cry. One of the men put his arms around her and hugged her.

"What is it?" Valena asked.

Hilario looked up and turned toward Valena. His eyes were dark with anger. "Steve's dead," he said.

21

Brenda Utzon headed down the ramp in Crary Lab. She had news, and she knew just who she wanted to share it with. She would tell Michael. She hurried to his door and knocked, but he did not answer.

She started back up the ramp toward phase 1 and her office. As she passed the middle of the ramp, where phase 2 branched left and right, she heard someone call her name.

She turned to see who it was. James Skehan was ambling toward her. She said, "Oh, hi there, Jim."

"Hello, Brenda. You look like a woman with a purpose."

Brenda blushed. "Well, I am. I was just looking for Michael to tell him the news."

Skehan raised his eyebrows to indicate interest. "Ah?"

"Well, it's about Valena Walker, so I suppose you already know, being both from DRI and all."

"She's with Emmett's project."

"Right. Oh, so you don't know?"

"I offer you a visage devoid of knowing. So tell me, what is new that is about Valena Walker, pray tell?"

"Oh, she's gotten on with Fleet Ops for the moment. That's very good news, because she was so disappointed to have to come all the way down here and not see anything of Antarctica."

"Oh. Right."

"Yes, just imagine, it must have been crushing. She has always, always wanted to come here."

"So Fleet Ops took her on? How was that accomplished so quickly?"

"Well, they're just borrowing her, what with Steve hurt and all. You heard that they flew him out to Christchurch. We're waiting for an update."

They heard the inner airlock door open at the end of the hallway. Michael stepped slowly through it. He was staring at the floor.

"Michael!" said Brenda. "I was just coming to tell you about—" She put a hand to her lips. "Something's happened."

Michael looked up slowly. "Steve's dead, Brenda. I just came from the Chalet. He was dead when they landed in New Zealand."

Brenda felt a sickening sense of compression.

Michael put a hand on her shoulder. "I guess that injury was worse than we thought."

Skehan said, "Injury?"

Brenda found her voice. "His head."

Skehan's voice deepened. "And how did this injury occur?"

Brenda said, "They figure he slipped off the bottom step of his tractor."

"In the middle of that storm, he was on his tractor?"

"I don't know how it happened. Cupcake found him." Brenda felt herself trembling and wondered if she was going to be sick. "So they asked Valena if she'd go, and she said yes. That's what I was coming to tell you, Michael."

Skehan's eyes widened. "Valena's driving to Black Island?" With urgency, he added, "Brenda, do you know where I can find Dorothy?"

"You know Cupcake?"

"She once assisted me with some field work."

Michael said, "I just saw her walking toward Berg Field Center."

"Poor Steve," said Brenda. She spoke unevenly, trembling giving way to silent tears.

Michael slid his arm around her shoulder and brought her up against his chest.

Without saying good-bye, Skehan strode toward the door at the end of the hall and through the outside airlock door, heading in the direction of Berg.

❖

NATHANIEL LANTHROPE—THE penguin guy—finished stowing the five-gallon water containers that he and his assistant had just brought in from their short helicopter ride from McMurdo. He adjusted the spigot, put a mug underneath it, and poured himself a drink, to which he added a couple of tablespoonfuls of Raro, New Zealand's answer to Tang. He favored the mango flavor.

Water was the limiting factor out here at Cape Royds. Satellite phone they had, and high-speed Internet, a busy colony of penguins, no dearth of volcanic rock, and millions of square miles of sea ice, but no potable water beyond these five-gallon jugs. The last patches of the winter's snows, which were in any case quickly melting on the sun-absorbent black rock, were full of salt from the mists that rode in from the ocean's edge a hundred yards away.

He walked out to a promontory from which he could survey the entire cape. He could see his assistant picking her way down the trail toward the Pony Lake and the penguin colony beyond. Summer was arriving in Antarctica, but the ocean was still frozen. Far below him on the rocks just above the frozen sea, fifteen hundred pairs of penguins had gathered, and he could hear their ruckus a quarter mile away. They had just completed their mating rituals and were beginning to lay their eggs, the meaning of their odd *rr-churring* sound shifting from "Hey baby!" to "Get off my nesting space, and gimme back that pebble."

The colony was struggling, still recovering from a five-year period during which the ice in McMurdo Sound did not break up. An iceberg the size of Connecticut—the infamous and mammoth B-15 berg—had broken off the Ross Ice Shelf and had grounded just north of Ross Island, blocking the two main agents that usually cleared the winter's ice from the sound: the warm summer ocean currents that usually melted the ice from below, and the ocean swells that flexed the thinning ice, shattering it so that a hard wind could blow it out to sea. Hence, the little Adélie penguins who congregated on Cape Royds each spring and laid their eggs and raised their broods had had to walk sixty kilometers across the ice to find the krill that formed bulk of their diet instead of a few meters. This had limited their rate of success in raising their chicks. The breakup of the Ross Ice Shelf thus provided the basis for his study of population response to climate change.

Nat drank his fill, then put on his jacket to protect himself from the incessant Antarctic wind, picked up his waterproof Rite-in-the-Rain notebook, and started down the hill. He knew the route through the odd mounds of volcanic rock by heart, so many summers had he worked here, watching the penguins, observing their births and lives, documenting their deaths. The crumbled rock that formed the path gave softly under his boots.

He descended past the camp where the New Zealand archaeologists were working to conserve the artifacts in and around Shackleton's hut. The little structure had been built in 1907 but looked remarkably fresh. He stepped past the dump where Shackleton and his men had thrown their disused bottles and other trash and continued past the little pond where they had watered their Siberian ponies. The Pony Lake was just starting to show some melt water around the edges.

The din of the penguin colony filled his ears now, waves of *k-kuk-ker-er-errr* and *err-kuk-err,* a raucous symphony of avian communication. They lay on their little piles of pebbles, staring into the wind. The watermelon-sized black birds with their guano-streaked white bellies lifted their heads and stared at him through emotionless eyes. A crescendo of warning sounds lifted from the nests as he came closer.

"Hey, something's strange here!" called his assistant.

He turned to see what had caught her attention. She was crouched near a group of nests inside a plastic snow fence that encircled them. They had erected the fence a week before. It did not prevent the birds from leaving the area, but did funnel them over glorified bathroom scales that recorded their weights as they left and returned from feeding. A small archway over the scales held an electronic reader that identified each bird from a small chip that had been inserted under its skin. "What's up?" he called.

She waved him toward her. "There are six eggs gone."

"What, did the skuas strike it rich?"

"I don't think so. Both eggs are missing from three nests, all in a tight cluster."

Nat pondered this as he closed the distance between them, stepping over the fence as he came. It was typical for the penguins to lose eggs to the skuas. There were always a few of the predatory, gull-like birds in attendance. But they tended to get one egg here or there but rarely both, and he had never seen them get eggs from each of three adjacent nests. "Have you found the discarded eggshells?"

"No. And that's another thing that's weird."

He stood beside her, seeing what she had seen. Three disconsolate male penguins stood sentinel over empty nests, waiting for their brides to return from feeding. "It's going to be a sad homecoming for those guys."

"Truly. But why the strange pattern of predation?"

"Here comes Nigel. Maybe he saw what happened." One of the archaeologists was walking quickly toward them from the direction of Shackleton's hut. "Hey, there, were you here the past few days?"

Nigel said, "Some artifacts have gone missing. Some bottles and a biscuit tin."

"That's odd."

"You didn't see anyone dodging about from your helo, did you? Somebody took those, we'll nail their right and left testicles to the hut here, leave them as a warning."

Nat raised his eyebrows. "No. So you were gone during the storm, too?"

"Right. Saw it coming, so we went out to Scott Base for a little respite rather than riding it out here. We just got back. Didn't cross paths with anyone coming up the route, so I suppose we're just getting daft from being out here too long. What's up with your birds?"

"It's almost like someone walked in here and helped himself to half a dozen penguin eggs. But who'd do that?"

The archaeologist took off his watch cap and scratched his head. "I don't know, mate. Maybe the same kind of idiot who'd steal Sir Ernest's tinned biscuits?"

◈

CUPCAKE ADJUSTED THE bindings of her skate skis with a focused fury. Steve was dead. Eight seasons she had spent on the ice, and risk of injury and death had always ridden beside her like a passenger who never speaks until it is too late, but this death had "wrong" written all over it. She had been in McMurdo during the helicopter crash of 2003, and that was bad enough, even though no one died. And then there was that pestilent journalist a year ago. Hardly anyone knew him, but still his death had cut everyone to the quick. But a coworker? Dying like that? And through malice?

Who in hell's name killed Steve? The question rattled in her brain, jabbing at her, bashing her, whipping her into a rage.

"Dorothy?"

She turned at the sound of a familiar voice. Sucking herself up into the hardened exterior she preferred to present to the world, she said, "What spider hole did you just crawl in out of, Padre?"

The man slowly closed his eyes and opened them again. "The name is Jim."

"Whatever. Come on, asshole, give a woman a hug." She grabbed hold of him and crushed him against her body. "So how's it hanging?"

Disentangling himself gently but firmly, he said, "A little respect for my vocation if you will, madame."

"Okay, stick to your vows if you must, but it's a waste."

He gave her a tired but patient look. "I want you to tell me about that tractor driver."

"Steve."

"You found him. You and a man named Dave."

"That's right. Me and Dave Fitzgerald. Why do you need to know?"

"Because I can't help but wonder if it has some connection with the other death."

"Last year. The journalist. Why, because of Dave?"

Skehan kept his face impassive, showing little of what he was thinking or feeling.

Cupcake said, "Yeah, it was the same Dave who was at Emmett's camp last year. And the official story about this year is that Steve slipped on the bottom step of his tractor and hit his head, but that's bullshit."

"You're sure of that."

"I am entirely sure. Or, like you scientists say, as sure as I can be without having seen it happen myself."

Skehan curled one side of his mouth in an ironic smile. "You're a quick student."

"You're a good teacher. Of course, I'd prefer a different subject."

"Let's not go there."

"Killjoy."

Skehan shook his head. "I understand that you are grieving, but does nothing slow you down?"

"I even have designs on the Grim Reaper. Imagine what a score that would be."

Skehan closed his eyes. "Steve," he said. "A man's been killed. Two men."

Cupcake looked away. "All I know is that Steve was out at the ice runway during the worst of the whiteout. The Boss sent him out there with one of the Challengers. He was supposed to be hanging out in the kitchen, but someone counted heads and noticed that he wasn't there. Next thing we know, he's out past Hut Point on the Cape Evans route, kissing something hard and on his way down. His tractor was back near the runway. You tell me how he got there."

"Did you see any tracks when you found him? Anything strange?"

Cupcake shook her head. "It was still blowing, kicking up fresh snow, and all we had in mind was getting him to safety. Fat lot of good that did him."

"Has anyone been back out there to take a look?"

"I don't know."

"I stopped by Science Support Center on the way over here and checked out a snow machine. How about you show me the spot?"

Cupcake thought a moment, then nodded. "Just let me put away these tools. But there's one thing I've got to tell you. Something that's bothering me."

"What's that?"

Cupcake turned and looked at the scientist. "You're right, it was Dave who was with me when I found him. Aw hell, Dave found him, not me. I was all but along for the ride. He . . ."

"Spit it out, Dorothy. Time's wasting, and you would not believe how much is riding on this."

Cupcake's usual tough-girl expression twisted with concern, then anger, then fear. Finally, she stared at the floor. "I do not like to rat out my coworkers, but . . . well, it was spooky. I'm not making any accusations, but Dave just drove right out there—it was miles—and—" She snapped her fingers. "There he was."

Skehan nodded, encouraging her to say the rest.

Cupcake said, "It was like he knew exactly where to look."

22

Valena felt the cold slice through her. She wrapped her arms tightly across her chest, trying to squeeze away the cold. "The man I'm replacing *died?*"

"Oh, yes," Hilario said. "Didn't even make it to Christchurch. Died on the plane. You'll excuse us, it's going to be a while before we're going to feel like driving anywhere."

Edith lifted her head and shoved a leather glove across her nose, sniffling. "No, I say we get going. There's nothing like a job to do to get things off your mind, and we can honor Steve by doing that job well. I'll take the first shift on his—the Challenger." She headed for the rig. "Come on!" she called over her shoulder. "We're falling behind schedule."

Hilario turned toward Valena and gestured toward the door to the Delta.

Taking hold of the grab handle mounted on the side of the cab between the two doors, Valena climbed back up into the cab and settled herself in the right front seat, which featured torn olive drab plastic upholstery over a brick of foam rubber. She felt oddly shaky. She hadn't known the man who had died, but she was walking in his shoes.

"*Mierde,*" Hilario said, rubbing his hands together to warm them as he settled himself into the driver's seat. "The man had a family, you know? And he had us."

Valena did not know what to say, so she said nothing.

"This sort of thing really shakes people up around here. *Es verdad.* They're still talking about that Air New Zealand flight that crashed into Erebus back in 1979."

"I'm sorry."

"Yeah. Well, like Edith said, we shall honor our man. They're going to do a memorial for him on Sunday, when we all have the day off. Meanwhile, it's business as fucking usual." He thumped the steering wheel, and then added, "*Perdona. Mi lenguaje.*"

"*No te preocupre.*"

"Right. Now, how you suppose this thing works?" He switched on the ignition, opened the heater up full blast, then wriggled out of his jacket.

Trying to bring up lighter topics, Valena asked, "Why's this thing called Flipper?"

Hilario shrugged. "Aw, it used to belong to the Fire Department, but they got to practicing maneuvers one day." He grabbed the huge, flat-mounted steering wheel and pantomimed turning it all the way to the right. "Rolled it. Guess you can only turn so sharp in one of these things, unless of course you're going some kind of reasonable speed. So we cut the box off it and here it is, the pride of Fleet Ops. *Bella*, eh?"

"Simply gorgeous." She felt the cab rock and turned to her right just as a large face appeared at the window beside her. It scared her and she jumped.

"Aw, don't get so excited," said Hilario. "It's only Willy."

It was another man dressed in the light brown Carhartt canvas ECWs. He was a big guy, as young as she or perhaps younger, but not blessed with even a single detail of physical beauty. He greeted her with an expression as lively as a cucumber, while banging on the door with one gloved fist.

She opened the door. "Hi," she said, trying to be friendly.

The man stared at her.

"Don't mind him," said Hilario. "He don't talk much. I guess he thinks you're going to sit in back so he can ride shotgun. Rank has privileges. You're the fingie."

Valena shoved some gear aside and moved to the back seat. Wee Willy lumbered into the cab. He was almost as big and about as pleasant as a bear who had just awakened from hibernation. With a motion like a bricklayer dropping his hod, he occupied the seat Valena had just exited, then turned, reached past her, and began digging through one of the flight lunches. Feeling her eyes on him, he fixed a glare on her.

Valena began to have doubts about just how much fun the trip was going to be.

Hilario fired the ignition. He sang, "We go cruisin' in the ma-chine!" swung the wheel, and off they lurched.

McMurdo Station flowed past in a tumble of steel and black road metal as they rumbled down the slope that led to the edge of the sea ice. At the transition onto the ice, Hilario stopped the Delta next to a cluster of snow machines and heavy equipment that was parked there.

Wee Willy lurched up off the seat and began to empty himself out the door.

"*Hasta luego, amigo. Vaya con dios,*" said Hilario.

Wee Willy did not reply. Heaving himself down out of the door frame, he dropped onto the ice and shambled off toward one of the snow machines, leaving the door open to the breeze.

Valena slammed the door with rather more force than was necessary.

"Oh, you'll get used to him," said Hilario. "Or not."

The snow machines were bigger and more utilitarian versions of what Valena would have called a snowmobile at home. They had the usual setup of skis in front and a single track behind and a saddle in the middle right behind motorcycle-style controls. But beyond that, they differed from their streamlined northern cousins in a matter of studied inelegance. As Wee Willy pulled the canvas cover off of one, she could see that the front cowling was one big, charmless expanse of blaze orange. The seat was a single slab of black plastic. And toward the back of the vehicle, a simple plywood box had been added to carry gear.

The heater in the cab had risen from pleasantly warm to full roast, so Valena cracked the window a few inches and shrugged off her big red parka, then turned and packed it onto the backseat, rearranging the duffels and equipment stowed there so that they wouldn't shift en route. "What's this?" she inquired, picking up a tube of fake fur that hadn't been there before.

Hilario let out a sardonic chuckle. "That's Wee Willy's hand warmer. His ma gave it to him."

"Oh." She put it up on the backseat.

The Challenger pulled up next to them, and Valena watched as the fifth member of their party climbed out of a jump seat in its cab and climbed down the steps to the ice. "Is that Dave?" she asked Hilario.

"Yeah. Good guy. Drove out there and found Steve."

Valena realized that it was the man who had stared at her in the hallway outside the galley the evening before. Her heart sank. *I'm replacing a man who died, one of the team glares at me, and another just plain stares*, thought Valena. *This is going to be a long trip.*

Dave crossed to one of the snow machines, checked its number against the tag of his ignition key, brushed the snow off its canvas cover, removed the cover and folded it neatly, then stowed it in a compartment. That done, he swung a leg gracefully over the saddle and lowered himself onto it. He stuck the key into the ignition and began clearing snow off other parts of the machinery.

Edith's voice crackled over the radio that was mounted in the ceiling of the cab. "Mac Ops, Mac Ops, this is Challenger 283, how read?"

"Mac Ops copies, go ahead."

"This is Edith Tanner. We are five souls in four vehicles—a Challenger, a Delta, and two snow machines. Contact is the Boss. Destination Black Island. We will traverse to KOA, then start setting flags at the edge of the dead zone. Intend overnight at Black Island Station and return tomorrow by eighteen hundred. Over."

Dave completed his snow-clearing task, set the primer and the choke, switched on the engine, and, with a few quick compressions of the hand-grip throttle, revved it to a level past which it kept running on its own. Then he set to adjusting his cuffs so that they would not become wind scoops.

"Mac Ops copies. Call from KOA before you enter dead zone, but in any case I want to hear from you by sixteen hundred, over. And you be careful, okay?"

"We will. Challenger 283 copies. Over and out."

"Mac Ops out."

Edith maneuvered the big Cat into place in front of the goose, which was an eight-foot-wide hydraulically operated grading blade mounted on a trailing chassis that was supported by skis. Once the machine was in position, she climbed down the steps out of the cab to secure the hitch and connect the hydraulic lines.

Dave continued to adjust his clothing, now pulling his polypropylene neck gaiter up over his nose, cinching his hood tight against his cheeks, and then putting a pair of goggles over the top. Last, he replaced his gloves, adjusting their cuffs over the cuffs of his parka.

Valena asked Hilario, "Why's he wearing red instead of tan?"

"It's a matter of preference. Most of us are more used to smearing grease all over tan. Ol' Dave here works as hard as the rest of us but somehow stays cleaner."

"Oh. What's the dead zone?"

"Oh, that's where we're behind Black Island and the radio can't 'see' us. We have to go all the way around the south side of the island to get to the station that's on it, because the ice is all screwed up on the north side, facing McMurdo here."

"Why isn't there a radio repeater?"

Hilario let out a rueful cackle. "Because there's nothing out there, that's why. What, you think a continent half again the size of the US with only, say, three thousand people on it—and that's in summertime—has a radio antenna in every little place you might like to go?"

"I suppose not."

"Then you suppose right. Look up there. That's all we got between us and Black Island Station." He pointed at the array of antennae on top of the building that housed Mac Ops and the Airlift Wing. "Black Island's got the big satellite dish, but it's there for telecommunications, not radio, and it ain't looking south."

"Where is it looking?"

Hilario rolled his eyes. "It's pointed north. It looks at a geostationary satellite over the equator. Damn thing is tipped up within four degrees of standing on its edge to see it. So you can do the math. It's seventy-eight degrees south latitude, looking how many thousand miles north—that puts that satellite up pretty high, eh? Like, so the dish can see it over the curve of the earth?"

"Doing trigonometry in my head has never been my forte."

Wee Willy had by this time finally made a match between his key fob and a snow machine number, had balled up the canvas covering on his machine and stuffed it into the wooden box mounted toward the back, leaving bungee cords dangling near the tread, and was having trouble getting it started. He cranked the ignition, hammered on the throttle, then stopped, waited a moment, kicked the machine, then repeated the whole routine, as if he could beat it into submission.

Dave sat adjusting his gear box, paying no attention to Wee Willy.

Edith opened the door to the cab of the Challenger and shouted, "Hey! You ever heard of the primer and choke, or what?"

Wee Willy shot her a scowl.

Edith hoisted herself out of the driver's seat and started down the steps toward her colleague. She closed the distance between her vehicle and his, pushed him out of her way with one hip, set the primer and the choke, gave the starter a switch and a yank, gave the throttle a couple of pumps, held it until the machine revved nice and high, adjusted the choke, and then stepped back and waited.

Wee Willy gave no outward evidence of noticing that Edith had assisted him. He settled himself back on the saddle like a load of turnips and pulled up his hood. As an afterthought, he pushed his hood back again, dug at the throat of his parka until he found his neck gaiter and pulled it up to the bottom of his nose, pulled his goggles down to meet it, then pulled his hood over the top of the elastic. He took off his gloves to accomplish this, dropping both on the ice. The wind caught one and blew it five feet away. Wee Willy climbed off his machine, galumphed after it, slipped and almost fell in the process of picking it up, then at last caught it and put it on, stuffing the cuff under the cuff of his parka.

"This is going to be a long trip," said Hilario.

Edith had headed back to the Challenger. As she placed her foot on the bottom step and started to raise the other, she slipped and took a tumble off onto the ice.

Dave instantly hopped off his idling snow machine and rushed to help her up. "You okay? You scared me, Edith. We don't need any more accidents around here."

Edith brushed snow off her Carhartts. "It's just like the Boss said. These bottom steps are all crammed with ice. He warned us about this in the safety meeting at the beginning of the season." Edith headed back up the steps, placing her feet with greater care.

Dave moved in and kicked the steps free of ice, then turned and strolled back to his waiting snow machine.

"But both she and Dave came down without slipping," Valena said, to no one in particular.

Hilario said, "She gets to rushing sometimes. Buckin' for pro-*mo*-tion," he said, singing the last word.

The Challenger, dragging the trail-grooming bar called the goose, swung out ahead of them and headed down the flag route that led out toward the ice runway. A snow machine shot out on either side of it, kicking up loose snow. Hilario swung in line behind them. They were off.

23

HILARIO LOOKED TO VALENA'S EDUCATION AS A DELTA DRIVER. "Watch and learn," he said, pushing the mammoth snow-crawler into higher gear. "You gonna be driving this thing in less than an hour." They began to roll faster. "This baby's got five forward gears, automatic shift. You can start it out set in high gear and it'll shift itself up there as it goes, or start in a lower gear and shift up when you're ready, but you always got to downshift by hand, except you don't have to work no clutch. Cardinal rule, don't let it break traction. You feel the thing beginning to labor, or hear the engine speed slow, you downshift like this," he said, demonstrating with an easy tug of the shift lever.

"Seems simple enough."

"Don't get overconfident. Pay attention all times."

"Check."

"Don't go off the trail. That Challenger's got treads, you got tires. With this load, you weigh fifteen tons. Especially don't go off the trail here." He pointed to the trail ahead of them, where it choked down to a narrows that led between two clusters of flags. Many of the flags were black.

"Big crack in the ice or something?"

"This is where the fuel lines cross from the island out to the ice runway. Don't go outside this slot or you gonna make yourself very unpopular round here." They rode up over a concealed bridge and down the other side. The route widened out again. "Okay, now here we got four lanes, closest thing to an Interstate highway on this whole continent. Outer two lanes are for tracked vehicles, inner two are rubber tires, that's us."

Training continued as they took a left at the first fork in the route, toward Williams Field—"Willy, they call it; it's named after this dude who drove a Cat through the ice over by Cape Evans," Hilario explained—then turned right a mile or two later, heading south toward Pegasus. "The third runway," said Hilario, "is for landing C-17s after the sea ice gets too soft to take the weight. We gotta resurface it every year, and it's farther from town, so we use the sea ice as long as we can."

The flagged trail dropped from four lanes to two. Finally, the turn to Pegasus swung off to the right, the route dropped to one lane, and they were on the Black Island route.

"Nothing beyond here but ice," said Hilario. "That flagged route to pole heads off down here. That's it. Nothing else. No man's land."

They moved at ten miles per hour. The Challenger ground along ahead of them, carving through snowdrifts, smoothing and compacting the trail. They had now left what Antarctica had in the way of civilization, and the human universe shrank quickly in contrast to the immensity of the ice on which they traveled. As they rode along, Hilario and Valena chatted sporadically, swapping unimportant facts about themselves, such as favorite foods and things to do in leisure time, and commenting on the variations in the crests and hollows the wind had carved into the hard-packed snow that shrouded the ice. Finally, Hilario said, "Time for you to start driving."

"Where are we?" asked Valena, searching the raw, white scenery for familiar landmarks. Hut Point and McMurdo Station had disappeared behind a rise and clouds had gathered about the towering heights of the Transantarctic Mountains and Mount Erebus. Their world had been consumed by snow and ice.

He pointed to a black smear of ice-dappled volcanic rock in the distance. "That's Black Island there, and that's—"

"I mean are we still on the sea ice or are we coming up onto the ice shelf? I saw a map that put the boundary between the two out here somewhere."

"Well, if you can't see an edge, then there's really no difference, now, is there?"

"Yes, there is. A huge difference. The one is ocean water that freezes and breaks up annually. The other is freshwater snow that refroze into ice thousands of miles from here and—"

"Oh, so you're going to split hairs. Okay, then, we're on the ice shelf."

"But where? I was expecting a cliff, or a climb of some sort."

"What are you, a glaciologist or something?"

"Well, yes, in fact I am."

"I heard you're a grantee. So why you in this bucket?"

Valena did not answer. She was thinking, *It's like McMurdo is one big communal organism, like a sponge or a jelly-fish.* The odd experience of being sent through the kitchen by the omelet man returned to mind. Somehow, between 10:00 p.m. and 6:00 a.m., half of McMurdo had heard about her change of plans, not to mention who she was and what she did here. This was not comforting, especially now that the man named Steve was dead. And how exactly had he died? It occurred to her that he might have been murdered.

She chided herself for thinking this thought, but murder had indeed occurred at Emmett's camp; there was no doubt of that now. Larry's information of the evening before had changed all that from speculation to certainty. Emmett himself had been taken into custody as a result, and . . . and who was she to say that he was innocent?

She hardly knew the man. *Was* Emmett Vanderzee a cold-blooded killer? His graduate students from the year before had gone on to other projects. They could have stayed on. Why had they jumped ship? Had they left him because they no longer trusted him? If so, what had changed their minds?

Somebody had prevented the journalist from getting the aid he needed, and that was murder. Had the feds fingered Emmett because he was the only one who had a motive to kill that man or because he was the only one who had had the opportunity? Perhaps one of the graduate students had buried that Gamow unit and had now separated himself from the whole situation by scorning his former professor. *Was that why Bob Schwartz ran off without answering my questions?*

Thus far, she had spoken to only three of the people who'd been present in the camp—Cal Hart, Bob Schwartz, and Manuel Roig—and they had each seemed reticent to talk about the situation. *No, wait, Cal Hart was interrupted by Jim Skehan,* she reminded herself. *But what was Bob's problem? And was Manuel Roig in fact too exhausted after searching for Steve? Or was the memory of watching a man die in Antarctica too painful to visit? But what if this was a foil, an easy explanation behind which to hide? Did he have a reason to want the journalist dead?* Valena's brain buzzed with the questions she had not thought to ask these men, such as, *Did you know Sweeny before you went to Emmett's camp?*

She ran down her mental list of possible killers. William the dogsbody was there by accident and was supposedly lazy or incompetent. She had no way of knowing whether he had a motive. David/Dave—the other muscle sent to the high camp—was a blank.

She looked out the window of the Delta, wondering if the David and William who had been present at Emmett's camp could possibly be the Dave and Wee Willy who were at that moment cutting lazy figure eights in through the drifts beyond the groomed trail. *No, too much of a coincidence,* she decided. *A thousand people work at McMurdo during the season, and David and William are common names.*

The cook she was about to meet. *What was she like? A bit cranky, having been alone with a tribe of men at high elevation? Would that make her a killer? And Calvin Hart: what was his story? What did he do for the project?*

Cracking into Valena's silence, Hilario repeated his question in a different form. "So really, what you doing driving out to Black Island?"

Valena blinked. "Sorry," she said. "I'm a little tired. Still jet-lagged, I guess."

"It takes a while to adjust," said Hilario. "First time on the ice, it takes at least a week. Dehydration, the endless daylight, all the weird people, eating food that comes out of a can . . ."

"I like it fine."

"And you are going to Black Island because . . . ?"

She tried to decide what of substance, if anything, she wanted to tell him. Clearly her story was getting around, but how much of it? "I wanted to see the Ross Ice Shelf," she said at last. "I'd read so many accounts by the early explorers of how vast it was, and . . ." Her grip on her mind slipped again. *And what?* Deep in her guts she did want to see it, if only a glimpse. Had always wanted to see it. Had longed for it, and for all of Antarctica. She shook her head and closed her eyes. Fatigue was definitely beginning to get the better of her. Fatigue and stress. She needed more sleep.

"Well, what do you think? Seen enough yet?" He fell into his low chuckle again.

It is beautiful, she wanted to say. *Painfully, astonishingly, joyously, se-*

verely beautiful, but instead she guarded her heart and, from her intellect, said, "I had expected something more dramatic, not that this isn't pretty awe-inspiring. But I thought there would be a cliff, or at least a steep rise." She had wanted an edge to cross, past which she could say, *Now I have been to that place that summoned me.*

She felt Hilario's eyes on her. "Any time this month you want to learn to drive this thing," he said, letting it roll to a stop. "Come on, it won't bite you. Climb over here."

They switched places and Valena settled herself behind the wheel, which was about eighteen inches in diameter and mounted almost flat, like that on a bus. Hilario showed her which gear to start out in—second for most purposes, first for soft snow or other questionable conditions. She gave it some gas and the big beast began to move. A smile spread across her face.

Hilario said, "You're a natural. Time for me to take a few minutes to myself." He climbed out of the shotgun seat, shoved everything that had been on the backseat onto the floor, and stretched out on it. "Wake me anything happens. Oh, and if I fall asleep or anything, wake me before we stop at KOA so Edith don't see me snoozing."

"Right. KOA. So what am I looking for? A campground?"

Hilario's sardonic laugh filled the cab. "Yeah, that's right. Only there's only one campsite. Just keep going until you see something that isn't ice or rock or flag."

The faster snow machines flew ahead of them going south along the route. The wind had grown brisk, driving spumes of snow from the crest of every drift, wrapping the snow machine drivers up in a blanket of gauze. Valena would wave to them as they barreled toward her or zinged by going the other direction, running circles around the Delta and the Challenger to stay with the bigger, slower machines. Sometimes it looked like they were chasing each other, and sometimes it appeared that Dave was herding Wee Willy, keeping him from getting lost. The big man seemed bent on finding a snowdrift that would buck his machine into the sky. He would find a big one, take aim, and hit it as hard as he could. Just for shits and grins, as her mother used to say.

A vision of her mother came to mind as she had looked in a photograph Valena had once found in the back of a book at her grandfather's house: sitting on her Harley, a can of beer resting on one knee, a skimpy tank top, and her huge Hollywood grin. It was the grin that always got people. Brought men to their knees. It was the Harley that had gotten her, late one night in the Snake River Canyon.

Valena drove onward across the ice, giving herself to its mass and dimensions. *I made it, Ma*, she wanted to tell her, but there was no email or conversation where she had gone.

The KOA turned out to be a survival hut, little more than a wooden box on wheels, a way station where a traveler could get in out of the wind. Edith called for a halt for lunch. "Come with me, Valena," she called as she disappeared behind the structure.

Valena stopped the Delta and joined her. Edith had not had to explain that this was the only place for miles around that they could drop their drawers and pee without being seen by the men.

"Your first dose of Antarctic girl bonding?" asked Edith as they squatted.

Valena smiled. "Yeah. Men sure have the advantage in such circumstances. We expose the full moon. All they got to show is the isthmus of Panama."

They shared a laugh, then zipped up again and headed back to their rigs.

With all four engines shut down, only the sound of the wind met their ears. They commenced their midday meal. Edith and Dave stood to eat, their paper sacks resting on the running board of the Delta. Valena and Hilario took seats on the two snow machines. Wee Willy sat inside the Delta, eating by himself.

Edith spoke to Valena as she smeared mayonnaise and mustard onto her cheese and bologna sandwich from little plastic packets. "I don't think you've met Dave," she said.

"Hi," said Valena, without looking up. She tried to cover her discomfort by putting a glove to her lips and clearing her throat.

"Hi, yourself," said Dave.

Valena could not read his face with the dark glasses and chewing, but he sounded friendly enough. People stared at her all the time, why had Dave's stare in the hallway of Building 155 bothered her so much? She turned to Edith. "So how many calories do you think are in one of these flight lunches?" she asked, inventing something to talk about.

Edith laughed. "I calculated that once. Just under two thousand." She pulled her sack down off the running board and dug through it. "Two big sandwiches, a couple granola bars, juice box, chips, mega-brownie—there's a weight-loss food—and don't forget the chocolate bar."

"You don't want to get cold," said Hilario.

Dave said nothing.

"Does NSF have some kind of a deal with Cadbury's?" asked Valena.

Hilario said, "You mean Raytheon; they do all the ordering. Yeah, must be. Cadbury's got a factory in New Zealand. Now, I like chocolate fine, "but this peppermint flavor just isn't my thing."

"Swap you for a fruits and nuts," said Edith. "Stick in my teeth."

Hilario looked at Dave. "What you got, amigo?"

Dave smiled, curling his mustache. "I ain't swapping. I got the mousse bar."

Hilario and Edith groaned with envy. "You luck!" said Hilario, heaving himself off the snow machine to make the swap with Edith.

Dave chuckled. "Too bad for you they don't make jalapeño flavor."

"You're a deep thinker," Hilario said.

"So this is what people do with their time in Antarctica," said Valena. "You argue over chocolate bars."

Hilario and Edith both stopped and stared at her. "Like there's anything more important in life?" said Edith. "I love to eat, and this place is food central." She shrugged. "Except for the freshies, which are few and far between. You'll notice there is no lettuce in your sandwich."

"I was wondering, but now you mention it, that makes sense. And it's a bit dry."

"Load on the mayo," said Edith. "Chowing on flight lunches is an art form."

Valena noticed that Edith's sack had become so light that it was beginning to blow along the running board "You've emptied that bag already? Woman after my heart."

Edith grabbed the sack and laughed. "You aren't doing so bad yourself, honey. That's what I love about this place. Eat, eat, eat, and you never gain an ounce."

"Amen on that."

Edith turned to Wee Willy, who had climbed down out of the cab. "So, how you like traversing?"

Wee Willy shrugged his massive shoulders. "Are we getting overtime for this?"

Dave said, "Ain't you liking this?"

Wee Willy shrugged again. "It's okay, I guess."

"Well, let's hit it," said Edith. "We got miles to go before we sleep."

Valena watched Wee Willy shamble away toward his snow machine, wondering who in his right mind would come to Antarctica for anything but love.

◇

FROM THE KOA, the route made a gradual turn toward the west around the south side of Black Island, rising higher onto the ice shelf. Valena knew that the ice was not standing still. It was flowing like putty, but on such an immense scale and so slowly that it took precise measurement with satellite-mounted radar and GPS to read its progress. This ice had been born a thousand miles away or more, perhaps even up on the Antarctic Plateau. It had crept here at speeds of no more than a few hundred meters per year. From space, NASA's satellites could read flow lines created as it streamed off the continent and onto the Southern Ocean, but from here, all she could see was unbroken whiteness.

As they convoyed along, the world opened up and out, their presence continuing to shrink as the immensity of the Ross Ice Shelf engulfed them. The world shifted to palest blue, and Valena's heart began to lift.

Twice, she felt the track beneath her wheels grow soft. She sensed this through her skin and muscles even before she heard the engine slow, and she quickly downshifted, easing the spin of the wheels over the soft patch, regaining her traction. The second time this happened, she glanced into the rearview mirror at the tires behind the cab. The surface of the snow immediately in front of them had begun to wrinkle, like a bow wake thrown up by a ponderous black ocean vessel.

Edith's voice crackled out of the speaker above her head. "Mac Ops, Mac Ops, this is Challenger 286."

"Go ahead, Challenger."

"We're at the edge of the dead zone. Reporting in. Over."

"Copy that, Edith. What's your ETA Black Island?"

"Eighteen hundred."

Valena slid up her sleeve and looked at her watch. It was 12:30. That meant five and a half hours without radio contact.

Mac Ops replied, "I want to hear from you eighteen hundred sharp, or earlier if you can pick up a signal."

"Roger that. We'll monitor radio and check in if we hear you. Challenger out."

"Happy flagging. Mac Ops clear."

Valena had been watching the flags that marked their route. Many were missing, leaving only the bamboo stake sticking out of the snow. Along one two- or three-mile stretch near the KOA, the flags had been replaced so many times that a veritable forest of bamboo stakes lined the route. Many were splintered or broken off near the surface of the ice. Now the convey had reached a stretch where only one or two feet of flagstaff showed above the snow. Here on the south side of Black Island, the wind blew relentlessly, sweeping the scant accumulation of Antarctic snow into a giant drift.

The Challenger pulled to a halt and the crew chief climbed out, waving the two outriders in from their wanderings.

Valena stopped also. "You awake, Hilario?"

"Yes. Gimme a minute; I got to find out where we are."

She turned and saw that he had switched on a global positioning system unit and was reading out their position. Pulling a paper copy of an air photograph of the area out of a folder, he marked their position. Valena could see the entire route marked between GPS readings a few miles apart. "Is that so we can keep going in the dark?" she joked.

"We could keep going in a whiteout with this gizmo," he said. "I done that when I worked up in Greenland one summer. We rode for miles on snowmobiles going only by the GPS and arrived right at the drill site no problem. Then I got off the machine and walked smack into the side of the building."

"You're kidding! Wasn't it dangerous to travel blind like that?"

"These satellite things are really accurate, you know? If the route's been mapped tight enough, you can do that. I wouldn't try it where you have crevasses or anything like that, but going over a groomed route like this? Sure." He completed his documentation, then said, "You're a good driver, Valena. You downshifted just right in those soft patches."

"Thanks."

"So you can continue. I'll take the first shift up on the load." He began to put on his outer clothing.

"How do we do this?"

Hilario's voice was muffled somewhat as he pulled on his neck gaiter and rigged into his parka. "The Challenger leads the way as usual, but you follow slower now. I throw a flag down off the load every two hundred feet." He swung his right arm like a javelin thrower.

Dave had climbed off his snow machine and was swapping his hood for a watch cap and his goggles for sunglasses with side protection flaps. He came over to the Delta, opened the door behind Hilario, reached under the backseat, pulled out two heavy iron rods with beveled points, dragged both irons over to where the snowmobiles were parked, and leaned one across each saddle.

Hilario said, "They use those pikes to jab holes in the snow so they can stick the poles in. You'll see. Don't get too far in front of them." Pulling the zipper to his chin, he climbed out the door, walked along the running boards and over the boxy fender that covered the wheel on that side, then stepped over the swivel that connected the tractor and trailer parts of the vehicle. Up on top of the load, he loosened the ties on the first bundle of flags and used the bamboo end of one of them to tap the roof of the cab, indicating that Valena could begin.

Valena eased the Delta into first gear and set it rolling. In the side rearview window, she watched the bamboo poles fly out every two hundred feet. Some landed upright in the snow or leaning at an angle; others, fell in places where the snow had blown away, baring the ice underneath, and simply bounced and skittered across the surface.

Dave and Wee Willy leapfrogged along behind her, setting flags turn and turn about, zooming from one position to the next, carrying their steel pikes like lancers at a joust.

As she drove along, Valena reminded herself that Antarctica was a desert. In the interior, annual precipitation averaged less than two inches of water, whatever that taped out to in snowflakes. Even here on the coast, where the snowfall was highest, it averaged less than eight inches. And yet the wind had rounded it all up and dumped it here, accumulating a thickness of five or six feet in a year. Was Emmett Vanderzee's high camp like this? Had the wind helped a killer bury the parachute drop?

Valena felt the morning's nervousness settle about her once again. She struggled to look on the landscape intellectually, as an object from her classes. Here the wind packed the snow hard, transforming it into solid ice in just a few seasons. Images filled her mind from the photomicroscopic slides Emmett Vanderzee had shown in his lecture during spring term. As the snowflakes accumulated in this perpetual deep freeze, they recrystallized into shards of granular snow. The shards then compacted, changing from snow into a more granular substance called firn. As additional snow accumulated on top, increasing the load, firn transitioned into ice, reforming into larger and larger crystals, finally interlocking into the massive ice of glaciers. She had read about this transition, and now she witnessed the result of the process in its immensity. Back home, glaciers were little things that lived in the high valleys of just a few mountain ranges, the exception to the rule. Here, ice was the rule, not the mountains it shrouded, and it formed not just alpine glaciers but huge glaciers and ice streams miles wide that flowed from the gigantic sheets of ice thousands of feet thick. The Ross Ice Shelf was as big as France. It was fed by the West Antarctic Ice Sheet, a mass half the size of the United States, and also by the East Antarctic Ice Sheet—larger than the whole lower forty-eight states by a considerable margin—which flowed through passes in the Transantarctic Mountains down which the monstrous glaciers flowed—in places, the ice in Antarctica was more than three miles thick. The sheer volume of all that bound-up water was beyond imagining, ninety percent of the world's ice, seventy percent of the world's fresh water.

As she rolled Flipper slowly along the trail, Valena stared out across the white wilderness. The variation in the patterns the wind carved into the snow and ice was fantastic. Here the surface snow and firn was sculpted into overlapping fish scales the size of her boot, there into waves as big as the Delta. *Sastrugi*, the Russians had named these endlessly variable sculptures; an alien name for alien forms.

Wee Willy pulled his snow machine to a halt in front of her and waved his arms for her to stop. She pulled up and rolled down the window, catching a blast of scouring wind in her face.

"I been out here for hours. Your turn," he demanded, pulling down his neck gaiter to speak.

Valena thought for only a second before deciding that she was only too ready to agree. She was enjoying driving the ponderous Flipper but envied the speed and maneuverability of the snow machines. In all her twenty-four years she had never ridden one ("You'll end up like your ma," Great Aunt Dilla had always said), and this was a grand way to start. "I'll be right down," she replied, and she began the process of layering on clothing to guard against the cold.

As she climbed down out of the cab of the Delta, she told Wee Willy, "I put your hand warmer into the top of your duffel. It had fallen onto the floor, and I was certain you didn't want it to get dirty."

Wee Willy had been on a trajectory to trudge past her without making eye contact, but at her words he stopped, turned, and looked at her, his lips slightly parted. He stared for several seconds, then said, "Thanks." He began to move toward the Delta again, but stopped again, turned to her, and said, "Remember to lift with your legs. It's heavy."

"The pike?"

"Yeah. Lift with your legs, then drop it into the snow. That way you don't hurt your back. And lay it across your lap while you drive to the next flag. If you try and put one end of it down on the running board and you hit a bump, it can fall off into the snow."

"Thanks." She took a seat on the snow machine Wee Willy had just vacated.

Hilario called out from the back of the Delta. "How about I take a turn on the snow machines, too?" he asked.

Edith had seen them stop and had looped around to rejoin them. "Dave, you want a turn on the Challenger?" she called out from its cab. "I'll take a turn on top of the load."

Dave gave her a thumbs-up, set his machine to idle, and headed for the tractor.

"But first give Valena the ten-second lowdown on driving a snow machine, will ya?"

Dave turned and crossed to Valena's snow machine. "Just turn the switch on the ignition and give it some gas," he said. "Should come right on. It's warm."

"Thanks," she said. She sat down quickly on the saddle and fired it up, then zoomed off down the trail, knowing that her haste was a little ridiculous, considering that there were as yet no new flags waiting to be set, but she wanted to show him that she could handle it. To her surprise and pleasure, she felt quite natural on it. Her hips rolled with the changes in the surface and, even as fast as she was going, she could feel the wind pressing at her back. When she thought she had gone about four hundred feet—two flag distances—she stopped the machine and waited.

The Challenger swept past her with Dave at the controls. He waved to her.

The Delta came lumbering down the trail with Wee Willy at the wheel. Edith tossed down a flag, and Valena hopped up and dropped the iron into the snow, lifted it out, and set the bamboo pole into the hole as the Delta continued down the trail. Sitting back down on the saddle with the iron across her lap as Wee Willy had suggested, she throttled up and zoomed off to the next position, where another flag already waited.

Valena continued along the trail, now setting the flags with the pike, now learning to use the hand augur to make a hole where the wind had blown the snow away from the ice. The wind increased incrementally, blowing in a bank of clouds that nibbled at the distant mountain range, gradually devouting it. She hummed as she worked, satisfied by the physical exertion and by proving herself a worthy member of the team.

A quarter hour later, the growing rhythm and harmony of the work were shattered by the sound of the Delta's engine stuttering and screaming. Valena turned and watched in horror as it wallowed into a soft patch in the trail. Willy gunned the motor and cranked the wheel hard left and right, making things infinitely worse. The huge vehicle flexed wildly on its point of articulation, digging itself deeper and deeper into the snow while Edith collapsed onto the load and hung on for dear life. The wheels spun faster and faster, the frame thrashed, and the entire machine sank down and down into the snow, digging itself in past its mammoth hubcaps.

Hilario whipped his snow machine around and thundered toward the Delta, hollering for him to stop, waving his arms. Wee Willy either could not hear or was not listening, and kept the monstrous beast thrashing. Finally, as the axles began to disappear, he stopped the vehicle, climbed out, shambled twenty feet off the trail, and sat down in the snow. He did not move or speak but instead just sat there, staring off across the ice.

Far down the trail, Dave turned the Challenger around and made a slow approach, ready to smooth the trail once the Delta was freed.

Valena got off her snow machine, walked over to the Delta, and began to kick loose snow away from around the wheels. "Got a shovel?" she asked Edith, who was very slowly climbing down off the load. "I've seen this kind of problem before on my grandfather's farm. Dead of winter, he once got a tractor trailer stuck out in the pasture. We dug away the loose stuff, got a low-angle slope, set the vehicle in granny gear, and drove it on out."

"Sounds like a plan," said Hilario, producing a shovel from underneath the back seat of the Delta.

They took turns digging.

Wee Willy sat and stared away to the south.

After taking her second turn with the shovel, Edith said, "I'll be back in a minute. I'm ChapStick dependent, and I left it in my other ball gown."

Valena asked Hilario, "Why do you guys let him get away with this crap? I don't see Dave letting him get away with this. For that matter, why am I doing this for him?"

"You? You're just a show-off. Dave had his fill of Willy long ago. Me, I don't get excited about Willy 'cause I figure he got dropped on his head somewhere along the line. And Edith? She's just shaping her charge. She's pretty even-tempered, and she knows that no matter how much this may look like a simple job of ramming flags into the snow, each and every moment it's also a matter of survival. Somebody gets twisted a little too tight out here, sometimes it's better to give them a chance to cool off." He laughed. "And we all know there's plenty of cooling off you can do around here."

"Yeah, but why not send along a stronger team member?"

Hilario laughed again, with an edge this time. "The Boss sent him along as sort of a morale booster. Hah. Total waste of a perfectly good boondoggle, if you ask me. I think he just wanted him out of Mac Town before someone murdered him. Okay, your turn with the shovel again."

With the snow excavated into a ramp, Valena had the pleasure of driving the Delta out of the rut Wee Willy had made, and Dave got to work with the Challenger and goose filling in the hole. When they were ready to proceed again, Edith took a turn at the wheel of the Delta and put Wee Willy on the top of the load tossing flags, and Valena and Hilario went back at it with the pikes.

The wind continued to rise. Clouds now filled the southern horizon. Streamers of snow wailed past them at an angle to the trail, immediately smoothing the tracks left by their vehicles.

By 1750 hours, they were climbing the lower slopes of Black Island. With relief, Edith made her call to Mac Ops while Dave dropped the goose from the Challenger and Hilario and Valena put the covers on the snow machines. They had set ten miles of flags, and they were a half-hour ahead of deadline. Wee Willy climbed along the side of the cab and heaved himself inside. Hilario climbed into the Challenger with Dave, and Valena joined Edith in the Delta for the ride up the steep pitch of bare rock road that led to the station.

Edith gave Valena a pat on the shoulder. "You're a real trooper," she said. "You didn't have to do anything but drive, but you busted your butt for us all afternoon. Thank you."

"You're welcome."

"Okay, then, next stop, Black Island Station. Hold onto your hat; the wind here knows no mercy. The food's amazingly good for a dry camp, and if you don't mind a little coarse language, the station manager's a kitten, but the bunkhouse . . . well, it's not my fault, so I won't apologize."

Valena realized that she was grinning. She was the happiest she had felt in years.

24

In McMurdo, Ted finished locking up the blasting equipment for the day and indulged himself in a regal stretch, pulling the front of his Carhartt parka taut. It had been a good day. The afternoon's blast had gone off textbook perfect, the heavy equipment operators tasked to him had moved the rubble quickly and efficiently, and Wilbur had not pissed him off even once. It was time for a quick shower, a hearty dinner, and a shot or two of good whiskey. The only blemish on the day was the crushing news that the man who had turned up lost on the ice was dead. *On second thought,* Ted decided, *I'll make that four shots from my secret stash of single malt.*

As he started down the hill toward his dormitory, Ted spotted the unmistakable form of Cupcake coming uphill toward him. There was a man next to her, a beaker by the look of him: big red, black wind pants, beard. Cupcake raised an arm and waved to him, the sort of stop-where-you-are motion that says, You're the guy we're coming to see. *What now?* Ted wondered.

"Ted!" Cupcake called out. "Wait!"

Ted hadn't realized that he had begun sidling toward an escape route until she spoke. "Who's your friend?" he asked.

"This is the Padre," she said.

The man stepped forward quickly and offered a gloved hand to be shaken. "Jim Skehan. Glaciologist out of DRI."

Ted tensed. Having someone offer the answers to McMurdo's first two questions of acquaintance caught him off guard. It indicated trouble, somehow. Why was it important what the guy did or where he was from?

And then the dime dropped and he realized that this man must be a colleague of Emmett Vanderzee's. What in hell was Cupcake up to now? He waited for her to explain herself.

Ted waited.

Skehan watched him wait. Something about the glaciologist's face bothered Ted. Skehan's almost expressionless mug, perhaps, or was it the laser-sharp eyes that floated in that impassiveness?

Cupcake said, "Okay, enough with the alpha dog act, fellas. Woof, woof, now you're friends."

"*Father* Jim?"

"He's a Jesuit. Get over it. "Father Jim and I have been out to the place where we found Steve," she said. We found something important out there. We found tracks."

Ted's eyes shifted to Cupcake. "After that blow?"

Skehan said, "Even a footprint compacts the snow just a little, moving it from snow toward ice. And more importantly, the layers are disturbed by anything that transits over the snow. Maybe you'd have a hard time finding penguin footprints out there, but anything as heavy as a man, or certainly a vehicle, will leave a trace. Then, unless the wind scours down below the level of compaction, you can still see the tracks. If they get buried, you can cut a small trench to find them."

"So let me get this straight: You two were able to find the exact place again in all that ice and went at it like a couple of archaeologists, or something."

Skehan shrugged. "Actually, the helicopter helped us. When it landed and took off to pick up Steve, it blew the newest layers of snow away. The spot wasn't that hard to find. Dorothy here isn't exactly a new hand, either."

Cupcake said, "The point is, we were able to examine the tracks around where Steve was lying."

Hunger to know what had happened to Steve won out over ego. "All right, what did you see?" he asked.

Cupcake said, "He was near the flagged route that leads out to Cape Evans, but not on it, so the footprints that led up to him had been cut into fresh, uncompacted snow." She turned to Skehan. "Tell him the rest."

Skehan said, "We went to the hospital afterward, and they still had Steve's boots. He had been wearing his own boots, not USAP issue. They had a different tread pattern from the ones we found out there. The pattern we found was exactly the same as FDX—you know, the blue boots."

"Beaker boots," said Ted. "Were the tracks bigger, smaller, or the same size as Steve's?"

"We didn't get perfect recovery on any of the tracks. What we saw were fragmental. When you walk in stiff-soled boots, you either walk flat-footed or you kind of mash the snow around, rolling off the toe and crushing the rest of your print. And whoever dropped him there took certain pains to step back toward the flag route using the same footsteps, which further disrupted them, and then there were the footprints of the rescuers. But we were still able to find three good prints that tell the story. What we could see seemed bigger than Steve's boots."

"And there were marks where Steve's feet were dragged across the snow," Cupcake added.

Skehan nodded. "Whoever did it was in a hurry. It was a hasty job. You can just see the little wheels in his head going, 'I've just hit this guy across the head, so what am I going to do with him? I don't want him waking up, and if I hit him again it sure won't look like an accident anymore, so what should I do? Let's see . . . I'd better let him freeze to death. To make sure that happens, I'll put him somewhere they won't find him in time. Now, where's a good place? It has to look like something he could have done on his own, so dumping him in a blowhole for some Weddell seal isn't quite the ticket. How about just dumping him near the flag route a couple miles out past the point? No one's going out there anytime soon, not in this weather, and when they find him, they'll just think he headed the wrong way in the storm.' "

Ted shook his head. "One little problem: the storm. If nobody else could get out there and back in that weather without getting lost, then how could our killer do it?"

Skehan said, I'd use GPS. I've done it myself in Greenland. You need to have mapped the route beforehand, set your waypoints, but you can do it."

"We're pretty far south here, lad. The satellite coverage can be a little sketchy."

"Maybe I get lucky."

"Nasty," said Ted. "I suppose it could work, on a long shot. Then let me ask another question: Why are you two telling me this? Why aren't you going straight to the Chalet with this?"

"We'll get around to telling Bellamy," said Skehan. "But you know the party line over there. They don't want the publicity. The muzzle he put on Emmett's arrest was appalling."

"But once again, why *me?*"

"Because you were there last year," said Cupcake. "Or almost. You know the players. We've done some figuring, and almost all the other people who were at Emmett's camp when the man died were in or around McMurdo yesterday when this happened. Calvin, Dave, and William were here. Sheila had come in by helicopter the day before to do her laundry and pick up supplies and was held up by the storm until evening. Bob Schwartz's flight to WAIS Divide was canceled, so he was here. Manny Roig led the SAR team. Dan Lindemann was supposed to be in the Dry Valleys, but I'm checking on him. The only person who was up at that camp when the man died last year who has a bomb-proof alibi for yesterday is Emmett himself, because he's locked up in Hawaii."

Ted said, "And what's your agenda?"

Skehan said, "Simple: I want Emmett's name cleared. He's more than a colleague, he's a friend, but even putting that aside . . . okay, I'll be entirely candid. When Frink attacked Emmett in the *Financial News,* he attacked all of us. He attacked the whole planet. He distorted the facts. He distorted how science is done. He was just plain wrong. He was selling a story designed to woo readers into believing that scientists who study climate don't know what they're doing. He was telling everyone to just sit back and keep comfy and keep burning all the oil and coal they want."

"It's that simple?"

Skehan stared him down. "He was supporting the guys who say, 'I don't care if greenhouse gasses heat up the atmosphere, because when we build our 120 new coal-fired plants in the United States, and more in China, yet more in India, we make money, so to hell with our grandkids! Let them make money selling ice to cool us back down!' Of course, there will be no ice left for them to sell, but that's progress!"

Ted said, "I'm not arguing with you, Skehan, but I was one of the last people to see that man alive. I didn't see any horns coming out of his head, and he isn't the one who wrote that article."

Skehan said, "Do you want any more deaths out here? No. And if we can connect the two deaths, then Emmett's in the clear, because he wasn't here for the second one."

Ted said, "But that doesn't clear him of the first one. Not really. And what if they aren't connected? Sounds like you have no concern for who killed Steve. After all, he wasn't a scientist. He was only support staff. A tradesman. A Carhartt."

Skehan closed his eyes. "Ted, I don't know who bit your ass," he said, keeping his voice soft and slow, "but I've worked on this ice five seasons, and two more in Greenland. When one is on the ice, death is always right there waiting for us. "He opened his eyes again." If we die by mischance, or through sickness, that's a tragedy that affects us all. But we don't often die out here, simply because we are a community. We work together, and live almost inside each other's pockets. It's a time-honored tradition, a necessity, that dates clear back to Scott and before. I do this work in part for that fellowship and that sense of shared honor, heartless intellectual though I may appear." He pulled off his right glove and reached out between them, palm up. "And if someone's out here purposefully causing people to die—out of cowardice, malice, greed, his motive matters not— I want him stopped. Is that good enough for you?"

Ted stared into Skehan's eyes for a long moment, then removed his own right glove and met him flesh to flesh. "I'm in."

❖

MAJOR MARILYN WOOD perched on a straight-backed chair in the conference room at the Airlift Wing offices, nursing her fifth mug of coffee for the day. "The Hummingbird," the others called her, when they weren't calling her "Wrong Way Wood," which inversely referred to her prowess as a navigator. It also made a joke about the strange business of flying "north" to the south, following the grid navigational system.

She blinked wearily, having just made the transit from New Zealand to the ice for the umpteenth time, returning with Major Hugh Muller from Christchurch after their depressing flight north with the dying tractor driver. Major Waylon Bentley, finished pouring his own cup of coffee and joined them.

Marilyn knew from years working with the Airlift Wing that Hugh preferred his caffeine fix in the form of cola and Waylon drank only water. One thing he liked about Antarctica was the ready supply of purified water that came out of the reverse osmosis system down the hill at the desalinization plant.

The three majors sat quietly together.

"Okay, this is what we've got," Marilyn said, breaking their meditative silence. "They had eight souls on board: Vanderzee, his graduate students Schwartz and Lindemann, Sheila the cook, two guys out of Fleet Ops— Dave Fitzgerald and the guy they call Wee Willy—and Calvin Hart. Oh, and of course, the deceased. They call for a replacement Gamow thirty-six hours after we pull the blaster out. It takes us six hours to get it to them, but they never find it, or so they claim. Waylon, you saw it this year when they dug it up."

Waylon twisted in his chair. "Yeah, the bundle was intact. Medical rig, pallet, fuel drum, and tracking beacon. The chute was buried underneath it, all crumpled up. It was absolutely not the result of a chance trick of the wind. No way."

Hugh said, "And the beacon had been disabled."

"Disconnected," said Waylon.

"You're sure," said Marilyn.

"Damn certain sure," Waylon affirmed. "And here's the thing: it wasn't like it had been smashed by chance or yanked apart by an amateur. Whoever did it not only turned it off, but knew how it worked, and he had to know what the thing was in the first place. The wires were neatly disconnected. So it was either ex-military or someone with electronics experience."

"But how did it all get buried?" asked Hugh. "I mean, all that weighed something. Was it all still rigged together?"

"Yes. The cargo straps were still in place. So you're right, it was heavy. Wrong Way, did you get into the loadmaster's records on that?"

Marilyn nodded. "It was rigged to exceed four hundred pounds. And have you ever tried to push a pallet when it was loaded? It's not like it's on skis."

Hugh said, "I've looked up the weather records. The wind was blowing from the camp toward the place where it was buried, but we dropped nice and low to minimize drift. Even if we were off in our calculations, someone still had to move that mass three hundred meters at least. So we're still talking major effort. With apologies to the fairer sex, Marilyn, I think that eliminates the cook."

"Unless she wasn't working alone," Marilyn said.

Waylon scratched his chin. "I hadn't thought of that. You're right, we haven't considered the conspiracy angle. We keep thinking it was one person acting alone. That rather opens the field."

They all looked at each other.

"They had a snow machine out there," said Marilyn.

Waylon pondered this. "Man, I would not like to try to drag a bundle with one of those hogs in that weather. Give me a nice, warm cockpit any day."

"Right," said Hugh. "So any way you slice it, we've got a defeated bundle. So it comes down to this: which one of them had the technology or the know-how to a) find it in full blizzard conditions, b) bury it, and c) defeat the beacon while he was at it? Surely that's got to narrow the field a little, now, doesn't it?"

Waylon said, "I'm still thinking ex-military."

"And trained in navigation," said Marilyn.

Hugh gave her a grin. "That would be your department. What would it take?"

She thought a while. "Well, if he knew to listen for a beacon, and had the technology for that, *and* had GPS . . ."

Hugh swatted his knee. "Just a few 'ands' there, eh? Surely if we can crack into the records—"

"Which we can't necessarily do, Hugh." Waylon said.

"Always the pessimist. Surely *when* we crack into service records, this guy will glow in the dark."

Waylon shook his head. "Hugh, this isn't a load of mousetraps this time. We're talking cutting the chain of command, we're talking special favors, we're talking military service and Raytheon personnel documents. That's not exactly according to Hoyle, my man. Just what do you think is the likelihood of pulling that off? And then you've got to figure out how to get the information into the hands of someone who can do something with it. What are you thinking, the colonel's going to phone the feds and say, 'We think you got the wrong guy?' Nice way to make us all very popular."

Hugh stood up. "I've got that all covered," he said, his eyes bright with excitement. "Remember Doris over in IT? She and I go back a ways. And once we get that information, she can pass it to Valena."

They all stared at each other awhile.

"Have a heart, Hugh," said Marilyn. "She's a nice kid, and perhaps she'd like to live to grow old."

"You got any better ideas?"

"No."

"Then let's get started."

25

SHEILA TUTTLE WAITED AT THE AIRLOCK DOOR AT BLACK ISLAND STA-
tion to greet the arriving traverse crew. She was blond and heavily freckled
and muscular and almost six feet tall and withstood the gale without a
parka, but she had to shout to be heard over the wind, her Australian accent twisting around their ears. "Ye'll want to take your gear out to the
bunkhouse now, before it blows any harder." She gestured toward a
smaller structure a hundred meters away that was anchored to the rock by
stout cables. "Then get on inside the station here, and we'll talk about ye
dinnah!"

All but Valena and Dave ignored her first instruction and instead
headed straight into the station house muttering words like, "Cocoa," and
"Whiskey." Dave was busy on the back of the Delta setting up the hose to
drain the water tank into its counterpart inside the station.

Sheila turned toward Valena. "So this is y' chance, woman!" she roared.
"They's only eight bunks out there, they's five of ye, and I got three
more already staying there while they dick around with the transmitter.
Go on out there and get a lower bunk before these louts double back
on ye!"

Valena grabbed her gear and turned to regard the bunkhouse and the
hundred yards of wind-scoured volcanic rock that lay between her and it.
It was a prefabricated trailer of sorts, an unadorned box made of naked
plywood with a few square windows, mounted on a chassis that rode on
skids instead of wheels. The cables that held it to the rock were as big
around as her arms. Beyond it, through a parting in the ragged clouds, a

short stretch of the ice-encrusted Transantarctic Mountains gleamed coldly in the chill evening sunlight.

On cue, the wind increased its roar and colossal buffeting. In the foreground stood a pair of wind generators. The angle of each generator was governed by a heavy spring that flexed with increasing wind, feathering the blades as the wind grew too strong for the mechanism. The current blow had laid them back within thirty degrees of horizontal. "How hard is it blowing?" yelled Valena.

"Sixty miles per hour," replied Sheila, at the top of her voice. "If ye so fascinated by meteorology, ye can watch our digital readout in the station house. We like it better than watching TV, and as ye can see by all these satellite dishes here, we've got the best reception on the continent. Now, git! I'll be waiting for ye inside; it en't a fit day out for idle chitchat."

Valena staggered off across the ground toward the bunkhouse. She had to adopt an awkwardly broad stance so that she could lean her shoulder into the wind and yet have a leg outboard to catch herself should the gale suddenly slacken and let go of her mass. At the steps to the bunkhouse, she had to brace herself again to heave the door open. She could imagine the people who had delivered the structure to this lone prominence trying to decide which way to mount the door: into the wind, where it would be torn off its hinges, or against it, where it would take Charles Atlas to open it? Or had they not thought at all and merely jammed it in where the ground happened to be level?

Inside, the atmosphere was dim, cold, and oddly suffocating. The small space had four double bunks crammed into it, and each window was covered by a heavy blackout blind, which nevertheless leaked light all around the edges.

"Well, it ain't much, but it's got character," she said out loud. There was something about the noise of the wind in this rawboned domicile that made her want to speak even though no one could hear her.

As Sheila had said, three out of the four bunks had already been claimed, all of them lower. Valena heaved Steve's sleeping bag and her backpack onto the fourth, then tested the mattress to see if it was acceptable. It wasn't much, but she suspected that the others were about the same. As her eyes adjusted, she noticed writings all over the walls, rowdy inscriptions by prior inhabitants. There were several choice limericks extolling the wonders of Black Island Station.

She headed back outside.

The station house was put together in sections, connected by passageways to two geodesic domes, which she assumed held satellite dishes. Valena stepped in through a long, narrow hallway lined with coat hooks, barrels for recyclables, and crude wooden shelves stacked with supplies. From there, she found her way into a large room that was kitchen, dining room, and lounge all in one. Wee Willy had loaded himself into an armchair and was watching an Armed Forces TV program. Hilario was playing cards with a couple of men she hadn't seen before. Dave and Edith had settled down at the table to share a bottle of Crown Royal with the station manager, a balding man in his fifties with a sweet smile. He greeted Valena with words that added up to "hello" but were studded with an astonishing riff of four-letter words.

Sheila cut across him with a more formal greeting. "Welcome to Black Island Station. Do ye have any special dietary requirements?" she asked.

"No," answered Valena. "I could eat shoe leather about now and savor it."

"Not on the menu. We are having pot roast of beef tonight, mac and cheese—homemade sauce, mind ye—and a nice mess of carrots, peas, and onions. For dessert I've made a berry pie, but there are cookies left over from lunch if ye prefer."

"I am in heaven."

"Nay ye aren't, but ye can see it from here. Dinnah be served in half an hour. Ye like a wee tour of the facilities while ye waiting?"

"Please."

Sheila led the way through a tight catacombs of hallways. "That's the shower room," she said, pointing into a dark little room about the size of a locker. "We don't partake of it often. Not enough water. If ye insist, kindly keep it to a minimum. Get wet quick as ye can, turn off the water, soap up, turn it on again briefly to rinse. Now, down here in this other room, we have the toilets. Ladies' urinal here, gents' there. Those are for the liquids. Anything solid, ye want this other option. Let me show you how to tie up the plastic bag when ye're done, so ye don't have any excess air to it. It all goes in this resealable barrel, which in turn goes out on the Delta with ye. What ye bring here ye takes with ye when ye go. Okay, now for the tour of what this station's all about."

Sheila turned left into a room crammed floor to ceiling with wiring.

"This is the telecommunications brain for all McMurdo," she said. "The fellows out there in the living room are adjusting the satellite dish to increase the bandwidth. And now, the pièce de résistance, the most amazing part of this whole mess." She indicated a laptop computer that sat on a shelf surrounded by hookups. "Ye just punch these two little keys, and it shuts down telecommunications for the whole shebang."

"The morning after I arrived I couldn't call out, because the lines were down."

"Yeah. The blokes weren't popular for shutting it down during everyone's day off. Now come along here. Ye've got to see the dish. But first, put on this hearing protection. The panels of the geodesic dome get to rattling a bit. When the wind blows, it's fit to puree ye brain."

Sheila handed Valena a set of ear protection muffs and led her through another airlock into the larger of the two domes.

Even with the muffs, the auditory channels to Valena's brain were instantly overwhelmed. The hammering of the wind on the panels of the dome was immense. Overpowering. Concussive. All that and colder than cold.

Valena stopped and stood still a moment, struggling to get her sensory bearings, trying to get a fix on what the noise reminded her of. Thunder wasn't quite it, nor was the largest drum roll on record or the pounding of eight diesel engines on the biggest drill rig she had ever visited. Standing underneath a metal bridge as heavy traffic rolled overhead came to mind, but it was infinitely louder than that, and constant, more frenetic, and she was locked up inside it.

She tilted her head backward, staring at the dish the dome protected. It was huge and tipped almost up onto its edge as advertised.

Sheila did not even try to speak to her over the din. After half a minute, she indicated that she had had enough and was going back into the room with all the wiring.

Valena followed quickly. She wanted a moment alone with Sheila to question her without being overheard by the others, and she had let her curiosity about the station burn up most of her chance. "Sheila," she began, once they had left the rumbling dome and they could hear each other again. "I've come here for more than just the tour, which was of course marvelous."

"Ye want to talk about what it was like last year, up in Emmett's camp."

Valena stopped short. "You know?"

"Yes. I've had an e-mail today from Jim Skehan. Nice fellah, that Jim. He told me to keep an eye out for ye."

"I'm stunned."

"Don't be. Some days the man of the cloth comes out in him."

"Man of the—?"

Sheila made a dismissive gesture. "What ye need to know is this: whatever your federal agents say Emmett might have done, that's a load of horse manure. Emmett hated what had been written about him—he wanted that man sent home alive and with the facts. He was obsessive about it. 'Make sure ye have the best foods for him,' he'd tell me. 'I want him fat and happy, so he'll change his story from fantasy to facts. This is hard, cold science, and he's got to be kept alert and comfortable enough to learn, so he can report what is true.' He'd go on and on, if ye let him."

"I see."

"Yeah, it was quite the situation. The man shows up and starts showing the symptoms right quick. Down he goes, and here comes the storm. Your Emmett, he was in a pickle. Sure, he thought the man was a prize anus, but he wanted to send him home a living and wiser anus. He jumped to that radio and arranged that airdrop so quick the handset was smoking."

"Then who buried the bundle?"

"Buried it? Is that the story?"

Valena winced, realizing that she had already halfway betrayed the trust of the Airlift Wing. "I've heard that rumor," she said.

"Not possible."

"Why not?"

"There was a storm on. It must have slid into a crevasse."

"But was anyone out of your sight long enough to have *pushed* it into a crevasse?"

Sheila fixed a look on Valena that would have fried eggs. "Who would do a thing like that?" she demanded. Then she closed her eyes and sighed with exasperation, and spoke more slowly and distinctly, as if trying to communicate with someone who was mentally impaired. "People were coming and going from tent to tent. We had lines stretched so ye could do that. I didn't keep track of their comings and goings."

"Who was with you the most?"

Sheila continued in a tone that told Valena she had answered these questions too many times. "We had the patient in there, to keep him warm. Had the stove running constantly. We had put it down on the floor and laid him out on the preparation table above it to keep him up off the cold, though that only raised him to something right around freezing. I wasn't paying much attention to who was there and who was not. Emmett was there with him continually, except when he went out."

"Did you hear the plane go overhead?"

"Aye."

"And Emmett went out to try to find the bundle."

"Yes. Maybe forty-five minutes or an hour after we heard it, he saw a break in the storm. He tied up with a rope and off he went. Never found it. He came back almost crying, he did. And he was right there caring for that man until the end. I've known Emmett maybe three seasons, and I've never seen him so distraught. Ye've got to understand—"

"I am quickly coming to understand. It's like everyone down here is part of one very tightly knit family."

"Yes. People here may be quirky, or eccentric even, or some of them downright antisocial, but when push comes to shove, they're there for ye."

"What about the others?" Valena asked. "Cal Hart, the grad students, and so forth. How did they take it?"

"Ye want to take a look at Schwartz and Lindemann, especially the latter. They haven't the loyalty I would hope for in that situation, and ye should have heard the way they spoke to the man. There was trouble between them and Emmett—and Lindemann, he got in terrible arguments with that reporter."

"What about?"

"Everything. About the work they were doing. About the state of journalism. About the weather. About the food. About the nose on his face."

"Can you recall anything in particular?"

"Nay. I tried to tune them out, y'know? I had work to do."

"What about the others?" Valena asked. "The men who were along to handle the equipment and the heavy lifting."

"Well, Willy there, he didn't show any emotion, but that's typical of him, and Dave, well he's a gent. And Cal—"

"Wait. You said Willy. The man's name was William."

"Nay, on his birth certificate it says that, maybe, but most everyone calls him Wee Willy. I can tell ye, I wasn't any too happy to see him at my door this evening."

Valena pointed toward the main room of the station. "That man out there. In the living room. Watching TV. He was at Emmett's camp?"

"Yes. And Dave, who's out there drinking with the man."

"That Dave?" *I was afraid of this*, thought Valena. *It's what's been bugging me right along.*

"Well, it's a common enough name, I suppose, but . . . if ye ask me, I'd stay away from chatting about this with just anyone, my dear. In fact, I'd stop about where ye are."

"Why?"

"Because if ye're right about it being foul play, and it wasn't Emmett, and I know it wasn't me, then it could be either of those louts. Hell, Willy could kill ye without even meaning to! All he'd have to do is fall on ye! But I do know this: it's a long way back to McMurdo through the dead zone, with too many bits of heavy equipment that could fly loose and hurt ye, know what I mean? And too many miles of ice that can kill ye either quick or slow as ye please. D'ye hear me?"

Valena stared into the cook's icy blue eyes. Her mind seemed suddenly to be running very, very slowly, like molasses exposed to the outside air. "Yes," she said. "Loud and clear."

26

VALENA FOUND DINNER HARD TO EAT AND EVEN MORE DIFFICULT TO digest. She barely tasted Sheila's cooking, being more focused on her words. Valena had torn off across the loneliest part of the planet looking for a killer—what had she been thinking of?

The others sat around the table wolfing down the savory meat and vegetables and pie, and called for more. Valena stared at the tabletop, pretending to read the map that had been placed there underneath a sheet of Plexiglas, trying to cope with the realization that she was in a tiny station house in an increasing gale on a tiny island of naked rock at the bottom of the earth.

She had known that the man named Dave could be the David who had been at Emmett's camp but had let the idea drift. Why? Because he was nice-looking and moved like . . . well, like someone with whom she'd enjoy dancing? Because he didn't take any guff from Willy? Because she wanted him to like her so that she'd know she was acceptable? She hazarded a glance at him, only to find that his eyes were already on her. He smiled at her. It seemed a calm and friendly smile. Was this the smile of a man who would kill another?

Valena looked quickly back at her plate. And Sheila, what of her? She was forceful, decisive, brash. *Can I trust everything—or, for that matter, anything—that she told me?*

Valena said a silent prayer, hoping that nothing she was thinking showed on her face. The whole maze of interactions among these people spun in her head in a dizzy array. She felt like she had stumbled through an imaginary door into a barroom fight in some Wild West movie just after a shot has been fired, with the gun smoke still hanging in the air. Who had pulled the trigger? And would he pull that trigger again?

What had she gotten herself into?

Edith cracked into her musing. "You're mighty quiet tonight," she said.

Valena managed a faint smile. "Just tired, I guess."

"You did great out there," said Hilario.

"I enjoyed it," said Valena.

"Can I buy you a drink?" asked Dave, curling his hand around the bottle of New Zealand wine he and the others were currently emptying.

Valena glanced his way, trying to determine whether his overture was in earnest or just good manners. His eyes were dark and soft, the kind that could hide a multitude of secrets. She shook her head. "No. I think I'll just turn in early." Having thus spoken, she pushed back her chair, thanked Sheila for the dinner, and headed out of the room. She braved the toilet, then found her parka in the mass of red and tan outerwear, opened the door into the wind, and headed across the way to the bunkhouse, adjusting her lean as she struggled to remain upright in what was now almost a hurricane-force wind.

The bunkhouse heater appeared to have given up the small ghost of warmth it had previously offered, but once she doffed her parka and slid into the giant sleeping bag, her warmth instantly returned. She pulled off her outer layer of thermal underwear, rolled it up for a pillow, put her head on it, and then rolled over so that the part of the sleeping bag that had been designed to lie underneath her head would instead lie atop it like a hood, covering her face. She did not wish to talk with anyone who came into the bunkhouse that night.

What seemed like hours later, she still lay awake as, one at a time, the others came in, each taking pains to be quiet except Willy, who, as he climbed into the bunk above her, put one huge stockinged foot up against her neck and rocked the bunk bed like he was trying to wrestle it to the ground. Fleetingly she wondered if the bed would take his weight. At length, the muffled sounds of sleep filled the room, and someone began to snore. Valena lay awake on into the night, wondering what, if anything, she could do to help Emmett Vanderzee—or, for that matter, herself.

27

DAVE LAY IN HIS SLEEPING BAG LISTENING TO THE SOFT SOUNDS OF breathing coming from the bunks all around him, trying to decide which inhalations and exhalations might be Valena's. The knowledge that she lay somewhere quite near him worked on him like an electric current, burning him wide awake.

He had drunk more than made good sense, trying to douse that fire, but instead, it had loosened his inhibitions and addled his thoughts. He had tried being the last one to walk out to the bunkhouse, letting the wind whip at his open jacket, hoping thereby to dispel what he was feeling, but the experience had only excited him further. The wild brilliance of the Antarctic midnight had glistened off the distant mountains, and he had lifted his eyes to see if he could catch a glimpse of the moon. He missed this nearest celestial body while on the ice; somehow, he could never spot it, and by this late into the Antarctic spring, the position of the sun began to lose meaning also. All spring it spiraled upward into the sky, and, making its zenith by late December, it then began its lazy descent back toward the horizon. He was sure that, no matter how many seasons he returned to the ice, he would never get used to this strange fact of the interaction of sun, earth, and latitude.

You're an incurable romantic, he told himself. Then, a darker voice within spoke: *you come all the way down here and it doesn't change a thing. You're in paradise and you'll screw it up. And she won't want you with your past. Give up.*

Now, lying in the darkness, he took these thoughts and pressed them like a nail through his consciousness, trying to keep his mind and heart from wandering, but thoughts of her uncertain smile filled his imagination. He listened, imagining that he could hear her breath flowing in and out of her strong, curvaceous body.

Was she dreaming? What dreams did she dream, lying so close to him? Or was she awake, listening to him breathing, too? Did she feel one tenth the attraction he felt for her? Or did she avoid him because she found him unacceptable, uneducated, rough? He liked to think it was because she was shy, or perhaps distracted with the problems his roommate Matt had told him about. Imagine, coming all the way down here only to find that ol' Emmett had been jailed.

During the long day driving the snow machines and Challenger along the trail from Mac Town to Black Island, he had caught glimpses of her. How fine and competent she had looked driving that Delta! And when she'd climbed onto that snow machine, she'd taken to it like a rodeo queen. She had a natural grace. He liked her determination, her will, her desire to learn.

But she was not from his place in life. She had a degree from a university and was working to get another. She would come to know a man who worked beside her in some laboratory and smile at him someday, and that would be that.

But it was more than that. Coming to Antarctica with Emmett meant that she had found that one break in a million that would put her on top, and she would know prestige. He had walked across the university campus near his hometown, watching from afar as regally dressed people strolled into gala celebrations overflowing with class and confidence. With his thick workman's hands and sun-leathered skin, he could never walk that walk, and though he counted himself as reasonably intelligent and read as much and as often as he could, he could never talk that talk. With her grace and intellect, she would climb that ladder with ease.

Or perhaps she had been born to it, and driving the Delta was the exception to the rule. He imagined that her exotic looks spoke of the union of two professors at some foreign institute and a patrician upbringing.

The truth was that he knew almost nothing about her. Matt had had little to report from his evening with her at the Tractor Club, except that she had once driven an antique tractor on her grandfather's farm. She had probably said little else. It seemed her style.

Willy began to snore. Dave let out a breath, wondering why the man had ever been hired, much less hired back for a second season. Where had he learned such ham-fisted handling of equipment? The army? Another place that Dave had never been. His had been the lot to leave school early. He'd picked up his GED a few years later. It hadn't been hard to do. Getting along in the world after his drunken father had thrown him out at sixteen had been a whole lot harder.

He'd done well, considering, he knew that, but still, the limitations of his rough beginning had narrowed his options to just about exactly what he was doing. No matter. He loved Antarctica, and that would have to do.

He closed his eyes and turned onto his side, letting his arm curl up around his opposite shoulder, and waited until the comfort of tired muscles drew him into sleep.

28

VALENA AWOKE EARLY IN THE DARKNESS OF THE BUNKHOUSE, UNCERtain of the time. For a while she lay wrapped in the suddenly cloying warmth of her sleeping bag, trying to regain the escape that night should bring, but the grip of whatever had awakened her only increased. Had she been dreaming? She could not recall, but she felt a gnawing at her gut just like too many times in childhood when she'd awake in the night in a room with all the cousins. She told herself that wasn't it. Had the heat finally come on in the desperate old heater in the corner of the room? No, it was the wind. It had stopped, lessening the advective draw on the heater's capacities.

At length the sure knowledge that she would not get back to sleep descended upon her and she looked at her watch. It was 5:36 a.m., far too late to dig into her tiny toilet kit in search of the over-the-counter sleep aid she should have taken the evening before. She wasn't a chronic insomniac, but she had to admit that over the past year or so—since when? since starting graduate school?—she had risen early and nervous with increasing frequency.

The only thing for it was to get up and start her day. But her day was under the control of others—their schedule, and that of the weather. These thoughts added to her anxieties.

She decided to head over to the station house. There would be water for tea there, or coffee. She wiggled out of her bag so as not to make a noise letting down the zipper, dressed quickly, and headed out the door and across the yard.

Outside, the world was bright and rugged and still. The cold air wakened her further. She could see a hundred miles or more in all directions. To the south and west, the Transantarctic Mountains danced in glistening splendor, and to the north, across the stretch of sea ice, lay Ross Island, on which McMurdo languished. The island was a meringue of ice sliding in its infinitely slow pace downhill toward the sea. Beyond McMurdo Station, Mount Erebus raised its angry fist in constant eruption, marked this morning by a trail of vapor that slid away to the west. She had not previously seen it completely naked, devoid of its customary veils of clouds, and it was the first time in her life she had seen an actual volcanic eruption. She stared at it, for a moment not breathing, then turned slowly on one heel and absorbed her surroundings in one long panorama. In answer, the scene wrapped its majesty about her heart and kept it for its own.

She was still high from this experience ten minutes later as she slipped quietly into the kitchen in search of a way to warm herself. She found tea, cups, and a container of honey laid out right next to a self-heating teapot. As she plugged in the pot, she heard someone moving beyond the heavy drapes that separated the room from the sleeping quarters beyond.

The station manager emerged, shuffling slowly in a pair of fuzzy slippers with leopard spots, his eyes swollen from sleep. "Howja sleep?" His voice rasped with early morning and too much drink the evening before.

"Okay."

"Yer lying."

"Yeah."

"Sucks."

"Uh-huh."

"Find whatcha need?"

"Mm-hmm."

He arched his well-padded body into a stretch, moaning. "Sheila said to tell you there's an e-mail message for ya. She printed it out." He pointed with his elbow toward the computer stand.

Valena grabbed the page and sat down on the couch. Sheila had folded it three times, stapled it as many times across the middle, and written VALENA on it. Quickly, she picked out the staples, unfolded it, and read it. It was from Cal Hart.

You're looking to talk to everyone who was at Emmett's camp last season. I join you in wanting to know the truth. I can't tell you how shocked I am that Emmett was not here on my arrival. Please e-mail back saying when you'll be in from BI and I'll meet you at Crary. Cal

Well, check that one off the list of suspects, thought Valena, and then, an instant later, *But maybe this is a con, a try at misdirection!* She turned toward the station manager, who was now scratching at his armpits and belly. "Can I use this computer to send an e-mail?" she asked.

He swept one arm in a small but regal bow to indicate that it was hers for the asking. "But you won't get through, at least not right away."

"Why not?"

"Some asshole's switched the dish off."

"Someone turned off the dish?"

"Yeah. You know, back in the wiring room, where they've got that little laptop that controls our universe. Someone's decided it's funny to go in there and play God over all of McMurdo. Punched the two keys. We're incommunicado with the outside world until our techs wake up."

"Has it been off all night?"

"I suppose so. I found it the last thing, as I was making my rounds before I went to bed."

"But who would want to do that?"

"Well, I sure didn't do it, and Sheila wouldn't, so it was probably one of you idiots, and as you can see, I'm not yet dressed to greet the world, so unless you'd like to sashay over to the bunkhouse and shake sleeping bags until you find the right guy, then we'll just have to wait. Meanwhile, you can send your messages, but they just won't reach their targets until we get the system back up."

Valena sat down in the task chair in front of the computer desk and turned on the machine. It was old and booted slowly. While she waited, she looked again at Cal's note, and then more closely at the paper on which it had been printed. Some of the holes through which the staples had been punched had been punched twice, slightly widening the holes.

Somebody had read her message and had tried to reclose it without being caught.

Sheila emerged from her room, scowling like she had a headache as she approached the task of making breakfast, but as Valena opened her mouth to speak to her, one of the men who was working with the satellite dish came in from the bunkhouse and spoke first, wishing Sheila a good morning.

"Screw you and the horse you rode in on," Sheila snarled in return. "All your fault with that cheap New Zealand pinot."

The man laughed. "No one told you to mix it with whiskey."

"And now ye're my father. Ye want breakfast, or are ye thinking maybe ye'd rather a day without food?"

"Eggs over easy," he said.

"We have no fresh eggs and ye know it. Ye'll have mummified bacon and waffles like the rest of us mortals."

The station manager wandered back into the room and addressed the tech. "Oh, so you decided to get up, did you? Well, some bozo turned your system off during the night. Would you mind turning it back on? The lady here is trying to e-mail her pen pals, and I'm sure that little research station down there on Ross Island would like to get back in touch with the real world, too."

The tech was busy sucking up coffee. He stared at the manager over the mug. "You're kidding me."

"No, I'm Mary Poppins. And Sheila, you've got to quit showing people how to switch the damned thing off. It was only a matter of time before someone decided to muck with it."

The tech wandered back toward the wiring room, grumbling.

Valena watched the station manager's progress toward the coffeepot, hoping that he would leave the room for a while. She wanted desperately to speak to Sheila again, to ask her when she had left the note and who might possibly have opened it. To ask a thousand questions. But she needed privacy, too and that was a scarce quantity here in Antarctica.

She turned and looked at the cook, who was now opening a rasher of precooked bacon that she had left thawing on the kitchen counter the evening before. Feeling Valena's eyes on her, she looked up. She was not smiling. She lifted a long, sharp knife, the type used to chop large amounts of vegetables, and brought it down with authority.

Valena returned her gaze to the computer, which was finally ready. Hoping that no one would look over her shoulder at what was on the screen, she opened her e-mail to write to Cal but found other messages waiting for her that interested her much more. The first was from Em Hansen:

> Valena, I thought I told you to quit. Oh well, if you insist on being as stupid as I am, here's my next best recommendation: stick with evidence that only you can understand, and gather it in a way that looks like you're only doing the job you were actually sent there to do. You have your undergraduate degree in geology, right? Well, think Sherlock Holmes. Was there any dirt in the dead man's shoes? Where did it come from? Where else did he get to? But watch your back. It's so easy to get all het up with crime being wrong that one forgets that, while the tragedy has already occurred, it's a gift that can keep on giving. Stay safe (hah), Em

Valena tucked that bit of wisdom into her brain and opened the next message. It was from James Skehan, dated Wednesday evening:

> Valena
>
> Thought you might like an update regarding Emmett. He has been formally charged with murdering Sweeny which we both know is a crock. I need to talk with you as soon as you get back here Thursday. I'm going to check out a beeper, so call me on it the moment you get in. I'll leave the number on your desk in Crary. Meanwhile, watch your back and don't ask questions while on the trail. You are traveling with two possible suspects.
>
> Jim

Valena closed this message immediately. She sat back and tried to think. Should she reply? In her haze of fatigue, she could not sort out what to think about any of the messages or what to write in a return. As she sat still, listening to her heartbeat pounding in her ears, all possibilities jammed on one logistical particular: she did not know when she would be arriving back in McMurdo. She was not in charge of that schedule. *No one is in charge of anything in Antarctica. The continent itself is in charge!*

"How'd you sleep?" Edith asked as she sat down at the table. She looked fresh as the proverbial daisy.

Valena squeezed her eyes shut. "Fine."

"Nothing like a day of good physical work to tucker you out."

"Right."

"Go get your gear together out of the bunkhouse and then come and have breakfast. We'll be loading up the empties to take back to Mac Town and be getting on the road ASAP. There's another storm coming, and I want to be in Gallagher's with a pool cue in my hands when it hits."

"Check." Valena logged off the computer and headed for the bunkhouse. Outside, she could see what Edith was talking about. The southern horizon was studded with clouds, and the wind was again rising.

The other two satellite technicians strode toward her across the yard from the bunkhouse, heads lowered against the blow. She hurried past them to the bunkhouse and pushed open the door, nearly colliding with Wee Willy, who was on his way out, duffel over his shoulder and fake-fur hand warmer dangling in front of the expansive front of his Carhartts. For the briefest of moments, he made eye contact with her. "Thanks again for picking this up," he said, patting the wad of fuzz.

Valena blinked in surprise. His eyes and voice had been filled with surprise, confusion, shy affection, and . . . she struggled to evaluate the last ingredient . . . longing.

Inside the bunkhouse, Hilario and Dave were just stuffing the last bits of personal gear into their duffels. "*Hola, chica!*" said Hilario. "Ready for another day of stoop labor?"

"Uh, sure."

"See you at breakfast, then. Last one gets no bacon." He brushed by her and left the building.

Suddenly she was alone with Dave. He looked up at her, smiling a sleepy good-morning smile. The low light in the room made his features softer, more intimate, and the fact that he was rolling up a sleeping bag with his large, thick-fingered hands added an entirely tactile aspect to their meeting.

She moved to her bunk and began doing the same. Turned her back to him. Pushed the silky fabric of the sleeping bag into the big duffel in which it had come.

Dave spoke. "Edith says you'd like to learn to drive the Challenger."

"Um, well . . . yes."

"Then it's a date."

For the space of several heartbeats, the only sounds in the room were the slithering of fabric being shoved into duffels and zippers being zipped. She heard his footsteps as he crossed the floor. The door opened, flooding the room with light.

The door closed again. She was alone.

She realized that she was perspiring.

❖

Valena managed to corner Sheila in the storeroom while everyone else was outside lashing down the return load. "I need more information," she said.

"I don't know what I can add," Sheila replied, appearing to focus her attention on which can of tomatoes to remove from the shelves.

"Anything. Any arguments you overheard. Anything that suggests that anyone other than Emmett had a gripe with the man who died."

Sheila rubbed a corner of her apron around the top of the can she had selected to remove a nonexistent coating of dust. "Well, I heard one . . ." she said, concentrating on a number 10 can of applesauce.

"Come on! Any moment, Edith's going to step through the doorway and tell me it's time to go."

"I only heard one side of the discussion. Though it appeared to have but the one side."

"Who's side? What was said?"

"It was the journalist. He kept his voice low, but I could tell that he was very, very angry."

"At who?"

"It was outside the tent the first day he was there. I was inside, cooking. So I don't know which of the men he was talking to, but he said, 'We meet at last,' and then, 'Yeah, you,' or words to that effect, and then, 'I've come a long way to find you, asshole,' and then I couldn't hear any more, because there were footsteps—you know how they squeak in that cold, dry snow—and Mr. Sweeny was following the other bloke away, nattering at him. At the time I didn't think much of it."

"Wow. Did you tell the feds about this?"

"Nay. They didn't ask, now, did they?"

The airlock door opened, and Edith stepped inside. "Valena!" she called. "Come on! We're waiting on you!"

❖

BY LATE MORNING, they had set another seven miles of flags along the route, picking up where they had started setting them the day before and progressing back toward McMurdo. Valena fell again into the rhythm of the work, engrossing herself this time in the art of pitching flags off the top of the load while Hilario drove the Delta. The task required that she closely monitor the bundles of poles. There was an abstract pleasure to pitching the poles just right so that they stabbed into the snow but hung at a slightly drunken angle, so that Dave and Willy, who were again riding the snow machines, would know which ones had been rammed into the snow at the proper depth and which ones still awaited their attentions.

As she watched the two men work, she noticed that Willy kept to odd numbered holes and left the evens to Dave, regardless of whether or not Dave was delayed drilling with the augur. In places where the wind had eroded the snow down to the ice, it was necessary to use the auger to get a hole deep enough to hold up the flag. This was harder work and took two to three times as long per flag as using the pike on soft snow, but while Dave moved from an even to an odd when Willy was delayed rather than moving ahead of him, Willy did not return the favor. At one point, Dave hit a long cluster of icy positions and fell far behind. Seeing this, Hilario stopped the Delta and waited for him to catch up. Wee Willy pulled his snow machine up beside the Delta and waited for his next flag.

Hilario leaned out of the cab. "Hey, Willy! Where you get off letting Dave do more than half the work?"

Willy stared at him, letting the blankness of his goggles speak for his mood.

Hilario growled, "I'll bet you were the *pendejo* that turned off the dish last night! Yeah, I saw the little wheels turning in your brain when the techs showed us which buttons to push on that computer!"

Wee Willy fussed with his neck gaiter, clumsily letting it slip low enough to reveal his smirk.

I'll be damned, thought Valena. *He's smarter than he looks. Either that, or a whole lot stupider.*

Half an hour later, they stopped for lunch. As they stood around in the lee of the Delta, they discussed the weather, the ice, and their position on the trail. Willy stood with them this time, closer to Valena than she liked.

"This is my point farthest south," said Edith. "We're at the southern-most point of this traverse. Seventy-eight degrees, eighteen minutes south. Not as good as Shackleton, but I ride in relative comfort."

"Yeah," said Hilario. "They didn't have ChapStick in his day."

Edith said, "So, Valena, how do you like driving the equipment?"

"I love it."

Willy stopped chewing and stared at her. "But you don't have to do this stuff," he said. "You're not even getting paid for it."

Valena realized that he had just given her an opening from which to ask questions while in the protection of the group. Starting with pleasant chitchat, she said, "You love it, don't you?" knowing that he didn't. Love and Willy were two things that didn't seem to connect.

Willy drew his eyebrows together in confusion. "It's work."

"Well then, let's put it this way: what brought you here?"

"I was looking for a job."

"Where?" she asked.

"On the computer."

"I mean, where were you when you logged onto the computer? In Kansas, New York . . ."

"Oh. Massachusetts. I was looking on the Internet for a job, and they said they had this job."

Dave said, "You didn't like it much last year, as I recall. So why did you come back?"

Willy shrugged his shoulders. "Dunno. It's a job."

Edith rolled her eyes.

Hilario said, "Well, let's get it moving, *muchachos*. We got miles to cover. Valena, you want another turn at the wheel?"

They continued setting flags through the first part of the afternoon. Finally, they saw the KOA ahead of them, a tiny box of cover in a wilderness of ice. Edith made her check-in call to Mac Ops and then announced over the intercom, "We'll pull up at the KOA and make a final shuffling of the vehicles, then head for the barn."

Hilario climbed down off the back of the Delta. "Edith says you're gonna ride with Dave this last pitch," he said. "He'll teach you good. That's the Cadillac of all Antarctic treads, and Dave's got a hand like velvet on those controls." He gave her a wink. "He don't bite."

Valena tried to force a casual smile but failed miserably.

Hilario threw back his head and laughed. *"O cariño!"* He chortled. "Dave is as gentle as a dove!"

So that was it, she was going to ride for two hours or more in that tiny cab with this man who made her that nervous. This man who might be a killer. And somehow, the nervousness and the possibility that he was a killer were two separate things. She pulled the Delta up next to the Challenger and climbed out. She walked across the open snow that separated the two vehicles. She climbed the steps up the fender.

Dave was waiting for her with the door open.

Edith roared past on a snow machine, gunning it for a fast return to town. Willy followed in hot pursuit. Hilario had moved into the driver's seat of the Delta. He lifted one hand from the steering wheel and made a little scoot-scoot-scoot gesture, urging her into the cab.

In for a penny, in for a pound, Valena told herself, and she stepped inside.

Dave moved to the jump seat and showed Valena how to adjust the driver's seat to her size. He reached in front of her to put his hand on the first of two levers to the right of the wheel. "Now, here's the transmission," he said. "You've got ten forward gears and two in reverse." He moved his hand to the second lever. "This one's the throttle." He pointed next to the floor. "The pedal on the left is the clutch. You can take off and shift through the gears without using it, but you'd need it for things like hooking up the goose, where you have to ease it back slowly and stop when the hole in the tongue is in line with the hole in the drawbar so you can drop in the pull pin. The next pedal is the brake, no different than a car. The third pedal is the decelerator, not the accelerator. It works just the opposite of the accelerator on a car. Pushing down on that pedal slows the engine."

"That's going to be a little hard to remember."

He laughed. "Then this is going to be an interesting ride. Now these levers are the hydraulics to lift and lower the blade. Keep it gentle. Okay, put it in gear, set it in eighth, and give it 2100 rpm's."

Valena set the throttle to a more conservative 1400 rpm. The Challenger eased forward. The big steering wheel moved like silk after the awkward swing of the Delta's. "Power steering," she said.

"Oh, you'd best believe it. Okay now, give it some gas; we don't want to miss dinner."

She ran the throttle up to 2100 and they began to accelerate.

"Keep an eye on this rearview mirror," said Dave. "You can watch how the goose is doing. If it gets too much snow building up, pull it up a little. No snow at all, let it down. Go ahead, try it."

Valena immediately dropped the blade too far into the snow, kicking up a spray that flew right over the top of the blade.

Dave laughed. "That's a little more than you need. Little movements. Try it again."

They kept on going, now moving a little faster, and, bit by bit, mile by mile, Valena gained confidence in both the tractor and in the instructor that came with it. By the time they came around the bend that opened up their view toward the sea ice, Valena was getting cocky and cut the curve a little too tightly.

"You want to try that third pedal on the floor when you feel it getting out of control like that," said Dave.

"I wasn't out of control," Valena answered tartly.

Dave grinned. "Oh, yeah? Ask that flag you clipped. It's spinning out across the back forty."

"I clipped a flag? You're kidding."

"Your secret is safe with me. But I got to tell you, you hit too many and Edith will give you a ticket."

"What for? Flag endangerment? Destroying government property?"

"No. Maybe for the same thing I got ticketed for once."

"And what was that?"

"Oh, I got pulled over in a little town for doing about double the speed limit. The old guy who wrote me up said it was for being 'careless and imprudent.'" The grin flashed again.

"Careless and imprudent," said Valena, trying on the words.

They rode in amiable silence for a while, then Dave asked, "I hear you're here to study the ice."

"That's right." She let it hang.

"I like to talk to the scientists, learn what they're learning."

"That's smart. Quicker than taking a degree, and cheaper, too." She immediately wished that she hadn't said that.

Dave's smile seemed a touch more abstract than it had been a moment earlier.

"I meant that as a compliment," she said.

He gave her a friendly smile. She received it like a flower.

He said, "So there's all that stuff about global warming. Are we going to be able to keep this place from melting?"

Now Valena's smile faded. "I don't know if we'll figure out what we need to know fast enough, or get people to change the way they do things at all." She shook her head. "And you know what? I love studying these glaciers, but if I was to do something more essentially to the point, I'd be working to help people have fewer babies. Thirty years ago, zero population growth was the clarion call, but now we seem to have forgotten all that and are just trying to figure out how to live high without fouling our nest. The bottom line is that there are just too many humans on this planet."

Dave's eyes softened. "I don't think you could have persuaded your parents that you shouldn't have been born."

She turned and looked him in the eye. "I have no idea how either of them felt about that, or if my biological father even knew I'd been conceived. I never met my birth mother. But the mother who raised me liked me well enough."

He was quiet a while, thinking through what she'd said. "Then I can't ask the question that's right here on my tongue. You must have been asked a thousand times, anyway. Where your folks come from."

"I have no idea of my ethnic background."

He smiled softly, looking at her with the eyes of a lover. "I think you're part everything. The first time I saw you, I thought, 'Dave, here's what we all will come to look like when we get over this foolish idea of race and just marry the people we love. And what a glorious result it is.' "

Valena felt her heart crash outward through her ribcage. She forced her gaze back toward the trail ahead of them and gripped the wheel more tightly. They continued in silence for many more miles.

❖

"You turn left up here," Dave said, as the route widened from one lane to two and then met an intersection. "Make sure to swing wide, out into the far lane, otherwise your treads will chew up the hardpack where the rubber tire vehicles need to run."

"Big ten-four on that." They careened around the bend, the goose slewing wildly to one side.

Dave laughed. "I said slow *down* a little when you make a turn!"

Valena grinned. "Careless and imprudent!" she sang. "My new motto!"

"Okay, we're on the interstate now. Lift the goose, push her on up into tenth, and take us on home."

Valena slapped it up to the top gear and gave it the gas. The great machine hurtled forward. "How fast are we going?"

"Flat out with a tail wind, nineteen miles per hour."

"Oh, feel the acceleration!"

Again Dave laughed. It was a wonderful sound.

Valena wanted him to laugh again. "So where was that little town?"

"Which town?"

"The town where you got that ticket?"

"Oh, upstate a bit from where I grew up."

"Where was that?"

"Another little town. Whoa! There's your right! Hit that decelerator pedal!"

Valena hesitated a fraction too long, and the Challenger slewed around the bend. "Did I clip any more flags?" she asked. Nineteen miles per hour this high off the ice felt like flying. "You get to do this all day long? You lucky dog!"

"That's me, ol' lucky dog."

Valena asked, "Don't you get lonely?"

"Not much. I listen to the radio, and there's the view . . ."

She could see the aircraft parked by the sea ice runway now. The C-17 had returned, waiting to take her back to New Zealand, en route to the States. They were almost to McMurdo. It was time to question him about Emmett's camp or there would be no time. *It's safe now,* she rationalized. *I can walk from here if I have to, and it's broad daylight from now until March.* "Dave, last year . . ." Her words stalled in her mouth. How could she ask this of him?

Dave turned his soft brown eyes in her direction. "You got troubles down here, I hear."

The broad, white roadway kept hurtling past them. The end of their trail was coming. Now they were crossing the fuel line, heading for the transition onto the land. She could see the Delta up ahead. Edith had finished parking her snow machine and was climbing into the cab of the Delta with Hilario. Now the communications radio squawked into life as Edith made her arrival announcement. "Mac Ops, Mac Ops . . ."

Dave said, "I'm sorry to ask."

"It's okay."

She hit the decelerator, cutting their speed in half. She wanted him to talk to her, to say most anything. Two other men—Jim Skehan and Cal Hart—were waiting in McMurdo and wanted to talk to her immediately, and for all she knew she would be hauled into George Bellamy's office for a good dressing down—*You've been where?* he'd ask her, *And under whose authority?*—and then she'd be marched straight up the hill to have her duffels loaded onto the C-17 for an early morning departure.

She took a breath to speak, only to find her lungs jammed against tensed stomach muscles. "It's just . . . well, I got here and things sort of got all snarled up," she said. "I'm trying to figure out what happened at Emmett Vanderzee's camp last year. And you were there, right?"

Dave's face went blank. He opened his mouth to say something, but in the next instant they both heard her name spoken in the middle of Edith's check-in conversation. The woman at Mac Ops was saying: "Is Valena Walker with you?"

Valena and Dave both stared at the radio.

"Affirmative," said Edith.

"I have a message for her. Can you get it to her? Over."

"I'm sure she is listening to this call, but I will double-check, over."

Dave grabbed the microphone and handed it to Valena. "Just press this key to talk," he said.

Valena slowed the tractor to a stop and pressed the key. Was this the bad news she had been bracing against? "This is Valena," she said, and managed to add, "Over."

The radio operator said, "Message reads: 'Meet Jim at Crary if back by eighteen hundred hours. If not, phone number will be on his door.' Do you copy? Over."

"I copy. Over."

"Thanks for your help, over and out," said Edith.

"Mac Ops over and out."

Dave gave her one of his smiles. "You look like your pet dog just died."

Valena hung her head in misery. "I'm afraid they're going to send me home tomorrow."

Dave put a hand on her shoulder.

She looked his way.

He smiled softly. Used one finger to slide a stray lock of her hair away from her eyes. He said, "Come on, things are always bound to get better." He pointed toward the line of snow machines. "Just park it right over there and I'll drop the goose."

She longed to drive up through the main street of McMurdo Station in this towering tractor with this handsome man at her side, smiling his smile, but she pulled up at the end of the line near the Delta and stopped.

Dave opened the door and stepped out onto the fender. "We'll ride up in the Delta with the others," he said, then hurried down the steps. The cab door swung shut behind him.

The constant daylight of Antarctica shone all around her, but Valena felt darkness closing in. Once again, she was alone.

29

VALENA RAN STRAIGHT FROM THE SPOT WHERE THE DELTA LEFT HER TO Crary Lab. She did not stop in her dorm room to drop her gear or take a shower. She did not stop in the hallway nearby to look at the flight manifests to see if she was scheduled to leave in the morning. She did not stop in her office in Crary or look for Jim's number, nor did she go looking for Cal Hart. Instead, she ran down the ramp all the way to phase 3 in search of Michael.

"What? Whoa!" he said, as she burst through the door into his shop and threw her arms around his neck. "What's going on? Hey! There, now. Hey . . ." As he realized that she was crying, he put his arms around her, taking in the great volume of her big red parka. "Slow down, little one. Tell me what's happened."

Valena could not say a thing for several moments. She was crying too hard. The sobs came with racking jolts from the very center of her soul. Finally, she began to relax against his body. "I don't know, Michael, it's all just so difficult . . ."

"What's difficult?"

"I'm trying to do the right thing, and . . ."

Michael quit asking questions and waited, swaying slightly to soothe her. He said, "I have it on good authority that the reason they made the cuffs as long as they did on the sleeves of your big red parka is so you can blow your nose on them."

Valena immediately put one to her face.

Michael went on talking stuff and nonsense to give her an anchor in the storm that was tossing her. "Really, it's true. I've been here long enough now that I've finished the initial training in the use of big red. Did you know that there are fourteen pockets in the damned things? Enough that you can load way too much into them. If you filled each one up to full capacity, you'd topple over onto your face."

"You're making this up," said Valena, beginning to smile through her tears.

"No, I'm not. First, there are the two big pockets at the sides, where you warm your hands and keep your gloves, right? There are four patch pockets on the front, and multiply that by two, because there's a hand warmer pocket behind each one of them. So that's eight. Then of course there are two inside breast pockets. That's ten. There's a double pen and pencil pocket on your left sleeve, just below the shoulder, and it comes with its own built-in pocket protectors." He patted it. "That's twelve. There's a bigger pocket in the same position on your right sleeve for your sunglasses."

"That's thirteen," she sniffed. "Where's the last one?"

"Ah, this is the extra-special one that you only get to know about when you're really, truly an Antarctican." He gently stood her back up onto her feet and helped her out of the parka, then turned it inside out and lifted the snow skirt that was built into it below the waist cinch. There was one more pocket there on the left. It was very large, just a panel of nylon. "See? This one's for your water bottle."

"Why down there? That's so hard to get to."

"Ah, yes, but it puts your water inside the parka where your body will keep it from freezing, and you can always unzip from bottom up to get it out. Sort of awkward, but I wouldn't want to have to chew my bottle open and lick ice in order to get a drink."

Valena smiled raggedly. "You're a pal, Michael."

"I'm pleased to be of service."

She looked at her feet, suddenly embarrassed. "You must think I'm nuts."

"No, I think you're under a lot of stress."

"It was a nice trip out to Black Island, really."

"Is that where you've been?"

She rolled her eyes. "I thought everybody in this town knew where I was. Heck, the omelet cook knew what was up."

"You know what I like about this town? As cranky or quirky as everybody is, they all look after each other. You heard about Steve, right? Well, it's like we're all one big organism that's lost an arm. People are grieving together, looking after each other. And even before that happened, I noticed that every person here, whether I know them or not, and no matter how quickly we happen to pass each other in the hallway or out between buildings, they look you in the eye, they smile, and they say hello. And there's always someone to eat a meal with. Which reminds me, it's past six. Would you like to join me?"

Valena sighed heavily. Jim Skehan was waiting for her, and so was Cal Hart, and for some reason all she wanted to do was go back to her dorm room and hide until it was time for her flight north. She was in over her head, she knew that now. No adventure or master's thesis or ethical principle was worth risking her life. She had cried it out now and was ready to concede the game. Something about riding over the snow with Dave had snapped everything back into proportion for her. "I'm sorry, but I can't. But thank you. For everything." She threw another bone-crushing hug on him, this time without the voluminous parka. Then she grabbed her things and headed out of the room in search of the note that would give her the number for Skehan's beeper.

She did not need the note. Skehan was standing in the middle of the hallway, waiting for her.

He crooked his finger for her to follow him and headed up the ramp. He wasn't smiling.

30

MICHAEL SAT FOR A MOMENT ON HIS LAB STOOL, TRYING TO COLLECT himself. *Valena's young and so . . .* beautiful *is the only word, though her beauty is as unconventional as . . .* Words escaped him. He reached up a hand and rubbed the back of his neck, trying to loosen a knot that had not been there before she tumbled into his laboratory. The skin felt hot and moist.

He turned and looked out the window toward the ice runway, taking in the view of neatly parked aircraft and distant mountains. He liked his life tidy. Valena's visit had been as wild as . . . *If she ran in here and knocked what I'm working on here onto the floor, scattering all the little clips and fittings, that would not have been quite as disruptive,* he told himself. And yet he wanted her to come right back and do it again.

He shook himself, trying to knock loose the urges that were running up and down his body. *It's one thing when I hug her,* he decided, *but when she threw that one on me . . .*

I'm almost old enough to be her father, for Christ's sake!

Michael, he told himself, *you thought you could hide out here in Antarctica, but for all the scarcity of people, it's wound up being more intimate than any place you've ever been, and it's telling you something: you've been alone too long!*

He hopped off his stool.

Quickly, he turned off his oscilloscope and unplugged his soldering iron, then grabbed his parka from its hook on the back of the door, switched off the lights, locked the door behind him, and headed up the ramp. *Maybe she's still there,* he told himself. *Please, let her still be there.*

He took the ramp in long, hearty strides, and at the top, turned right. *Ah, good, her door is open!* He closed the distance quickly and burst through into Brenda Utzon's office. She was sitting at her desk. She smiled tentatively when she saw him. The little crow's feet around her eyes and the first few gray hairs on her head looked dear, and very, very welcome. "Brenda," he said. "I was wondering if you were on your way to dinner. Would you join me?"

Her smile broadened, and a bright light came into her eyes. They were lavender, he noticed. Why had he never seen that before?

A snorting sound from the farthest desk in the room alerted him to the fact that they were not alone. He looked up and only then saw that Doris was at her desk, leaning forward into her laptop computer. She was fighting back a hearty smirk. *To hell with you,* he thought merrily, *I've finally made my move.*

Turning his attention back to Brenda, he waited confidently for her answer.

"Sure," she said, moving her mouse around to close down her computer for the night. "I'd be delighted."

◆

"MAC OPS, MAC Ops, this is Cape Royds," came the call.

The woman on shift at Mac Ops reached for the microphone. "Mac Ops," she replied.

"Hey, I need you to pass a message for me," said Nat, his voice garbled by the radio and the wind.

"Standing by for message. Over."

A second voice, this one with a New Zealand accent, came over the air. "Hi there, Mac Ops! We've been having a little cocktail hour up here in Nat's tent, and . . . over."

"What's your message?" she asked.

"Tell Bellamy I think whoever pinched the penguin eggs also stole some artifacts," Nat said. "We need to have a council of war on this."

The New Zealander added, "And tell him that if he's coming out here tomorrow, he should see if that girl who worked for Emmett Vanderzee still wants to join us. Nat says she's kind of cute. Oh . . . over."

"Mac Ops copies. You boys behave yourselves. Over."

She could hear a sea chantey being sung in the background as Nat toggled his mike one more time to say, "Royds over and out. Oh, and we're doing fine, so don't expect an eight p.m. check-in call."

She said, "Mac Ops clear," then switched off the microphone. She smiled, thinking what fun they were having out there. She knew the Kiwis had some good recipes for mixing Raro with various other beverages, but the sweetness in the mix made the drinks hit the brain even harder than it hit the liver.

She dialed George Bellamy's phone number, knowing that he had already left his office, so when it rolled over to his assistant's answering machine, she left the message there, not knowing that that woman had gone to her dorm room with a fever and would not find the message for two days. Then she sat back and tried to reason out how to reach "that girl who works for Emmett Vanderzee." She felt sorry for Valena. She had really gotten hosed, coming all the way down here only to find that her professor was gone. Maybe there was something she could do to help, if only to tell her to watch out for inebriated Kiwis.

31

JAMES SKEHAN SIGNALED FOR VALENA TO FOLLOW HIM AND LED HER UP the ramp. His stride was long and he moved quickly. He opened the door to the stairwell and took the steps up toward the library two at a time. "Come on, hustle!" he told her. "We've got people waiting!" Once inside the library, he headed toward a group of people who sat drinking coffee on a cluster of couches arranged in a semicircle. Changing swiftly to a more congenial tone, he said, "Hey, everybody, I've found someone else to join our little party. Valena, I think you've met a few of these people. Kathy Juneau is a biologist, and Ted is a blaster. I think you've also met our own dear Cupcake and Cal Hart. We also have Julia Rosserman, geology; Ken Phelps, atmospheric science; Bill Williams, glaciologist."

Valena did her best to look calm and collected. "Um, yeah. Kathy, nice to see you again. Cupcake? Cal?" she said, wondering why Cal was there. Hadn't he been scheduled to fly north?

"Sit down, Valena," Skehan said. "We're all just having a little chat about what happened to Emmett. We're rather concerned."

Valena lowered herself onto the couch. *Skehan's trying to sound casual, but he's wound up tighter than a watch spring,* thought Valena, recalling one of her grandfather's aphorisms. It was becoming an anachronistic aphorism, because now most watches ran on batteries. *Of course, if I'm going to be anachronistic, it might as well be over a timepiece,* she decided, then realized, *I'm starting to dissociate, focusing on the details instead of the way they fit together. This is not good. Something's wrong here. Why is Cal still here? I though he was scheduled on the flight out yeasterday.*

The man named Phelps sat with his shoulders held as high as Ed Sullivan's. His skinny knees jiggled inside his baggy chinos.

Skehan said, "What went down out on the ice with the man from Fleet Ops really troubles me."

Kathy Juneau tapped her pen against the pad of paper on her clipboard. "I'll bet I'm not the only one who wonders if there's a connection between what happened to Steve and what happened to that man in Emmett's camp last year. I wish to hell we could get a flight up there and have a look ourselves."

"That occurred to me, too," said Cal. He sat sprawled back in his couch with both elbows over the back and one ankle crossed over the opposite knee.

Valena's brain was running at high speed, picking up every detail and plugging it into position on a game board of infinite dimensions. *Should I tell them everything I know? No, because the Airlift Wing could get in a world of trouble.*

It occurred to her to wonder why they were including her in this gathering. *Do they know that I was investigating this problem myself? But I'm done now. They can have it! And don't they know that I'm being sent home on the next plane?* She turned and looked at Cupcake. "What have you told them?" she whispered.

"Nothing."

"What's that, Valena?" Kathy inquired.

"Nothing," she said.

"Nothing substantive or nothing at all?" asked Skehan.

She fidgeted with the zipper on her big red parka. "Nothing of much note," she said cautiously.

Cal said, "You were on the traverse with two other people who were in Emmett's camp. What did they tell you?"

Valena said, "You mean Willy. He strikes me as a prize stumblebum."

"And the other man?" said Skehan. "What was his name? Dave? Cal has described him as something of an operator. A bit sly."

Cal said, "And I hear he's a womanizer."

I don't like you, Valena decided, but she tipped her head to one side, indicating polite inquisitiveness. "I happened to speak with Manny Roig," she said. "I got the impression that being in that camp at that time was nothing less than traumatic for him. Would you concur with that, Cal?" she added, pushing the question back at him.

Cal knit his brow and nodded. "It was terrible for all of us."

The beeper on Skehan's belt went off. He read its message and then picked up the telephone on the coffee table and dialed. "This is Jim," he said. "Yeah, sure. She's here." He handed it to Cupcake.

Cupcake gave the phone a quizzical look, then spoke into it. "Cake here. Oh, really? Now? Shit, can't it wait? Okay, okay." She put down the phone. "Sorry, got to run. Can't be helped." Glancing at Valena, she said, "You can fill me in later."

As the heavy fire door at the top of the stairs closed behind Cupcake, Cal said, "What's the problem? Is Cupcake that much of a sieve for information?"

I really, really do not like you, thought Valena.

Ted chuckled. "I have a long and mutually supportive relationship with the Boss over at Fleet Ops. What can I say? It just happened that he needed her to fill out a report about her part in the search-and-rescue effort."

"Slick," said Cal. "We got her input on Dave Fitzgerald and the search and rescue, and then we got her gone. I like the way you guys operate."

Skehan's face darkened ever so slightly. "I don't like to *operate,* Cal. I prefer to do science."

Point to Skehan, thought Valena.

Skehan said, "In fact, it's time to end this little gathering. Cal, Valena, you are excused. I don't mean to be abrupt, but the rest of us need to meet on project matters."

Wondering what Skehan's prior urgency had been, Valena stood up, nodded to each person, and headed for the door. She was relieved to be excused. Cal's manner had gotten under her skin and she was angry. She slipped through the heavy fire door at the top of the stairs and waited. She knew that he would be the next to exit. A moment later, Cal opened the door and nearly bumped into her.

"Hey," he said.

"You said you needed to talk to me."

"Right—uh, but that was before this came up."

"You mean, this meeting?"

"Yeah. Imagine. They're having a strategy meeting and trying to make it look like an accidental coffee klatch." He shook his head. "They got rid of Cupcake, so why shoo us away?"

"You don't have to second-guess everyone, Cal."

"What's that supposed to mean?"

"And why are you still here?"

"Emmett's my best friend! They should let me help."

"Did you help Emmett look for the Gamow bag?"

Cal lowered his gaze to the floor. "We tried, but in that blizzard? We couldn't see our hands in front of our faces, so we went back to the tents."

"So you stayed at the camp."

"Yeah. I helped with the patient. We were trying to keep that man alive!"

"And the others? Schwartz and Lindemann?"

"Those putzes stayed in their tent. Regular Akbar-and-Jeff team. No help whatsoever."

"And Sheila? And Dave and Willy?"

Speaking to himself, Cal said, "Shit, they can't keep me from trying to help Emmett." He turned and pushed the door open, heading back into the library.

Valena headed down the stairs and into the lab equipment storage room, looking for a pad of paper and pen to write up some notes for Jim Skehan. While she searched through the shelves, the lower fire door opened again and Cal Hart walked out. Not seeing her, he stepped across the hallway into the doorway of Brenda Utzon's office. Looked around. Stepped quietly inside. Valena heard the sounds of drawers opening and closing. Two minutes later, he came out eating a handful of chips and headed down the hallway toward the main entrance to the building. She heard the doors open and close.

Easing out from her hiding place, Valena stepped out into the hallway. *So you are an opportunistic little filcher,* she mused. *Not as lily-white as you put on!*

The fire door to the stairwell opened again and Skehan stepped out. "Valena?" he called. "Are you still here? Come back upstairs."

Valena emerged from the storeroom and followed him back up the steps. "I thought you wanted me to leave," she said.

"I wanted to keep you out of the limelight," said Skehan. "Make you seem incidental to this investigation. Just in case."

"In case of what?"

"Call me paranoid, but I'm going to stick only with those people who I know well to trust with my life." He opened the upper door and strode into the room.

"But you don't know me," said Valena, "and—"

"I know you better than you might suppose," he replied. "You had the guts to argue with me."

"Does that make me trustworthy?"

"It'll have to do." He sat back down on the couch. "Okay, what have we got?"

"I like the program you laid out before Cal and Cupcake joined us," said Bill.

Valena remained standing. Turning toward her, Skehan explained, "We're each going to request through our universities that NSF make a formal inquiry into what has happened to one of our most distinguished scientists. He's been treated like a thug, whisked off the ice like some support staffer who's gotten into a fight in a bar. And we're each doing what we can here, and we need your help. Valena, you're the most flexible, being at loose ends, as it were, and NSF will hardly notice what a graduate student is up to. That is, if you keep your head down. You can do that, can't you?"

"It would have to be what help I can provide from New Zealand or the US," Valena said cautiously. "If the weather holds, I'm on my way to an early morning departure."

Skehan tossed one hand to the side in a dismissive gesture. "We've already taken care of that. Your stay has been extended."

"It *has?*" A shock ran through Valena. For the first time, she was not so certain that she wanted to stay.

"The strings weren't all that difficult to pull. Kathy asked for your assistance over the next week because one of her people is down with the crud, I said I needed you the week after that, Bill said he might need you as well, and about then Bellamy caved and just told us to get back to him when we didn't need you anymore. So that's taken care of. Now, don't thank us," he said. "You have not yet begun to comprehend the long hours we work down here."

He grabbed at the beeper mounted on his belt, which was again summoning him. He read the instrument and then leaned toward the phone on the coffee table and dialed. "Skehan," he said into the instrument. "Yes, she's here." He passed the phone to Valena.

Valena gripped the receiver, wondering who would know to contact Skehan in order to reach her. "Hello?" she said.

"Hi, Valena? This is Lulu over in Mac Ops. I have a message for you from the guys out on Cape Royds."

"Who?"

"Nate the penguin guy, and there are some Kiwi archaeologists working out there at Shackleton's hut. They're nice enough guys, but they were hitting the sauce, and something about someone stealing artifacts and penguin eggs. If that's true, I suppose they were getting stinko because wow, that would really bother them, you know? Anyway, the message is that you're supposed to come visit if you like." She giggled. "But I'd watch out if I were you, because . . . well, it sounded like they thought you were pretty cute."

"Yeah. Okay. Thanks for the message. And for the heads-up."

"Hey, we gotta stick together! Southern girls rule!"

"You got that one, sister," said Valena, and added, "Over."

"Mac Ops clear!" sang Lulu.

The connection ended. Valena took her time hanging up the phone. It was one thing to burn off her disappointment at Emmett's colossal change in plans by thinking that she could clear him, but she was over that now, convinced that sticking her neck out was not such a good idea. And here was a group of PIs—full-scale grantees—who wanted to use her as a probe or a decoy, and they had her staying right here where things didn't seem safe. She need time to think, to figure out how to protect herself.

"Who was that?" asked Skehan.

"Lulu in Mac Ops," said Valena. "She said I'm invited out to Cape Royds and that someone's stealing artifacts and penguin eggs."

"Someone's *what*?" asked Kathy. "That's not only theft, it's against treaty protocols!"

"They've got to be hallucinating," said Bill. "How could anyone get out there without anyone knowing it?"

Skehan said, "How indeed? Anything out of the ordinary around here is grist for this mill."

Ken Phelps said, "I agree. Kathy, you're headed out there tomorrow, aren't you?"

"Yes. I could take Valena along, and it would fit inside our cover that she's working for me. You have a tent and sleep kit, don't you, Valena?"

Now you're talking, thought Valena. *I can go out to Cape Royds and mind my own business, stay out of trouble, not have to wonder who my friends are and who is my enemy . . .* She said, "George Bellamy had the people at Berg Field Center retrieve all the field gear out of Emmett's office."

Ken Phelps said, "No problem, have BFC put a replacement set on my account."

"Get that gear and meet me here ten o'clock tomorrow morning," said Kathy. "You'll need a tent, too. Make sure to ask for a mountain dome. Those other ones take too long to set up, and they make a lot more noise in the wind."

"I'll be here," said Valena. "And I'll be ready."

"Okay, getting her to Royds is taken care of," said Skehan. "Now, how about getting her out to the Dry Valleys to talk to Dan Lindemann. Anyone?"

The Dry Valleys? thought Valena. *I'm going to the Dry Valleys?*

Julia Rosserman said, "I'll get a message to Naomi. She's in charge of their project. I could have Helo Ops pick Valena up at Royds and continue across to their camp on Clark Glacier, drop her off there. I'll let Naomi know she's coming—tell her it's part of my transect or something—and get Helo Ops to add her to the manifest under my account."

"That's great," said Skehan. "How and when are we getting her back?"

Bill Williams said, "Naomi is bringing up a lot of core. I'll bet they'll have a helo coming back every couple days to pick up a load, and they can pull Valena out as accessory pax when they do that."

In spite of her newfound caution, Valena began to tremble with excitement. *I'm going to a penguin colony and the Dry Valleys, just like that! How life can change!*

Skehan shook his head. "That's too open. If there's a problem there, she needs to be able to make a pullout on her own. And we'll need a signal to send through Mac Ops."

Julia said, "Hey, I'm not made of helo hours! I don't know about you, but NSF really put the limits on my flight time this year. I'm stretching it to pick her up at Royds and drop her at Clark."

Ken said, "I'll supply the backup. I'm not flush, either, but it's the least I can do. If Emmett goes down, we can all kiss the freedom to do science in an honest, straightforward manner good-bye. It's the camel's nose under the hem of the tent: don't like the results a scientist is getting? Attack him in the press, drag his butt before Congress, and then, if he still doesn't get the message, accuse him of murder!" He shook his head with fury.

"Congress?" said Valena.

"There's more to the story," said Kathy. She glanced at Ken, who was calming himself, and artfully changed the subject. "So what did you learn from Sheila while you were up at Black Island?"

"That she can play the cards even closer to her vest than you can, Jim."

One corner of Skehan's mouth almost curled into a smile, but he caught it. "Just as I thought. Okay," he said. "I think we all have our tasks well in mind. Now, from here, let's all wander off separately, or in groups no larger than two or three. This meeting never happened, are we clear on that?" He stood up and looked at his watch. "We can still make it to dinner."

"Absolutely," said Ken. He stood up and headed for the door without further discussion.

"You don't have to tell me twice," said Kathy. "I like coming down here." She was twiddling her pencil now, batting it nervously against her clipboard. "You know, the NSF is in a bad situation here. I can understand why Bellamy has tried to put a lid on this."

"You understand this how?" asked Skehan. "Our colleague has been arrested like a common criminal. You're telling me you can understand that?"

Kathy said, "I don't think Emmett hurt anybody any more than you do! But everybody wants to hang this on the middle manager, or on management in general. You know the old adage, 'Shit from above, shit from below.' George is out here at the end of a very long chain of command, assigned to keep a town full of rebels in line while serving a raft of scientists, all of whom think that their work is the most important work in the world."

Skehan gave her a wry smile. "I happen to think that whether the climate is going to heat up so far that we get intense species die-off is important, yes."

Kathy went on. "And of course George Bellamy can't know what we're doing, or he would be required to try to stop us, but I think that in this case what he doesn't know would rather please him."

"You might be right," said Skehan. "Let's leave our egos at the door and presume that he would be a member of this team if he could. Okay, we're done here."

Several of the others nodded, and they all stood up.

"Ones and twos," repeated Skehan. He watched as the assembly sifted out of the room. When everyone else had left, he turned to Valena and said, "Well, sorry to say it, kiddo, but a lot rests on your shoulders. As grantees, we have a lot of stroke around here, but just in case you hadn't noticed, McMurdo is not a part of the United States."

"Can you enlarge on that statement, please?"

Skehan awarded her a sardonic smile. "I like you, Miss Walker. You're smart. Really, really smart. I meant only to suggest that this little patch of humanity does not operate as a democracy." He put a hand on her shoulder to steer her toward the doorway. "And please be careful. I'll do everything I can to cover you, from buying wine for Cupcake to getting you around to see the people you need to see without Bellamy half noticing that it's happening, but there are so many ways to die it doesn't take a wizard to weigh the risks. Okay, now get going. I don't want to be seen walking with you."

32

Dave Fitzgerald headed across the road toward dinner in Building 155 with his hair still wet from the shower. He liked to think that the soap he had used made him smell like springtime, which was exactly how he felt. Two hours in the cab of the Challenger with Valena Walker had been quite the tonic. He was in an exceptionally good mood after his sojourn along the trail to and from Black Island, and the pleasure of a clean shirt and the possibility of bumping into Valena in the galley were like extra toppings on a sweet dessert.

He met the Boss coming the other way. "Oh, there you are, Dave," he said. "I left a message for you at Building 17. Did you get it?"

"No, sir. What's up?"

"You asked if you could help me out if any good boondoggles came up, didn't you?"

Dave gave him an appreciative smile. "I just had me a perfectly fine boondoggle, but I wouldn't turn down another. Why, do you have another one up your sleeve?"

"Yeah, but this one's a bit outside my jurisdiction, so it can't be on the clock."

"That's okay with me. I would have done Black Island off the clock. It was a great trip."

The Boss broke eye contact for a moment, a shadow sliding across his gaze. "Well, I'm glad you appreciate all that. To be candid, I've been dealing extra goodies your way because you work hard. And because you had one blow up on you last year, like."

"Oh, you mean that business up at Vanderzee's high camp? Hell, that could have happened to anyone. Sure, it was hard being there when the guy died, and having him lying around out there in his tent froze solid until we could get him out of there, but still I appreciated the chance to see such a different part of Antarctica. I really did."

The Boss slapped a hand down hard on Dave's shoulder and gripped it. "You're a sport, Dave. Well, anyway, things are still sort of a mess around here after Steve and all, so I thought you'd like another day outside of town."

"Always willing. What's the job?"

"There's this grantee, a biologist lady, and she needs to get out to Cape Royds. That's a real plum of a trip. You get to go around by the Erebus Glacier Tongue and maybe see some seals, then by Cape Evans and see Scott's hut, then Barne Glacier. You'll need someone to ride back with you, so I asked Matt, and he said yes also. You know where to find Matt—you guys are roommates, right?—and he'll give you the details. See you back at the shop on Saturday."

"Sounds great! Thanks."

"And if the grantee needs you to stay out there longer, well, just give me a call and say you'll be late. You might want to take your sleep kit, just in case."

Dave's smile cooled a bit. "What's up, Boss?"

"Maybe you'd better get your food to take out. There's some real bullshit running around here just now."

"No idea what you're talking about. What's up?"

The Boss waved a hand about as if trying to dispel a bad odor. "Forget it. Forget I spoke. It's nothing." He began to move past Dave and then stopped. "Oh, one more thing: you know anyone who borrowed one of those snow machines parked out on the line?"

"We took two of them out to Black Island. Why?"

"No, the day before."

Dave shook his head. "In that storm? Why would anyone do that? And you have to check the keys out from Science Support, don't you?"

The Boss shook his head. "Looks like someone hot-wired one of them. It's not difficult to do. They used to teach us how to do it in case we lost a key out there. Anyway, the guys at Science Support are asking around."

"I'll keep an eye out."

"You do that, champ. Now, if you'll excuse me, I've got to run."

Thinking that he'd be whistling right now if he was any good at it, Dave continued down the hall, hung up his parka in the alcove, washed his hands at the hand-wash station, glanced at the monitors to see if anything interesting was going to be on TV that evening, then stepped into the line to get his dinner. After selecting chop suey, fried rice, egg rolls, and a big piece of chocolate cake, he scanned the dining room in the hope of spotting Valena. He didn't see her, so he chose a table for four that had nobody else sitting at it, figuring that if she came through the line soon, she'd be more likely to sit with him if he was alone. Just to make sure that he didn't look too hopeful, he chose a chair that put his back to the food lines.

His plan quickly failed. "Hey, lover boy," said Wilbur, lowering his tray onto the table across from him. "I hear you scored with that grantee with the nice ass."

Dave quelled an urge to push his plate into Wilbur's face, managing to instead greet him with a serene smile.

Joe dropped into the seat beside him. "You pork her for the Steve-o, y'hear?"

Dave felt his breath go tight. "I miss Steve, too, boys," he said, trying to steer them off the subject of Valena.

"Cupcake thinks you did him," said Joe.

Dave was just raising a fork full of chop suey to his mouth. He set it down again carefully. "She . . . *what?*"

"She says you knew right where to find him. You ought to hear her. Makes it sound real spooky."

"Or dark," said Wilbur.

"You guys are just messing with me."

"Nope. Scout's honor. And she's got Cal Hart talking about you, too."

Dave sat very still and contemplated his next move. He breathed deeply, staring at his chop suey. Deciding that finding another place to eat was in order, he gripped the edges of the tray and began to stand up.

Cal Hart's hand came to rest on his shoulder. "Where you going, dickhead?" he said, his voice loud enough to be heard at least three tables in any direction.

Dave continued to stand up and turned toward him all in one move, shoving the tray in between them. "Joe and Wilbur here were just telling me you've been talking about me," said Dave. "Anything you'd care to say straight to my face?"

"Yeah. But not in here. Come on outside."

Dave's mind sped up. There was something weird about Cal's manner, like he was reading from a script, but he said, "Suits me." Brushing past him, he continued to the dish room, scraped his meal into the bins, and dumped his plates and silverware into the wash line. He hated to waste the food, but was too proud to leave it sitting on a table for someone else to clean up for him. He knew he would not be returning to the galley this evening. He was done eating for tonight, entirely done.

Outside in the cold air of the driveway, he shoved his hands firmly into his jeans pockets, stared at the man who had given his foolish friends something to flap their jaws about, and waited. Joe and Wilbur had followed them outside, and others were slowing their gaits as they passed, gathering to watch. *I will keep my hands firmly in my pockets,* he told himself. *I will not get duped into a fight and get thrown off the ice.*

Cal said, "You're a real stud, you know that, Dave?"

Now on top of boiling mad Dave felt a wave of nausea. "If you're passing lies about me, stop it now. This is too small a town for that kind of—" He couldn't think of a word strong enough.

Joe said, "Don't let him get you mad, Dave. You know the rule: zero tolerance for physical fighting."

Edging closer, Cal said, "What I want to know is this: did you kill Steve?"

"Did I *what*?" Rage rose in Dave's chest and his ears began to ring, but he fought to keep his mind rational. *Joe's right, this asshole wants me to take a swing at him. Why?*

Cal's face now hovered inches from his own. "It just seemed so strange that you knew exactly where to find him. So call me paranoid, but I got to thinking that maybe you hit him, dumped him out there, then took Cupcake out there to make it look like you'd just sort of stumbled on him. And you were there at the high camp last year. Too much of a coincidence."

Dave shook his head slowly from side to side. "The Cake chose which route we'd follow. Ask her." He turned and began to walk away.

Cal came after him. "So you say. Well, this guy Jim Skehan's got a real hard-on about finding out who killed Steve."

Dave turned back and faced him. "And why should this be a concern of mine?"

"Because it looks like Skehan's organizing a posse, and you're right smack in his radar." Cal stepped closer to him. "Skehan's trying to figure out who really killed that reporter Emmett had up in his camp, and you're on that list, too. I'm not the only one who got a little paranoid. You get it?"

"So what?"

"Valena Walker is 'so what.' Watch out for her, man."

Dave closed his eyes. The image of his companion of the afternoon sitting in the seat of the Challenger smiling, filled his mind. Beautiful Valena smiling. That smile fading as the conversation careened toward what was so clearly troubling her. He shook his head, but it didn't free him. So he did the one thing he could do for himself: he kept his hands in his pockets and walked away.

33

IN HER DORM ROOM, VALENA PACKED AND THEN REPACKED HER DUF-
fels for field deployment. As she moved through the task, she nibbled at
her dinner, which she had brought from the galley on a take-out plate.
She had laid the dish on the bunk below hers, chancing spilling chop suey
on the comforter, but she was too wired to be concerned with such details. If food spilled off the plate she'd deal with it and take things from
there. This seemed a metaphor for the way her entire life seemed to be
playing out of late. Besides, on the comforters and Army blankets issued
from Housing, a spill might go unnoticed. Like everything else in
Antarctica—the so-called furniture in the room, the buildings, the
Deltas, the whole town of McMurdo—they had a scavenged look to
them. *Skuaed*, thought Valena, remembering the local term. *Picked over
by predatory gull-like birds.*

When she was done eating and confident that she had forgotten nothing
she would need to survive in a remote Antarctic field camp—short of the
equipment she would check out from the Field Center in the morning—
she sat down with Emmett Vanderzee's computer on her lap. She began to
skim through the files she had noticed before, looking for anything that
seemed connected to his arrest.

She began with a transcript of the article Frink had published in the *Financial News* almost two years earlier. It purported to debunk a scientific
paper Emmett had published in a scientific journal. She knew the paper
backward and forward: it examined data from a wide range of paleocli-
mate records, including ice cores, lake cores, ocean cores, tree rings, and

historical records, and showed that the modern-day climate was warmer than it had been at any time during the last two thousand years. It also showed that this increase had occurred during the last fifty years. The increase was so large and abrupt, in fact, that the graph of temperature increase versus time looked like a hockey stick laid on its side. For the first 1,950 of those two thousand years, the shaft of the hockey stick lay horizontally, with little or no increase. Then in the last fifty years—the puck end of the stick—the temperature had shot upward. Al Gore had emphasized this information by standing on a lift in his movie, *An Inconvenient Truth,* rising with the line on his graph in a horrifying swing toward the ceiling.

Frink's article attacked Emmett's findings by stating that his data were scant, self-contradictory, and subject to misinterpretation, and concluded with a strong statement about Emmett's motivation for having published his analysis: "Clearly, Mr. Vanderzee wishes to scare citizens back into the Stone Age. One wonders to what lengths he will go to obtain his next dole of grant money from public funds."

"Whoa!" said Valena out loud. She read on. The next file in the sequence was a compendium of letters to the editor of the *Financial News* that had been sent in response to the article. Emmett had written an eloquent rebuttal to the article, as had Jim Skehan and other scientists. Following each letter was a transcript of the way each had actually been published in that newspaper. As Skehan had told her, the letters had been severely edited, changing them into confused prattle.

Rebuttals to the edits followed, Skehan's particularly vitriolic. Responding e-mails from the editor stated only that they were "looking into the matter." Next in the file were a flurry of e-mails from colleagues indicating that the edited letters to the editor had done their damage within the scientific community.

Things got even worse from there. The next file was a scanned photocopy of a letter to Emmett Vanderzee from the United States senator who chaired the committee on science. The letter "requested" that he come to Washington to appear before the committee and explain his analysis of the data. The senator demanded a list of documents: not only Emmett's published analysis but also his raw data, his colleagues' data, a listing of his funding sources, and justification for all current and planned climate studies. Finally, it required that he open his books, showing how all project funds were being spent.

The letter was a shotgun approach to fact finding, a witch hunt, an attempt to intimidate, so outrageous that Valena thought at first that it must be a joke letter sent by a colleague, and she reexamined the letterhead to make certain that it was authentic.

Why would the US Senate presume to review scientific research? Was that within their purview or, more sensibly, within their expertise?

She understood more fully now why Emmett had invited Frink to his camp. He had wanted to teach the man how science was done, and what it meant. He had wanted the journalist to understand that while scientific interpretations of data were open to debate, that debate belonged between people who understood not only how to analyze the data but also how those data had been gathered. He had wanted Frink to call off his dogs.

But instead of Frink, he had gotten Sweeny. What was Sweeny's piece in all of this? Why was a political reporter looking into science?

Valena read on. After Sweeny's death, the *Financial News* articles went for Emmett's jugular not just as a scientist but as a man, painting him blacker and blacker through innuendo and almost direct statement that he had set Sweeny up to die. "Emmett Vanderzee, who is under investigation by the Senate Committee on Science, was not content to take criticisms," began one article, and, "Having attempted to incite widespread panic with his flawed analysis of climate variations, Vanderzee greeted criticism by leading Morris Sweeny to his death," read another. There were accusations that he "would do anything to protect his funding."

The date of the latest article was three days before Emmett had invited her to join him this year in Antarctica. Was that because Schwartz and Lindemann had just that minute jumped ship?

Flicking the cursor back into the list of programs, she opened her professor's stored e-mails and set the pointer to group them alphabetically by sender. She scrolled to *F* for Frink, but there was nothing there. She then scrolled to *S* for Sweeny and found a short list. The first few were no surprise, questions about what to expect in the camp and what to bring. They were all dated within just weeks of Sweeny's arrival on the ice, suggesting that he had signed on late in the game. The last one caught her interest:

Mr. Vanderzee

Am in receipt of the image taken in your camp yesterday. Wanting to know name of second man from right. Is this Edgar Hallowell?

Morris Sweeny

She backed up one e-mail and found what she expected: Sweeny's original request for a photograph of all personnel who were working with him that year. Why would he want that? And who was Edgar Hallowell, and why was Morris Sweeny interested in him? She closed her eyes, concentrating. *The only name even close to that is Ted, which could be a nickname for Edgar. But why would a political reporter coming to Antarctica to learn about climate change be interested in a guy who blows things up?*

Pondering these questions, Valena turned on the word-processing program, opened a blank document, and began to write, making notes of the conversations she had had with the people who had been in Emmett's camp:

Emmett Vanderzee—arrested
Bob Schwartz—stayed in tent, doesn't want to talk about it, argued
    with deceased?
Manuel Roig—saddened by events, was in cook tent, cook is alibi
Sheila Tuttle—Roig her alibi
Willy?—seems unmotivated and slow-witted, but crafty? Mischie-
    vous? Could he be stupid enough to get into trouble?
Calvin Hart—says he helped EV, but did he? Where was he?
Dave Fitzgerald—

She could not bring herself to make an entry next to the last name, so instead she added Ted's, just in case he had some previously undisclosed connection to the deceased.

It was getting late. Valena turned off the computer and once again hid it inside her closet. She rolled her bath kit and pajamas into her towel, stuffed them under her arm, and headed down the hallway toward the showers, where she crammed herself into one of the tight, worn-out shower stalls with the plastic curtains too narrow to fill the gaps they were meant to cover.

The water became hot very quickly. Abstractedly, she thought of Peter the energy efficiency engineer. Had he fitted the system with a recirculating hot water system so that people wouldn't have to run the water long to get it hot? *It's all resources,* she thought. *Antarctica is all about the resources. So if that's so, what resource came into play at Emmett's high camp?*

She was at last beginning to relax a little, enjoying the sensation of hot water coursing over her body, when she heard a familiar voice call her name. It was Cupcake. *Oh, good, I can ask her Ted's full name,* she thought, as she turned off the water and pulled the shower curtain across her body. "Hey, what's—"

"Just looking for you, darling." Cupcake wobbled a little, the effect of several stiff drinks. "You know, I'm good. Real good."

"Aw, come on, Dorothy! I'm in the shower!" Valena pulled the scanty curtain closed as far as it would go and turned the water back on.

"I can see that, not that you're showing me much."

Valena's blood began to boil, an old habit of getting mad so she wouldn't have to know that she was scared. "Get out of here! I mean *now!*"

Cupcake began to back away. "Don't get so touchy. Wha' happened at the rest of that meeting? 'At's why I'm here. I jus' wanna know what's up . . ."

"I said go away!"

Another woman came into the bathroom. "Hey there, Cakes, wassup?"

"Oh, I'm just having a little chat with my friend here, tryin' ta calm her down. She's sort of upset."

Valena stuck her head out again. "Upset? You want to see upset? Just push it an inch farther!"

The third woman grabbed Cupcake by the arm. "Come on, Dorothy, you know better than to screw with a grantee."

Cupcake yanked her arm loose. "Screw with her? Hell, I came in here to warn her about her new boyfriend!"

The woman grabbed Cupcake by both arms now and hauled her out the door. "You're drunk! Come *on,* Dorothy!"

As the door swung shut, Valena heard Cupcake yell, "He looks real sweet, but it's just a candy coating! You don't want to know what's hiding inside!"

Valena huddled against the back wall of the shower. Adrenaline coursed through her naked body. She began to tremble, shivering with cold even under the hot water, and she wondered if she was going to throw up. She tried to think, to get herself under control. *It's just been a hard few days,* she told herself firmly. *Get a grip. Yeah, there's bad shit happening around here, people getting killed, but I've got that under control now. I'm leaving for Cape Royds in the morning, and I'll be safe where I'm going. Okay, maybe it's not smart to go to that field camp where Lindemann is, but what's he going to do to me? Screw up his doctoral position? Not hardly.*

The water began to warm her skin, but deep inside she still felt cold. She turned off the water and pulled her towel inside. Tried to rub herself dry. Her skin felt like it was crawling around on her body.

Cautiously, she stepped out of the shower, dressed, and headed down the hallway, glancing both ways to make sure Cupcake wasn't waiting for her there.

Back in her room, she climbed into her bunk, pulled the blankets and comforter up to her chin, and closed her eyes. Slowly, by inches, she admitted to herself that she was scared, not angry, and that what had scared her most was the chance that Cupcake might be right about Dave Fitzgerald.

34

VALENA ONCE AGAIN AWOKE EARLY. SHE DRESSED QUICKLY AND, LEAV-ing her gear in the room, slipped out the door and across the way toward the building where the Airlift Wing had its offices. There she left a note with Master Sergeant John Lansing, with instructions to give it to Larry. It read:

One of the men at Emmett's camp may have been using an alias. Sweeny may have been looking for someone named Edgar Hallowell.

Thanks, Valena

She wrote her e-mail address across the bottom of the page.

This task dispatched, she jogged back across to Building 155 and headed down the hallway in search of a hearty breakfast. Glancing neither left at the flight manifests, nor right at the monitors mounted near the galley door, she grabbed a tray and headed into the food lines, steering a course directly toward the omelet man. "Good morning," she said, awarding him her best smile.

"Good morning to you," he said. "What can I get for you today?"

"I want three *fresh* eggs with tomatoes, black olives, mushrooms, green peppers, and jack cheese," she said.

"It's yours," he said, cracking the eggs onto the griddle. He chopped the yolks expertly with the edge of his spatula and started adding the toppings.

"I wonder if I could ask you kind of a personal question," she said.

"Shoot."

"The other day, how did you know I needed privacy?"

The omelet man continued to stir and fold the eggs, indicating not a flicker of change in the tenor of the conversation. "I'm in the room next to your friend Matt in the dorms," he replied. "There was a discussion out in the TV lounge." He turned the eggs, flicking a runaway bit of cheese onto the heap. "It had been quite a day for news, as you'll recall."

"I'm not used to this place yet. I don't know how people do business."

He scooped the eggs onto his spatula and slid them onto the plate. "There's good folks down here, by and large," he commented. "Everybody's got their reason for being here and not somewhere else, but once they get here, they usually find a place here. Those that don't, you seldom see. They hide."

They hide, thought Valena. "Thanks for the omelet," she said. Completing the circuit of the service area, she poured two glasses of water and one of orange juice, grabbed a muffin, and headed toward a table under the windows.

She was four forkfuls of egg into her meal when a woman with gray hair and gentle blue eyes appeared with a tray at the opposite side of the table. "May I join you?" she inquired.

"Certainly."

"You're Valena Walker, am I right?" She settled into a chair and arranged her breakfast in front of her. She moved methodically, removing each item from the tray and laying it out as Emily Post might have done.

"Yes," she said, "Emmett Vanderzee's student." She tried to sound cheery as she added, "Why, am I wearing a sign on my back?"

"No, it's on your big red parka," said the woman. "It's my job to know who all the grantees are." She extended a hand. "And how rude of me to not introduce myself. I'm Nancy Saylor. I'm in charge of Berg Field Center."

Valena shook her hand. "Well, what luck, then. I need to come see you this morning to check out some equipment."

Nancy set about consuming a large bowl of the homemade granola topped with yogurt, canned peaches, and milk. "No need to. When George told me to reinventory the gear Emmett had checked out, I sent someone to fetch it but simply put it back into Emmett's cage. Like you, I am hopeful that he shall return this year."

"His cage?"

Nancy smiled. "It's a system we have so that people can come and go at whatever hour to work with their field gear. In the back of BFC, we have a series of screened alcoves with combination locks on them, and you can get in there and get your gear anytime you want. That way I don't have to lock the whole place up or be there twenty-four hours a day."

"I see."

"Before he came south this year, Emmett filled out a request for the equipment. That way we know we have enough, and if we don't, we can order more." She waved her spoon concisely in the air to describe things shuttling back and forth. "At any rate, when he arrived this year I already had his order waiting for him in his cage. He took his part of the kit when he went to the high camp last week and left it in his office. They weren't planning on spending the night"—she gave Valena a look that said *little do they understand this place*—"but of course they had all the equipment they might need, including sleep kits, tents, stove, food, and a Gamow bag."

"A Gamow bag."

"Of course, I don't handle that gear," she said. "The Gamow is issued through Science Support Center, I believe, but for some reason, it was returned to me last year instead of going directly to them."

"You mean the one that was air-dropped?" Valena asked. "But I thought—" she managed to stop herself before saying, they only found that this year.

"I mean the one Emmett had with him when he first went up to the high camp last year." She paused from her eating to study Valena's face. "You don't think that Emmett would go to high elevation without proper precautions, do you?"

"I . . . to tell you the truth, I don't know Emmett all that well." She paused, then stated, for what felt like the fiftieth time, "I was brought onto the project just a short while ago."

Nancy went back to her granola. "Of course. Yes, I heard about that. His other fellows decided to come down with a different event this year." She shook her head. "Irritating fellows. You're much more pleasant. What were their names?"

"Schwartz and Lindemann."

"Ah, yes; Schwartz and Lindemann. I always thought of them as Rosencranz and Guildenstern, only with attitude."

"And Emmett is Prince Hamlet?"

"Very good. Yes, the one with the conscience." Nancy shook her head again. "He gets himself so wound up. But that shouldn't be your problem. You are here to do research and get your degree."

"I'm here to get my degree, yes, but also do something worth doing and to see Antarctica."

"We all like to feel that we are making a contribution down here. That's why we're all here, you know. To support science. It takes this whole support staff"—she lifted her spoon and made a circle in the air to encompass the entirety of McMurdo Station—"to send you scientists into the field each year. I forget what the ratio is, but there must be four or five of us to send each one of you into the field. But it's worth it. Do your best to preserve this place, Valena. Help keep the ice from melting. It's so special. No, that's trite. It is an extraordinary place, and I personally believe that our continuance as a species depends on humbling ourselves before such mighty and fragile places as this."

Valena could think of nothing to add to that.

Nancy set down her spoon and took a sip of her tea. "You know how quickly it's melting, don't you?"

"No, I don't know. Not for sure. That's part of what we're here to study. But there are indications that it is accelerating, and that scares me."

"Good. Pay attention. I am pleased to support you in your work."

Valena felt like she had received a benediction from a priest. "Thank you. You remind me of my high school history teacher."

Nancy smiled more broadly. "Perhaps because I was one, before I started coming here."

"What an interesting change of jobs. How did you come to make such a change?"

Nancy smiled sadly. "One has one's reasons."

Valena took several more bites of her eggs before her mind swung back to an earlier part of the conversation. "Tell me more about this Gamow bag that came to you. The one that Emmett took up originally. How did you get it, and why wasn't it at the camp when it was needed?"

Nancy shook her head. "I'm not sure why, but it came back with some field gear they weren't using. The guy who unloads the Twin Otters down on the flight line brought the load up. It had apparently gotten put into the plane . . . by mistake."

"But how could that happen? What do these things look like?"

Nancy continued to consume her breakfast with utmost serenity. "You're talking about a bundle about a foot and a half square, rolled up. It's made of a flexible material, rather like an overlarge sleeping bag. You open it up, put your patient inside, zip it shut—special zippers that don't leak air—and then pump it up to pressure, simulating sea level or even below. But it doesn't work if it isn't there."

"Did it look like it had been stuffed in with the other gear intentionally?"

"Perhaps it had merely been placed inside the wrong duffel. A poor arrangement, obviously, the duffels looking so much alike."

"No one's mentioned this to me before."

"Interesting. I suppose they were all rather embarrassed."

"Embarrassed? There's not a bigger word than that?"

Nancy took another sip of tea.

Valena had finished her eggs and muffin and was working to get enough water down her throat.

Doris arrived at the table and set down a tray full of food, her lascivious boyfriend in close pursuit. "Hey, guys," she said. "So, Valena, you got everything you needed off of Emmett's laptop?"

Valena gagged on her water.

Doris continued, "Hey, you got to watch that stuff. It's got a kick. Just come and see me if you're having any trouble getting into anything you need," she said. "You got me?"

"Thanks," said Valena.

Nancy said, "Oh, did Emmett have books on disc or something?"

"No, just scientific gobbledygook," said Doris. She gave Valena a sly wink.

Valena stared in wonder. Everybody seemed to know her business, a sensation that had her strung between relief and paranoia.

Nancy had finished eating. "I'm heading over to BFC right now if you'd like me to show you how to get into that cage," she said.

Valena hopped up and grabbed her tray.

Doris offered a casual wave, as if nothing of importance had been said.

Along the road that led toward the Berg Field Center, Valena asked, "How many seasons have you come to the ice?"

"Ten," said Nancy. "Not every year, but most. I took a few off. There aren't many who have been here more than I have. I'd say Dorothy has me by a season or two."

"Dorothy? You mean Cupcake?"

"People call her that, yes."

Valena's pulse quickened. "Is she kind of . . ."

"A shit-stirrer?" asked Nancy.

"Yeah."

"Valena, this is an unusual community. Of course you've noticed that. People who come here like the wildness of the place, and yet most are all but cooped up on this island. I dare say Dorothy's never been past the runways. The rec department tries to arrange Sunday outings for people, but once you've been out to Pegasus packed into the Delta with twenty other people to see the wrecked plane, you've done that. People get to living out of each others' pockets. There are people you'll never see do essential jobs, like running the power plant, or keeping the trash sorted out. Just imagine if it was allowed to stack up. They're like troglodytes. They don't want to talk to anyone, so they don't. They eat their meals in their rooms. And then there are others, like Dorothy, who get overly involved with each and every person. Dorothy gets particularly personal with grantees. Forgive me if I speak plainly. This is not a classless society."

"Please explain. I thought I understood things, but obviously I do not."

"If you scientists don't come here, then we can't be here. We aren't exactly your servants, but if you don't come here, we don't either. We are dependent on you. And then there are the military. It used to be that this whole place was a Navy base; that's why there are so many terms that hang over—galley for kitchen, pax for passenger—but they stay separate. They're more conservative in their politics than us townies. They call us liberals." She laughed. "In fact, we're Marxists. Have you noticed? There's almost nowhere to spend money down here, and we all do our parts as little cogs in a big machine. The ultimate in mutual support."

"I hadn't thought of it that way."

They had reached the large Quonset that housed the field equipment, and Nancy opened the door and showed Valena in. Inside, she found a large work area in front of a forest of folded Scott tents, and behind that, a series of wire cages. Nancy unlocked the door to Emmett's and led her inside. "Here's your sleep kit," she said. "And you'll want this tent." She pulled out a yellow stuff sack about a foot and a half long and ten inches in diameter. "It's intuitively easy to set up, and quite comfortable. It'll be hard to figure out how to tie it down out at Cape Royds, but Nat's assistant will help you get settled. Will you need a set of skis up on Clark Glacier?"

Valena shook her head in amazement. "You already know everywhere I'm going."

"It's my job to know these things. And Kathy Juneau found me at dinner last night. I've said that this is a Marxist society. That's not exactly true. There are others who use their position to . . ."

"Play power games?"

"Aptly put. It is inevitable in such a close, paranoid setting."

"Paranoid?"

"Again, inevitable. It's us against Nature. Us against each other. Imagine what happens when you get someone down here who is confused."

"You mean, someone who feels isolated."

"You're catching on quickly. One never needs to feel alone here. In fact, few ever get that luxury. Well, here's your gear. Do you need a pair of cross-country skis? Take these. They're pretty beat up, and bindings aren't much, but they'll work with the FDX boots. Can you get it all? No, of course you can't, and you won't need the skis until the helicopter takes you out to the continent anyway. Take the sleep kit and the tent now—and here's your pee bottle and water bottle; I'll just tuck them inside the duffel—I'll call a shuttle to take you and the gear down to the helo pad. Have them tag the skis so they'll be on that load when it picks you up tomorrow at Cape Royds. Don't forget them, now."

Valena smiled. "I won't."

❖

AFTER CARRYING HER gear down to the helicopter pad to be weighed and tagged and stepping on the scales herself, Valena left the skis in a bin marked with Naomi Bosch's event number and carried her duffels over to her office in Crary. She then went to the library and looked for e-mails. There was one informing her that she should present herself in ten minutes' time for a briefing on the Dry Valley Protocols, which would teach her how not to damage that delicate cold desert ecosystem. The only other message was from Em Hansen:

Valena

I don't mean to encourage you in any way, but I have opened a line of communication with a friend at the FBI lab just in case. I understand you have some sort of lab facilities there. Do you have basic petrographic microscopes? Anything else?

I have asked around through other channels and have nothing to add regarding Emmett Vanderzee's status. Sorry.

I did manage to contact Morris Sweeny's wife. She says Frink wooed her husband to go to Antarctica because he wanted him to cover the Senate subcommittee angle, hoping to blow the story up much bigger, but that Sweeny had no interest in taking the assignment until Frink showed him Emmett's Web site. Sweeny thought he saw a man he was looking for, a guardsman who served during the invasion of Iraq with Morris's brother Jacob. Jacob wrote home to ask his family to get him some of the new ceramic plates for his body armor. Early in the war there were not enough vests with this new kind of armor to go around, so they were issued to the soldiers with the greatest need. Jacob said that there was a guy in his unit who had a compulsion for stealing things, among other things the plates out of Jacob's vest. The guy who stole them already had a set but had a reputation for selling all sorts of things on the black market, so Jacob knew it was him and said he was going to report him. It was Jacob's last letter home. The unit was ambushed the day after the plates went missing and Jacob was killed because he didn't have them.

Watch your back and don't be stupid.

Em

Is this the answer to the Edgar Hallowell question? Valena wondered. *And yet it answers nothing, because I still have no idea which of the men he is.*

She opened an Internet browser on the computer and requested Emmett's Web site, hoping for a look at the picture Sweeny had seen. The machine returned the answer that it could not load the site, please try later. *Okay, I will*, she told herself. Then, switching back to Em Hansen's e-mail, Valena replied:

Em

Thanks for all. I shall investigate lab equipment. And will report a few days hence. And don't worry, I am going to Cape Royds and Dry Valleys, where I will be around scientists only. No sociopathic kleptomaniacs, I promise . . . or at least, I expect none there. Just the usual antisocial scientists and a lot of penguins.

Valena

Valena headed down the stairs to Brenda Utzon's office. She found the woman humming a happy tune. "Oh, hi, Valena! Lovely day, isn't it? That storm swung a different direction. Want some chips?"

"Thanks, I just ate. So, I was wondering if you could tell me what kind of lab equipment we have here for doing petrographic analysis."

"Oh, you'd need to see Lennie about that, down the hallway." She pointed. "He could help you."

"Thanks, Brenda."

Valena headed down the outer hallway of the western arm of phase 2 and eventually came across a laboratory with Lennie's name on the door plaque. Someone had artlessly added, in Sharpie, LENNIE'S SPIDER HOLE. *Ah, another ornate McMurdo personality,* Valena mused. She knocked on the door. No one came. She turned the knob, rattling it. It was locked. She had begun searching through her pockets for a bit of paper to leave a note when the door was yanked open.

"What?" barked the man who had opened it.

"Lennie?"

He continued to stare at her.

"Okay," she said. "Well, my name is Valena, and I am told you can help me with some lab equipment."

Lennie glared at her. "I'm really busy right now. Come back later."

"Okay . . ."

The door slammed shut.

Here to serve science, eh?

Valena walked back down the hall to Brenda's office. "Can you tell me where to find Ted the blaster this time of day?" she inquired.

"Oh, he'd be up at the blast site, setting charges. Let me show you on this map." She got out a little folding map of McMurdo Station and indicated how Valena could wind her way to the place where Ted was working.

Valena zipped up her big red and headed out through the air lock. The breeze had died, and the sun felt warm in its northerly transit across the sky. She trudged happily up the labyrinth of gravel streets, soon leaving the land of scientists behind and achieving the realm of heavy equipment operators. She passed yards parked with tractors, loaders, and trailers of varying descriptions and ages. The older ones had names. A pair of small green airline tugs were labeled CLOSET CASE and BASKET CASE. FUEL MULE was a tank truck. A backhoe was emblazoned with JECKLE, and she imagined that HECKLE was not far away, or would it be HYDE?

Hyde, thought Valena. *Hiding . . . is Ted more than he lets on?*

She passed yards laid out with fuel drums stacked on pallets and wondered if this was where the Airlift Wing had come to get a barrel to add weight to the bundle they had dropped on Emmett's camp. She passed shipping containers and neat piles of scrap. At last, she came to the place above town where Ted the master blaster was working to straighten the road.

"Hello, Valena," he said, rubbing his face as if it hurt.

"Hey, Ted. I had a couple more questions, if you have time."

Ted sighed heavily. "Can it wait?"

"I want to know about the Gamow bag."

"They never found it, like I said."

"No, I mean the other one. The one which Emmett took along when you first went to the high camp."

Ted was distracted by a large front-end loader that was coming toward them at high speed. He grabbed Valena by the arm and towed her out of range of the three-cubic-yard bucket that preceded it along its trajectory.

Valena said, "Sorry, I didn't mean to get in the way."

"You weren't in the way. He's a lousy shot." He shook his head and began to mutter, talking to himself more than to Valena. "They're supposed to know how to handle this equipment before they're sent down here or they don't get the job, but not this one. Just look at the way he slams that bucket into the muck pile. Wham! No finesse. You're supposed to move into it, not ram it, and you lift the bucket as you go." He held both hands out, indicating the motion that should have occurred. "This one slams into the pill, spills half his load . . . rough on equipment . . ."

Valena stepped further back as the operator backed out of the spoils pile, swung the vehicle around, and charged off toward where he was dumping it. "I was asking about the first Gamow bag," she said.

"What first Gamow bag?" said Ted. "What are you talking about? Golly Moses, this crazy son of a bitch!"

The front-end loader once again slammed into the rubble, this time at an angle. For the first time, she could see the driver's face. It was Wee Willy. "Tell me about him," she said, pointing a glove his way.

"William? He's got military written all over him. Does nothing unless told to directly. A regular sloth."

"Which branch of service?"

"I only suppose he was in the military. In fact, I know nothing about him," said Ted. "And I don't *want* to know anything about him, either. He's a trog. He keeps to himself. We're all the more fortunate for it."

"A trog? As in, he hides out a lot?"

"Everybody around here is hiding something."

The great machine spun its wheels. It was stuck.

"I'm not going to help him this time," Ted hissed. "I'm just not going to help him. Absolutely no feeling for the machinery. None."

Willy slammed the loader back and forth between forward and reverse, eventually working his way free. He swung the load. Stopped, staring at Valena.

She waved.

He waved back.

"Shit," said Ted. "Don't distract him. You never know what he might do if he loses what concentration he has."

Valena made a sweep with one hand, guiding Willy's attention toward the direction he should be moving. Willy nodded, gunned the engine, slipped it back into gear with a horrendous scream of tortured metal, and lumbered away.

"You'd better get out of here before he returns," said Ted.

"With pleasure," said Valena. "But first, two questions."

"Shoot."

"What's your full name?"

Ted tore his eyes off the waddling front-end loader long enough to glare at her. "Theodore Xavier O'Hare. Who wants to know?"

"I do. And if I want to find out who hid the Gamow bag that originally went up to the high camp with Emmett inside a duffel so that it would 'accidentally' be returned to McMurdo, who would I ask?"

"You're looking for an accident, ask this guy," Ted growled, pointing at the front-end loader. "You want some other explanation, why not ask your new boyfriend?"

Valena did not even say good-bye as she stormed away down the hill.

35

GEORGE BELLAMY READ THE NOTE A SECOND TIME, AND A THIRD. IT still said the same thing. He crumpled it, squeezing it this time into a tiny knot. What was he going to do?

He leaned forward onto his desk. Put his head down on it. Raked his fingers through his graying hair. The National Science Foundation did not pay him well enough to deal with problems like this. *I'm going to wind up like that other fellow they had to medevac out to Cheech with a heart attack*, he told himself. *And right now, that thought has its appeal!*

He uncrumpled and smoothed out the note and read it one more time. It had been typed to keep it anonymous, untraceable, just like all the infernal rumors that sluiced around McMurdo like oily water in a ship's bilges:

Mr. Bellamy—
You need to know that certain scientists currently in McMurdo are con-spiring to investigate the death of journalist Morris Sweeny. These peo-ple will stop at nothing to gather evidence. They are threatening to go to the press themselves. You know what that means. Once the negative pub-licity bottle is opened, the genie is out. The left will bring up the question of why we're spending so much money to be here instead of spending it on schools and will ask why we are using huge volumes of carbon-based fuels instead of solar and wind power. The right wing will agree with them if only to stop the investigation of rapid climate change which Sweeny was here to attack.
Stop them while you have the chance.

Bellamy crumpled the note a second time. Considered eating it. Knew that ingesting it would solve nothing. *Fifty years we search for the best, the brightest, the most talented scientists in the world,* he grieved. *We build the finest infrastructure the funds can provide. We build them a laboratory, supply them with air support and field equipment, food, assistance of every type. We defend their findings and the importance of doing the work. We beg Congress for every penny. We have built a world-class reputation for doing groundbreaking research, and now this. Why don't they listen to me? Why don't they just do their work and leave their political fights back home in America?*

What can I do? Call Black Island and tell them to shut down telecommunications for the foreseeable future? No. I can't do that. I am mandated to keep this station running at full capacity, and that means making it possible for each and every scientist to have access to the Internet. Besides, he realized, *that wouldn't work, because even if I shut down the dish at Black Island, some of them have iridium phones. And even if I took away the ones we have supplied, some of them brought their own damned phones, and they all have shortwave radios!*

Scientists! You can't control them!

With a feeling of impending doom, Bellamy lifted the receiver from his telephone and dialed the extension for his assistant. "I want you to schedule a meeting for eleven a.m. in the Crary Library with all of the scientists who are in McMurdo at this time. It is urgent. I require full attendance. Here are the names . . ."

36

VALENA PRESENTED HERSELF AT THE DOOR TO KATHY JUNEAU'S OFFICE at five minutes to ten and snapped a brisk salute.

Kathy smiled a hello. "We're loading into the Pisten Bully that's sitting right off the loading dock. Our drivers will be here in just a few minutes. You can go ahead and put your gear in the rear compartment if you like. I need to load this equipment." She gestured toward a rude assemblage of pipe fittings. "That's a coring rig for taking small samples out of the Pony Lake."

"Right. What's a Pisten Bully?"

"Tracked vehicle. Bright red. Says 'Pisten Bully' on the side in big, friendly letters. You can't miss it."

Valena took a hint and headed toward her office to pick up her gear. It took two trips to schlep it up the ramp to the door by the loading dock. She then moved it outside.

A cute little tracked vehicle waited below the dock. Valena jumped down off the dock to take a look. It was about twelve feet long and was composed of a cab with two bucket seats and a separate but attached back passenger compartment, which had two benches.

A husky man was approaching from the direction of the dorms. "Hi, there, Tractor Valena," he said.

"Ah, Tractor Matt! Arrrr . . ." Valena replied, making the pirate gesture with bent forefinger.

"Arrr."

"Say, are you our driver out to Cape Royds?"

"The same."

"What luck!"

Kathy appeared on the dock with her drill. Matt hoisted it, carried it to the vehicle, and put it inside the passenger compartment. Valena set to work transferring her duffels and Kathy's into the compartment beside it.

Kathy asked, "Is your companion driver here yet?"

"No," said Matt. "He's picking up the flight lunches. I expect him any moment."

Valena heard footsteps on the gravel behind her. She turned.

"Hi," said Dave. He smiled uncertainly.

"Hi," said Valena. She was simultaneously happy and sad to see him. The two emotions instantly tied themselves into a knot in her stomach, and she cast her eyes downward. When she looked up again, Dave had looked away, suddenly fascinated by something far away. Then he turned toward the Pisten Bully and loaded the lunches into the driver's compartment.

Kathy opened the door by the shotgun seat, stepped up onto the track, and climbed in. "We'll all swap around," she said as she buckled her seatbelt, "but it's a gorgeous day, I'm the PI, and what the heck, I'm pulling rank."

Her stomach still twisted sideways, Valena climbed into the passenger compartment, climbed over the load, and sat down on the rear bench seat.

Outside, she heard Matt speaking to Dave. "I'll flip you for first turn at the wheel," he said, then added, his voice now carrying a tease, "Or would you prefer to start out in back?"

She couldn't quite hear what Dave was saying.

"Fine then," said Matt. "Ro-sham-bo." He lifted his fist and began to pump it to start the competition. On three, he shot out two fingers, indicating scissors. "Dang," he said. "Okay, you choose." A moment later, Matt climbed into the compartment with her. "Happy days," he said. "I get to start out with you."

She felt the vehicle shift as Dave climbed into the driver's seat. She could see the back of his head now through the glass panel that separated the compartments. She saw Kathy turn her head to the right, heard her open her door to talk to someone. She climbed out.

A moment later, Kathy opened the door to the passenger compartment. "Give us a minute, Matt," she said. When Matt had climbed out, she climbed in and lowered her voice. "Bellamy's just called a meeting of all the scientists in town to discuss a security breach regarding the Vanderzee investigation. I have to be there at eleven." She glanced over her shoulder and lowered her voice even further. "But here's the deal. He did not list your name and apparently does not know that you are with me. So you get going before anyone spots you. Just drop this drill with the Kiwi archaeologists, okay? They'll get it to my people."

"But how are you going to get there?"

"I'll figure that out later. Now, go, before George figures out where to find you!" She stepped out.

Matt stuck his head in. "You want to ride up front, then?"

Valena shook her head. "You take it," she said, thinking, *I'll hide back here where I won't get spotted.*

Five minutes later, the Pisten Bully was at the transition onto the ice, and fifteen minutes after that, they were rounding Hut Point with the broad, frozen expanse of McMurdo Sound opening out before them. Valena stared out at Mount Erebus. High stratus clouds lay in a thatch above its crystalline summit, and a long, white plume of vapors led from the crater out across the ice. The plume had grown so large and thick that it was throwing a shadow. Ten minutes more, and the vehicle stopped. She heard the driver's door open and climbed out to see what was up.

A quarter mile to the north, a long line of broken ice rose before them. Blocks the size of automobiles lay in a rhythmic line of complex curves and blue shadows, crossing the field between them and the edge of the island.

"Do you see them?" asked Dave, suddenly quite close to her.

"See what?"

He moved closer to her and extended an arm so that she could sight along it, pointing toward the blocks of ice. "The dark things. Like logs."

"Yes . . . oh, they're seals!"

"Weddells. Neat, huh? They come up through the holes made when the ice heaves. Sometimes they have their pups there."

"What makes the ice heave like that there?"

"The Erebus Glacier Tongue. It's a glacier that pushes off the land into the sea ice for several miles, kind of wrinkling the sea ice. Up here a ways, we have to test the ice to get around the end of it."

"Test?"

"We don't want to drive into a crack. The rule is, you can drive over a crack that's a third as wide as your treads are long, but still . . . no need to find out the hard way whether a Pisten Bully really floats."

They continued north along the flag route another few miles before Dave stopped the vehicle again, close enough to the end of the ice heaves that Valena could see the whiskers on the seals. They lay on their sides basking in the sun, occasionally curling a flipper.

The men got out and tested the ice, then continued around the end of the glacier tongue, and a little way farther along, the Pisten Bully left the flag route. The shore of Ross Island arched westward here, and as they approached, it resolved slowly into a long, low cliff of black rock with a small yellow shack at its foot. Valena had noticed other shacks like this one. There was one just below Hut Point and another closer to the transition.

She could see a truck parked next to the shack now, a truck with tracks. It was a Ford pickup, painted red like most of the newer vehicles around McMurdo, but its wheels had been replaced with individual tracks, one where each wheel had been.

They pulled up next to the shack. As Valena climbed out, Matt said, "This is a dive shack. Sweet, huh? Looks like we're going to view a dive! How cool is that!"

Valena replied, "I should imagine the correct word would be 'cold.' "

Matt hailed the occupants of the hut and they stepped inside.

Three men were rigging into dry suits and wrestling their way into layers of gloves. A fourth man assisted, lowering a string of plastic flagging down the hole, which was a two-foot-diameter bore through the ice. The floor of the shack was plywood, with a hatch centered over the hole.

"How thick is the ice here?" asked Valena.

"Ten feet," said one of the divers. "And the water's at twenty-eight degrees Fahrenheit."

"Twenty-eight? Isn't that below freezing?"

"It's saltwater," said the man. "Damn, I'm getting overheated." He reached into the hole and fished out a handful of slush, which he patted onto his head.

"You're out of your mind!" said Matt.

"You don't know how many layers of insulation I have on," said the diver. "Enough to stay warm in twenty-eight-degree water is enough to roast in twenty-degree air, especially inside here, where there's no wind.

But if I jumped in here without this suit, I'd be dead in minutes. Head first, and the shock might kill me quicker."

Valena asked, "What are you diving for? I mean, are you looking for specimens or something?"

"Foraminifera," said the man. "*Adamussium colbecki*. They're little—"

"Single-celled animals," she said, completing his sentence. "My undergraduate degree is in geology. We studied them in paleontology class."

"Well, then, your professor should have taught you to call them protists, not animals. Or single-celled creatures, or organisms. But not *animals*. Gah!"

Valena smiled at his chiding. "Are they just lying around on the bottom?"

"Oh, hell no. These encrust other organisms, in this case Antarctic scallops. Cheeky little devils. And they're not so small, by foram standards; they're in fact considered giants."

"Why are you studying them?"

"What interests us is that they secrete a sort of superglue that works in salty water. Not to mention *cold* water. That glue has important medical applications. Salty human armpits are perfect for delivering drugs to humans who don't want to deal with suppositories, but we can't figure out how to get the meds to stick. This glue will hold the meds in place."

Matt said, "Amazing what we learn from creatures adapted to extreme environments. Like that fellow who's studying the Weddell seals."

"Yes. Their diving physiology changes from pup to adult. From looking at that, he learned how their muscles change over their lifetimes, and that has relevance to human cardiac patients. And there's a group studying the Antarctic codfish. How do they survive twenty-eight-degree water? It's got to do with the way they metabolize salt, and also they have a natural antifreeze. Again the cardiac patients win."

Valena asked, "Well, better you than me. You'd never get me into that water, much less down such a narrow hole."

"Neal here just loves that part. The tighter the better for him. Once the bore is cut, it starts freezing in again, making it tighter and tighter. Of course, we didn't bring him along because he was sane."

Another diver grinned. "Oh, yes, we're regular heroes. We usually just come out for the dive—forty-five minutes, at these temperatures—but the other day we got pinned down out here by that storm and had to eat the rations in our survival bags. That sure sucked."

"Yeah," said Neal. "Sam here snored all night. At least we had the heater and all, and the trash novels they put in the survival bags were pretty good once we figured out to read them aloud with proper theatric modifications."

"We read parts. Henry played the part of the ingenue. He was a natural."

"So you were out here Monday night?" asked Valena.

"Yeah, that was it. Condition 1. We weren't expecting it for hours. Caught us with our pants down."

"Or our dry suits, as the case may be," said Sam.

"Notice anything strange out here Tuesday morning?" asked Valena.

"No, we just rigged up and took another dive while we waited for the weather to clear."

"I saw something strange," said the dive tender. "I stepped outside the shack a moment to see if the weather was clearing. Seemed to be breaking up in the west first. Anyway, I swear I saw some nut zooming by out there on the flag route. It was still snowing some, just not anywhere near so hard."

"What was nutty about that? asked Valena. "Was he going too fast for the visibility?"

"Well, that, and he was alone," said the tender. "Going hell-bent on a snow machine."

"That is strange. Did you tell anyone about it?"

The man shook his head. "Nope. Henry here came up with a leak in his suit, so it sort of slipped my mind until just now, when you asked." He laughed. "Henry's suit was flooded clear up to his chest. I asked him if he was cold! Tell them, Henry."

Henry said, "I told him, 'My feet are numb, my legs are numb, and when I started to lose the feeling in my penis, I figured it's time to come up.'"

They all laughed. Good, cold fun. All in a day's Antarctic dive.

"That snow machine," said Valena. "Which way was it going, and when?"

The tender said, "When did we dive, boys? About nine a.m.?"

"Yeah, that was it."

"Yeah, so call it 9:30. He was heading south."

"Towards McMurdo," said Valena.

"I suppose so. I figured he was going to turn around though, because it was still snowing pretty thick over toward Hut Point."

"What color parka?"

"Red. That's why I could see him. Red parka, black pants, blue boots. Your basic beaker."

Valena thought, *Not just beakers wear the red parkas.* She asked, "How far could you see from here?"

The dive tender thought for a moment. "Now and then, I could just make out Tent Island, very vaguely. That's about two kilometers. An hour later, it was all but clear."

Sam slid into the dive hole, raised a thumbs-up, and descended out of sight. A boil of bubbles filled the opening in the ice, then subsided. Neal followed, giving a merry wave, and finally Henry.

Matt said, "Well, that's the show, I guess. We'd better get going."

The tender saw them to the door as they walked out to the Pisten Bully. Dave opened the shotgun door for Valena.

She stood ten feet from it, trying to decide what to do. The day before, she had ridden for hours with this man alone across the ice, but today, everything was in a jumble. She had been told point-blank not to trust him, but by someone she in turn no longer felt she could trust. And yet someone had ridden past this point heading toward the place where Steve had been found. Could that have been Dave?

Taking a deep breath, she climbed up over the treads into the shotgun seat. Matt climbed into the passenger compartment.

Dave climbed into the driver's seat, buckled up, restarted the vehicle, and turned the vehicle into a vector that would intersect the flag route around Cape Evans.

Valena said, "Could that man on the snow machine have been Steve Myer?"

"I don't think so. Steve was in a Challenger. Or he'd taken one out to the sea ice runway that morning, anyways."

"But he didn't take the Challenger to where you found him?"

"No, it was pretty near the runway galley."

"Where exactly did you find him, Dave?"

Dave stared out through the windshield. "We passed the place before we got to the seals. Why?"

"Why's Cupcake on your case?"

His voice came out tight and angry. "I do not know."

"Did you say no to her once?"

He let out an ironic chuckle. "Let's call it more than once. But that don't separate me from the crowd."

Valena didn't say anything for a while.

Dave shifted uneasily in his seat. "I have a lot of respect for the Cake, but . . ." He let the subject drop.

Valena wanted to change the subject, too. "What would anyone be doing bombing along here in a snow machine by himself in a blizzard?"

"Wouldn't I like to know."

"You think that man at the dive shack was hallucinating?"

"No."

"Did you see something where you found Steve that fit with that?"

"It was still blowing. Some of the time I couldn't see my own feet."

Valena said, "I notice that some . . . tradesmen here wear a big red parka instead of Carhartts." She forced herself not to look at Dave's red parka.

Dave glanced at her. "At Clothing Issue, we're given our choice," he said. He drove onward, his face set in silence.

He knows what I was thinking, thought Valena.

They came back onto the flagged route and rounded Cape Evans. The route swung toward shore again, leading them up into a shallow cove that held a splendid view of Mount Erebus in its embrace. Dave pulled the Pisten Bully to a stop at the edge of the ice, where it formed a shallow heave against the land, and parked it next to another tracked vehicle that was painted a soft ocher. "This is as close as we can get," he said, climbing out.

"To what?"

"The hut."

"There's another dive hut here?"

He turned and smiled quizzically. "You *are* new here. This is the hut Scott lived in the winter before he headed to the pole. His *Terra Nova* expedition."

"You're kidding!"

Dave's smile widened into a grin. "Why do you think I took a day off to come with you guys?"

"Can we go inside?"

"Let's find out!" said Matt, who had already climbed out of the passenger compartment and was heading toward the shore.

Valena tumbled out of her side of the vehicle and skidded across the ice. The wind had blown the snow off the ramp of frozen ocean where the expansion of freezing had shoved it onto the land. It was as slick as glass. Gingerly, she corrected her course to climb the ramp where there was still an armoring of snow.

Dave moved past Valena and probed the snow. "Here's a crack," he said, as his pole jerked down into the snow. "Just follow my footsteps."

Valena stepped along behind him, watching his shoulders roll with the effort of finding his footing in the drift. Tucked into a hollow on the land, a roof was visible now. As she walked higher up the drift, she could see the walls below its eaves. It was a much bigger hut, taller, wider, longer. Clearly, Scott had learned from his first attempt at Hut Point and had come back better prepared with a structure that would house him and his men for as long as necessary. Snow had drifted in scoured tongues around the entrance, and as they approached, Valena saw the rusted metal of spare skids for long-gone sledges leaning against its sides, as if still waiting for Scott's return. "This is magic!" she cried. "And look—the door is open!"

At the sound of her voice, a man dressed in yellow ECWs stepped out through the doorway. "Greetings," he said. "Want to come inside?"

Valena clapped her hands together in delight. "Yes!"

"Step this way. We were just locking up to head over to Cape Royds, but we can certainly delay a few minutes. Be sure to brush the snow off your boots with that brush in there," he said. "And don't step beyond any black lines. Here, you'll need this." He handed Valena a flashlight.

She stepped inside and found herself in a vestibule that led to an inner door. An ancient snow shovel rested against the jamb to one side, and beside it, a row of long, wooden skis and a wheelbarrow. Behind her stood a rusted bicycle, crazily bent by some mishap.

Valena cleaned the snow from her boots and then stepped cautiously toward the inner door, letting her eyes adjust to the lowered light. It had no lock, only a rope pull with a wooden handle. As she reached out to grasp it, she realized that the hand of Sir Robert Falcon Scott had touched it also . . .

She pulled. The catch eased. The door swung inward.

She stepped into a world lost in the age of heroes, when men crossed Antarctic ice on foot, hauling sledges. Inside, it was dim—the only light coming from a few small windows far inside the long room—but Valena did not turn on the flashlight. Instead, she let this world envelop her.

The trusses of the room arched high above her, with equipment stored in the rafters. A sledge. A ladder. There was a cast-iron stove, and shelves made of packing crates filled with tins and jars of food stores. Mustard, ketchup, cocoa, biscuits, oatmeal. Down the center of the room stood a long table sparsely laid with crockery, and to either side, crude bunk beds.

I've a photograph of men dining here, she realized. *A holiday feast, with pennants hanging from these beams. And I've seen a picture of the men lying in these bunks.*

Valena moved quietly into the room, almost afraid to breathe. She switched on her light now, letting its thin beam search in among the shadows of the bunks. In the picture of the men lying in these crude beds, their faces were tired and grimed with oil from their food and soot from their lamps. How patient they had looked, as they survived the long winter they must endure before their leader headed toward the pole. Or was that photograph taken as they waited, praying for a return that would not come?

How they must have suffered!

Suddenly feeling a strong need for companionship, Valena turned to the door. Matt and Dave had followed her inside and were absorbing the magnificence of the living relic in silence, eyes roaming, mouths agape. The New Zealanders followed close behind them.

They wandered here and there, leaning carefully over books left open on a table—a headline on an Australian newspaper declared, SPRING HAS COME!—and shaking heads in amazement over the reindeer-hide sleeping bags that rested on the surprisingly short bunks.

These men were smaller than I am, thought Valena. *And yet they endured.*

"This was Scott's bunk," said one of the New Zealanders, moving up beside her. "And here's his desk." A penguin collected for study lay across the table, as fresh as if it had been left the day before.

In another corner of the room, a set of chemist's glassware rested on a wooden bench, awaiting the scientist's return.

"We should get going," said one of the archaeologists.

Valena thought, *I don't want to leave, but I've absorbed all I can for now, it's that overwhelming.* After thanking the archaeologists for the incomparable treasure of visiting the inside of the hut, she turned to follow.

BACK OUT ON the ice, Dave, Matt, and Valena climbed back into their Pisten Bully and followed the archaeologists' Haaglund as it left the flag route from McMurdo behind and continued on a less-traveled track to the north, rounding Barne Glacier, a wall of ice that glowed a neon blue. They were no longer in the Antarctica of jet aircraft and flush toilets but the one of lone huts and little-used trails.

Valena rode in silence, her world far away, an abstraction.

Dave broke the quiet. "So you came down here to work with Emmett Vanderzee."

"Yes."

"You know I was up there last year when it happened."

She turned and looked at him. "Yes."

"If there's anything I can do to help . . . You know, I'd hate for you to have to go home."

Valena thought, *He's going to make this easy for me.* She studied the angles of his profile. He was a fine-looking man, handsome in a gentle, kind sort of way. Unassuming. A comforting presence. "I need to know as much as I can about how it went down," she said.

"Like what?"

"Like . . . well, like did you hear the plane? That sort of thing."

"Sure. It was low overhead. You could hear it even through the wind."

"Where were you when you heard it?"

"In the cook tent. I was keeping the stove going so Emmett and Sheila and Manny could concentrate on the patient. They had him up on the table on top of a couple of camp mats to keep him as warm as possible. I had the stove on a packing crate underneath. I wanted to keep an eye on it so it didn't melt its way down into the ice and go out, or ignite the tent fabric."

"Who else was there with you?"

Dave thought a moment, conjuring the scene in his head. "Willy was there eating cookies a lot. Bob and Dan were in their tent, and Cal was in the one he shared with Emmett."

"You're sure that they were in those tents, and not somewhere else."

"I checked on them when I went to the latrine once. Bob was sleeping, or just lying there with his eyes shut, and Dan was reading. And Cal was alone in his tent. Then the plane came over, and we took a look but the wind got so bad Emmett was on his belly using an ice axe to hold on, so he made us return to the tents until it let up. He went out again after a while but couldn't find it."

"Did Cal go with him?"

"Yes."

"And when the plane first made its drop, did you have radio contact with the pilots?"

"Yeah, through Mac Ops, we did. They reported seeing the chute open, but they couldn't see our tents. And we couldn't see a damned thing."

"You needed the ropes to find your way ten feet from tent to tent."

"Right. That or that GPS they had."

"Who had?"

"Emmett and Cal."

"I see. So what was it like when Emmett couldn't find the bundle?"

Dave shook his head. "He was frantic. He kept pacing up and down in the cook tent, looking out every few minutes to see if it had let up."

"Did you tell all this to the feds?"

He shook his head. "They didn't ask me."

"What? They came down here and arrested Emmett but didn't speak to all the witnesses?"

"I hear they talked to Willy once." He smiled at the thought. "I guess they decided us Fleet Ops guys aren't too smart." He chuckled. "Anyways, I suppose they meant to question me, but I was doing my shift at Pegasus, and about then they got their weather window to fly up to the high camp, and . . . well, that was the last I saw of any of them, including Emmett." His smile faded. "I wished I *had* spoken to them, now. Maybe I could have helped."

Ice surrounded them on every side.

"Anything else you need to ask me?" asked Dave.

"Yeah," said Valena. "Why did you come here?"

Dave pondered her question a moment, then, with his usual easy smile, said, "Well, I was at something of a crossroads," and left it at that.

They reached another point of land, one less shrouded with snow or ice. Black volcanic rock protruded everywhere through shallow drifts of snow. The Haaglund drove a short distance up the rocky slope and pulled to a stop. Dave parked the Pisten Bully next to it.

The landscape was humpy and confusing, a maze of lava flows. They unloaded Valena's gear and started up a steep hill over knobs of black volcanic rock all knotty with dark crystals the size of Valena's fingernails. Far away to the left, she could hear a strange chattering noise. "What's that sound?" she asked.

"Penguins," said Matt. "Come on, let's get your gear stowed, and then if it's okay with Nat, we can go see the birds."

"You need a permit?"

"You most definitely need a permit," said Matt. "Nat Lanthrope's your man, so you'd better smile prettily and convince him you're not out to mess with his birds."

At the top of the rise, a small valley opened out among the naked rocks, facing north toward the Ross Sea and the Southern Ocean. Endless ice rolled out before them, for the winter's pack ice had yet to break. It was a landscape of contrasts: white on black, snow and ice on darkest rock. To the south, the slopes of Mount Erebus rose toward a steaming summit, their own private Fujiyama.

Tucked into the lee of a curl of crumbling rock stood a large tent with a wooden frame. To one side of the entrance stood a large solar collector mounted on a staff with cables running off it into the tent.

"Ahoy, Nat!" called Matt.

A young woman stepped out to greet them. "Hey there. Nat's out taking his afternoon constitutional. I'm Jeannie Powers, Nat's assistant. I know important things, like where the chocolate bars are hidden."

Matt returned to the Pisten Bully to unload the drill. Dave and Jeannie helped Valena pitch her tent on a broad patch of disintegrating lava, fighting a nattering wind that wanted to take it off the cliff onto the pack ice. Jeannie showed them how to scout first the least abrasive rocks to use as dead men inside the tent and, next, rocks of just the right size to hold down the guylines and secure the rain fly.

"It doesn't rain here," said Jeannie, "but you'll need the fly for the warmth, and to make it just a little bit less bright inside, so you can hope to sleep. The latrine is that drum-and-bucket arrangement up against the side of Nat's tent. Dry Valley Protocols here, which means liquids in the fifty-five-gallon drum and you-know-what in the bucket. They gave you a pee bottle?"

Valena produced the quart Nalgene bottle Nancy had given her that morning. It had PEE written in several places around the sides of the bottle and a large letter *P* boldly emblazoned on its cap. "I guess they want to make sure I don't confuse it with my water bottle."

Jeannie nodded. "You'll get the hang of it. Superior bladder control is the key to Antarctic survival. That, and good aim."

Valena stared at the latrine with concern. The right side of the bucket was up against the bank of lava and the back was to the tent, but the front and left sides faced the view.

"We don't get many visitors," said Jeannie dismissively, turning her attention to Valena's sleep kit. "It really hasn't been that cold out at night, only down to about ten Fahrenheit."

"Downright balmy," said Valena. She knelt down and unrolled the mats and sleeping bag into the tent, then shoved her personal duffel over into the windward side to supply additional deadman weight. She then gathered up her camera and climbed out of the tent. "Thank you," she said.

"You're welcome. I'm going to get back to my work," said Jeannie. She headed back into the frame tent, leaving Valena and Dave alone together.

Valena faced into the wind that was blowing off the frozen ocean. "Lovely day."

"Care to take a walk?" said Dave. "Maybe visit another archaeological treasure?"

Valena nodded, and they began their stroll down among the odd volcanic rocks of Cape Royds. "It's weird walking between lava flows," said Valena.

"Is that what this is? Lava flows? Why are these so black? They're darker than the rocks over by McMurdo."

"Different flows. The darker lavas have more minerals that are rich in iron and magnesium—olivine, amphibole, pyroxene. The lighter-colored ones, like you'd get in the Andes, or the Cascades, have more feldspar and even quartz, which lack the iron and magnesium."

Dave laughed. "Really? It minds me of double-chocolate cookie dough. What are those big crystals sticking out all over the place? The chocolate chips."

Valena leaned down and picked up a handful. "You mean the phenocrysts."

"That's a pretty big word. What's it mean? Big crystal?"

"Pretty much. It means, 'crystal big enough to see with the naked eye.' So much for trying to boggle the imaginations of wandering tractor drivers. But they're nice phenocrysts, eh? And it's interesting . . . they seem to crumble out to an even size, about like peas."

Dave gave her a saucy grin. "It's cute the way you scientists get all wound up about grit and critter glue and things."

Valena took a playful swipe at him. He dodged.

They continued down the narrow pathway between the knots and lumps of rock, now following the increasing sound of birds as much as footprints. The trail zigged and zagged and finally opened up into a natural amphitheater. Beyond it, along the sea cliffs, the rocks were peppered with black birds with white bellies. The few who were standing upright were less than two feet tall. The other birds all lay on their nests, bellies down, beaks pointing south into the wind.

They stopped and watched the birds for a while at a line of do-not-pass signs that announced the boundary of the penguin colony. Dave said, "They look like two-tone rugby balls."

"And how about that ruckus they're making," said Valena.

"Like a couple thousand squirrels screaming at someone who's trying to steal their nuts."

"There you are," said Matt, striding up from their left. "Let's check out the hut."

Valena had been so taken by the birds that she had hardly noticed Shackleton's hut. It was smaller than Scott's, a humble gray structure nestled against a particularly large snow drift. Unlike Scott's hut, the ground downwind from it was naked of snow, revealing a heap of broken bottles and twisted strips of rusted iron.

Dave's voice dropped to a whisper. "Matt likes Scott, but Shackleton was my man."

"Why?"

"He always got his people home alive." Dave walked over to the entrance to the hut and followed Matt inside.

Valena took a moment by herself to absorb the panorama of black rock and its towering mother, Mount Erebus. The hut looked inconsequential by comparison, a pale afterthought of human habitation. At last she stepped inside and was once again lost in a world of men who sailed on tiny ships across wild oceans in search of dreams.

It was soon time for Matt and Dave to leave. Valena followed them to the Pisten Bully to say good-bye. To her surprise, she found herself fighting off tears. She didn't want them to leave, especially Dave. *What's happening to me?* she wondered. *I'm not used to caring this much.*

"Are you okay?" Dave asked. He waited, a hand resting lightly against the back of her neck.

She could feel his hand even through her parka. She no longer tried to choke the tears but let them slide down her cheeks.

"Isn't it amazing," said Dave, his voice soft and soothing, "to be in a place where all day long, the sun goes from east to west but in the northern sky, and all night long, it goes back west to east in the southern? I can't get over that. I really like it, but it's kind of confusing, just the same."

Valena began to smile through her tears. "Everything about this place is different from everywhere else."

He pulled her closer and nuzzled his lips into her hair. "That's why I come here," he said. "That's why really."

VALENA FOUND IT hard to watch the Pisten Bully dwindle away across the ice carrying the gentle man whom she was, against all caution, beginning to trust. She watched it go until it was a just tiny speck on the giant white landscape. It rounded the corner at Barne Glacier and was gone. A soft welcome from the cold wilderness engulfed her.

Still she watched the place where the tracked vehicle had disappeared, unable to tear herself away. She was stuck to the spot, stuck inside, just plain stuck.

The wind shifted, bringing the chattering calls of the penguins to her ears. At last she turned and hiked back up over the hill toward their nesting grounds. She stopped politely ten feet outside the line of barrier signs.

She heard footsteps behind her and turned. It was Nathaniel Lanthrope, the penguin guy, approaching from the direction of Shackleton's hut. For a moment, she thought she had slipped back a hundred years in time and that this was someone from that great man's party coming to invite her to tea. It was something in his ice-blue gaze that threw her off, a broader reckoning, a deeper vision.

"Welcome," he said, mapping her face with those thousand-mile eyes.

"Thanks for letting me come to your camp," said Valena.

"You're welcome. And you're welcome to enter the colony on my permit, but you have to stay with either Jeannie or me at all times. Do not approach the birds, and do not move quickly around them. Be smart. They're stressed enough without humans looming over them. Recently, the sea ice didn't break up for over five years, so this colony has had to march sixty kilometers over the ice to get a meal. It's been hard on their reproductive success."

"Then the ice usually breaks up here?"

"Certainly. Shackleton anchored the *Nimrod* just down there. Scott sailed the *Discovery* all the way to Hut Point, and the *Terra Nova* to Cape Evans. You've seen the photographs, I'm sure."

"Yes, I have, come to think of it."

"In the meantime, these birds are stressed. A lot of them have moved quite a distance to other colonies." Nat abruptly changed the subject. "I hear you're investigating the murder at Emmett Vanderzee's high camp."

"So much for trying to be discreet," said Valena.

"Word gets around," he said. "Well, if you're good at the puzzles criminals leave, I have one for you here."

"The missing eggs?"

"Come," he said, crooking a finger.

She followed the biologist like a duck following its parent across a lake. The sound of the penguins grew louder, and louder, a surging *krr-uk-uk-uk-uk, arr-kuh-kuh-uk*. Their nests were in groups of twenty or more, little piles of angular pebbles arranged and coated with guano right on the naked, ice-cold rock. Nat led her to a low plastic fence that had been constructed around two groups of nests.

"I hear the skuas steal their eggs," said Valena. "Am I going to hate seeing that?"

Nat thought about that. "I'd feel sorrier for the skuas. The penguins hit them with their flippers. I'm here to tell you, it's like getting hit with the edge of a ping-pong paddle about thirty times a second. But what I wanted to talk to you about is this," he said, pointing to a footprint just inside the fence in a small patch of snow.

"Not yours, I take it," said Valena.

"Nor Jeannie's, nor any of the archaeologists, nor the biologists. Nobody crosses this fence but Jeannie and me, and we cross over there." He pointed to a place where the plastic sagged a little.

Nat pointed to another footprint on their side of the fence, and another, and another. "They lead off to the far side of that tall lava flow south of Shackleton's hut," he said. "Or more accurately, they come from there. Nobody goes that way. It's too much work. You'd have to be sneaking around, trying to avoid being seen. That, or ignorant of the best ways to walk around here."

"You seem to have this all figured out," said Valena, pulling a small photographic scale out of one of her multitude of pockets. "Could you lay that next to that footprint? I want to take a photograph of it."

"Here, give your camera to me. I can get a better angle." He took several exposures. "And like hell I have this all figured out. Who would do this? Six eggs are gone, and a few things from near the hut as well. The archaeologists had some packing cases waiting for removal to Scott Base, where they're conserving all the artifacts."

Valena considered the puzzle for a while. "Ask it this way: what would anyone need a penguin egg for?"

"Need?" said Nat, his tone rising in anger. "No one *needs* a penguin egg. People may *want* a penguin egg, but no one *needs* one. No one starves to death around here anymore. And these eggs are *protected*!"

"I'm sorry, I didn't mean it that way."

Nat's face writhed with barely controlled emotion. "It had to be someone from McMurdo," he said finally.

"Is there nowhere else a person could come from?"

Nat threw out an arm. "Do you see anywhere? Anyone? McMurdo is the only place that people can come from or go to for a hundred miles."

Valena stared out across the ice toward the continent. "The Dry Valleys are over there," she said.

"That doesn't make sense. If you want to come here from there, you go by air. People have gone from Mac Town to the Valleys over the ice, but it's a big undertaking. Traversing is no laughing matter. There are considerable hazards. When the ice breaks up, the tourist ships come in and invade the Valleys a short distance, but do you see any ships out there just now? None. The only ways in here are over the ice or by helicopter, and we know nobody's landed here—the pilots have logs to fill out, and schedules to keep, they aren't stupid enough to have done it—so whoever did this came in over the ice from Mac Town, just as you did."

"And you know it wasn't one of the New Zealanders."

"What self-respecting Kiwi would do that? These men are archaeologists, not egg-stealing morons!"

"I understand that. I'm just checking all the angles. Being systematic. We are scientists," she said, trying to calm him down.

"I'm sorry," he said. "Yelling at you won't help."

"I understand," she said. "Or I think I do. You're working to understand these birds, and—"

"This *ecosystem*," he said. "The Ross Sea is the last unbroken marine ecosystem in the world, or at least it is until the Japanese 'harvest' all the beluga whales. I come here to study these birds because they are part of that ecosystem. I treasure them. It's simple rape to mess with this colony of birds."

"Okay, let's start from another angle. When did you notice that the eggs were missing?"

"Wednesday. Two days ago."

"So they were there Tuesday?"

"I wasn't here Tuesday, so I don't know. I had been in town for a couple of days."

"That's right, I spoke with you in the galley that evening."

"Yes. I had meant to return here Monday but was delayed by the storm. I came out Wednesday and they were gone. And this footprint was there."

"It certainly doesn't have any fresh snow in it, so that suggests that the print was made after the snow stopped on Tuesday."

"Good point."

"And the eggs were on the nests before you left for town. When was that?"

"Jeannie and I went to town Saturday with the New Zealanders. And the answer is yes, they were on the nests. Each bird lays two eggs. They might lose one to skuas, and maybe both, but seldom at the same time, and not in inner nests all in a group. The skuas attack from the edges. For three nests in a tight cluster to lose both eggs . . . well, I've never seen it before. And there is the matter that the shells are not here."

"The skuas don't carry them away?"

"No. They have trouble lifting a whole egg, so they knock it away and then peck it open and eat it right there, and very quickly." He swung both of his hands with fingers bunched together to look like beaks pecking at a rolling egg.

"And the archaeologists said they have something missing, too."

"Yes, some old bottles. Artifacts."

"Where were they located?"

"They were under tarps in boxes in their layout yard, over by where they park their Haaglund."

"Do the errant footprints lead there?"

"No. But you can cross to there without walking through any snow-drifts."

Valena thought for a moment. "And were there any Kiwis here Tuesday?"

"They came back Tuesday night. They had gone to Scott Base for the skirt party Saturday night and to take Sunday off. The weather looked bad enough Monday morning that they stayed put. They were just down at Cape Evans today to see if anything was missing from Scott's hut."

"Skirt party?"

"The men dress in drag and drink and dance about. It's a time-honored custom that dates to before the tender sex joined us on this God-forsaken rock."

"I see. They have dresses? Really?"

"Togas made of old sheets and packing materials and mops for wigs. You're getting off the subject."

"Indeed I am. Packing materials?"

"Think bubble wrap."

"*Bubble* wrap?"

"Yes! Okay, so the situation is that someone was here between Saturday afternoon and Tuesday evening, otherwise the archaeologists would have seen or heard him."

"Ah. And that footprint says after the storm abated, so Tuesday morning at the earliest."

"Yes."

"Then it must have been the guy the dive tender saw zooming by on the snow machine."

"Which divers? Where?"

"The dive shack by Cape Evans." She explained.

Nathaniel Lanthrope's mouth sagged open. He pulled it shut. Thought. Said, "What a damned crazy thing to do! He could have been killed! Is anyone missing up there? I mean, aside from that . . . oh, no."

Valena nodded. "You're thinking like I'm thinking," she said. "Steve was found right next to the Cape Evans flag route, a few miles north of Hut Point. The man who drove me out here found him."

Nat turned and stared out across the ice, arms folded. "Those eggs would be worth a lot of money to some monster somewhere who wants to raise his own little colony on his swank estate. That is, if you could get them back to McMurdo fast enough and somehow smuggle them north without their freezing, but that's not the only reason a man would bludgeon anyone who spotted him returning from stealing. The Antarctic Treaty protects the huts and those eggs. Anyone caught even crossing into the colony is subject to prosecution, but actually absconding with the wildlife? We're talking huge fines, and *years* in prison."

37

Alone in her tent, wrapped in the luxuriously thick embrace of her Arctic Storm sleeping bag, with the constant winds buffeting the tent, Valena slept long and hard. She slept to digest the wonderful tuna, cheese, carrot, and mashed potato casserole that the Kiwi archaeologists had fed her for dinner. She slept to metabolize the wine that Nathaniel Lanthrope had contributed to the feast, and the berry and granola cobbler Jeannie Powers had invented. She slept to make up for all the nights in the past ten days that she had not slept enough. She slept to let all the jumbled facts that she had amassed begin to knit together in her head. And she slept because her soul was finally, deep in this wilderness, away from the longings and madness of humanity, at peace.

She did not awake until almost 9:00 a.m., and even then, she did not look at her watch and did not hasten to rise from her tent. She instead lay on her back with her hands folded under her neck, watching the wind ruffle the fabric of the tent, soaking up the joy of simply existing on this remote point of land in the last unbroken marine ecosystem on Earth.

Finally, her full bladder drove her to wriggle out of her sleeping bag and pee into the quart bottle. After carefully screwing the bottle cap on tightly, she pulled up her various layers of long underwear and wind pants, shrugged her way into her parka, opened the front flap of the tent, put on her boots, slid her hands into her gloves, picked up the still-warm bottle of urine, and wandered over toward the latrine to empty the bottle into the drum. Once finished, she put the bottle into the secret pocket of her parka and stumbled up onto the front porch of Nat's hard-framed tent.

"Nat?" she called. "Is it time for breakfast?"

He opened the wooden door to the tent. "I've been up for three hours. Come on in. I've got some hot water on the stove."

"You're a prince." She began to knock the grit from the path off her boots so that she would not track it inside the tent.

"Don't worry about that," said Nat.

Valena stared at the wooden floor of Nat's tent. "But these boots pick up so much of this disintegrating lava."

"I just sweep it all down through the gaps between the floorboards."

A thought occurred to Valena. She lifted a foot and examined the sole of her boot. "Nat, look." She pointed at the fragments of mineral crystals that were stuck between the treads.

"What's so amazing about that?"

"It's stuck," she said, picking at one of the crystals with an index finger. "Really, really stuck."

"I fail to see the significance of this phenomenon," said Nat.

"You don't? Well then, you've forgotten your one bit of evidence that will tell you who stole those eggs."

"The footprint?"

"Exactly. That man—or large woman—wore FDX boots, just like these. Glorified couch cushions with Vibram soles, but if you're interested in riding a snow machine around in a blizzard over the sea ice, you'd want to stay warm, right?"

"I follow you so far."

"The rock here is different than the rock around McMurdo. Here it has these huge phenocrysts, and they crumble out of the rock at exactly the size that sticks in the treads of these boots. Now, how many people from McMurdo get to come here?"

"Almost none. You've already met everyone authorized to come here this season: me, Jeannie, the three Kiwis, Kathy Juneau's group, the two men who brought you out here yesterday. I count ten. Two men who helped set up my tent and so forth, that's twelve."

"Thirteen, counting me. How many pilots have landed here?"

"Three. No, all four of the helo pilots have landed here, though they don't tend to get out of the aircraft, and they don't wear FDXs."

"So that's seventeen people out of thirteen hundred who have an excuse to have these crystals at this diameter stuck in their boots, and maybe half of them even have a pair of FDXs, let alone that size. Now, name me two other things that might get caught in a boot here that wouldn't show up anywhere else on the island. Or would not be likely, at least."

"Why two?"

"Three's a good number. One is happenstance, because these crystals might show up in at least one other lava flow between here and McMurdo. Two is coincidence. Three begins to be a trend."

"Well, there's the penguin guano. I've sure picked a lot of that out of my boots."

Valena said, "Let's try bottle glass. Shackleton group liked to break bottles, or perhaps they were just lousy shots when they pitched empties out the door of that hut, trying to hit their dump."

"Let's go take a look," said Nat.

Down at the hut, they picked through the loose gravel, picking up shards of bottle glass. One of the archaeologists sauntered over to look at what they were doing. "I realize this looks like trash," he said, "but it's actually part of this archaeological site. Kindly do not remove it."

Valena handed him the shards. "Are these all from the *Nimrod* expedition?"

The archaeologist raised his palm and examined them. "Looks like it. The pale violet started out clear. This green is common, as you can see in the dump, and this rust red is as well. It was all brought from England in 1907. There were not yet as yet any glass manufacturers in New Zealand."

"And the impurities that made these colors? Would they be diagnostic?"

"Certainly," he said. "The colors are various iron oxides, except the bright blue, which is cobalt oxide. And this pale purplish one might have fluorite."

"Could you possibly make a formal loan of some shards? For the investigation of this case?"

The archaeologist thought a moment, and then said, "If it would get those unbroken bottles back, I would loan you my right arm. But I have a selection of tiny bits. Let me get them for you." He strode away to the depot where they were storing the carefully cataloged artifacts.

Valena smiled. "That's three. But I'd say that simply finding these phenocrysts and a little penguin guano on the boots of someone who was not supposed to be here would be fairly conclusive."

"Right," said Nat. "And finding six penguin eggs and antique bottles in his foot locker wouldn't hurt, either."

◈

VALENA WALKED SLOWLY through the penguin colony, trading stares with the birds. *I am a detective now,* she realized. *Shorn of the role I came down here to play, I have stepped into another. What do I need to accomplish here? Only to walk through the colony, then clean my boots into a sample bag. How strange . . .*

She crouched to line up a photograph, zooming in on one individual who had stood up to stretch. The bird stared back at her through eyes that revealed no warmth or emotion. She clicked the shutter, then panned down the bird's shoulder to examine its wing. The tips of its short, thick feathers were not black but blue, the same shade as the sky.

Valena lowered the camera and watched the bird as it flipped its head about, looking to its grooming. *How clever you are,* she thought. *I sure couldn't make it, trying to live out here on this rock. I wish you best of luck.*

Valena followed Jeannie as she wove a route up and over and around the penguin-dotted lava flows, mimicking the pace and languid motions of the biologist as she turned her head slowly this way and that, peering to see who still had eggs.

"How long do they sit on the nests?" Valena asked.

"Until the job is done," answered Jeannie. "Egg-laying occurs over a three-week period, ending about now . . . hatching begins mid-December . . . they're off the nests by February. Off to a life on the ice floes: swimming, eating, wandering around, just being penguins."

"You come here every year?"

"This is my first year. I think this is Nat's twenty-sixth time on the ice. He knows these birds personally, maybe better than he knows most humans."

"Is that true about the marine ecosystems?"

"Being broken? Too true, sorry to say. You take out the apex predator, you throw the whole game off. Take out the krill or fish, again it's out of whack. And things don't regenerate as fast as they do in warmer waters. When you buy Chilean sea bass at your market, sometimes it's actually Antarctic cod. The Antarctic cod takes years to grow to breeding maturity in these waters. They are delicious, I don't argue that, but when a fishing boat comes in, the captain is thinking return on investment, not, 'Am I taking too many?'"

"I get you. Like too many other resources we consume, we harvest faster than the resource can regenerate."

"The word isn't 'harvest.' When we take faster than it can regenerate, it's 'mine.' We are mining the edible populations of the ocean."

"So we should eat farmed fish?"

"Farmed fish tend to be carnivorous species, such as trout. That means that some other edible species is being mined to feed the farmed species. I think the answer is to make fewer humans, not more fish."

"I agree."

"You and I are at that age when we have to decide these things. Do we have babies? How many? I come from a big family. I'm one of five. It will be strange to limit myself to two children. Do you have brothers and sisters?"

"I don't know."

"Huh?"

"I'm adopted."

"Oh." Jeannie was quiet for a while, continuing her slow, rhythmic search through the colony. "What was it like, being adopted? I suppose that's an option I should consider."

"Depends on how important it is to you to be genetically close to your children."

Jeannie laughed. "But we're all genetically close."

"Try thinking that when you look like me."

Jeannie turned and faced her. "There is no such thing as race."

"What do you mean?"

"All the research done in the past half century has said the same thing: we are all one race with only minor variations, but the mixing is spread all across the globe, the result of constant intermarriage, not just this tribe splitting off from that. And surely you've heard about mitochondrial Eve? Each woman on this planet, including you and me, carries the same genetic coding in our mitochondria, with only minor, minor variations that have built up over the millennia. In a manner of speaking, we are all daughters of one ancient mother. We all carry her heritage. We are sisters." She had begun to make emphatic gestures.

Valena smiled. "You're upsetting the penguins."

Jeannie pulled in her arms and spoke more quietly. "We all trace ourselves to one small population that lived in southern Africa less than two hundred thousand years ago. Less than two glacial cycles, putting it in the time frame you glaciologists think in."

"Interesting."

"I was reading a book called *Mapping Human History* while I was flying down here from the States. Then when I was waiting to change planes in Sydney, I looked around at all the faces of the people who were waiting with me. They were from every part of the globe—Asian, European, African, Polynesian, you name it—and we were all standing in line, all facing into the light, and suddenly I saw what was similar about every face, instead of first seeing the differences."

Valena could think of nothing to say, except, "I'd like to see that, too."

At noon, Valena picked from her boots the grit and other material she had accumulated during her time on Cape Royds. After splitting the sample into two, she put each half into a separate plastic bag, labeled them, signed them with the date, and passed them to Nat and Jeannie to do the same. She then taped the ziplock edges shut and ran staples all along through the tape so that no bag could be opened and reclosed without leaving an obvious path of disruption. She repeated this process with grit from Nat's boots, and then Jeannie's, and added to the pile the tiny collection of glass shards lent by the archaeologist.

"Take care of those glass shards," said Nate. "Conserving all the artifacts in those huts is a mammoth undertaking, being done with private contributions. The Kiwis take the job very seriously, as well they should."

"I hear you." Her data-collecting chores done, Valena turned to Jeannie's laptop, clicked onto the Internet, and brought up Emmett Vanderzee's Web site. She turned to the pages that would already have been in place the year before, trying to figure out what had caught Morris Sweeny's interest.

Dan Lindemann had posted a blog of preparations for that year's deployment to Antarctica. There were two photographs on the page: one of Emmett, Bob Schwartz, and Dan Lindemann giving thumbs-ups in front of a map of Antarctica; and another of Emmett and Cal Hart packing crates to be shipped south from Reno. The picture with Cal in it interested her. Dan had caught him in profile, but he had noticed the camera out of the corner of his eye and was not smiling. In fact, he appeared to be lifting his hand to ward off having his image caught for the Web site.

Valena typed out an e-mail:

Em

Am at Cape Royds penguin colony. Have photographed boot prints of uninvited visitor presumably responsible for illegal removal of six penguin eggs and two artifacts. Suspect seen scramming to McMurdo at edge of storm. Possible—or probable—connection between this suspect and contemporaneous bludgeoning death of tractor driver whom I'll guess was unlucky enough to witness arrival.

Also have samples of grit that collects in boots here. Visual observation indicates phenocrysts (feldspars?) and lithic fragments of decayed lava from Mount Erebus and penguin guano; also have samples of bottle glass fragments from Sir Ernest Shackleton's 1907 *Nimrod* expedition as microscopic fragments might be present in boot samples. Glass was manufactured in England and possibly France (ship's manifest indicates several cases of champagne).

Emmett Vanderzee still in custody, though evidence builds that others had opportunity to spoil efforts to retrieve key airdrop of medical supplies to his camp last year. Person seen driving snow machine through heavy storm raises question was same person in Emmett's camp and did he get to airdrop before Emmett could find it?

Come on Em, admit it, you are fascinated by this. Kindly write back with advice on analyses and who to contact with results.

Valena

P.S. Don't worry, I'm out of harm's way, or just about.

"There," she said. "We now have a representative sampling of what we might find in the boots of our mystery guest, and samples from which to ID the missing bottles. My colleague back in the States will hopefully tell me how to proceed with the analyses."

"Who's your colleague?" asked Jeannie.

"Emily Hansen. She's cracked a bunch of murder cases using geologic evidence. Technically speaking, the glass here is man-made geology. Em knows people in the FBI lab. The FBI would call this trace evidence."

"Nicely done," said Nat. "But I shall admit to having a heavy conscience about asking you to help with this. If you're right that there's a connection between the eggs and bottles and the dead Cat driver, then please leave it to the professionals."

Valena said, "I'm on my way to the Dry Valleys, and I think I'll be safe there. As soon as I get back to McMurdo, I'll turn in my evidence, and then everyone will know what I know, and I'll no longer be a target."

Jeannie said, "I think I hear your helo."

Valena cocked an ear. The distant throbbing of helicopter blades had invaded the wilderness of Cape Royds.

They walked outside Nat's tent to watch the helo approach around the shoulder of Mount Erebus, a tiny dot of machinery suspended in a frozen sky. Its far thudding grew louder as it increased in size, blades a blur of movement, its skids now swinging overhead, the sound concussive and deafening, snow and grit pounding into a wild dance. The machine hovered, slid sideways, chose a landing site, and settled, the blades still spinning.

"Lucky you," Jeannie said, shouting to be heard over the engine and rotors. "You got the AStar. The sports car of all Antarctic helos."

The blades continued to whirl. "Looks like he wants to load you hot," Nat hollered. "You ever done this before?"

"No!" Valena's heart was hammering in her chest. In survival training, Manuel had told them that although the roar of the helicopter would urge them to hurry, they must keep their heads and not approach the craft unless beckoned by the pilot.

Nat walked a wide arc around the field until he stood fifty feet in front of the helicopter, making eye contact with the pilot. He grabbed the front of his pants with one hand and put the other across his chest, then pointed at Valena.

The blades crooned to a stop.

Valena hefted her duffels and walked over next to Nat. "What did you say to him? Your semaphores, I mean."

"I told him you're a virgin."

Valena started to laugh. Impulsively, she gave Nat a hug, and then she shared a longer, womanly squeeze with Jeannie.

The pilot popped his door open and stepped out. "Where's mine?" he called, in a crisp British accent.

Jeannie wiggled her eyebrows. "You got Paul. Stand by for major flirtation," she said. "Underneath that helmet he's a looker."

"We'll put your gear in this external basket with your skis," said Paul, indicating a pod on the side of the aircraft. He hefted each duffel and checked them for weight tags. "And you, my dear, shall ride up front with me. Discussion of your charms around Mac Town had prepared me for a happy flight, but you far outreach their capacity for description."

Valena averted her eyes in embarrassment.

"Helmets, your choice of sizes." He produced two helmets and helped Valena find the one that fit best. Then he showed her how to climb up into her seat, buckle the restraints, and latch the door.

Valena smiled and waved at Nat and Jeannie. *I'm in a helicopter!* she told herself. *I am in Antarctica in a helicopter, and I'm about to fly to the continent!*

The helicopter was no larger than a passenger car inside, and the whole front seemed to be made of Plexiglas, even down to a panel of it beneath her feet. Paul restarted the engine, soon bringing its squeal to a screaming pitch. The blade in front of them began to swing, disappearing around behind them to be replaced by its opposite, and again, and faster, and faster, until they formed nothing but a blur. Paul gripped the stick and the collective, twitched them this way and that, and up they went.

The ground dropped away. Contracted. Nat and Jeannie shrank into mice, and then gnats. The helicopter began to slide forward, tilting slightly toward its nose, still rising. The penguins went by, tiny dots of black and white on the splattered rock. The helicopter was over the frozen sea now, the Transantarctic Range spreading across the horizon to greet them.

They flew across trackless miles of ice, their world reduced to a tiny bubble that cast a vague shadow the size of a pinhead far below them. The edge of the continent slowly resolved from a thin line to a scrabble of rocks, and then they were over it, continuing onward, now cutting up a valley between two ranges of mountains, following a river of ice toward its source. The glacier filled the valley in a fractured cascade, frightening in its instability. "I wouldn't want to walk on that," she said to Paul through her tiny microphone.

"No, you would not. But beautiful, eh? In a terrifying sort of way? And look at this one." He pointed to their right, to a lobe of ice that hung like a tongue from a high side valley. "Incredible, all the shapes. Before I came here, I thought ice was ice, but it's a world unto itself, infinitely variable. This will be Clark Glacier up here to our right." He lifted the controls, raising them up higher and higher, climbing like a mosquito up over an elephant's hide, skimming up past dry, empty walls of rock until they came out over a notch in the mountains. "This is the Olympus Range," said Paul. "Just one of many ranges that make up the Transantarctics here in the Dry Valleys. And here on this saddle sits Clark Glacier. Just a little thing, only two miles wide and how many long. A nice, quiet little glacier with no cracks in it for you to begin your studies."

"I'll take my ice as crevasse-free as I can get it," said Valena. "Where's the camp?"

"Just there," said Paul. "Can't you see it?"

Valena peered out across the smooth expanse of snow-covered ice looking for the line of tents she knew must be there. They had a drill rig going, so there would be at least one very large tent, but where was it?

Suddenly, she saw it: a minuscule group of pinpoint dots. The dots grew larger now, and larger yet, until they were a line of tents: two yellow Scotts, a few small domes, one large orange dome for the drill, and something that looked like a brightly colored pill bug. A tiny person was waving at them, pointing to a position in which he wanted them to land. No, *she*, Valena realized, as they descended low enough to make out the smiling face of a woman.

They settled onto the snow, and Paul shut down the engine, bringing the rotors to a stop. Valena unclipped her seat belt and shoulder restraints and hopped out. "Dr. Bosch?" she inquired.

"Please call me Naomi," said the woman. She was in her late thirties or early forties and very fit, dressed in nicely fitted overalls and a thick fleece sweater. A bright red knit cap did not quite cover a head full of busy brown curls, and her alert brown eyes took in Valena in detail. Naomi was a smiler, and her welcome was clear and hearty.

"Thanks for having me to your camp," said Valena.

"Glad to have an extra pair of hands. Let's get these core boxes un-loaded," said Naomi. "Hey, boys! Hop to it!"

A flap on the side of the big drilling tent opened, and two young men stepped out and hurried to help Naomi with the core packing boxes. When they were done, one of them stood off to one side, eyeing Valena through his dark glasses.

Valena recognized him from brief sightings around DRI: here, at last, was Daniel Lindemann.

38

Naomi reached inside the helicopter, selected a helmet, and put it on. "Climb back in," she told Valena.

Valena gasped. "I'm not staying?"

"Oh, we'll be back later," said Naomi, "but first we've got to scout our next drilling location." She gave Valena a wink. "Come on, I know it's a lot to ask . . ."

"I'm in!" said Valena.

Naomi turned to the men. "Now, don't look so hangdog. You'll be living there in a few days."

Dan Lindemann slunk back off to the drilling tent.

"Surly," Paul whispered, so that only Valena could hear him. "Unfriendly. I saw him watching you."

Valena gritted her teeth. "If I have any 'accidents' in the next day or so, you remember that, okay?"

Paul's eyes widened, but he didn't say anything.

They loaded up and lifted off, peeling away to the northwest toward the next valley. As they crossed over it, Valena saw why the Dry Valleys were thus named: this one had no ice in it at all. In fact, it was carpeted with sand dunes. The valley did not at first appear to be very large, but when they swung out to cross it, it seemed to expand and swallow them. Once again, the terrain had tricked her mind.

They flew along a great, dark cliff that stood in pillarlike columns. *More volcanics,* thought Valena, but, looking far to the left and right, she saw that this flow had not come out across the surface of the earth but had instead been injected between layers of rock. *A sill,* she thought, recalling the correct term from her geology classes. And it went on and on. Never had she seen one so clearly exposed, nor so large, even in photographs.

Naomi's voice came to her through her headphones. "That's the Ferrar Dolerite," she said. "Pretty impressive, eh? That cliff will be a couple hundred feet high, and you know how far it goes?"

"I can't possibly guess," replied Valena.

"Three thousand kilometers. The length of the Transantarctic Mountains. Imagine all that magma," she said. "That's one hell of a lot of liquid rock."

"All at *once?*"

"Exactly. Mind-bending. It marks the breakup of Gondwanaland. Tear Antarctica away from Africa, South America, Australia . . . and up comes the hot juice." She indicated with her hands big plates of the earth's surface ripping apart.

Valena's jaw dropped. Throughout her undergraduate geology training, she had studied plate tectonics, the unifying theory of geology that described the movement of the earth's crustal plates, and had understood it. Moreover, she had found the evidence for it compelling, convincing. It had become a cornerstone of her understanding of the world around her. It explained why the fossilized remains of dinosaurs and delicate ferns had been found on this continent, the remains of life that inhabited it when this land was farther north. Then the convection of heat within the earth's mantle had ruptured the supercontinent of Gondwanaland into its current chunks two hundred million years ago and had moved Antarctica slowly south, then parked it here thirty million years ago.

The Ferrar Dolerite, one long, black cliff of evidence. Data like this was why scientists came to Antarctica, and this was why the nations that had called Antarctica their own had suspended their claims and set it aside, under the Antarctic Treaty, as a scientific and ecological preserve.

As they flew deeper into the continent, the mountains rose above them into minarets and castles. Mammoth tongues of glacial ice licked down wide valleys from the impossibly broad reaches of the Antarctic Plateau. Ice and rock, rock and ice rolled out all around them, a symphony of harsh beauty. The brute strength and naked vulnerability of the land called Valena to its icy breast, claiming her forever as its own, speaking to her of her tininess. The frenzied scurryings of civilization did not exist here.

She leaned her face against the cold Plexiglas of the helicopter window, sighing, falling irrevocably in love, grateful to the bottom of her soul that there existed this one place on earth that could not be tamed.

◈

THE LITTLE HELICOPTER crossed over another wild knuckle of mountains and landed in a wide bowl of snow-covered ice. Naomi spoke over the headphones. "We'll be about a half-hour here, okay?"

"Right-o," Paul answered. "Guess I'll just have to take a break, eh?" He shut down the engine, and all climbed out and turned slowly around, taking in the spectacular scenery. The bowl of glacier rose up on three sides like a great cresting wave lapping against a craggy shore of Ferrar Dolerite. To the east, it fell away in sensuous folds, flowing toward a far range of mountains that flew like sails glimpsed at the mouth of a harbor.

Naomi threw her parka into the helicopter and began to dance a boot-clumsy minuet, arms aloft and legs akimbo, her face blooming in an exquisite smile. "Yes! Yes! I like it, I like it," she sang.

Paul leaped into the air, whooping, "It's so beautiful! Three seasons I've been coming to Antarctica, and this has got to be the most incredible . . . ye-*ow!*"

Valena was quietest in her receipt of beauty. She turned a complete circle slowly, drinking in the landscape. She moaned softly, more a relaxation of breath than an exhalation, the sound rising from deep inside her and drifting away on the breeze.

Paul bounded off along the crusted snow. The air here was still and the sun bright, making it surprisingly warm. He threw off his helmet, and then his gloves, prancing like a great stag.

Naomi said, "I'm going to pace things off here and make my GPS measurements. Why don't you two take ten?" She walked away across the glacier, singing.

Valena was alone in a world of soft curves. Words ran though her mind: *I am home.* All the sad confusions of her former life turned into vapor, rose high into the atmosphere, and ceased to be. Time fell away. All dimension froze. There was only ice.

◈

NAOMI WORKED HER way back down the bowl of ice, making notes in a book. When she arrived where Valena was standing, she took her by the elbow and walked her farther away from the helicopter. "I hate to bust a high," she said, "but I've got something I need to talk to you about."

"And what's that?" asked Valena.

"You're not here just to take in the sights. You're Emmett's student, right?"

"Uh . . . well, yes."

"And word travels here, even way out here in the field camps. A crew hiked up from Wright Valley the other day doing a recon for some kind of organism that lives in between the grains of the rocks, and they told me what happened. So tell me the developments."

"I don't have anything much to report," said Valena. "I arrived a week ago today, and Emmett was gone."

"And of course you're trying to get him back. I would, too. So what have you accomplished so far, and who's helping you?"

"There are some people—we're—I'm—trying to . . ."

"Ah. So it's like that. And you've come here to talk to my young idiot."

"Idiot?"

"Dan Lindemann. He was with Emmett at the high camp last year, so you need to interview him if you're going to be thorough."

"Idiot?" Valena asked again.

"Don't get me wrong, he's top-notch, and I was lucky to get him as a student, but he's being an idiot about Emmett's situation. Is there anything in particular you need from me?"

"Maybe you can tell me this: why did he come to you, instead of sticking with Emmett?"

"I'd like to believe it's because I'm doing the kind of work he wants to do, but on the face of it . . . well, he'd finished his master's with Emmett, or at least, he's defended his thesis and has just a few things to clean up and hand in to call it complete. So he was all but done and wanted to get on with another Antarctic project, or at least that's what he said."

"What are you working on?"

The same old ice core stuff. The oxygen and hydrogen isotopes in the ice will tell us about temperature. The chemistry of the dust will tell us how hard the wind was blowing, and the amount of salt tells us how far the sea ice extended into the ocean, and we're working with a dozen or more other stable isotopes and trace elements. But it's otherwise a different game from WAIS Divide. Emmett and his team picked a spot on the ice sheet as flat and white as spilled milk on glass. The scenery sucks, but he wanted ice that does not have much of a local climate signal. WAIS is more of a global record. My sites here in the mountains have lots of local influences caused by wind and ice flow through the mountains. To figure out what's been going on around here—to understand how the ocean, sea ice, and land ice interact and form climate—we need to have a varied array of ice cores. We are collecting five cores around the Dry Valleys so we can make sure the changes we see are widespread and not caused by some little bump in topography."

"Trace elements. That's what I hope to work on with Emmett's cores. Though if I can't get him back down here . . ."

"You'll get him back," said Naomi. "He didn't do it."

"How do you *know* that?" asked Valena, keeping her voice as level as she could. "I don't mean to sound like I suspect him—Jim Skehan already bit my head off for that—but the reality is that I don't really know him. I replaced Dan, just as Taha replaced Bob. Which gets me back to my original question: why did Dan come to you instead of staying with Emmett? Clearly he had the work for him."

Naomi considered the question. "On the face of it, there's nothing mysterious about that. Dan put in his application clear last year. February, I think it was. Well, come to think of it that would have been about five minutes after he got off the plane returning from Antarctica. Hmm. Anyway, I was delighted to get one of Emmett's students for a PhD. I'm still starting out in the profession myself, you know, not all that well established, and it was a feather in my cap to get the baton handed off from the great Emmett Vanderzee. He wrote Dan a brilliant recommendation, when asked. Of course I had heard about the trouble, but . . . well, I prefer to keep my nose out of other peoples' troubles."

"And Bob Schwartz? He jumped ship, too."

"That does not tally with my experience of him," Naomi said, the precision in her choice of words the only hint that she might be perturbed. "He began talking with the PI he's with clear back in March . . . my husband, to be precise . . . and they had an understanding by the time the funding for their part of the WAIS Divide project was confirmed in early April."

"Did Emmett write him a recommendation, too?"

"It did not occur to my husband to ask. Bob is a fully fledged professional. My husband had heard him speak at WAIS Workshop meetings, and it was clear that Emmett thought highly of his work. We read Bob's dissertation." She narrowed her eyes as she stared out across the ice.

"Maybe I have all of that wrong," said Valena, knowing damned well that she didn't. Taha had told her. Had described Emmett's shock at his departure. She did not speak of this to Naomi. It was not her place to do so.

Naomi asked, "Emmett picked you up when?"

"September. After I returned to school in late August at the end of the summer break. I had to withdraw from my classes and add thesis-study units to be available for this deployment, another reason I'd very much like this field season to end happily. Spring term starts the fourth week in January, and I have ten more units of classwork to take before I can qualify to hand in my thesis, which of course will be all about nothing if I can't get any data."

"I can fix you up with enough data to keep you going for a doctorate," said Naomi. "But don't worry, you'll get your master's with Emmett. And he may expect that you'll simply hand in your master's thesis, keep taking classes, and swap over into a doctoral program."

Valena turned and gazed into Naomi's eyes. "You're willing to help me out? But I haven't even applied for your program, you haven't seen my transcripts, I—"

"If Emmett took you on, you're qualified, last minute or no. Weren't there other students lined up for the spot?"

"Yes, but—"

"He chose *you*. There are people who've been through PhD programs and several fellowships who would jump at the chance to work with him. There are professors who'd take the semester off from work to come down here with him. He chose you. End of topic. If this debacle leaves you stuck for a degree program, I'll take you on and figure I've made out like a bandit. But first, let's get the poor man out of jail. You'd be better served to finish your master's with him anyway. His name still looks better on your vita than mine, controversy or no." She grinned and swept her arms out across the scenery. "And then come back here with me for your doctorate. Much nicer weather than WAIS Divide."

"This is . . . so *kind* of you!"

"Think nothing of it," said Naomi. "We are family down here." She turned and hiked back over the rough *sastrugi* toward the helicopter.

"Okay, Paul, sorry to break up your nap," she said, nudging the sun-bathing pilot with her boot. "I'm sure you want to be back in Mac Town for Saturday night with all your girlfriends. Come on."

"Right-o," said Paul. "Home for tea and medals."

Paul flew Valena and Naomi back to Clark and then lifted back up into the pale blue Antarctic sky. The overwhelming buffeting of the rotor wash diminished into a flutter and the AStar into a tiny spec as it sailed away over the hard knuckles of the Olympic Range.

Valena turned to Naomi. "Put me to work," she said.

Naomi sent her off with another of her students to make a radar survey of the glacier, a task that involved dragging a transmitter across its surface to record reflections off the rock beneath it. When she returned, Naomi asked, "Are you any kind of a cook?"

"I haven't had many complaints."

"Good. We share the work here, so you're expected to contribute, and to be frank, we're sick of our own cooking."

One of the drillers said, "How about she whips up some stir-fry? We still have a kilo of prawns, and I keep coming across bags of mixed veggies in the freezer pit."

"I'll see what I can do," said Valena.

The other driller picked up the bucket of drill cuttings and carried it down to the cook tent to show Valena around. "The dry food is all here, in these boxes we use to weigh down the skirts of the tent so it won't blow away—no problem with critters getting into it, as there aren't any this far inland, not even skuas—and you'll find a storage pit out the back door." He grinned. "Refrigeration is not a problem when you work on glaciers. We use the drill cuttings for drinking and cooking water. This particular ice fell as snow about two thousand years ago."

"Vintage water," said Valena.

"You know to put some water in the bottom of the pan before you start to melt the ice?"

"Yeah, so it doesn't scorch the pan."

"Good. There's some water in the half-gallon thermoses in the cook tent. We set them up boiling, morning and night, so we always have some starter water."

"I'll take care of it."

As Valena set to work creating dinner, she noticed that she had all but forgotten her urgency to find out who had killed the journalist in Emmett Vanderzee's camp or, for that matter, who had stolen the eggs and bottles from Cape Royds. The riveting importances of the preceeding days seemed months in the past and light-years distant. This was why she had come to Antarctica!

The stove was a two-burner Coleman that ran on propane. She lit the right-hand burner and set to work melting the chipped ice, listening with amazement as the bubbles of ancient atmospheres popped.

It proved difficult to thaw the prawns. While she had adjusted to the constant cold, the prawns still seemed to know that ten degrees Fahrenheit was well below the point of freezing. When she had some water heated, she poured some into a second pan and put the prawns into it, but the water cooled so quickly in the Antarctic air that the little arthropods still floated as a solid brick and refused to thaw.

Even rebellious prawns could not dampen her mood. She turned toward the open door flap to admire the wide sweep of snow that had been blown and scoured into zigzagging *sastrugi* in wild fractal variations, coating glacial ice that swept up to the rocky peaks of the Olympus Range in curves unbroken by the devices of humankind. She could glimpse the float of Mount Erebus, paled almost to invisibility in the frigid distance.

The sound of a footfall jerked her from the sweetness of the moment.

Dan Lindemann entered the tent. He dug through the litter of snacks that had been left out on the dining table and selected a Pecan Sandie cookie. Watching her with brooding interest, he shoved it into his mouth in two bites and chewed. Still staring, he unscrewed the cap on an insulated water bottle and emptied half of it down his throat in one long guzzle, behavior that might have struck her as grotesque in the real world. Food and drink was not a social matter in Antarctica; it was requisite, a job to get done, and if it felt or tasted good going down, that was a bonus. Dan swallowed the last of the cookie he had ingested. Still staring, he addressed her with an abrupt, "Why are you here?"

"I need to talk to you," she replied.

"Well, at least you're honest."

"I trust I can expect the same from you."

He shook his head as if to clear it. "This is about Emmett."

"Yes, it is."

"Hell."

Valena waited, occupying the time by crumbling the mass of frozen vegetables into separate bits.

Dan reached past her to grab a ladle and dipped some hot water from the melting pot into his water bottle, then took another swig. "I hear they arrested his ass."

"In fact, they arrested his whole body, ass and all."

"Huh."

"They took him to Hawaii. He's been arraigned, or whatever they call it when you get charged with something."

"What was the charge?"

"Murder."

"No shit."

"None whatsoever."

"Huh."

She waited.

"Murder one or two?" he asked. "Or is it three? You know, manslaughter. Kind of an accident."

"I don't know. NSF is keeping a lid on things, but I suppose by the time I get back to McMurdo the *New York Financial News* will have it on its front page."

Dan fumbled another two cookies out of the bag and wolfed them down. He stared out the doorway. He chewed. He swallowed. "So why are you *here*?"

"Like I said, to talk to you about it."

"Why?"

"To clear him. I need your help." Valena was beginning to feel annoyed.

"He got himself into this. I sure can't help him."

Valena detected evasion in his voice. Or was it outright deceit? "Don't you even *want* to help him?"

"No. In fact, I am not the least bit interested." He spoke decisively, and with heat.

Valena silently counted to ten, then said, "You know, I'm having a hard time featuring this. The man was your thesis advisor. He gave you the break of a lifetime bringing you down here, and that's the best you can do? Not even, 'Wow, the poor guy,' or, 'I wish I could help but I'm brain dead?'"

"You weren't *there*," he said. "And yeah, I got my master's with the guy, but it was supposed to be a PhD, you know? He gets his ass in a crack with these guys and it costs me an extra year to get through graduate school. A man could starve to death. You know?"

Valena fought to keep her voice steady. "I'm still not clear on this. Why did you have to leave? And why was it going to take an extra year?"

Dan Lindemann's voice rose and cracked. "When that business with the newspaper article hit, it was one big shitstorm. It was all he had on his mind for weeks. Then he had the US Senate dragging his butt into chambers and cutting him to bits. I was doing all the work. Me and Bob. We were running all the lab analyses and even beginning to write the papers."

"Isn't that what graduate students do?"

Dan bared his teeth in frustration. "We hardly ever saw him! He was either flying back and forth to Washington to testify, or he was in his office with his door shut. Or God knows where. Bob finally pulled the ripcord. He would have stayed, but no, there was no funding all of a sudden for a postdoc, let alone an actual research associate. Jeez, Valena, don't you get it? He's down to running his research on cheap labor! It's grad students or nothing!"

"I can't believe this."

"You don't want to believe it. Why, have you had a different experience? How many times have you actually had five minutes of Emmett's time? I'll bet he had Taha tell you what you needed for coming to Antarctica, and Taha's never even been here! Just look at you, you're wearing FDX boots! He didn't even take enough care to tell you to bring boots you can actually walk in!"

Valena tried to focus on the vegetables. Doggedly, she said, "I came here to talk to you because I'm trying to get a handle on what actually happened last year at the high camp."

Dan grabbed two more cookies, said, "I'm not even going to talk about that," and abruptly exited the tent.

DINNER WAS A silent affair, as much because everyone was exhausted from a day's physical efforts at 4,200 feet above sea level on a glacier as because there was nothing to talk about. All sat about the table in their parkas and fleece hats, eyelids sagging from the week's work. Naomi Bosch made small talk for a while and then slipped into some puzzle she was working out in her mind. Dan Lindemann stared at his plate. One driller ate with his head bowed over one of the newspaper summaries that the helicopter pilot had dropped off. The other fiddled with little drawings he was making in the margins of page two of another.

When Valena produced a pan of gingerbread that she had baked in the Coleman oven, it was gone in two minutes, but the only formal reaction she got was from the driller who was drawing pictures, who made brief, rapturous eye contact with her as he announced, "I love ginger. You may stay."

Dan left the instant dinner was over and did not return. One by one, the other members of Naomi Bosch's Clark Glacier crew mumbled good nights and stumbled off to bed. Valena brought the melt water back up to a boil and refilled the thermoses, then filled her own water bottle, climbed down inside the sunken latrine to empty her bladder into the pee bottle, emptied that through the funnel into the local fifty-five-gallon drum, and shuffled off down the line of tents to her own.

Ensconced in her sleeping bag with the warm water bottle up against her belly, she thought long and hard about the day, the week, and her life, and once again about the joys of discovering herself as a scientific colleague. She had never fit in anywhere like she fit here in Antarctica. Dan Lindemann might be sorry she was there, but everything else was so perfect that he was easy to discount.

Finally, with the bright light of the Antarctic night still shining through her eyelids and a fine rime of ice crystals forming on the inside of the tent from her exhalations, she slipped off into a deep and dreamless sleep.

39

SUNDAY MORNING FOUND MCMURDO STATION IN A SOMBER MOOD. Sunday breakfast, a meal usually frequented only by those who had not found a party the evening before, was mobbed with those who did not feel that they could handle Steve Myer's memorial service on an empty stomach, and those on the night shift who had stayed up to join them. In anticipation of the hike up Observation Hill to the place chosen for this observance, most had already dumped their trays into the dish room and had returned to the dining hall to drink an extra cup of coffee to help keep them warm. They sat quietly, watching a gathering snow flurry obscure the landscape outside the windows.

George Bellamy's voice boomed out over the public address system. "Good morning. This is to announce that the memorial service for Steve Myer, which was to be held on Ob Hill, will be held instead in front of the chapel. This is because it is snowing. Once again—"

The voice coming over the speaker was drowned in a rising tide of grumbling, growling voices. There was a great scraping of chairs as every person in the room stood up and filed out past the dish room, leaving their coffee cups by an untended window, the dishwashers having already left to get their coats.

A great tide of red and tan parkas filtered out through the falling snow and flowed toward Observation Hill, funneling now into a file four wide as the slope steepened. The only sound was that of boots crunching through crusted snow into scoria. As the first reached the summit and gathered around Scott's cross, others began to spill out around the slope below it.

They were consumed in a soft, white world that deadened sound, a cocoon of opacity that fell from the sky like frozen tears.

Father James Skehan stood in front of the cross, eyes closed in prayer, a violet stole draped across the shoulders of his big red parka. A PhD in geology and years working on the glaciers unlocking the secrets of climate had not washed his earlier seminary training from him. He held in his gloved hands his copies of the *Rite Book* and the *Holy Bible*. The fine leather of his Bible was soft and frayed from all the years he had carried it with him to his field locations. He opened his eyes, looked out across the multitude, and said, "Let us pray."

As Father Skehan led the citizens of McMurdo through the liturgy for the dead, the falling snow thickened, and the world continued to lose its edges. The cadences of the familiar words brought comfort, and in many, released tears.

At length, Father Skehan turned to the Boss and asked him to say a few words. The Boss reached out a hand for Father Skehan's Bible and read from it, his strong, paternal voice both soothing and heartbreaking. Then he closed the book and said, "I chose to ask Father Skehan here to offer a Mass because Steve mentioned to me once that he was of the Catholic persuasion. More often he spoke of how this place filled his heart. We come from far places to work here, places where it's warm and we have family and where you can take long showers, but we always leave a part of ourselves here. I think of how the Greeks might have seen it: they had the myth of Persephone. She's the girl who ate those seeds from the pomegranate. She was beautiful, body and soul. Everybody loved Persephone, including Hades, the god of the underworld. One day while she was gathering flowers, he abducted her, just split the earth open and swallowed her up.

"Things got bad on earth after Persephone was abducted. Her mother Demeter grieved her so intensely that the plants ceased to grow. It was so bad in fact that Zeus went down to the underworld and demanded the girl's return and got it. But she had eaten those seeds, and that bound her to the underworld, where nothing grows, for that many months each year.

"I'm not a young maiden who gathers flowers and neither was Steve, but I think on Persephone each and every time I come down here. This place gets into your soul. Although nothing grows here, it's like a passionate fruit of intense flavor, and we return to eat of it year after year. And that's where we turn that myth inside out. We long for this underworld.

We know something about it that few people ever get to know. It is bright and clear, and it sings to us in our dreams, like a mirror in which we can at last see ourselves clearly.

"I like to think that Steve hears that singing still. Well, that's all I have to say, except that when we're done here, we've got a barbecue going down by the Heavy Shop, and the first round's on me!"

A great roar went up. A few others stepped to the summit to speak: Cupcake as the one who had been coming south the longest, then a few others, and then Father Skehan closed with a final prayer, and the moment fell away as the crowd dispersed into the snow.

Halfway down the hill, Dave Fitzgerald felt a jab at his ribs, a poke blunted by layers of down and polypropylene. "Hey, why didn't you say something?" asked Wilbur. "You found him."

Dave turned to see whether his workmate was looking on him with kindness or craziness. It was the latter. He sighed. "Just give it a break," he said, and continued down the hill.

MAJOR MARILYN WOOD stood with Major Hugh Muller at the foot of the hill, a tiny knot of camouflage brown and black as a sea of red and tan parkas flowed past them, hoping to spot Valena in the crowd.

"Did she answer the message you left for her?" asked Major Waylon Bentley as he moved through the crowd to join them.

"No," said Hugh. "I put a note on her door in Crary. I'm thinking that she isn't anywhere in town, but she hasn't left the ice. Her name never showed up on the pax manifests."

"She went off with that traverse to Black Island," said Waylon. "But she came back, right? You're sure of it?"

"I'm sure. I saw her. Then she went walkabout again or something."

"Let's ask Paul here," said Marilyn, grabbing the arm of the helicopter pilot as he walked by her.

Paul looked up in surprise, as if he had been woken from a dream.

Marilyn said, "Any of you guys carry a beaker named Valena anywhere recently?"

Paul smiled. "In fact I did. Lovely girl. I took her up to Clark Glacier in the Dry Valleys yesterday."

"Whew!" said Marilyn.

"Why, what's up?"

"Oh, nothing," said Hugh. "Any idea when she's coming back?"

Paul shook his head.

"Whose event is she with?" asked Marilyn.

"Naomi Bosch. Glaciology. I forget the number."

"Did you take anyone else up there?" asked Waylon.

"Just her."

Marilyn asked, "Who else is in that camp?"

Paul rolled his eyes up in thought. "A couple of drillers and two graduate students."

"Names on those students?"

"The new one I didn't catch, but Lindemann I remember from other years. A bit of a sniveler if he doesn't get the front seat."

"Thanks," said Hugh. With Valena checked off his mental list for the moment, he began scanning the crowd for another face.

Marilyn shook her head. "There are wheels within wheels with this puzzle."

Waylon said, "This guy we're looking for . . . did the service record give a photograph of him?"

Hugh said, "Everyone looks alike in these damned red parkas. Besides, I wouldn't go by appearances, or the name he's got on his parka. He's here on a false passport."

"Imagine," said Waylon. "A dishonorable discharge, right here in Mac Town."

"You think this guy knows Valena is on his trail?" said Marilyn.

"Let's hope not," said Hugh, "but assume he does. We're just going to have to figure out how to reach her before he does, and pray that he's not Dan Lindemann."

40

On Clark Glacier, Naomi Bosch looked out the flap of the cook tent. "It looks like it's clearing. I was thinking we should ski down to the terminus of the glacier," she said.

Twenty minutes later, everyone had bottles of hot water in their packs and rations of chocolate and granola bars in their pockets. The drillers had their skis on first and shot out ahead of them. Dan Lindemann and the other student followed second, and Naomi and Valena brought up the rear.

"I'm sorry I don't have better equipment," said Valena, noticing that Naomi was wearing gear that looked like it must be the latest, greatest thing.

"Never fear. We do things on the buddy system here. We'll all swap off. Did you get much out of Dan yesterday?"

Valena stared at her. "You sent him to talk to me?"

"I did. He would have hidden in his tent until you left if I'd let him."

"Well, he wasn't all that informative."

Naomi took this in. "Then I'll have another talk with him, let him know that he has a choice: he can help or he can walk home."

They skied away across the wide expanse of Clark Glacier, the fresh snowflakes glinting at them like a thousand separate gems. They were soon warmed from the effort and shed parkas into their packs, switching to wind jackets. As they left the center of the saddle, the glacier began to curve downward—the reverse of a ski slope, which has a concave curve toward its base—and the skiing became easier and easier until it was in fact too steep for the equipment Valena was using. Waving for one of the drillers to stay with Valena, Naomi shot away down a half-pipe-shaped chute that descended along one side of the glacier.

The wind had blown the snow away, revealing blue-green ice. The edges of Valena's skis were too dull to cut into it, so she took off her skis and began to kick steps in the side of the pipe, working her way down. The others waited at the foot of the glacier, examining it, waving their ski poles as they discussed it.

She arrived at last, stepping for the first time onto the dry ground for which the Dry Valleys had been named. The surface was a fine trash of ventifacts—stones that had been polished into smooth facets by blowing grit—and broken on a much larger scale by the odd frost-fracture pattern called polygonal ground. Valena was in a world of magic, the coldest dry ground on earth. She wandered out across the patterned ground.

She knew the simple facts that had rendered these valleys ice-free—at this low elevation and in this location, the ice sublimated away faster than it could accumulate—but still it seemed strange. All but two percent of Antarctica was covered with ice, and the lion's share of uncovered ground was here.

The terminus of Clark Glacier was a cliff about a hundred feet high and draped with icicles. Valena wandered closer. She could see layers in the ice, great festoons of strata etched by melting. She was just considering walking even closer to it when an icicle several times her mass detached with a ballistic snap and crashed to the valley floor, scattering chunks of ice like shrapnel.

"That one almost got you," someone called from a position well behind her. "You might want to back up."

Valena turned. It was Dan Lindemann. "Thanks for the tip," she said. "Do you have any other key intelligence for me?"

Lindemann scowled. "Naomi says it's my turn to babysit you."

Valena closed her eyes to blot him temporarily from her world. She had heard this scornful tone a thousand times from cousins and schoolmates who would not accept her, but she refused to let it sting her as it always had. This was her place now, and he could not take it from her. *When I open my eyes,* she told herself, *I shall see only a sad person who cannot sneer his way out of a wet paper bag.* She opened her eyes. Dan Lindemann was still looking at her, but his demeanor had shifted from disdain to uncertainty.

She looked around to see where everyone else was, and to her horror realized that they were already climbing back up the glacier. She wanted to question Lindemann but not be left alone with him in a dangerous place. Hefting her skis onto her shoulder, she led the way.

Dan put on his skis and shuffled along behind her. "Too bad you don't have skins for your skis," he said. He made it sound like a taunt.

Valena stepped lightly over the snow, following the steps she had kicked coming downward. She had put on both layers of boot liner and had tightened the laces as tight as she could, but it was still tough going.

"I don't have anything to tell you," said Dan, pulling up beside her.

"That's too bad," said Valena evenly. She was becoming interested in the way the snowflakes refracted the light. They were like diamonds, and here and there lay a ruby, an emerald, a sapphire, or richest citrine.

"Emmett was going down, and if I'd stayed with him, I'd be sitting in Reno right now with Taha. Or I'd be in your shoes."

"Mm-hm." She glanced up the slope. The distance to the others was widening. She picked up her pace.

"Okay, what do you want to know?"

"I want to know who was where when it happened."

"What do you mean?"

"When the Airlift Wing dropped the bundle. Where were you?"

"I was in the cook tent. We heard it go overhead. But it was blowing and snowing so hard . . . well, we stayed put."

"You stayed put."

"No, I followed the ropes down to my tent. The one I shared with Bob. We were together the whole time. Emmett told me later that he and Cal went out right away, but they were nuts."

"Okay."

"Okay? That's it?"

"Okay, and who was in the cook tent?"

"Sheila. Morris. Dave."

"That's interesting. You called him by his given name."

"Who?"

"Morris Sweeny. He was a real person to you."

"Oh, sure. Kind of an ass, but he was a good writer."

"Even if he misrepresented Emmett's work?"

"It was Frink who wrote that article, not him, though we had some lively debates about all that. But Morris seemed more intent on . . . well, like he was looking for something here in Antarctica. Another story. Maybe his own story."

They were on the steepest part of the slope now. Valena tilted her head back to look for Naomi. She was just disappearing up over the convex curve of the glacier. "What sort of story?"

Lindemann said, "I don't know . . . human interest, more. He asked a lot of questions about the people he was going to meet in camp."

"Who in particular?"

"He was pretty cagy, didn't focus on anyone in particular, but asked lots of questions about who had been in the military, or how long they'd been around the university. How well Emmett knew everybody."

"And how well *did* Emmett know you all?"

Lindemann stopped to take a drink of water from his pack.

Valena looked upslope. The two drillers had disappeared. Only the second graduate student was still in sight.

Lindemann started moving again, but he changed the subject. "Like Frink, Morris didn't get the science. Just didn't have a clue about how it's done. You know how it goes: he thinks a theory is a fact, and thinks the facts are negotiable based on who observed them. Doesn't understand the scientific method, or what it's good for and what it's not. Basically clueless. Educable, perhaps, if you get him away from his neo-con buddies. That's why Emmett invited him down, or at least, that's why he said he did."

"And was he getting educated?" She looked again uphill. They were alone. She quickened her pace.

Dan shook his head. "It was kind of a mess. The storm hit just after we got him to the high camp, and then he got sick. It sure put an end to our arguments."

"You argued with him?"

"About the science."

"Had you ever met him before?"

"Huh? No. Why?"

"Then how do you know so much about him?"

"I was down in McMurdo when he arrived."

"I didn't know that." She was sweating from the pace.

"Yeah. I'd gotten sick, so Emmett left me behind when he went up to the high camp. In fact the only way I got up there at all was because they had the plane scheduled to fly in to pick up some of the fuel barrels that had gotten buried to another site."

"I don't understand. Why drop the barrels and then move them?" She was panting with the effort. She dropped her skis and put them on, hoping the gradient was now shallow enough that she could ski and pick up the pace. She slipped, then the skis caught, and began to surge forward.

"I don't know, really. The Airlift Wing had dropped them, and someone needed some over in another camp, so NSF sent in the Otter to pick a couple up. That meant there were two seats for us going in, and Morris push his way into the high camp because there had been such delays and he hated McMurdo. Too many liberals."

"I can just imagine."

"So NSF went along with it. They should have called his bluff, but they didn't."

"So you had kind of gotten to know him while waiting in McMurdo." Lindemann nodded. "The Coffee House."

"Wine."

"New Zealand merlots. We had that in common."

"And women."

"Yeah, he liked women. So do I," he said, sliding an evil look her way. "So what?"

"Okay." She was making better time now, the slope of the glacier shallow enough that she could really begin to move.

"And I was making progress with him. Helping him understand things a little better."

"That's good. So then you were at the high camp, and Ted the blaster flew out with the Otter pilot, and the storm hit, and Morris got sick, and that was that." Her breath burned in her lungs from the effort of speaking while she pushed so hard on the skis. "Have I got all that straight?"

"Yeah."

"So how did the other Gamow bag find its way back to McMurdo?"

"That—" Dan shuffled along for a while, thinking. "I don't know," he muttered.

"All right then, here's another question: did you notice anything unusual or unexpected after you got there? I mean, as regards Morris's conversations with the others. Before he got sick."

"What do you mean?"

Valena thought carefully about how to phrase her question. Whoever had visited Naomi's camp to pass the word of Emmett's arrest would not have known the particulars she knew, so if Dan offered them up, he knew them from having been there rather than from having been filled in after the fact, and she did not want to contaminate him as a witness. "Well, the feds assumed that Emmett was the one who caused the death because he was the one who was angry with the deceased. But perhaps someone else had a beef. So who else did he communicate with?"

"Oh, I see what you mean." Dan thought a while. "It's hard to remember after all this time. Mostly what I recall was how scared Emmett and everyone was when the guy got sick."

At last, they were back up on top of the glacier and could see the tops of the Scott tents coming up over the curve. "Let's put it another way, then. Who wasn't scared?"

"Oh, that's easy. That Wee Willy guy. But I figured he was just too damned stupid to get scared." Dan stopped skiing. He stood still, thinking. "And come to think of it, there was another guy Morris didn't like." He gave her an appraising look. "Exactly what's it worth to you to know?"

Valena pushed ahead. Over her shoulder, she called, "It's worth your damned doctorate!"

"Dave," called Dan. "He didn't like Dave."

41

ON MONDAY WHEN THE ASTAR THUDDED OUT OF THE SKY ONTO CLARK
Glacier, Valena was ready and waiting next to the loaded core boxes. The
downdraft from the rotors of the descending helicopter blasted her and
everything within fifty yards with flying snow. She said her good-byes and
thanks to Naomi, waved to the others, and climbed aboard. Her departure accomplished, she greeted the liftoff with the sharp focus of the single-minded.
She had narrowed her search to two suspects, and it would soon be one.

The pilot on duty was not the talkative type, which was fine with
Valena. Her brain was already in Crary Lab, where she would requisition a
microscope just as quickly as she could. The gorgeous ridges and valleys
rolled past beneath them as they flew south to pick up another passenger.
There were stunning views of volcanic dikes, swarms laid naked along
glacier-polished mountain tops. Like a settling leaf, the little craft spiraled
down into the steep-sided valley that held the frozen length of Lake Bon-
ney. They barreled out from the edge of the continent out across the ice,
passing the big rig run by the ANDRILL project. When they landed at
McMurdo, she refused a ride to her dorm, instead heading straight up the
hill to the lab, saying that she would be back for her gear.

In Crary, she stopped only an instant at Emmett's office to check for
notes—there were none—then set down her duffel and parka and relocked the door before heading up the ramp in search of a binocular microscope, which she found in the storeroom near the head offices. She
peered at the contents of the plastic bags. Instantly, she saw more than she
had expected. Not only did the sample from her boots have lithic frag-

ments and phenocrysts, it had tiny little penguin feathers, their short, thick barbules unmistakably belonging to flightless birds.

To identify the phenocrysts, she headed down the hallway and found a young woman from the Erebus team.

"Anorthoclase," said the vulcanologist as she squinted through the lens. "Yeah, that's the main feldspar phenocryst you get around here."

"Do you find it only in the basalts on Cape Royds?" asked Valena hopefully.

"Oh, heck no, it's pandemic. And to be more specific, those aren't basalts, they're phonolites. It's more alkaline than your basic basalt."

"Oh. Okay. But I don't see the anorthoclase phenocrysts here in Mac Town."

"No, but half the flows on the island have it, though the size of the crystals may vary."

Valena thanked her, stuffed the samples into her pockets for safekeeping, relocked the door to the office, and headed off to find Jim Skehan. He wasn't in his office, so she went to the library and looked for e-mail messages. There was one from her friends at the Airlift Wing:

Valena

Edgar Hallowell served during Iraqi Freedom. Went AWOL en route court martial for theft of body armor. No current address.

Signed, Your friends

There was also one from Em Hansen:

Valena

I checked with a friend at the FBI lab, here forwarded. Try to stay warm. Stay out of trouble. Em

The forwarded e-mail from the FBI lab began:

Feldspars and broken antique glass—well how cool is that?

Shackleton's discards would be worth money even if they were Budweiser bottles. In 1907, quality control still wasn't the big thing in manufacturing processes. There would be a lot of variability— measurable variability—in the composition of those bottles, even within a single bottle. Also, they didn't have the respect we have today for heavy metals leaching from containers, and there would probably be some interesting trace elements in the bottles too. The light green and brown glass were probably colored by iron oxides (differing oxidation states), and the blue was usually cobalt oxides.

There was a long paragraph on analytical equipment she could use to identify the bottle glass, how large a sample she needed for each, but the lab tech had assured her that that the binocular microscope was as good as it was going to get here in McMurdo. She was going to have to find a lower-tech way of establishing a connection between boot grit and Cape Royds. She read onward:

Volcanos are as distinctive as people. Each one spews out its own unique output, and each eruption is a little different. Chemically, even the start of an eruption is different than the end. If you had a decent sample and the right reference material, you could tell which volcano produced which ash, and that will tell you where someone/something has been.

Valena pondered this. *So petrography as it is practiced at the FBI lab is a little more detailed than a volcanologist can manage here with a hand lens. That's a relief!*
She read on to the closing salutations:

As for the penguin guano, well, the defense community always said that the FBI Lab doesn't do shit, and in this case they'd be right.

Valena threw back her head and laughed. But her mind was still racing. She had come up dry trying to figure out who had killed the journalist, but if she could nail the penguin egg theft to the man who had been seen riding south along the route from Cape Evans to Hut Point the morning Steve was killed, and if that person had also been at Emmett Vanderzee's high camp when the journalist was killed, then she might be able to tear a hole in the whole picture, at minimum opening the way for doubt in the minds of the feds. And she thought she knew exactly how to identify that way.

42

HUGH MULLER STOOD UP FROM HIS TABLE IN THE GALLEY AND scanned the room for any sign of Valena. He unconsciously stood in almost full brace, his major's leaves flashing on his fatigues.

"She'd be coming through the food lines, wouldn't she?" said Marilyn.

"Sit down, Hugh," said Waylon. "You don't want to draw attention to this."

Marilyn said, "It may be time to come out into the open with this, Waylon."

"There's Matt, I'll ask him if he's seen her," said Hugh. He moved through the crowd to the table where the heavy equipment operator was sitting with a few other men. "Tractor Matt," he said, making it sound like a social call. "You heard from our newest recruit lately?"

"You mean Tractor Valena?" said Matt. He wasn't smiling. "I was just talking about her with Father Jim here. Jim, Hugh flew the mission last year to the high camp."

Skehan stood up and shook Hugh's hand. "We sent her into the field. She was expected back on a helo this morning, but she has not reported in. I left a note for her, but it's gone now, and I don't think it was her that took it down."

"That's not good," said Hugh.

"No, in fact, that's bad."

Hugh said, "I left a note for her yesterday. I don't suppose it was there when you last checked."

Skehan shook his head. "I put my note up early this morning, well before she was due, and there were no notes waiting for her."

Hugh leaned closer to the scientist. "I'm going to take a chance here. We military generally keep to ourselves here on the ice, but this is a special case. When that man was killed up in the high camp, it was because our drop bundle was tampered with, and that makes it personal. So I think it's time we told each other everything we know, and put our heads together on this."

"Amen, brother."

Hugh said, "Valena asked us to look into the military record of a man named Edgar Hallowell. There was an Edgar Hallowell who served in Iraq at the beginning of the war. He was suspected of a number of petty thefts, but when he got to stealing body armor, the investigation went onto the fast track. They brought him back to the States for court-martial, but he went AWOL. We were able to obtain a photograph of him. Well, I was the pilot who flew Vanderzee's event into the high camp last year, and guess what?"

Skehan's eyes narrowed. "Cal Hart."

"Got it in one."

Skehan's face grew dark with anger. "We do our very best science, and an opportunist threatens to take us down."

Matt said, "That problem goes all the way to the White House."

Skehan stood up. "I'm on my way to Bellamy's office."

43

VALENA STOPPED FIRST AT THE POST OFFICE, WHICH WAS HOUSED IN one end of a large, white building just down the hill from the Boss's office in Building 17. At the end of the room, she found a window where stamps were sold and packages weighed. She presented herself to the clerk.

"Hi," she said. "Is it true that I can mail things from here just like I was shipping something locally at home?"

"Yes," said the woman. "This is an Army post office, which means that you pay as if you were shipping from our port of entry into the United States. Well, actually, things have to go through customs in New Zealand, which means that you can't send anything that would be hazardous to New Zealand wildlife. They have very strict rules about that."

"I see. So you X-ray the packages."

The woman shook her head. "No. We weigh them and sell you the postage. You fill out the customs form, just like at home in the States."

"And what if the contents are particularly fragile? Or . . . temperature sensitive?"

The woman smiled. "We supply all the bubble wrap you can stand. If you need to send something especially fragile, you can get heavy cartons over in BFC or Crary Lab. Everything gets recycled around here, and the scientists get special equipment shipped to them all the time, so it's easy to skua a really good box over there. And they have wonderful stickers you can put on the boxes that say 'Do Not Freeze' or 'Keep Frozen,' depending on what you need." She smiled. "They have little penguins on them."

Little penguins, thought Valena. *How ironic.* "How does something with a sticker like that get home?"

"The scientists can have boxes shipped home on the cargo vessel that comes in at the end of the season, or they can ship things through here. This is much faster, and costs very little. I once sent my skis all the way home for six dollars."

"Fantastic. And how long do packages sit here before they go out?"

"Oh, usually only a day or two. We can usually get them on the next flight. This time of year, it's the southbound flights that are overfilled."

"So if someone brought you a package say, last Tuesday, when would it have gone out?"

The clerk looked at her askance. "You mean during that big storm."

"Yes, that was the day."

"Well, we had a flight go out that evening, but it took off in a hurry, too fast for us to get the mail on board. You'll recall that was the day Steve Myer died." Her face tightened and she gazed down at her fingertips for a moment. "But there have been two flights out since."

"Do you remember any particular boxes? Perhaps one marked 'Do Not Freeze'?"

The woman laughed. "Half of them say that."

"Are you able to guarantee that they won't be frozen?"

"We do pretty well," she said, but her eyes were beginning to ask, Why all the questions?

"Do you recall a man bringing you a 'Do Not Freeze' box last Tuesday about this time of day?" She indicated a tall man with her hand. "Good-looking guy with blond hair, or a big, scary guy with darker hair?"

The woman gave her a crimped smile. "Now, you know that's none of my business to answer a question like that."

"But if it had to do with the murder of Steve Myer?"

The postmistress gave Valena a long, evaluative look before saying, "Then I'd have to answer that only one person came in at lunchtime that day, and that yes, he was tall and blond and good-looking. And he had a large box to ship, and as I recall it was marked 'Fragile' and 'Do Not Freeze.'

Valena thanked her and let herself out the door. She cut around the back of the post office building and through an equipment storage yard to reach her next target, which was Chad Hill's office. If she was going to be successful, she needed the authority that was vested in the marshal of McMurdo Station.

Chad Hill had gone to lunch. The woman who managed his office said that he would be back in half an hour.

"May I leave him a note?" Valena inquired.

"Sure." She began looking around for notepaper. She fished a discarded notice out of the paper recycling and handed it across her desk.

Valena lifted her pen and wrote:

Mr. Hill:

I have in my possession trace evidence that I believe will connect theft of protected wildlife and antiquities from Cape Royds to the murder of Steve Myers. The fact that this theft was accomplished during last Tuesday's storm connects it to Steve's murder, but also to the murder of Morris Sweeny. The connection is that whoever drove a snow machine out to Cape Royds in that storm would also have been able to use GPS and a snow machine to find the missing drop bundle at Emmett Vanderzee's camp and bury it in one of the fuel drum excavations. GPS was present at Emmett's camp and was used by his assistant, Calvin Hart.

I have questioned every person who was in Emmett's camp last year, and only Cal's testimony varies from the others in important details. Raytheon studies the backgrounds of potential employees and would be harder to fool than my professor, who is too busy researching what is true to notice when someone is lying to him. It is my belief therefore that Calvin Hart is an alias, and that his true name is Edgar Hallowell.

When Edgar Hallowell was a soldier in Iraq, he stole plates out of fellow soldier Jacob Sweeny's body armor. Jacob died in an ambush because he lacked these plates. His brother Morris became obsessed with finding Hallowell, who disappeared after being dishonorably discharged. Morris came to Antarctica in search of him after spotting him on Emmett's Web site.

The postmistress states that someone answering to Hart's description mailed a package from McMurdo's post office last Tuesday. Please take steps necessary to track and seize this package. I believe it contains live penguin eggs and antique bottles from Shackleton's Nimrod hut, which will prove his guilt in that matter at least.

I request also that you use your authority to search clothing in Hart/ Hallowell's possession for trace evidence. In particular seize his FDX boots and check materials lodged in the treads for anorthoclase crystals, penguin guano, and feathers, and possible shards of antique bottle glass. Meanwhile, I will be at Emmett's office in Crary Lab with corroborative trace evidence.

Sincerely, Valena Walker

Valena folded the note, stapled it, taped the edges, and handed it to the woman. "Please see that Mr. Hill gets this the moment he returns. It's urgent."

The woman looked at her as if she had just sprouted a new head. "Okay."

"It has to do with Steve Myer."

"Oh! Okay!"

"Thanks." She smiled and relaxed a little, knowing that her job was almost finished. Chad Hill would return from lunch within the half hour, and she would be waiting in Emmett's office with Jim Skehan.

She let herself out through the air lock, automatically popping her sunglasses out of her sunglass pocket on her upper right sleeve and putting them on. Outside, as the outer door swung shut behind her, she strolled down the steps and tipped her face up into the great Antarctic sunshine. She closed her eyes and for a moment took off her sunglasses, confident at last to enjoy the sting of the cold and the blast of the sun. *I'll get a quick shower,* she decided, *and slather on some more sunscreen, then take a slow stroll through this glorious twenty-four-hour sunlight on my way to Crary Lab, where I'll—*

Her face cooled as something slid between her and the sun. She opened her eyes, and was confronted by the presence of a tall, blond man who had just stepped into her path.

"Valena," said Cal Hart, smiling sweetly. "How nice to see you. Where are you going? May I offer you a ride?"

"No, I don't—"

"But you do," he said, firmly grasping her arm and steering her toward a red pickup truck.

Valena began to shout, and then to scream, but her voice bounced off all the double-paned glass and heavily insulated buildings, rose, and flew away with the lone skua that was hovering overhead. Then everything went black.

44

George Bellamy grabbed his phone off its cradle. "George, this is Chad Hill," said the caller. "What is this about stolen penguin eggs and artifacts on Cape Royds?"

"How fast can you be here, Chad?"

"I am in Crary and I am coming over. What we need to discuss is Valena Walker. She has left me a note, and we must act. Now. But I do not know where to locate this woman. I am in her office—Emmett Vanderzee's office, George, do you get me?—but she's not here. Brenda Utzon and her people have scoured Crary. They've looked everywhere. She is not in her dorm. She is not in the galley. She is not checked out with the fire department. She is not checked out with Mac Ops. I even called Fleet Ops, damn it! Where *is* she? She says that Calvin Hart killed Steve Myer and Morris Sweeny! You didn't tell me that!" The connection ended.

George Bellamy set his phone down slowly and faced Father Jim Skehan. "Chad and I were detaining Mr. Hart for observation because a few days ago, he mailed some very elegant mineral samples out through the APO. They were discovered as the package went through customs in New Zealand. As Mr. Hart does not have a collecting permit this was of course illegal. We bumped him off the flight north last Wednesday to see what else he might be up to."

Skehan said, "He didn't know you were watching him?"

"I don't believe so."

"Then there's hope. If he knows he's cornered, he might do anything."

Chad Hill burst in through the air lock and stormed into Bellamy's office. He was still shouting, as if continuing his tirade on the telephone.

"And she says that Hart is an alias for Hallowell, and that Sweeny was after him for killing his brother. We have to take action. Now! Do you get this picture, George? She leaves a note saying she has evidence against this man and then is not where she said she is going to be! If Hart—or whatever his name is—is indeed guilty of murdering two men, I will gladly escort him to Honolulu, but I will be damned if I will escort him there for killing a woman, too!"

Bellamy crossed the room to the doorway. Felt himself moving through it, as if in a dream. Crossed to his secretary's office. Spoke. "Get me the microphone for the public address system, and turn it on, will you? And patch it through to all buildings that are wired. And then I want you to relay this message to the main offices of all buildings that are not."

Eyes popping with surprise, she handed the instrument to him.

He pressed the key to activate the microphone. Stared at the far wall, as if the words he needed to say might be written there. "All hands, all hands, this is George Bellamy. This is an all points bulletin. I request an immediate search of McMurdo and environs for either of two people: Valena Walker or Calvin Hart. Repeat: Valena Walker or Calvin Hart. If anyone knows the whereabouts of either person, call my office immediately. Repeat: call my office immediately! Notice: approach Hart with extreme caution! Repeat, extreme caution!"

He set down the microphone and put a hand out to steady himself against the wall, his eyes squeezed shut. The image of the young woman's face floated across the insides of his eyelids. *So young,* he thought, *and so much promise. I did my best to protect her. If only they'd let me send her home!*

◈

DAVE HEARD THE Boss calling over the radio on the Fleet Ops frequency as he drove toward Pegasus, returning from lunch: "All hands, all hands, this is the Boss speaking. Anyone seen our girl Valena?" He sounded angry, very angry.

Edith's voice came next. "Edith here, Boss. Haven't seen her. Is she supposed to be with us? What's up?"

The Boss answered, "There is an APB to locate either her or Calvin Hart, pronto. Approach Hart with caution. If you see Valena, offer aid. Over!"

Dave turned the truck toward the sea ice, the place he knew how to search best.

MASTER SERGEANT JOHN Lansing ran downstairs with the all points bulletin ringing in his brain. "Hugh!" he called. "Waylon! Did you hear this?"

"Got it," said Hugh. He was already shrugging on his parka. "The damned thing is, I have no idea what else we can do to help, but I can't stand still and do nothing. I'm on my way to the fire department. If they put together an organized search, I'm on it."

"Me, too."

Waylon and Marilyn followed them out the door.

◈

FATHER JAMES SKEHAN ran out of the Chalet into the yard that lay between it and Science Support, trying to figure out what to do. He had assisted the others in the search of Crary for Valena. He had personally looked into the bottom of each fish tank in the aquarium.

He saw Dustin, the teacher from Happy Camp, hurrying toward the Science Support Center and ran to him. "Is the SAR team forming?"

"Yes. Cal Hart took a truck mid-morning. I was just out checking its parking space and it's not there. Have you seen him since then?"

"No."

"Let's get back inside. Manny and the rest of the SAR team are putting together a plan."

The two men hurried inside and up the stairs to the warehouse space the Search and Rescue team used as a nerve center. Skehan could hear radio calls coming through people's hand units as they rigged—units checking in, questions asked, messages relayed. Team members were arriving from other tasks, pulling on clothing and equipment on the run.

Manuel Roig stood next to a wooden crate with a notebook open in front of him, talking on a radio. "Right. Okay, good. You got lift-off." He turned to Dustin and Skehan. "The first helo is up looking for that truck."

Moments later, the radio squawked again. Manuel picked it up, said his name, and listened. "What? We'll be right there." He slammed down the phone and keyed the microphone on his radio. "All SAR, we have located a vehicle checked out to Cal Hart. It is parked at the dive hut on the sea ice off Hut Point. Repeat, Dive Hut 4 off Hut Point. Approach with caution, but hurry. Over."

◈

DAVE HEARD THE calls and swung the truck toward Hut Point and the dive shack and pressed the accelerator as hard as he could without breaking traction on the ice. A helicopter hovered overhead like a beacon shining the way. As he neared the hut, he saw Chad Hill skid his truck to a stop, clamber out, and slide to one side of the door to the hut. He pushed it open. Looked inside. Suddenly, all caution drained from his body and he rushed inside.

Dave was out of the truck and across the ice to the building at a run. Adrenaline crashing through his brain and muscles, he crossed the threshold into the tiny hut, taking in the scene at a glance.

The cover over the dive hole open, filled to the brim with freezing slush, traced in blood.

Cal Hart, soaking wet, sprawled across the floor.

Chad kneeling, his hand to the man's throat, feeling for a pulse.

Valena, alive. Pounding on Cal's chest, her lovely face covered with blood and running with tears. "Breathe, damn you!" she roared. "Breathe!"

Search and Rescue personnel began crowding into the hut. Manuel Roig shoved Valena out of his way as he and the others prepared to administer cardiopulmonary resuscitation. Valena tried to get back at Cal, but they firmly pushed her aside.

Dave knelt beside Valena and gathered her up in his arms, squeezing her until she quit struggling. "Are you okay?" he said.

She nodded. Then she began to collapse and leaned against him.

"What happened?" Dave asked.

Beginning to tremble with unspent adrenaline, she put her lips near his ear. "D-dragged me to his truck. Hit me. Was . . . blacked out. Until here. He . . . w-was going to stuff me down that hole. I—I—"

"There, now. You're going to be okay, and that's all that is important."

Her voice came between her teeth. "I think I killed him!"

"He was going to kill you, Valena. You had to protect yourself."

"I have to tell you!"

"Then tell me."

"You won't hate me?"

"How could I hate a woman as fine as you?"

Valena put her arms around him and buried her face against his chest. "He dragged me out of the truck. I fought like hell, but he had me by the arms, p-pinned behind my back. Dragging me in here, trying to get my neck. I fought! Braced my feet either side of the door. I could see he'd been down here already, had the lid off the dive hole. I knew what he was going to do!"

"I am so glad you didn't let him." Dave began to rock her, soothing her.

"He kicked my leg to break my hold. I fell forward. He kind of . . . rolled over me. It slammed my head. Stunned. When I came to, I saw him there in the hole." She squeezed him harder, looked up into his eyes, begging him to understand. "All I could see was the soles of his boots. He kicked once, and then . . ."

Dave shuddered at the idea of hanging head-down in a hole that narrow, encased in ice, in twenty-eight-degree water. . . .

"He's dead," said Manuel. "The ice is thicker than he is tall. There was nothing to grab hold of to push himself up, and the hole was too tight to turn around in."

"No!" Valena cried. "I did everything I could to pull him out!"

Chad Hill put a hand on her shoulder. "That's okay," he said.

"I want him alive, damn it! I want him to stand trial, so everyone can know the truth!"

Chad said, "We all do know the truth now, thanks to you."

"But I want it in the papers! People have to know what's happening in their world!"

Chad smiled. "We have our own paper here, *The Antarctic Sun,* and it's online. And you'd be amazed how a story like this will be picked up by the wires."

Valena took that in. A moment later, she hung her head. "Are you going to arrest me?"

"No, I am not," said Chad. "You didn't do this to him, Valena. He did it to himself. And I think there's been far too much arresting of innocent people going on around here."

Dave helped Valena to her feet and led her out into the bright Antarctic sunshine, where her great, big, mixed-up, miscellaneous new family had begun to assemble, some arriving by vehicle, and others coming by foot or on skis. Paul, who was flying the helicopter that was hovering overhead, waved to her and headed back to the helo pad. Marilyn Wood stepped forward, took off her scarf and used it very gently to wipe the blood off of Valena's face. Hugh Muller gave her a big smile. The Boss grinned. Edith slapped her on the back.

"Hey, Valena, we were worried!" people were calling.

"We're so glad you're all right!"

"We want you to stay!"

Valena looked from face to face in happy disbelief and the simple joy of being alive, tightening her arm around Dave Fitzgerald's waist. In the privacy of her mind, she thought, *I've finally found my heart, right here in Antarctica, and it's broken wide open!*

45

THE C-17 MADE A LONG, STATELY APPROACH ONTO THE SEA ICE RUN-
way at McMurdo. When it had finished back-taxiing and had pulled to a
stop, Ivan the Terrabus pulled up next to it, and out of the passenger door
spilled thirty-five men and women dressed in big red parkas, black wind
pants, and blue or white boots. They turned and took in the view: the
broad sweep of ice, the grand mountains, the endless sky.

"Keep moving!" called the driver. "You can take your pictures later on!"

One tall, angular man stood in the midst of the crowd, oblivious to the
driver's urgings. He had been here many times before and was not to be
hurried. And he was looking for someone, a special someone who had
helped him in a way he could never hope to repay.

A Challenger 95 tractor pulled up next to the bus. The cab door swung
open, and a young woman dressed just like the others, in United States
Antarctic Program ECWs, emerged from the jump seat and climbed carefully but joyously down the steps that led out over the fender and down to
the ice. The driver of the tractor smiled and gave her a wave good-bye as
he headed out to Pegasus for another shift of rolling the runway smooth.

The young woman grinned and waved when she saw her professor.
"Emmett!" she called. "Over here!"

A man with black hair and rich, tawny skin tugged at the tall man's
sleeve. "There she is!" he said.

"Where, Taha?"

"There!" Taha was grinning, waving a greeting to his fellow graduate
student.

Emmett Vanderzee turned and saw Valena. "Ah, there you are, my clever, clever one." He held out his arms and gave her a fatherly hug.

Thus anointed, Valena grabbed one of his orange duffels and pointed him toward the bus. "Right this way, gentlemen. We'd better hurry. We have a lot of work ahead of us, and we're burning daylight!"